# Trapped in a reality TV game show unlike any other . . .

"I'm Alex Everett," the bald man said. "Before we do the rest of the introductions, let me explain for those of you who still don't understand what you're doing here." He winked at Amy, who kept her face as blank as she could manage. "You lucky seven have been chosen from hundreds of applicants for Taunton Life Network's newest show, *Who Knows People, Baby— You?* Myra Townsend and I are the producers, and this is how the show works."

As he explained, Amy seethed. So the dog in the tree had been a setup and she'd been filmed. The "robbery" in the lobby. The "rats" outside the doctor's office—which she had believed were a legitimate student-film project. She had been played, and she didn't like it one bit.

"I quit," she said loudly.

Everyone's head swiveled to look at her.

"Of course," Alex said, watching Amy closely, "you're free to quit if you choose. This is a job, not serfdom. There is a long waiting list of girls ready to take your place. But then we'll expect repayment of the advance you've received."

Mrs. Raduski's rent. Gran.

Violet, in the chair beside her, found Amy's hand and squeezed it.

Amy choked out, "I'll stay."

# OTHER BOOKS YOU MAY ENJOY

| | |
|---|---|
| *Black City* | Elizabeth Richards |
| *Crossed* | Ally Condie |
| *Gamer Girl* | Mari Mancusi |
| *Incarceron* | Catherine Fisher |
| *Legend* | Marie Lu |
| *Matched* | Ally Condie |
| *Nightshade* | Andrea Cremer |
| *Origin* | Jessica Khoury |
| *Phoenix* | Elizabeth Richards |
| *Prodigy* | Marie Lu |
| *Reached* | Ally Condie |
| *Shock Point* | April Henry |

# FLASH
# POINT

# FLASH POINT

A NOVEL

NANCY KRESS

PUFFIN BOOKS
An Imprint of Penguin Group (USA)

SPEAK
Published by the Penguin Group
Penguin Group (USA)
375 Hudson Street
New York, New York 10014, U.S.A.

USA / Canada / UK / Ireland / Australia / New Zealand / India / South Africa / China
Penguin Books Ltd, Registered Offices: 80 Strand, London WC2R 0RL, England

For more information about the Penguin Group visit www.penguin.com

First published in the United States of America by Viking,
a division of Penguin Young Readers Group, 2012
Published by Speak, an imprint of Penguin Group (USA), 2013

THE LIBRARY OF CONGRESS HAS CATALOGED THE VIKING EDITION AS FOLLOWS:
Kress, Nancy.
Flash point : a novel / Nancy Kress.
p. cm.
Summary: "In an America decimated by economic collapse, teenage Amy jumps at the chance
to star in a reality show—but what she doesn't know is that it may kill her before it pays off"—
Provided by publisher.
ISBN 978-0-670-01247-3 (hardcover)—ISBN 978-0-14-242746-0 (pbk.)
[1. Reality television programs—Fiction. 2. Interpersonal relations—Fiction. 3. Conduct of life—
Fiction. 4. Sisters—Fiction. 5. Poverty—Fiction. 6. Grandmothers—Fiction. 7. Orphans—Fiction.]
I. Title.
PZ7.K8842Fl 2013
[Fic]—dc23
2013013052

Speak ISBN 978-0-14-242746-0

Printed in the United States of America

1 3 5 7 9 10 8 6 4 2

The publisher does not have any control over and does not assume any
responsibility for author or third-party websites or their content.

For Leslie Howle,

friend to so many writers

# One

ALL THE OTHER girls were better dressed and prettier than she was.

Was dress going to matter? Was prettiness? Of course it was—it always did. But how much, here and now? What were the interviewers looking for anyway?

No clues in the room, which was a bare, ugly concrete square in a warehouse close to the waterfront. It wasn't even warm. Outside, homeless huddled against the east side of the building, out of the March wind. Inside, rows of hard wooden chairs overflowed with a few hundred girls. The chairs faced two doors, one labeled RESTROOM, one blank. Two uniformed guards flanked the uncommunicative door, their faces as blank and hard as its wood.

1

Amy turned to the girl on her right, a tall blonde in skinny black jeans and a red pea coat. The coat looked warm. "May I borrow a comb?"

"Sorry." The blonde didn't even turn to look at her, but a sneer curled her bottom lip.

Amy fought down her temper. Maybe the blonde was right. Amy could have lice, or even worse, considering the diseases loose in the city. She shouldn't have asked.

She rose and made her way to the ladies' room, carefully picking her way between the rows of tightly packed chairs, trying not to put her ratty sneakers onto polished boots, four-inch heels, red flats with perky bows, and—were those a pair of vintage Manolos? So many girls here to interview! And probably none of them as desperate as she was.

*Oh, Gran, what are we going to do if I don't get this job?*

The bathroom, packed with girls, was even colder than the waiting room. Maybe that was a good thing—no one lingered in the stalls, or even in front of the fly-specked and flaking mirrors. Amy smoothed her hair with her fingers, splashed cold water under her eyes, and straightened her green sweater, the nicest thing she had left. Actually, the nicest thing Kaylie had left. Her sister had been asleep when Amy left the apartment at four a.m. to take the bus here, which was a good thing because Kaylie would have thrown a royal fit about lending the sweater. It was nearly noon and Amy's stomach rumbled with hunger. Dammit, why hadn't she brought a sandwich! And a comb.

"Here," a voice said to her left, "borrow mine."

The girl who held out a comb was even taller than the blonde, and breathtakingly beautiful. Long black hair, smooth and shiny as glass, and legs that seemed the length of a football field. Amy blinked, said thanks, and wondered why she thought she had a chance at this job. Or any other.

"What's your number?" the girl asked.

"One hundred twenty-three."

"Catchy." She sang, "And a *one* and a *two* and a *three!*" and did a graceful little dance step.

Amy laughed. "What's yours?"

"One sixty-eight. No music there. Why don't you tease the top just a little? Here, let me." She took the comb from Amy, deftly teased an underlayer of hair, combed the rest over it, and stuck a hairpin at a strategic angle on one temple. Instantly Amy's hair, honey-colored but thick and unwieldy, looked better.

"Hey, thank you!"

"Don't mention it. But you better go, One Two Three— they were up to number one eleven when I came in here."

Amy held out her hand. "I'm Amy Kent."

"Violet Sanderson."

No one was named Violet, and even if they were, Amy had

never seen anyone less like that shy, delicate flower. This Amazon radiated confidence and charm. Amy said, "Good luck, Violet."

"Good luck, One Two Three."

Someone had taken her chair. Amy leaned against the wall for another hour, shivering and hungry, until a PA system boomed, "Number one hundred twenty-three," and she walked toward the wooden door. *Just like a bakery. Take a number and be served. Or be served up.*

It didn't matter. She would take this job, if she could get it. They had to have the money. Gran was dying.

Beyond the wooden door was a short corridor fitted with an X-ray machine. Amy walked through it, knowing it was viewing everything on her for every possible kind of weapon. The next machine blew air at her, sniffing for explosives. After that, she pressed her fingers onto an ink pad and waited while a computer matched her fingerprints to those in a database somewhere. Amy dipped her fingers in the cleansing wash and dried them carefully. She couldn't get ink on Kaylie's sweater, the last decent thing either of them owned.

Finally, after another long, shivering wait—couldn't these people afford to heat their buildings?—a green light went on over the door at the far end of the corridor, a lock audibly clicked, and Amy pushed open the door and stepped through.

Into another world.

In the moment it took for her eyes to adjust to the soft light after the fluorescent glare of the waiting room and corridor, she got a phantom, sharp and clear in her mind as they always were: a maze of red velvet trees, with something radiating cold at its hidden center. After a searing moment the phantom dissipated, as they always did. In its place was the kind of room she'd seen only in the movies, with apricot silk walls and a herringbone-parquet floor. Three men and a woman sat in leather chairs grouped around a small marble table. The woman gestured toward a fifth chair. "Please sit down, my dear."

Amy sat. The chair was warm, the room was warm, the woman was warm, with kind eyes in a middle-aged face. She was dressed in camel-colored pants and silk blouse, with a cashmere vest in a deeper brown. Two of the men, one gray-haired and one bald, wore dark, expensive suits that made Amy even more aware of her old sneakers and faded jeans. The third male, African-American and far younger than the others, wore jeans and a black leather jacket, but even these made Kaylie's silk sweater look shabby. Well, so what? Amy was here to apply for a job, not to fit into their moneyed world. She made herself smile. "Hello. I'm Amy Kent."

"Yes, you are," the woman said, making a comic little moue and holding up her tablet, which, of course, held all the information from the application Amy had filled out seven hours ago. "Tell us about yourself, Amy."

Tell them what? They already knew she was sixteen, lived at an address none of them would be caught dead anywhere near, and had finished short-form high school. They could see from her clothing that she hadn't had the money for a full-term school, the kind that prepared you for college, let alone for college itself. *Sell yourself, Amy. That's what you do on a job interview.*

"Well, I graduated third in my class, and I did especially well in math, my favorite subject. I'm a very hard worker. One of my teachers said he'd never seen such a persistent student, even for things that don't come easy to me."

"What doesn't come easy to you, Amy?" the woman asked.

Damn, why had she said that? On a job interview you were supposed to talk about your strengths, not your weaknesses. But she answered honestly. "I'm not good at music. Totally talentless, I'm afraid, and there was a breadth requirement at school to learn a song on the virtual keyboard. It took me weeks to learn a song, and even then my two hands weren't completely coordinated." She smiled, hoping to seem charmingly self-deprecatory. "But I'm good at other things that involve hand-eye coordination."

"Was it about your keyboard playing that the teacher praised you for persistence?"

"Yes."

"What was the song you learned to play?"

Why were they asking her so much about this? If the job involved music, she was already disqualified. "It was 'Mary Had a Little Lamb.'"

"I see," the woman said. The gray-haired man smiled faintly. "What non-school talents do you have, Amy?"

"I have a good eye for clothing." Not that she could afford any of it. "And I play chess."

"Chess? How well?"

"I used to have a United States Chess Federation rating of 1900." Would that mean anything to any of them? She couldn't tell.

"You said 'used to have.' What is your rating now?"

"I don't know. I had to drop out of competition."

"And why was that?"

"I couldn't afford the dues." She stared directly at the woman, who probably could afford anything she wanted, let alone the paltry amount that the Chess Federation demanded.

The young black man in the leather jacket, clearly bored, pulled out a tablet and bent over it. All Amy could see was the top of his head, with thick brown hair that needed cutting. The bald man said, "Do you have any athletic skills?"

"I did gymnastics, years ago." A lifetime ago, when Gran

had been well and so had the United States economy.

"Can you still do a backflip?"

She stared at him. A backflip? What *was* this job? But the supercilious amusement in his half-smile riled her. She got out of the deep, cushiony chair, walked away from the furniture, and did a backflip and two cartwheels across the parquet floor.

Immediately she felt like a fool.

"Thank you, Amy," the woman said, with no change in her kindly, poised tone. "You may sit down again."

As Amy sat, she caught the glance exchanged among the three older adults—the young man hadn't even looked up from his tablet—but she had no idea what their glances meant. The woman leaned forward. "We'd like to give you some tests now."

"Tests?"

"Yes. Simple things, I'm sure you'll do well." From a compartment in the arm of her chair she drew a tablet and handed it to Amy. "Just sit there and work on them for a few minutes."

The tablet was a Li 6000, the newest and best Chinese tech. Amy had never even held one before, only seen them on TV. When Gran still had TV. The tablet felt sleek and light in her hand, yet with the right apps it could move satellites in orbit. Her thumb found the On button.

"Go ahead, dear," the woman said. All four interviewers watched her closely.

A home screen appeared, with one icon: a pencil and little blue test booklet of the kind last used fifty years ago. Amy smiled. The icon brought up a written paragraph followed by questions. Amy scanned them: reading comprehension, very basic stuff. She read the paragraph, spoke her answers, and tackled a series of increasingly difficult paragraphs, followed by math questions, also increasing in difficulty. The "few minutes" became twenty. The three adults never took their eyes off her, which was unnerving.

Then the questions grew weird.

"If you saw a child being beaten by two older teenagers on a deserted street, what would you do?"

"Call 911," Amy said, although she herself had neither phone nor tablet. Both pawned, like everything else.

"What if, instead of a child, the victim were a ragged and diseased homeless person?"

"Call 911."

"Your tablet has died."

"I guess . . . scream for someone to help."

"No one comes. The child—let's say it is a child—is writhing and crying in pain."

"I would pretend to call 911, very loudly—the thugs don't know my tablet has died. I'd also yell that I was taking pictures to identify them. Then I would run like hell. I'm very fast, and I could probably reach a store or other people before they caught up to me. And they'd have left the child."

"They do catch you, grab your tablet, and try to smash it."

"I'd let them have the tablet. The point is to save the child, not my tablet."

"What is your favorite color?"

*What?* "Blue."

"What did you eat for breakfast this morning?"

"I didn't." What *was* this?

"Why not?"

"I wasn't hungry," Amy said, just as her stomach growled loud enough to echo.

It was the final insult. "Look," Amy said to the interviewers, "I don't mean to be rude, but before I answer any more personal questions, I'd like the chance to ask one. What exactly is this job?"

The kind-faced woman said, "What did you hear about the job, Amy? And how?"

"I overheard two girls mention it yesterday. On the bus." She didn't add that she'd only been on the bus because she'd taken Gran to the free clinic again, where again they had done nothing for her. Gran couldn't possibly walk that far. On the bus she'd fallen asleep and Amy had cradled her with one arm and listened for anything to distract herself.

"Did the girls on the bus say what company was hiring?"

"Only that you're a TV station."

"And were you hoping for an on-air job?"

"No." That had never crossed her mind. What, as a weather girl or something? Then she had another thought. "This isn't a porno station, is it?"

The bald man laughed. The woman said, "No, dear. We're TLN."

Amy was stunned. Taunton Life Network was the edgy, upstart station that in the last five years had surpassed even NBC and Fox in the ratings. Couldn't TLN afford to hire experienced personnel for any position they wanted, on- or off-air? And what was with the tacky, barely heated concrete waiting room?

She rose. "I think I'm in the wrong place."

"Maybe not, dear. We're looking for a hardworking, intelligent, physically fit girl to fill a new job, with union pay and full medical benefits. And I promise you there is no porn involved."

The only part of this that really registered on Amy was "union pay and full medical benefits." *My God, that could mean hospital care for Gran, a safe apartment, enough to eat* . . . Much more fiercely than she intended, she turned on the woman. "Would I be able to put my grandmother on my medical care? I'm her sole support."

The woman blinked. "You're guardian for your grandmother? At sixteen?"

"Not legally. But she's ill and I take care of her." Gran was Kaylie's guardian and had been Amy's until she turned sixteen. But that was irrelevant. Suddenly she wanted this job, wanted it so badly her chest ached. She *had* to get it. What had the woman said? *An intelligent, hardworking, physically fit girl.* "I can build sets, move furniture, keep track of supplies—I'm very organized! And strong!"

"Where are your parents?"

"Dead. I'm a fast learner—I can do anything you need!"

"We'll let you know," the woman said. "Thank you for your time, Amy. You can exit through that—" The gray-haired man, who had so far said nothing, shifted his weight in his chair and instantly the woman stopped talking.

He said, in a quiet and deep voice that she had heard somewhere before, "What TV shows do you watch?"

*Oh, shit.* She was going to lose this job because the TV had been pawned six months ago and the only programs she ever saw were those playing in the restaurant kitchen: sports or fashion parades or, when Charlie was the only one there, porn. Could she lie? No, he'd catch her at it. She choked out, "Not . . . not too much TV. I read a lot."

"And take care of your grandmother."

"Yes."

"Your application says you work part-time at a restaurant. Why not full-time?"

"I couldn't find a full-time job. I looked."

"You may go."

Amy took a stumbling step toward the door, then straightened. The hell with them. She walked the rest of the way as regally as she could manage—she was Queen Elizabeth I, Anne Boleyn on her way to the scaffold, Mary Queen of fucking Scots. Quietly she closed the door behind her, proud that she hadn't slammed it.

Another guard, another short corridor, another door, and she was out on the street, the cold March wind blowing through Kaylie's thin silk sweater.

"I vote we use her," said the kind-faced woman.

"She's not really pretty," the bald man said. "Our viewers will want—"

"She could be prettier," the woman said, "with some makeup and decent clothes. That green sweater is all wrong for her coloring. She won't be a startling beauty like some of the others, but pretty enough."

"Chess?" the bald man said. "Not exactly a ratings grabber."

"She's athletic."

"That's not enough, by itself. Although the poverty might help. She'll be willing to do anything."

"She's clearly intelligent."

"But not pretty enough!"

"I'm a bit worried about that defiant streak in her—although it could be an asset."

"Could also be a liability. If it's us she gets defiant toward."

"Even then. Viewers might like it."

"I vote instead for the redhead with the great boobs."

"Alex, this isn't the program you used to produce! Mark, what do you think?"

The young man shrugged without looking up from his tablet. "I don't care. I don't know why I'm in on this meeting at all. My tech will work with whomever you pick."

The bald man said, "She has a likeable quality—I'll give her that. Worth a screen test to see if it comes through on camera."

The woman said, "Shape that hair a bit, enhance the eyes . . ."

The gray-haired man cleared his throat. The others immediately fell silent and turned toward him. "Take her," he said. And that was that.

# Two

**THURSDAY**

AMY WALKED HOME to save the bus fare: 102
blocks. *The city in miniature*, she thought, and then snorted because the thought was so unoriginal. Even graffiti on the side of
a crumbling building said TIMES BE TOUGH MAN. Like everyone
didn't already know.

First the waterfront: idle rusting machinery that used to
bustle with container ships coming and going. Empty ware-
houses on streets that she would never have dared walk after
dark. A lot of the buildings had been colonized by homeless
people, including the packs of abandoned children that roamed
the city, begging and thieving. Farther on was a shopping area
with half the stores boarded up—but at least that meant that
the other half were open. Then uphill to an actual thriving

neighborhood with pretty houses, flowerbeds, and heavy-duty electronic surveillance. The pretty houses gradually grew shabbier until Amy trudged past the kind of apartment houses where the "courtyard" was full of discarded syringes. More stores, becoming brighter and cleaner the farther she walked, until she passed a high brick wall topped with barbed wire. Back in there, she guessed, were houses for the rich—not that she would ever find out for sure. Then more houses, these sub-divided into apartments, becoming seedier and cheaper until she reached her own.

Two blocks before she got there, the bottoms of her feet ached so much that she sat for a moment on a crate left out for the trash. Since trash pickup was erratic at best, a crate could be there a very long time. Now, however, it was still solid and relatively clean and Amy sank down gratefully. At least with all that exercise she was no longer cold.

A half-dressed girl ran out of the nearest house.

The phantom that sliced into Amy's mind was so sharp it brought her to her feet. *A baby rabbit, struggling to free itself from an iron trap around its leg, the cruel teeth cutting into the bloody flesh.* How-ever, this girl was no baby. She was about Amy's age, beautiful and wild-eyed, her bright red lips drawn back and her exposed breasts turning blue-veined with cold. A man dashed out after her, caught her easily, and pinned her arms to her sides. He began to drag her back inside.

"Stop!" Amy cried before she knew she was going to say anything.

The girl and man both looked at her, and it was the girl who spoke. "Mind your own business, slut!" She twisted in the man's arms and snarled, "I said twenty, and I mean twenty!"

"All right, all right!" He let her go and glared at her. They both walked back into the building.

*Well, I certainly misjudged that.* So why the rabbit in a trap? Were her phantoms becoming inaccurate? No—the images that leapt so unpredictably into her mind were always true. This particular rabbit was so deep into the trap that she didn't even know there could be anything else but the leg iron.

*Not me. Not ever me, nor Kaylie either. No matter what I have to do.*

She unlocked the front door of her building, an uncared-for house subdivided into too many too-small apartments. The vestibule was once again filled with trash. The landlady, Mrs. Raduski, poked her head from her ground floor apartment, followed by her growling dog. The schnauzer was the terror of the building, biting unpredictably and without provocation. Mrs. Raduski said, "You the one who dumped all this—oh, it's you, Amy."

"Hi, Mrs. Raduski."

"You know who dumped all this here?"

Amy did, but she said, "No, sorry."

"None of you tenants worth your rent." She slammed her door.

*But you need our rent. You have to live, just like the rest of us. You and that mangy dog.* Not that Amy would ever say that aloud. Why not? Was it politeness or need that made her meet Mrs. Raduski's rudeness with courtesy?

No contest there. It was need. Need made you tolerate a lot that you shouldn't. But there were limits.

Amy climbed the twisting stairs to the third floor. Inside the cramped apartment, Gran was asleep and Kaylie was out. Kaylie hadn't closed up the sofa bed where she and Amy slept, or done the lunch dishes. Bread sat out on the counter where it could attract rats. Amy dreaded rats. The rodents would have horrified her even if they hadn't been the carriers of so many fast-mutating diseases. The Collapse had brought new diseases to the city and dried up funding to fight the old ones. There had even been a few cases of bubonic plague, as if this were medieval Europe—and Kaylie knew all that! But there the bread sat.

Amy put it away, wiped down the counter, and carefully folded Kaylie's sweater back into their shared dresser. The apartment had only two rooms: a small bedroom for Gran and the front room with one window overlooking the street. One wall held a stove, a tiny fridge, and one square foot of counter space. Into the rest of the room crowded the sofa bed, a rickety table with four chairs, a shabby easy chair for Gran, and the dresser.

It was all so different from the house they'd lived in before the Collapse: Gran's house with its bright kitchen, big living room lined with bookshelves, pretty bedrooms for Kaylie and Amy, trees in the backyard. Gran hadn't been sick then. They hadn't been rich, but Amy had gone to a good magnet school; Kaylie had guitar lessons; a woman named Rosa had taken care of them both while Gran was at her lab. There had been camping trips, museums, new school clothes each year. For some reason, Amy especially remembered a blue coat with gold buttons on the shoulder, from sixth grade. She'd loved that coat. She'd worn it too long after it no longer fit, just to feel the fine wool in her fingers.

Now Gran—so fragile and thin—lay in bed with a flimsie across her chest: SCIENCE NOW. Amy had printed it yesterday at a publishing kiosk downtown. Gran's body might be dying but her mind was still sharp with the wonderful pre-Collapse education Amy would never have. Once she had been a biologist, earning advanced degrees when that was still rare for a woman. She still liked to keep up with the world, and Amy intended to squeeze out money for flimsies no matter what else she had to do without.

She woke. "Amy?"

"Hi, Gran. I'm back."

"Did you get the waitressing job?"

"No, the job was filled. What can I get you, Gran?"

"Nothing. I'm fine, honey."

Gran was not fine. All but one of the blankets in the house were piled on the bed, yet goose bumps prickled the forearm exposed by her hold on the flimsie. Amy reached over to pull the blanket up to her chin. The free clinic had made a tentative diagnosis but had no equipment or funds to do anything about it except provide pain pills. Some days the pills worked, some days they didn't. Amy accidentally jostled the bed and Gran moaned. Amy said, "Oh, I'm sorry, I didn't realize—"

"Open up in there!" Pounding on the apartment door.

Amy and Gran looked at each other. Gran said, "Don't—" but Amy was already at the door, peering through the peephole. A cop stood gripping Kaylie by the arm.

*A trash can, slimy with something rotten at the bottom . . .*

"Open up!"

Amy undid the chain and deadbolt. Kaylie cried, "Let me go, you fucker!" The cop dragged Amy's sister inside.

"You this girl's guardian?"

"Yes," Amy said, even though she wasn't. In the bedroom Gran tried to rise and couldn't. "What happened?"

"Shoplifting," the cop said. His small, piggish eyes traveled around the apartment, taking in the shabbiness but also the teak dresser, which Gran had saved from before the Collapse, and the George III silver tea set that had been a wedding gift to her and Gramps sixty years ago. Not even Kaylie had suggested pawning that.

Amy said, "Is Kaylie under arrest?"

The cop met her gaze. He looked again at the silver, then pointedly back at Amy. "I might let her off with a warning. Depends."

"On what?" Amy said. Did he know her knees were trembling?

"You wouldn't want her in prison. Pretty little thing like her."

"She's a juvenile."

"Them places are worse," he said, and Amy knew he was right. Everybody heard the stories.

Kaylie yelled, "If you don't let me go, you fucker, I'll—"

"Shut up," Amy told her. She went to Gran's desk, took out the envelope with Mrs. Raduski's rent, and handed it to him. "This is all we have."

He let go of Kaylie, who for once stopped yelling. Maybe even she realized what could happen—and wouldn't it be nice if just once she had thought of that *before*? The cop opened the envelope, counted the money, and made a face. His eyes went again to the silver.

"Please," Amy said, "it really is all we have. It's the rent."

Wordlessly he pocketed the envelope and turned to go. Probably he realized that the silver would be too easy to trace at any pawnshop. *Just don't say anything, Kaylie, just for once shut up—*

She did, at least until the door closed. Amy locked it and whirled on her sister. "How could you? Don't you—"

"I didn't do it!" Kaylie cried reflexively. But a minute later she reached into the waistband of her jeans, smiled slyly, and produced a long piece of rich silk, which she carried into the bedroom. "Anyway, it's for Gran. Look, Gran, what I brought you!"

The scarf hadn't been for Gran, not from Kaylie and not in that color. The green just matched Kaylie's eyes, that clear and startling emerald that made such a contrast with her pale skin and black curls. Six inches taller than Amy's five-two, Kaylie had the kind of figure that made men ride their bicycles into oncoming traffic. The sisters looked nothing alike, and next to her gorgeous, larcenous sister Amy usually felt washed out. Right now she just felt furious.

"Kaylie, do you know what you've just done? The rent is due in three days!"

"Oh, you'll come up with something," Kaylie said. "You always do. Saint Amy."

Amy wanted to kick her. Gran gazed at Kaylie with reproachful, helpless eyes. Amy pulled Kaylie and her silk scarf out of Gran's room, closed the door, and pinned her sister against the peeling wall. "If you ever again dare to—"

"Shut it off, Amy—you don't own me!"

"The rent—"

"All right, all right! I'll get the money by Friday!"

That was worse. *The girl with the exposed breasts, the rabbit in the trap*— "How? How will you get it?"

"That's my business!"

"No, it's mine! If you think you're going to—"

Kaylie flexed both arms and threw Amy off her. Amy staggered against the table, righted herself, and prepared to lunge back, even while the rational part of her mind said *Don't don't don't don't do it*—

She didn't. Another pounding on the door stopped both girls. They stared at each other until Mrs. Raduski's raspy voice came through the door: "Amy! You got a phone call! Who said you could give out my number for your own personal business? Huh?"

"I didn't," Amy said, to no one. She opened the door. Mrs. Raduski, followed by the snarling schnauzer, shot her a look that could wither a cactus, but she held out a cell phone, one of the few in the neighborhood not owned by drug dealers. The mystery of why Mrs. Raduski would bother to bring the call upstairs was solved with her next words. "It's TLN," she said reverently, as if in church. "The *television people*. Why do they want to talk to *you*?"

Amy took the phone. "Hello?"

"Amy Kent?"

"Yes."

"This is Myra Townsend. We interviewed you this afternoon for a job. We'd like you to come back tomorrow for a second interview, ten a.m., same place. You're one of our final candidates for the job."

Phantoms almost never sprang from voices alone, but this one did: *a deep hole, lined with silk as rich and luxurious as the scarf that dangled from Kaylie's suddenly rigid hand.*

# Three

GRAN HAD EXPLAINED Amy's phantoms.
Before the Collapse and her long illness, Gran had been Dr.
Amelia Whitcomb, working in a genetics lab, decoding how
genes determined personality. Amy, she said, just happened
to have a combination of genes especially good at assimilating
unconscious observations of people's body language, subtle
facial shifts, tones of voice, and perhaps even pheromones.
Lightning-swift, Amy's brain put these all together and, because she also had genes for strong visual imagery, translated
these observations into metaphorical pictures.

The only thing problematic about Gran's analysis was that
it felt wrong.

Amy knew there was more to the phantoms than genes, although she didn't know what. She sensed it. There was more. If she could have gone on to college, it would have been to study neurology and investigate that "more."

None of this was on her mind the next morning as she loitered outside the warehouse at nine thirty. Fortunately, the weather was much warmer than yesterday; you could almost believe spring might come to the city. The air held a sweetness unaccounted for by the polluted river and uncollected trash. Where did it come from, that mysterious spring sweetness that always seemed to promise so much? It made your heart ache for something you couldn't even name.

Amy was early because she hadn't wanted to take a chance on the bus schedule, which could be wayward. Also, from her position across the street and partly hidden by a Dumpster, she hoped to catch a glimpse of other candidates for "her" job.

Was that boy a candidate? Wiry, only a few inches taller than she, dressed in jeans and a faded brown sweater. He was twenty minutes early but marched right up to the door, knocked, and was admitted. Amy prepared to follow him when a bus stopped and a girl got out. Violet Sanderson! Was *she* Amy's competition? Amy figured she might as well go home right now. Violet, her long black hair so gleaming it practically reflected the building, wore high-heeled sandals and one of the new dresses set with tiny mirrors. Not a designer original,

Amy's expert eye decided, but a decent copy. Violet disappeared into the building. Amy crossed the street.

A guard guided her through security; no sign of Violet or the boy. This time she was led in a different direction, down a long cinder-block corridor to a small room containing only a metal desk, a chair, and another door. "Wait here."

"Is there a mistake?" This looked nothing like yesterday's luxury. "I'm here for an interview with—"

"Wait here."

Amy waited. The room was cold. The chair was cold under her ass. The desk drawers were all empty. The second door was locked. There was nothing to look at on the walls. Amy was just about to go back to the corridor and shout for somebody—anybody!—when the guard returned, crossed the room, and unlocked the second door.

"You can go now."

"Go?"

"They picked somebody else."

Amy stared at him: his impassive face, his hard eyes. No phantom came to her, but outrage did. "That's it? That's *it*?"

"That's it."

"Not even a . . . a courtesy of some sort? 'Thanks for coming in, we had only one slot and there were so many great candidates'? Nothing?"

"You need to go now, miss."

Amy glared at him. But he was probably just doing his miserable job. She lifted her chin and stalked out the door, hearing it lock behind her.

And she had hoped for so much.

She faced an alley, so narrow that looming buildings darkened it to shadows, lined with high, closed blue Dumpsters. Trash littered the ground. Amy picked her way through, keeping a sharp eye out for rats. She passed the largest Dumpster and came upon a man lying on the ground, moaning. Blood soaked one sleeve of his ragged jacket.

"Hey! You all right?"

"Help . . . me . . ."

"OK, yes. I don't have a phone but I'll run to get—" Fresh blood gushed from his shoulder. *Apply pressure to the wound before he bleeds to death.*

She knelt beside him. "Stay still. I'm going to stop the blood flow. Just stay still. . . ." She yanked off her sweater, an old one with a hole in one elbow, put it on his shoulder, and pressed hard.

The man screamed in pain, then began to gasp for breath.

"Oh God . . . Just a minute, I'm going to—" He passed out and stopped breathing. Keeping one hand on his shoulder, her own heart gonging in her chest, Amy pushed down on the man's chest with her other hand. *Keep the rhythm going, breathe breathe dammit breathe. . . .*

He seemed to be breathing again, but his face was still slack. Unconscious. The shoulder seemed to have stopped bleeding, too. *Should I go for help now?*

The man reached up and grabbed her.

Instinctively Amy threw him off; he was in an awkward position without much leverage. She scrambled to her feet but then he was on his feet, too, and from somewhere he had pulled a knife. No breathing difficulties, no wounded arm. She'd been played.

"You fucker," she said.

He smiled.

His body blocked her from running down the alleyway. She hadn't brought the pepper spray she carried when she came home from the restaurant at night. Wildly she looked around for something to use, anything. A broken piece of lumber leaned against a Dumpster, short but thick, a four-by-six. She snatched it up. "Let me go by!"

"Not a chance." He didn't move.

If she went toward him, he could probably get the wood away from her before she could hit him with it, since it was a clumsy weapon and he looked strong and fit. So she stood still and tried screaming. "Help! Help!" That went on for a full minute. No one came. The man kept smiling.

"I'm going to do some interesting things to you," he said.

All at once she put the stick of lumber vertically on the

ground by the nearest Dumpster, set the ball of her right foot on it, and leaped. The wood wobbled under her weight but by that time she was on top of the Dumpster.

"Hey!" the man called. He started toward her.

Amy leaped to the next Dumpster. The blue plastic was slippery and she barely kept her footing. She was now a short distance farther down the alley than he was, and above him. He grabbed for her, but the Dumpster was too wide to reach across and by then she had gone to the top of the next Dumpster. One more, leap, *dismount*. A perfect landing and she was running, ahead of him by a few feet. A blank wall ahead but the alley turned and Amy turned and—

Another wall, with a recessed door. Amy grabbed the handle. It was locked. "Help!" she screamed again, rattled the lock. Nothing. He was right behind her. *All right, if it's a fight, then it's a fight—go for the eyes, the instep, the crotch—*

He had stopped several feet short of her. "Hey, Amy," he said.

She gaped at him. The door behind her opened and the kind-faced, middle-aged woman stepped out. "You did very well, Amy."

"What—"

"That was the interview, dear. And you did very well."

Amy thought she'd known rage before—at Kaylie, at hunger, at fear—but not like this. Not like this. "You fuckers—"

"Now, dear—language. Yes, this was perhaps unfair, but it was an interview and the young man there is of course an actor. You were never in any real danger; we wouldn't permit that. You were carefully observed. And you did very well."

"I—"

"We would like to offer you a job with TLN, on a new show we're developing, aimed at young people. It's a rather unorthodox show, but I can promise you it will be interesting. And of course, as I mentioned before, it carries full union salary and medical benefits for your entire family."

The phantom slammed hard into her mind: *a mountain of glass, with tiny figures sliding helplessly down the mountainside to fall onto sharp mirrored splinters.* But . . . full union salary. Rent due Friday. Mrs. Raduski. Gran, too weak to get to the clinic. *Medical benefits for your entire family.*

"How much salary?" she choked out past the rage.

The woman told her.

Amy gaped at her. The actor said, with sullen envy, "Take it, idiot."

Amy said, "I'll take it."

"Good," the woman said briskly. "Then come inside. We have contracts ready, and a lawyer for you."

Lawyer? "Why do I need a lawyer?"

"Just a formality," the woman said. "Nothing you need to worry about at all."

She gave Amy a friendly smile.

A long polished table in a small polished room. Legal papers. Legal talk. Hurry, hurry, hurry, the job needed to start right away. Why? Amy couldn't seem to get an answer; so many people talked so fast on so many topics. *You want the job, don't you, Amy? Sign here, initial here, sign here.* . . . A few things she did get straight.

The lawyer worked for TLN but she signed something that said she accepted him as her representative.

Since the Collapse, sixteen-year-olds were considered adults, so she didn't need Gran's signature. Well, no one need-ed to tell Amy *that*—she knew sixteen-year-olds had been de-clared adults in order to save the debt-ridden government bil-lions of dollars in welfare aid to children.

The woman who had hired her was a producer, Myra Townsend.

The job was for three months only, a probationary period. "To see how you work out," they said.

"Thank you, Amy, you can go home now. Report for work on Monday," Ms. Townsend said. She and Amy's lawyer and the other people—more lawyers?—all stood.

"No, wait! I have some questions!"

Ms. Townsend said, "I thought I said that your duties will be explained to you on Monday."

"Other questions. Please. I need to . . . to know some things."

Ms. Townsend shot a look at the other people, who all left the room. The woman sat down again, frowning. Even then, her face looked kind. "How can I help you?"

Amy said, "Are you the person who called me on the phone?"

"Yes."

"And you're my boss?"

"Yes, I am. Myra Townsend. You report to me."

"What will I be *doing* on this job? Just generally, not the specific duties."

"You will be testing products which we hope appeal to young people. Video games, mostly."

"In that alley why did you—"

"It was a game scenario, obviously," Ms. Townsend said. "Amy, I have another meeting now."

"With other candidates? Did you hire more than just me?"

Ms. Townsend hesitated, then smiled. "Yes, we did. You're quick, Amy."

"If the thing in the alley was a video game, why test it on me in real time?"

"Because that's the way we do things here. Now, I have another meeting. See you Monday."

"Wait, I—no, please, one more thing . . . I need an advance on my salary. I'm sorry, but I do. Today. Now."

Ms. Townsend turned back to gaze at her. Amy, to her intense discomfort, felt herself redden. "I'm sorry, but I need the advance. Our rent is due Friday. I'm sorry."

"Of course," Ms. Townsend said with sudden and bewildering gentleness. "Just stay here and I'll have the guard bring you a check."

"Cash," Amy said. "We . . . I don't have a checking account." Banks charged fees.

"Cash, then. And on Monday we'll open an account for you."

"Thank you."

The cash appeared with startling promptness, along with a family health-insurance card. Amy signed a receipt—at least this paper was short enough for her to actually read!—and was ushered out. The money and her precious card both safe in her bra, Amy treated herself to a bus ride home. *I have a job, I have a job, I have a job*—but like hell it was "testing video games." They were testing something else in that alley. What? And why lie about it? Well, whatever it was, she hadn't been hurt, only scared. And for this amount of money, the scare was worth it.

Whatever else was going on, Amy would discover it eventually. Meanwhile, she had the rent for Mrs. Raduski and health care for Gran and money for groceries—

*I have a job, I have a job, I have a job!*

The words sang in her head all the way home, acquired a beat, and then a tune. Her foot tapped on the bus floor, her head bobbed in time. Amy couldn't stop smiling. She didn't notice the boy with the sunglasses and heavy backpack. She didn't notice the woman emerging from the grocery store as Amy got off the bus. She didn't notice any of the microcameras.

"So we have our five," Myra Townsend reported to the gray-haired man in his exquisite hand-tailored suit in his penthouse office. He sat behind an antique mahogany desk, the city forty stories below like his own personal carpet. She stood on the actual carpet and held up one manicured finger after another. "The slumming socialite that viewers can despise, the desperate little climber they can root for, the gorgeous hunk they can drool over, the dummy they can laugh at, and the geek they can be confused by. Plus Lynn, of course."

The man looked up from his desktop, the surface of which shimmered with changing graphs. "What about the dancer?"

"We eliminated her."

"Put her back in. We can have six plus Lynn."

"Yes, sir."

"I want to see the completed pilot by the twenty-first."

She looked startled. "But that's only—yes, Mr. Taunton. By the twenty-first."

"And on Saturday a rough cut of the first footage."

"We already agreed on that."

"Fine. And Myra—this time, no legal ends dangling. No room for lawsuits, no matter what you devise for those kids."

"There won't be any legal issues."

"There better not be," the gray-haired man said, and went back to studying the graphs shimmering on his desktop like living jewels.

# Four

BY THE TIME Amy's bus reached her neighborhood, her elation had been replaced by cunning. She was going to need a strategy. Two strategies: one for dealing with Gran and one for dealing with Kaylie.

She pondered tactics while buying bread, milk, cheese, butter, and sliced turkey at the ramshackle grocery store two blocks from her building. The store, no bigger than Gran's apartment, was run by Mr. Fu. His name, he had told her once, meant "happiness" in Chinese, but Mr. Fu never looked happy, and neither did his wife. He gazed at her mournfully from behind his sagging counter.

"Mr. Fu, do you have any bananas?" Gran loved bananas.

"No bananas."

"Oh. Well, just these things, then." The Fus had emigrated from Beijing just before the Collapse. Very bad timing. America, its economy in such a shambles that many had predicted the country would not survive, had disappointed the Fus. This made Amy try extra hard to be nice to Mr. Fu, which in turn made her feel vaguely resentful at being someone bouncier and more upbeat than she actually was. Amy Pollyanna.

"Bananas no come. Times be tough man," said Mr. Fu.

"Do you think the bananas might come tomorrow?"

He shrugged. "Who knows? Banana country very far. Boats have no oil. No go, maybe never."

Amy doubted that every boat importing bananas was completely out of fuel, or that bananas would never show up in the grocery store again. She smiled wider, felt stupid, and paid for her groceries. "Have a nice day, Mr. Fu!"

He shook his head sadly and she escaped. *Have a nice day*— she never said stuff like that. Mr. Fu had a bad effect on her by making her too sweet. Just as Kaylie had a bad effect on her by making her too sour.

Kaylie and Gran were both in Gran's room, Gran in bed and Kaylie perched on a chair jammed in beside it. On the wall behind Kaylie hung her double: their mother's picture, beautiful and unsmiling, her dark curls cut in an old-fashioned style.

Gran gazed often at the picture, although she never spoke about her dead daughter. She was not one to dwell on the past. Amy knew little about her mother and even less about her father, a journalist kidnapped and murdered in Iraq when Amy was barely three. But she did know that she had his coloring, so much less dramatic than Kaylie's.

Gran and Kaylie were eating lunch or maybe a late breakfast: oatmeal again. Amy said, "Wait! I brought stuff for sandwiches! I got a new job!"

They both stopped eating, spoons halfway to their mouths, looking so identically comical that Amy would have laughed if she weren't so tense about the coming conversation. She had decided on her strategy.

"Well, actually, it's not a great job, but it pays better than the restaurant, if only because it's full-time. So it really doesn't matter that it's going to be so boring."

"Is it at the TV station?" Kaylie demanded.

"Yes. I'm going to—"

"Are you going to be on *television*?"

"God, no. I sit in a back room, call people on the phone, and ask them questions about what TV shows they watch and do they like them, blah, blah, blah. You know, ratings surveys."

Kaylie relaxed. Amy could *see* the jealousy leave her, the green monster subsiding behind those green eyes.

Gran, who was not so pale this morning and even seemed to be eating, still looked suspicious. "Amy, why would a TV station give a full-time job to an untried sixteen-year-old when unemployment is over twenty-seven percent?"

"Because the shows I'm calling about are aimed at teenagers. So they wanted somebody young to talk to the survey takers. You know, more relatable."

Gran bought it. Amy saw the moment she, too, relaxed, her head sinking against the pillow. Kaylie hadn't brushed Gran's hair. And as Amy moved closer, she could smell the burned oatmeal.

"Don't eat that," she said, keeping her temper under control. "Kaylie and I will make sandwiches—I brought turkey! And Gran, I didn't even tell you the best part—I got full family medical! As soon as I can get an appointment, I'm taking you to a real doctor!"

"Amy . . ." Gran said softly, and didn't go on. But the single word, plus Gran's soft, admiring gaze, was enough for Kaylie. Her eyes narrowed; she bit her lower lip.

"Kaylie," Amy said, "come help me make sandwiches." She dragged Kaylie to her feet and into the other room, "accidentally" bumping the bedroom door closed behind her. This would be the tricky part with Kaylie.

Her sister said, "Well, aren't you just the little family savior. Saint Amy, swooping in to save us all."

Amy pulled out the envelope with her advance. She had carefully divided it; the remainder stayed in her bra. "This job you're sneering at saved your bacon. This is Mrs. Raduski's rent, Kaylie, plus ten dollars over. They gave me an advance on salary. You're going to take the rent downstairs and then you're going to take the ten dollars for yourself, because we're a family and my good luck is everybody's good luck."

Kaylie stared at her. Amy got what she'd hoped for: a phantom in her mind, just for a quick second, of the Kaylie that Amy remembered, the bouncy little girl who had adored her big sister. The phantom Kaylie, dressed in pink overalls with a bunny embroidered on the front, laughed and reached out her arms to Amy before vanishing.

The sulky fifteen-year-old beauty in front of Amy said, "You'd trust me with the rent?"

"Yes."

"How do you know I won't just spend it instead of giving it to Mrs. Raduski?"

"I know." Was knowledge the same as hope?

"You're right," Kaylie said. "I'll go now."

"Then come back and have a sandwich."

"OK." But at the door Kaylie turned back. "Is there an extra ten dollars for you, too?"

"Yes," Amy lied.

"Good. Then get yourself something to wear at the Thrift

Value so you don't have to steal my good sweater again."

Amy didn't answer. Kaylie took the rent downstairs. Amy opened the apartment door a crack and held her breath as she listened to Kaylie's footsteps on the worn wooden stairs, her knock on Mrs. Raduski's door, the frantic snarling of Buddy on his choke chain. Kaylie started back upstairs and Amy darted back to the tiny counter in the galley kitchen. Kaylie had given over the money. Of course, Amy had warned Mrs. Raduski how and when it was coming, and if Kaylie had headed out the front door instead, she would have been followed by both the landlady and her vicious dog.

Always best to hedge your bets.

"Amy?" Gran called feebly.

"Right there, Gran!" She opened the bedroom door.

"Are there any bananas?"

"No, Mr. Fu said the delivery didn't come. But I'm making you a cheese and turkey sandwich. Here, drink this milk—just like you used to tell me to do!"

Gran said quietly, "But you were a child, and I am not. Amy, is Kayla in trouble?"

"No. She was. It's OK now, I fixed it. Kaylie's just . . ." What? Trouble, yes. From the time she'd outgrown those pink overalls, Kaylie had been trouble.

"Is she using?"

Looking at the intelligent old eyes in the pain-ridden face, Amy couldn't lie anymore. "I don't know for sure. I hope not. But she's running with a rough crowd."

"Tell her that anything harder than pot will eventually affect her looks."

Amy blinked. It was a cynical piece of advice, based on a thorough knowledge of both her granddaughters. Amy nodded.

"And tell Mr. Fu," Gran added, "that he should read the flimsies more, or however he gets his news. Agricultural imports rose half a percent last month. We're in economic recovery. Even the president says so."

Amy smiled uncertainly. Sometimes she couldn't tell when Gran was being ironic and when she wasn't. Was the country going to stop trailing behind China and India and even Europe in everything? Was Amy's new job due to some fragile economic recovery?

It didn't matter what it was due to. It only mattered that she had it. She and Kaylie made thick, satisfying sandwiches. Kaylie even helped Amy clean up. Then, while Gran slept and Kaylie went to spend her ten dollars, Amy went to her Friday-night shift in the restaurant kitchen, her last shift. She told Charlie she was leaving. She bussed tables and scraped dishes and loaded and unloaded the ancient, unreliable dishwasher.

By eleven o'clock she was exhausted, sweaty, and stinking. She caught the bus home, got off in front of Mr. Fu's grocery, which was closed and shuttered, and that was when she saw the dog up in the tree.

A dog? In a *tree*?

At first Amy wasn't sure what she was seeing. The street was deserted and dark. Amy hurried along, cold in her thin old jacket, her can of pepper spray in her hand, anxious to get safely into her building. When she heard barking, she stopped and gazed around. More barking. She looked up. An animal cowered in the crotch of a March-bare maple, fifteen feet above the ground.

A cat. It had to be a cat. But then it barked again, Amy squinted and the animal slightly shifted its precarious position. It *was* a dog, high up in the tree.

Kids must have put it there. Amy's blood roiled; she didn't understand cruelty to animals. What did people get out of it? How could they? This was just a puppy!

It barked again, piteously. Amy called, "Just a minute, tiny dog, just a minute don't move! It'll be OK!"

A ladder. Whoever put that dog up there had used a ladder, and it didn't make much sense to carry a tall ladder a long way. So it might still be around somewhere.

Pepper spray in hand, pocket flashlight turned on, she

peered cautiously down a nearby alley. Three trash cans, one overturned, and something scurrying away from the flashlight. Her heart stopped until she saw that it was an alley cat, not a rat. However, no ladder. Could she stand on the trash can? No, not high enough. She saw nothing else she could climb on, either.

Back to the tree. It wasn't full-grown; she could reach her arms around it easily. A lower branch, not very sturdy-looking, grew from the trunk about six feet above ground. Amy jumped, caught it, and tried to pull herself up onto the branch. It broke and she fell.

"Ow!"

Fortunately she'd landed on the stretch of dirt, sparsely covered with dead grass, between the street and sidewalk. She'd torn her jeans but nothing on her seemed broken. If her old gymnastics coach had seen that move, she'd have been off the team in a New York minute.

The dog shifted again and yelped sharply. Amy leaped up to catch it. "No, puppy, don't jump! Don't jump! I might miss you!"

The dog whimpered.

Cursing, Amy put both arms around the tree and started shinnying up it. The rough bark tore at her hands. But she reached the place where the broken branch had joined the tree, grasped the stub of branch still attached, and got herself up

onto it. The palm of one hand was bleeding. By balancing carefully, she could extend the other hand to within a foot of the
dog, but no farther. Now she could see it more clearly: a little
mutt with curly gray fur, floppy ears, and terrified dark eyes.

"Now, come here, puppy, that's it, come closer—come on,
now, you can move—dammit, come to me, you stupid animal!"

The dog vanished.

Amy gasped and looked down. It must have . . . but no,
it hadn't fallen. Neither had it shifted to a position where she
couldn't see it. The dog was just *gone*—there one second and
not there the next.

A chill ran over her, as distinct from the cold she already
felt as a blizzard from a snow flurry. The dog hadn't been there.
It must have been a phantom in her mind. . . . Oh, God, what if
she couldn't tell her phantoms from reality. . . .

The chill passed. The dog had not been a phantom. She
had seen it. Whatever it was, she had actually seen it. Once, in
the science museum on a sixth-grade field trip, a curator had
demonstrated a three-dimensional hologram. He had made
a rose appear on a table, a rose so real-looking that the kids
had all exclaimed and rushed forward to touch it. Amy still remembered the eerie feeling when her hand had gone through
the rose. Had she just seen a hologram of a dog in a tree?

But who would do that? And *why*? This wasn't the sort of

neighborhood to host high-quality tech equipment. Also, the hologram of the rose had shimmered around the edges, especially when you got close to it. She had been a foot away from the dog, and she would have bet her life that it had been a solid, fleshy, breathing, terrified animal.

In a way, she had bet her life.

Still, getting down from the tree was easier than getting up. On the ground, Amy gazed upward. Nothing. Her left palm was bloody, her jeans had torn, the bruises on her body were beginning to ache.

"Damn you," she said loudly, to anyone who might be listening. Then she went home to a hot shower.

# Five

THE SCREENING ROOM held eight black leather chairs, each deep and wide, arranged in two staggered rows. Small tables between the chairs held drinks. The screen, ten feet wide and seven feet high, shone blackly in the reflection from recessed lighting. Dark red cloth covered the windowless walls.

At ten a.m. on Saturday, six people settled into the seats. James Taunton, front and center, reached down to pick a tiny piece of lint off the carpet, an action rightly perceived by the two people on either side of him as a reproach, even though of course they had nothing to do with the cleaning staff. But this was their event, their TV show, their room for the next two hours on this sunny Saturday. If a meteor hit Taunton Life

Network in the next two hours, they were responsible.

"Sir," Myra Townsend said on Taunton's right, "you understand that it's very rough. We only shot the final participant last night."

"Of course he does," said Alex Everett, on Taunton's left. "How many screenings do you estimate you've been to, sir?"

Taunton didn't answer. He held out the piece of lint to Myra, who took it. In the far seat, tech genius Mark Meyer blinked and tried to stay awake; he was *never* up at this hour of the morning. Also, his hands felt naked without a tablet in them. But it was only a few hours and then he could go back to bed. The two underlings seated behind the four said nothing, and would not have dreamed of doing so.

"Roll it," Myra said. The screen brightened.

Music started low, gradually becoming more audible: rap set to keyboards performing atonal music. The rap words were indistinguishable and stayed so, but the strange music sounded both energizing and slightly menacing. Two teenage actors, preternaturally beautiful, materialized as if floating in black space, although it was clear that their trendy boots stood on firm, unseen ground. Neither smiled.

The boy growled at the audience, "You think you're a good judge of character? Yeah, you do. Well—here's your chance to prove it."

"What you're going to see," the girl said, "might shock you

sometimes. This isn't just one more sorry reality show. The people you will see don't know they're being filmed—they *never* know for sure. We put them in unexpected situations—but not to see how they react."

"To see how *you* react," the boy said. "Can you predict what each of them will do? You predict right, and you can win big."

"Really big," the girl said. "Every week we're giving away five million dollars—just for being a good judge of human nature. Are you?"

Now pictures with names flashed behind the actors: huge close-up shots of Amy, Rafe, Violet, Lynn, Waverly, Cai, and Tommy. Each face held for three seconds; the whole loop repeated while the girl spoke again. For the first time, she smiled, a smile with a hint of nasty relish. "Seven people. We show you each of them encountering an . . . *interesting* situation, different every week. Then we list five responses they might have made."

Film of a short brunette, provocatively dressed in short shorts and a crop top, buying an ice cream, leaving the store with it. The film disappeared, replaced by a wall of glowing letters:

LYNN:
1.  Ate the ice cream!
2.  Dropped it in the gutter!

3.  Offered it to a crying child!
4.  Gave it to her dog!
5.  Threw it at a cop!

"No, nothing that lame," the boy said scornfully. "This isn't Sunday school. We're not interested in do-gooding—we're interested in your ability to judge people." The screen resumed its montage of the seven teens. "You'll get to know Lynn and the others, none of whom is an actor. You'll see them react week after week to situations they don't anticipate or understand—because some of the things that we'll arrange to happen to them aren't filmed at all. They'll never know which events are part of the show, which aren't, and which are just their widely diverse lives. They'll never see the cameras, and we've got cameras everywhere. Then you text us your vote on what *you* think they'll do in situations far edgier than buying ice cream."

"Each week," the girl said, "seven participants, five possible responses, seventy-eight thousand one hundred twenty-five chances to get it completely right. Way better odds than the lottery! And if you're one of those that get it right within the first two hours after the show ends, you split five million dollars with the other winners."

The photos on the wall cycled faster and faster, until one

face blurred into the next. The music rose to deafening levels, eerie and menacing. The title came up in scarlet:

WHO KNOWS PEOPLE, BABY—YOU?

James Taunton shifted in his chair.

"Of course," Myra said, "Mark can tweak any of the tech you think needs it. Anything."

A film started of Amy spotting the holographic dog in the tree. It ran through, followed by the return of the music as a list appeared on the screen:

AMY:
1. Walked away from the dog!
2. Called authorities to get the dog down!
3. Brought other people to get the dog down!
4. Climbed the tree to get the dog!
5. Made the dog jump in order to catch it!

Film rolled of each of the other six encountering a treed dog. Mark Meyer leaned forward to study his tech. Each film ended with a close-up of the unwitting teen's startled face after the dog vanished, followed by the list of options. The whole list and all the names, identified by small head shots, stayed on the screen while the music pulsed and, presumably, watchers phoned in their predictions.

"No," James Taunton said in his deep, oddly musical voice. "No."

Myra and Alex looked at each other. Alex spoke first. "What is—"

"This show is supposed to be edgy," Taunton said. "*Edgy.* And you give me a dog in a tree? Why not the opportunity to help an old lady across the street? No."

Myra said, "We thought that for a first, introductory show we could start simple and then escalate to—"

"No. What else do you have?"

"Right now there isn't—"

"We're done here." Taunton rose, elegant in his suit of Italian wool. Immediately a flunky in the second row of seats leaped to turn on the lights.

"Mr. Taunton, we can—"

Alex cut Myra off. "We can show you the audition footage in the alley. It's far edgier."

Mark looked up sharply. Myra said, "But it isn't even— OK, yes. Jackie, roll it!"

Taunton sat down again. Another drink was deposited soundlessly at his elbow. Jackie, clearly terrified, jumped to the computer and fumbled among files. Random shots came up:

Waverly answering questions, Violet dancing, Tommy talking slowly, without sound. Finally Jackie found the right file.

When the film, unedited and too long and occasionally jerky, without lists or music, ended, Taunton said, "Yes."

Myra said eagerly, "It can be——"

"Give me more like that. Exciting. Dangerous. Rough footage by Monday morning."

Mark said, "But my tech with the dog was so——"

Myra put a hand on his arm and squeezed hard. "You'll get more tech scenarios, Mark. By Monday, sir, certainly."

Taunton left. Alex motioned Jackie and the other minion to leave with him. When the two producers and the tech head were left alone, Alex said to Myra, "Well, do you think you kissed his ass enough?"

"Shut up, Alex. We're still in, which is all that counts. What do we do for the next scenario?"

Mark looked up from his tablet, which he'd pulled out of his pocket the moment Taunton left. "We move up scenario number five, of course. To tomorrow."

Alex frowned. "I don't know if everything for that can be assembled on such short notice, and——"

"Bullshit," Mark said. "You can do it if you have to. And my guys are ready."

"Mark," Alex said with exaggerated and condescending

patience, "you seem to think your piece is all that matters. The tech is interesting, sure, but let me tell you yet again, since you seem to have forgotten it, that the heart of this thing is—"

"We can do it," Myra said. "And I think Mark is right. We should. Then if we edit all night, we can show Taunton something on Monday."

"Aren't you going to be a little busy on Monday, Myra?" Alex said. "Think again. That's the day the kids all report for 'work.'" His fingers made little quotes in the air.

"Alex, don't you ever get tired of throwing up roadblocks?" Mark said.

"Mark's right, Alex," said Myra. "We can do it if we have to. And we have to. Taunton needs to see something spectacular. We've got forty-eight hours to pull this together."

"Shazam," Mark said.

# Six

AMY WAS HAVING a suspiciously good Saturday morning.

Gran felt much better; she even got out of bed and sat at their tiny table for breakfast. Kaylie woke early enough to join them for breakfast, a rarity. Kaylie folded up the sleep sofa without being asked. Amy had turned up the thermostat and made a big pot of coffee. If you didn't look at the peeling walls and exposed overhead pipes, it was almost like old times.

"Yum," Gran said, carefully setting down her cup. "Good coffee. What are you girls' plans for the day?"

"I have a lot of homework," Kaylie said.

Amy and Gran stared. Homework? *Kaylie?*

"Don't look at me like that," Kaylie snapped. "I have to graduate, don't I? Two stinking months and twelve days left."

Amy recovered herself. If Kaylie was voluntarily doing homework, there was some ulterior motive. Carefully monitoring her tone—not too eager, not too big-sister, not too anything—she asked, "Do you want some help?"

"Yes," Kaylie said promptly. "You can do all the math assignments."

"I didn't say—"

"Kayla Jane," Gran said, leaning forward, "what's going on? Are you in trouble at school again?"

"No. Really, I'm not. But I want to compete in All-City with the band, Friday night at the Arena. A 'talent show' might be lame but what the fuck, it's publicity, and I can't be in it unless my grades are 'current.' Bunch of bullshit."

Amy had heard Kaylie's band, Orange Decision. Amy, with her lousy ear for music, had no idea if they were good or not. They were certainly loud. But anything that got Kaylie doing homework was terrific. She said, "We can start right after I make an appointment for Gran at her old doctor's." Full medical benefits!

"How are you going to do that? On Mrs. Raduski's phone? She won't let you. And incidentally, Buddy nearly bit me when I got in last night. Fucking dog. Oh, sorry, Gran—sweet misguided canine."

"With fucking bad genes," Gran said, and Kaylie nearly choked on her coffee, laughing.

Definitely a good day.

"No, not on Mrs. Raduski's phone," Amy said. "I have just enough left from the job advance to buy three of those cheap cells with prepaid minutes. But they're only for emergencies, Kaylie. There won't be many minutes on any of them."

"Good idea," Kaylie said amiably. "I'll stay with Gran while you go buy them. Gran, maybe you can help me with this essay I have to write for history?"

Kaylie must really want this All-City gig.

Amy bounced down the stairs and through the vestibule—no Buddy—into a warm, clear spring day. She tilted back her head to let the sunshine fall on her face. Some children tore past in a grade-school pack, chasing a soccer ball in some made-up street game of their own. One little boy flashed her a smile as rich and sweet as chocolate cake.

Mr. Fu stood sadly behind the counter of his cramped store. Amy bought three of the cheapest prepaid cells. "Still no bananas," Mr. Fu said. At the print kiosk three blocks over, Amy printed a flimsie of the *Post-Herald* for Gran. When she returned home, a truck blazoned CALLAHAN MOVERS stood across the street, with men unloading furniture.

That was unusual in this neighborhood. People moved

often, seeking lower rents or fleeing rent due, sometimes in the middle of the night. But they borrowed friends' pickup trucks or they loaded what they could carry into a taxi and abandoned the rest or they rented a flat dolly and laboriously wheeled furniture ten blocks to the next temporary residence. Real movers cost money.

A woman came out of the building and directed the movers. Behind them on the sidewalk, a boy of about Amy's age sat in a wheelchair beside a small table. On the table was a chess set. Amy crossed the street.

He didn't notice her at first, so intent was he on replaying the game notated in a book beside the chess board. Amy, gazing at the game, recognized it instantly.

"Hey," she said. "The Immortal Game."

The boy's head jerked up, startled. He wasn't handsome but he had beautiful eyes, gray with flecks of silver. A thick blanket lay across the wheelchair, hiding his legs. His tone was cautious. "You know the Immortal Game?"

"Sure. Adolf Anderssen versus Lionel Kieseritzky, London, 1851."

His silver-gray gaze sharpened. "You play?"

"Yes."

"FIDE rating?"

"Was 1900. I don't belong now."

He didn't ask why not. She recognized his type immediately, from countless tournaments in her pre-Collapse life: the superbright, socially challenged chess nerd. Amy felt at ease with him in a way she never did with hot guys.

He said, "Wanna play?"

"I can't right now, but maybe I could come over later, if it's all right with your family."

He looked around vaguely, as if he'd forgotten he had a family. The woman emerged again from the building, saying, "No, no, I told whoever I talked to on the phone that the sofa wasn't going to fit through the doorway and would have to—oh, hello."

"I'm Amy Kent, from across the street." Amy held out her hand.

The woman took it, her gaze focusing suddenly as she realized that an actual girl had been talking to her nerdy son. "Hello! I'm Ann O'Malley and this is my son Paul. We're just moving in, as you can see." She laughed, a sound tinged with embarrassment. She didn't want to find herself in this neighborhood, Amy thought. Well, who did? Still, she seemed nice.

"Ma," Paul said, "she's coming over later to play chess."

"Oh, well . . . sure." Amy saw her glance around at her disassembled household, scattered on the sidewalk. The kids with the soccer ball tore past in the other direction. The ball bounced off a lacquered Chinese desk. And the woman's sweater, although old, was beautifully made. These people had had some money once, and had it no longer. Amy warmed to them.

"If it's too much trouble, Mrs. O'Malley, Paul and I can play another day, after you have a chance to—"

"No, no, come tonight. Say, seven o'clock? Paul never finds girls—I mean, people—who can play chess with him. And call me Ann."

"OK." Amy smiled and moved off. But first she couldn't resist reaching out to make the next move in the famous game that every serious chess player knew by heart: black knight to g7.

"Hey!" Paul said, somewhere between indignation and delight.

Definitely a good day!

But the next one was not.

On Sunday morning Gran awoke feverish. Her doctor's appointment wasn't until three. Kaylie, out late last night practicing with her band, slept past noon. Amy rushed back and forth between the bedroom and kitchen to bring Gran hot tea, aspirin, cold cloths for her forehead, food she didn't eat. Every time Amy passed Kaylie, lying in an insensible lump, her resentment grew. It didn't help that last evening Amy had played three games of chess with Paul and had lost two. Paul had remained monosyllabic throughout. Outside, a sullen sky spit rain.

When Kaylie finally woke, she was grumpy. "Do you have to make so much noise?"

"Do you have to be so little help?"

"Lighten up, for chrissakes."

"You're helping me take Gran to the doctor's, do you hear me?" Amy said fiercely.

"I said I would, didn't I? What the hell's wrong with you? You cream for that crippled chess player and he push you away?"

"No!" Despite her familiarity with Kaylie's nastiness in this sort of mood, Amy felt stung. It was true that she'd liked Paul more as the chess games went on, but it was also true that Amy had learned to be wary about boys. She knew—now, after a few bad attempts at relationships—that she got attracted too soon, too often, too indiscriminately. Her sister's barb hurt precisely because there was some truth in it. Keith, for instance, at the restaurant. Two dates and Amy had been hooked, and then Keith had switched his interest to one of the waitresses. Even Gran had said gently to her, during her stupid heartache over Keith, "You feel too much, Amy."

Kaylie followed up her advantage by saying scornfully as she disappeared into the bathroom, "You always have to be in *lo-oo-oo-ve*."

Kaylie, who loved nobody. Sometimes, Amy thought, not even Gran.

But Kaylie was patient and careful as they got Gran to the bus stop, onto the bus, to the doctor's office, which was located in a small, old-fashioned strip mall. Half the shops were boarded up and the parking lot was nearly empty. Another of the huge red graffiti sprawled across the side of a brick building: TIMES BE TOUGH MAN. More and more of them were appearing around the city, and every time Amy saw one she wanted to say: *Put in a comma*. Which was really not the appropriate response.

In front of the doctor's office, three steps led up to a small concrete terrace set with big flowerpots, all of them empty and a few broken. A low roof shielded the terrace from the intermittent drizzle. Gran negotiated the steps with difficulty. The doctor took her into the back of the office, alone.

All Gran would say as she emerged, clearly in pain, was, "They took blood, ran tests. He'll call me later in the week with the results." She held up her new cell and tried to smile. But it was so hard for her to walk out of the building that both Amy and Kaylie had to support her. Oh, why hadn't

Amy saved enough money out of her advance to pay for a cab!

"Hey," Kaylie said as they pushed through the glass door and stood at the top of the steps, "what's all *this*?"

"Run!" a woman screamed, racing from a narrow alley between stores toward her car. "Plague!"

A siren sounded, so loud that Amy couldn't hear whatever Kaylie screamed at her. Two more people, a boy and girl with terrified faces, ran across the parking lot. Then Amy saw them.

Rats. They poured from the alley, a dozen of them, then another dozen. Some ran jerkily, staggering; some walked normally. No, not normally—there was foam around their mouths. And blood.

"Get inside!" Gran cried. Kaylie was already tugging at the glass door behind her. It was locked. Two of the rats, perhaps attracted by the noise, stopped at the bottom of the steps and turned. Amy stared at their long, ugly snouts and flat black eyes. One drew back its lips and bared bloody fangs.

Over police sirens coming closer, Gran's voice came clear and strong right beside Amy's ear. "Rabies or plague or some mutation—*climb*, girls. Climb!" She raised a skinny, trembling arm to point at an iron flower trellis bare of flowers. The trellis rose from a huge stone flowerpot, now full of cigarette butts and Doritos wrappers, up to the low roof over the terrace.

Amy couldn't think. Jumbled thoughts invaded her

mind—that was the word, *invaded*, like a conquering army. *Rattus rattus*. Black Death, and a third of Europe dead in the Middle Ages. Rabies: rabid squirrels, rabid raccoons, rabid dogs—Atticus Finch in *To Kill a Mockingbird*—rabid rats. Rats could climb, but these might be too sick and the trellis was thin-runged and slippery. Winston in George Orwell's *1984*, forced to wear a cage of rats on his head until he betrayed the revolution. *They go first for the eyes. . . .*

The rat with bared teeth had already climbed the first step, where it stood hissing at them, the most horrible sound Amy had ever heard. In the parking lot the girl had fallen and a rat leaped on top of her body. "Go!" Gran said.

Kaylie stood on the lip of the flowerpot, one foot on the trellis. She looked at Gran, obviously unable to climb, shouted, "Fuck fuck fuck!" and jumped back down again. Kaylie grabbed Gran's purse and held it like a weapon. "Come on, you fucker, just try it! Amy! Don't just stand there—fight!"

Into Amy's mind came a phantom, clear and sharp as the knife Amy didn't have: *an empty cardboard box, flaps open, so void of contents that the box didn't even contain air.*

She said, "They're not real."

"What?" Kaylie screamed. "Don't you have that pepper spray?"

"They're not real," Amy repeated, just as two cop cars

squealed into the parking lot. The rats were like the holographic dog in a tree, and this was—

Someone somewhere above her shouted "Cut!"

The rats all vanished.

Cops heaved themselves from their squad cars. The girl on the ground got up, fastidiously brushing dirt off her jeans and sweatshirt. One of the policemen stared up at the roof, the other demanded of Gran, "What's going on here?"

Kaylie said, "I think it's a movie! Gran, we walked into a movie shoot!"

A man climbed down the iron trellis. "Is there a problem, officer?"

Kaylie said eagerly, "Are the cameras on the roof?"

The cop said, "You got a permit for this?"

They began to argue. The man, who looked not much older than Amy, said it was a film for his college course and he didn't need a permit because it was a "noncommercial endeavor." The cop, unimpressed, wanted to know just what had happened. Amy stopped listening to them.

She'd been wrong. Wrong to think that some lame student movie was actually connected to the dog that had vanished from a tree, and that both were some kind of plot against her, Amy Kent, by her new employer. Why? What would they gain? And who was she to think she was important enough for anybody to follow her around, setting up weird situations and filming them? This was just a movie—now more young people carrying camcorders spilled from an empty shop next door— and she was an idiot. The young people wore sweatshirts say- ing MIT and even Amy knew that the Massachusetts Institute of Technology had the nation's most advanced robotics and optics labs. Wrong, wrong, *wrong*.

And wrong most of all in not even trying to defend Gran. Kaylie had grabbed a purse—a purse!—to do that. Amy had pepper spray in her pocket and, frozen with fear, hadn't even reached for it. She was a coward, a wuss, wrong wrong wrong.

Gran staggered. Amy caught her before she could fall and eased her to sit on the edge of the flowerpot. The cop stopped arguing with the movie guy long enough to say, "Is the old lady all right?"

"No!" Amy said, trying fiercely to keep back tears. "She's my grandmother and she's very sick. Please, can you give us a ride home? I don't have any money and—please!"

The cop said gently, "Sure, kid." Over his shoulder he bel- lowed, "Murphy! Take this family home!"

Murphy, his face young beneath his cap, helped Gran into the backseat of the squad car, all the while staring hungrily at Kaylie. She scowled back; cops were emphatically not her style. Amy sat miserably squashed in between Gran and

Kaylie, staring at the metal grill that kept dangerous criminals from assaulting Murphy and his partner. *Wrong, wrong, wrong.* A movie. Special-effects rats. Kaylie leaping off the trellis to defend Gran. Amy frozen, her pepper spray untouched in her pocket.

But . . .

Why had the glass door to the doctor's office suddenly been locked?

"She froze," Alex Everett said, gazing at the screen.

"Good," Myra Townsend said.

# Seven

**MONDAY**

MONDAY MORNING AMY arrived for her first day of work at Taunton Life Network on Sixth Avenue, downtown. She'd left at seven since she had to walk and had no money left for the bus, but at least it had stopped raining. The building was huge, a glass-and-blue-steel skyscraper that occupied the entire block. Amy found the entrance she'd been instructed to use, a small side door on Remington Street. A security guard had her put her fingertips to a scanner, then consulted a tablet.

"Go ahead, miss. Through those detectors, elevators on your right. Go to Room 864-B."

She was nervous. Was she dressed OK? She wore her best pants and Kaylie's green silk sweater, swiped again before Kaylie woke up. Her shoes, though, were her old school flats, comfortable for walking but worn and with a tiny hole on one side. Would jeans and sneakers have been better? Myra Townsend had said they wanted an "athletic" employee. Still, the pants had enough stretch for good movement—

She needn't have worried. The elevator took her to the basement, where she wandered low-ceilinged, featureless corridors until she found room 864-B. A bored-looking man with another tablet said, "Name?"

"Amy Kent. I'm new today and—"

"Cubicle 96."

More than a hundred people, all doing . . . *something* in their separate cubicles. In cubicle 96 Amy found a phone, a headset, a thick sheaf of papers, and a list of instructions:

Call each name on the list. Follow the script EXACTLY as you conduct the survey. If the initial response is that no one in this household plays video games, don't waste time in chitchat. Politely say "thank you," hang up, and go on to the next name on the list. Remember, your calls may be monitored for training and quality-control purposes.

Telephone surveys. She would be doing exactly what she had lied to Gran and Kaylie that she would be doing.

No. There had been a mistake.

"There's been a mistake," she told the bored man with the tablet after she'd wended her way back through the cubicles and found him again. "This isn't supposed to be my job."

"Says here it is."

"No. I need to talk to Myra Townsend."

She hoped the name would impress him. It didn't. He consulted his tablet again. "Ms. Townsend will come get you later in the morning to take you to Human Resources to fill out paperwork."

"Maybe, but meantime there's been a mistake. I was hired for a different job!"

"Yeah? What job?"

"Well . . . I don't know."

He sighed. "Miss, do you want to get to work or do you want to be escorted out of the building? I can arrange that. You have something to take up with Ms. Townsend, you can do it when she arrives."

"But—"

"You in or out? Choose."

"In," Amy said. There didn't seem to be any choice. She went back to cubicle 96.

For two hours she conducted telephone surveys, trying to find out what people thought about a computer game from TLN's game division and recording the results on photocopied forms. Thirty-seven people hung up on her. Two men tried to talk dirty to her. Three lonely souls wanted to chat. Forty-one people had never heard of the game; sixty more had heard of it but had never played it. Sixty-one if you also counted Amy. Twelve people actually answered the survey questions.

Did people really spend eight hours a day at this mind-numbing task? Amy couldn't hear what the people in the other cubicles were doing, but surely TLN didn't need more than a hundred people doing phone surveys all day, every day? Even her restaurant job, hot and muscle-straining and messy, had been better than this.

At ten Myra Townsend arrived, and Amy nearly sprang at her. "Ms. Townsend! I thought—I mean, you told me—"

"Oh, Amy, I'm so sorry! There's been a mix-up. This isn't your job at all. Come with me, dear."

Amy relaxed. So it *was* a mistake. And Ms. Townsend's kind face and warm brown eyes were the most welcome things she'd ever seen. She followed the older woman from the room, automatically noting her gray pantsuit—Jil Sander, Amy guessed—gray-and-pink silk scarf, just-right Cuban heels. Ms. Townsend kept up a flow of apologetic chatter, delivered in a discreet cloud of rose perfume.

She led Amy up in the elevator to the main lobby, a vast expanse of marble floor, uniformed guards, a forest of plants in marble pots, and crowds of well-dressed people. A wall with three revolving doors gave onto Sixth Avenue. A side door was open to an alley, through which more uniformed men wheeled metal boxes on handcarts from the open back door of an armored truck.

Amy saw Violet Sanderson in the crowd, walking beside a middle-aged man.

"Hey," Amy said, pleased, "I met that girl over there, the one with long black hair, at the——"

"Everybody down! *Now!*" someone shouted.

Men in hoods, armed with automatic weapons, suddenly surged into the lobby. The men with the metal boxes drew their own weapons. The rat-a-tat of guns deafened Amy, along with screams and shouts. She and Myra Townsend dropped to the floor just as the man pushing the dolly dropped, spouting blood. Hooded men blocked the doors. Alarms sounded.

Just like yesterday——

But this was no movie, no holographic special effect. One of the guards bringing in the metal boxes moaned as he lay dying, a sound that pierced Amy's gut. Ms. Townsend had flung one arm protectively if uselessly over Amy's body, as if to shield her.

"Nobody move!" one of the gunmen shouted. "Don't move and you don't get hurt!"

Amy saw a girl move.

The girl crept slowly across the floor toward a baby. The baby hadn't stopped screaming and its mother lay still, blood on her back. She'd been hit in the exchange of gunfire with the box-deliverers. A gunman shouted into the terrified silence of the lobby, "Shut that kid up! You, hold still!" He waved his gun at the girl on the floor.

She only crawled faster, rising now to all fours. Amy, sprawled flat behind her, could see only a blonde head, a shapely rear in expensive jeans, and the dramatic red soles of Christian Louboutin sandals.

"I said stop, bitch!" a hooded man screamed, waving his gun at the girl.

She kept going, reaching the baby just as the gunman let loose a spray of bullets above everybody's head. The girl threw her body on top of the baby, shielding it. Just as a boy rose to his feet on the opposite side of the lobby, Amy felt a tug on her shoulder. She turned her head.

Violet Sanderson crouched beside her, whispering fiercely, "Do something!"

Do something? Was Violet crazy? The blonde girl had taken an admirable risk to protect that baby, but during an armed robbery the best thing to do was lie still, follow orders, hope to not get *shot* . . .

Across the lobby the boy launched himself at a hooded man guarding the revolving doors.

At the same moment Violet said, "Here we go, One Two Three," and yanked Amy hard. Violet, eight inches taller than Amy, was *strong*. Amy was pulled to her feet.

"Stop!" she cried, but Violet launched both of them forward, straight into the nearest gunman, who went down under the girls' combined weight. He didn't fire but instead said mildly, "Hey!"

*No no no*, robbers didn't behave like this! This was—

And then the phantom in her mind: *the empty box again, holding nothing.*

"That's enough," Myra Townsend's voice called loudly. "Thank you, everybody."

The gunman untangled himself from Violet and Amy, rubbing his elbow. Men pulled off black hoods. The dead mother rose from the floor and hit a switch on the baby doll, which stopped screaming. The dead guard rose, seized his handcart, and wheeled it away. People brushed off their clothes, chatting and shooting amused glances around the lobby. And Amy rushed over to Myra Townsend, grabbed her gray Jil Sander, and screamed in her face, "You tell me what's going on and you do it this very minute!"

"Really, Amy," Ms. Townsend said, freeing her sleeve from

Amy's clutch, "why don't you already know? Everybody else does."

Violet Sanderson pulled Amy away. "Come here. I'll explain."

"Explain what!" The "second interview" had been bad enough; Amy had never been this furious in her entire life. Her stomach acids boiled, her chest was about to explode. One more word from Myra Townsend and she would slug her.

Violet said softly, "Look around you, One Two Three."

People were crossing the lobby toward them: the blonde girl who had "saved" the baby, now looking smug. The boy who had assaulted the "robber." Two more boys and another girl. The real TLN security guards, some looking pleased and some sulky, resumed what Amy guessed were their normal positions.

Ms. Townsend said, "Follow me, everyone," and set off briskly toward the elevators.

Violet said, "It was a setup, One Two Three. We were being filmed."

Well, Amy had figured out that much! She snapped, "I didn't see any cameras!"

"And you never will. The latest microcams are supersmall. Come on!"

Ms. Townsend led them to a small conference room on

the second floor. Amy recognized the bald man who was waiting there: he had interviewed her the first time. Everyone sat around a polished wooden table. Ms. Townsend, looking harried, excused herself: "I'm needed in editing."

"I'm Alex Everett," the bald man said. "Before we do the rest of the introductions, let me explain for those of you who still don't understand what you're doing here." He winked at Amy, who kept her face as blank as she could manage. "You lucky seven have been chosen from hundreds of applicants for Taunton Life Network's newest show, *Who Knows People, Baby—You?* Myra Townsend and I are the producers, and this is how the show works."

As he explained, Amy seethed. So the dog in the tree had been a setup and she'd been filmed. The "robbery" in the lobby. The "rats" outside the doctor's office—which she had believed were a legitimate student-film project. She had been played, and she didn't like it one bit.

And what kind of lame title was *Who Knows People, Baby?* Give me a break!

Had everyone else figured out what was going on? Obviously Violet had, and the blonde, and the boy who had attacked the guard. Also, from her knowing expression, the small girl with the sharp-featured face. But not the other two boys. At least she wasn't alone.

Not that it helped. She'd been made to look like a fool. She interrupted Alex, who was now explaining how viewers could vote on a slate of the "players' possible responses to each scenario." Amy wasn't playing.

"I quit," she said loudly.

Everyone's head swiveled to look at her.

"You lied to me, and you filmed me without my consent, and I'm not even sure that's legal!"

"Actually," Alex said, "no one lied. You were deliberately not told the details of the job you accepted until we had completed the first few scenarios. That some people guessed when you did not perhaps means that they are more sophisticated about television. Nor did we do anything illegal. You gave your consent to film you in the contract you signed."

All those papers thrust in front of her: *Sign here, initial here, sign here* . . . All those lawyers. And she'd been too elated at the prospect of a good paycheck and full medical benefits to read anything. Medical benefits . . . Gran . . .

"Of course," Alex said, watching Amy closely, "you're free to quit if you choose. This is a job, not serfdom. There is a long waiting list of girls ready to take your place. But then we'll expect repayment of the advance you've received."

Mrs. Raduski's rent. Gran.

Violet, in the chair beside her, found Amy's hand and squeezed it.

Amy choked out, "I'll stay."

"Good," Alex said, "we're happy to have you. Now, the next important thing—none of you are allowed to blog about the show, or Tweet about it, or post anything about it on Facebook or anywhere else on the Internet until Myra and I give you the go-ahead. That's in your contracts, and we mean it. You can send private e-mails, messages, or Tweets to your family about your participation, but nothing public. Doing so will result in not only dismissal from the show but legal action. Everybody understand?"

Everybody did. Alex finished explaining the show, adding that the first episodes would air very soon as a replacement for a show that had been abruptly canceled.

Until then, Amy realized, she would never know whether anything that happened outside of her apartment was real or not. Well, she would just spend a lot of time in her apartment! Unless—

"Can you film us in our homes?"

"No, of course not," Alex said.

"Will we come to work here each day?"

"Yes, and your hours here are eight thirty to six, with an hour for lunch, which is free to you in the company cafeteria. You'll be doing a variety of tasks, including previewing new TV shows, testing computer games from our games division, even assisting on the sets of different programs. It's great training for anyone wanting a career in TV, or a spectacular assist to your résumés."

Violet said, "I was promised a spot in the chorus line of *Dance Dance Dance*."

"With one guaranteed appearance on air, I know," Alex said. "You'll get it, after this show has filmed all its episodes. You'll all get whatever you were promised in your contracts. Now, let's introduce ourselves. Lynn? Tell us a little about yourself."

The small, sharp-faced girl to Alex's left said, "Well, I'm Lynn Demaris; I'm eighteen years old. I just graduated in December from a full-form high school, and I want a career in TV production. That's why I'm here. And I'm grateful for the opportunity, Alex." She smiled, eyes downcast as if overcome with gratitude.

The abrupt phantom in Amy's mind astonished her: the same empty box that had appeared twice before. But about this girl—what did it mean? Lynn Demaris, dressed in undistinguished jeans and sweater, had nondescript features and brown hair that would frizz at the first hint of dampness. She looked completely ordinary.

Alex prompted, "And do you have any hobbies, Lynn?"

"Playing computer games. And I'm *good*."

A few laughs and smiles around the table; everyone was relaxing except Amy. Alex said, "Waverly?"

The blonde who had thrown herself on the doll gave them a practiced smile. She wore clothes that Amy thought of as "punk socialite"—expensive jeans, silk top artfully sewn in ragged layers, and the Louboutin red-heeled sandals. Her spiked jewelry, including a nose ring, said *trendy* and her perfect teeth said *money*. "I'm Waverly Balter-Wells. I'm seventeen and I'm an actress. This is my first big break, but it won't be my last. I hold a brown belt in karate and I enjoy golf and racing my parents' sailboats."

"La di da," Violet whispered to Amy.

Amy had to lean forward and crane her neck to see the next speaker, mostly hidden by the huge bulk of another boy. The moment she glimpsed him she knew two things: that he was the one who had assaulted the fake criminal in the lobby, and that he was the most gorgeous person she had ever seen.

"I'm Cai Marsh," he said.

His thick black hair fell over his forehead; instantly Amy wanted to run her hands through it. Pale brown skin like warm sand. Eyes like pieces of blue sky. Full red mouth. Amy felt her body grow taut and she crossed her arms across her chest. *No no no.* This job was complicated enough without any stupid yearning for a boy who would never look at her.

"I'm eighteen, half Hawaiian and half Welsh, which is where I get such a weird name. 'Cai' means 'full of color' in Chinese and 'rejoice' in Welsh. I surf, or at least I did when we lived in Hawaii. I have no idea what I want to do for a living eventually, and I didn't know what I would be doing here until the dog-in-a-tree thing Thursday night. But I'm really glad to meet you all."

Oh, God, he sounded as if he meant it. Nice as well as hot. Amy deliberately looked away from him.

"I'm Violet Sanderson, a dancer. I trained with the Caroline Mallard Company for six years. I'm eighteen, and with dance class every day and now this job, I don't have time for any other hobbies. Although I do like shopping."

Waverly rolled her eyes. She and Violet seemed to have taken a dislike to each other on sight.

Next to speak was the thin, brown-haired boy whom Amy had glimpsed at her callback audition. "Rafael Torres—Rafe," he said flatly. "I'm here for the money."

Amy looked at him more closely, both liking and surprised at his bald honesty. He said, "I'm sixteen. I work a crappy job, or I did until now, doesn't matter what it was. I'm interested in politics and science. Someday I'm going to med school and becoming a doctor, and after that I'm going to solve the Riemann conjecture."

Everyone looked puzzled. Apparently only Amy knew that the Riemann conjecture was math's holy grail, a problem the best mathematical minds in the world had not been able to solve in over a hundred and fifty years. Rafael Torres was very smart, and either he was very arrogant or his brusqueness covered up massive insecurity. There was a little silence.

"Tommy?" Alex prompted.

The tall boy sitting next to Amy blinked twice. Slowly, as if dragging the words from memory, he said, "My name is Tommy Wimmer. I'm eighteen. My address is 643 Sycamore Lane Apartment 3B. I live with my uncle Sam. His phone number is—"

"That's fine, Tommy," Alex said as shock replaced the dregs of Amy's anger. What was this boy doing here? Either his IQ was subnormal or he was mildly autistic. A girl like Tommy had lived next door to Amy pre-Collapse, before Gran's investments tanked and she got sick and lost both her job and the house. Amy had tried to be extra kind to Elise, because most of the other kids were not.

Alex said, "What do you like to do, Tommy?"

"I like insects and spiders. I make plastic models of spiders. There are over thirty thousand species of spiders. The hairy mygalomorphs like—"

"Good, good. Amy?"

"I'm Amy Kent. I'm sixteen, and I like chess, math, and gymnastics." Let them know right away how much of a nerd she was. "Anybody else here play chess?"

Nobody answered, unsurprisingly, although she'd thought that Rafe might play. Well, at least she had Paul O'Malley across the street. Waverly's lip quirked with superior amusement.

Alex Everett opened a box on the table and pulled out papers. "Well, then, let's fill out the paperwork that Human Resources demands. Now, these forms are W-2's—"

Afterward, as they all left the conference room, Amy put a hand on Violet's arm until they trailed behind the others, out of earshot. "Violet, you told me to 'do something' in that fake lobby attack, and you were going to take me with you when you leaped up for the cameras. Why are you helping me? Aren't we supposed to be rivals?"

"No, it's not a direct competition, One Two Three— weren't you listening? But if it becomes one, and I wouldn't put it past that bitch Myra Townsend, I want an ally. Together we can come up with more camera-pleasing ploys than one person alone. You in with me?"

Amy didn't want to "come up with camera-pleasing" anything. Nor was she ambitious to succeed at this show. But she didn't want to be fired, and she liked Violet. "Yes, I'm in."

"Great!" Violet said. "Now look at that Cai! Too bad I already have a boyfriend. Did you ever see anything so hunky in your life?"

"I didn't notice," Amy said.

Violet laughed. "Sure you didn't. You're not exactly a poker face, One Two Three. But don't worry, nobody else was watching you."

"Actually," Amy said, desperately hoping to deflect Violet, "I already have a boyfriend, too. His name is Paul. He plays chess."

"Ah," Violet said, which could have meant anything. "I see."

Violet saw too much. Myra and Alex staged too much. And Amy—"*You feel too much, Amy,*" Gran always said. Well, not this time. Amy had a job to concentrate on—even if she still, after three scenarios, two holographic species, and one gallon of fake blood, wasn't exactly sure what it was going to demand of her. Or when.

# Eight

ON THE LONG WALK home, every time some-one passed Amy on the sidewalk, every time a car slowed for a stop sign, every time a window opened in a building beside her, Amy expected the start of another of TLN's "scenarios." Anything could happen at any minute; she had to be ready, she had to respond—

A squirrel ran down a tree and darted across her path, and she cried out.

"Hey, relax, kid, it's just a squirrel," a man said, smiling at her.

Was he part of a scenario? No, he just kept walking. The squirrel ran away, just a squirrel. The children running past were just children—but why was that one girl looking back over her shoulder, directly at Amy?

No reason. Just children.

*Calm down!*

It was with enormous relief that she finally unlocked the door to the apartment, her refuge from Taunton Life Network. The delicious smell of stew wafted toward her. Kaylie stood at the stove, stirring. The table was set, the apartment clean. Gran sat in the easy chair by the window, a blanket across her knees.

"Kaylie," Amy said, "that smells so good—wait, stew? I didn't buy any stew meat."

"I did," Kaylie said.

"With what?" Amy couldn't imagine her sister shoplifting a package of cubed beef, but with Kaylie, anything was possible.

"With your money," Kaylie said serenely. "I told Mr. Fu you got a really good job and so he let me have some things on credit until Friday. You get paid every Friday."

"How did you know that?" Amy said. She herself hadn't known that.

"I called the TV station and said I was doing a research paper on the economy and had hard times changed how often they paid their employees? And the woman said no, they'd always paid weekly instead of biweekly, for a lot of boring reasons I didn't listen to."

Gran rolled her eyes. To Amy she said, "How was the first day on the job?"

"Boring but easy," Amy said. Gran looked at her more closely and frowned.

Kaylie was enormously pleased with herself. She pushed Gran's easy chair to the table, served the stew, and informed Amy that she had attended school that day: "The whole lame thing, even math," so that she could turn in all the back assignments she and Amy had done over the weekend. "So I'm cleared for All-City on Friday night, as long as I go to school every single day this week. That'll be hell, but it's worth it. Orange Decision is going to *kill* at that show. And I'll bet that talent scouts show up from the big music companies and everything, and they'll see us play."

"Talent scouts?" Gran said. "At a youth show?"

"Why not? Kids are where the talent is."

Amy and Gran exchanged looks. Gran said, "Kayla, I don't want you to get your expectations up too high and then the—"

Kaylie scowled. "Why are you always knocking me down?"

"I'm not, I only—"

"If it was Amy doing something, you'd be telling her how she could conquer the world! But me you just put down!"

"I do not," Gran said with a touch of the steady, level-tone authority she'd lost ever since she got sick. "I just want you to be realistic, Kayla. I'm sure your band is good, but there are so—"

"You're not sure we're good," Kaylie said. "You've never even heard us. And now I don't want you to. Either of you. Stay away Friday night!"

Amy said, "Kaylie, of course we're coming, or at least I am and if Gran feels well enough to—"

"I said stay away! I don't want you there, bringing us down!" Kaylie stood up so fast that her stew sloshed over the rim of her bowl. She grabbed her jacket off the peg by the door. "I'm going to practice! Saint Amy can clean up!" She slammed out.

"That was my fault," Gran said. "She's all on edge about this band performance. I'm going to be there Friday night, Amy, no matter what."

"Let's see how you feel then."

"Don't talk to me like a child," Gran said sharply. "I'm ill but I'm not five."

It was too much. The weird job, money, Kaylie, now Gran—Amy put her head in her hands and let the tears come.

She felt Gran's hands on her shoulders. "I'm sorry, honey. I shouldn't speak to you like that. You're holding it all together here and you're only sixteen. . . . Please forgive me."

The words were like all the lollipops, all the kisses on all the booboos that Gran had given over the years. Amy raised her head, leaned back, and let her grandmother massage her shoulders.

"God, your muscles are knotted as macramé. Let me knead them."

"Mmmm, that feels good."

But after just a few moments the old hands faltered. Amy got up. "Gran?"

"Just a little dizzy. . . ."

Amy helped her into bed. Pale and drawn against the pillow, Gran said, "You remind me so much of your mother."

She almost never mentioned Amy and Kayla's mother. Gran didn't believe in what she called "wallowing in grief." Amy glanced at her mother's picture on the wall and waited, in case there was more.

Gran said, "Kayla looks like Carolyn, but you have her sweet and trusting nature. She would be proud of you, Amy."

Amy didn't know what to say. This wasn't like Gran. Was it her illness that made her so emotional? At the same time, Amy sucked up the praise like a vacuum cleaner. This place *was* her refuge.

But then Gran said, "Why are you lying to me about your job?"

"I—I'm not . . ."

"Yes, you are. You didn't have a 'boring but easy' day. You had the workday from hell, and you're trying to protect me from knowing why. Please don't do that. It just makes me feel older, sicker, and more useless than I already am."

"You're not—"

"Amy," Gran said, and now there was a dangerous glint in her eyes.

"OK," Amy said, "it wasn't boring and it isn't easy. I'm a . . . a contestant on a new kind of game show, and it's nerve-racking because today we got our first set of problems and I didn't do well."

"Like *Jeopardy!*?"

"Not exactly."

"What kind of problems?"

"Logical." That was true, sort of. Amy was not going to worry Gran any more than she had to.

"You should be good at logic. You are at math."

"I'll do better next time."

"I know you will."

Amy could see Gran's strength ebbing. Her eyes closed. "Maybe I'll just sleep a little. . . . Kayla was wonderful today but it's tiring when she's home, sort of like inhabiting a closed space with a small tornado. Amy, why don't you go play chess with Paul? Chess always calms you. I don't know why, with all its mock warfare, but it does. Kayla can do the dishes after band practice. Use up some of that energy."

"I will," Amy said. Suddenly chess looked as tempting as a couture dress. "But here's your cell by the bed, and you call me if you need anything."

"I will," Gran murmured, already half asleep.

Chess did calm Amy. Paul, silent and awkward, wanted no small talk from her. Mrs. O'Malley watched TV in the shabby living room, merely fluttering into the kitchen during commercials to offer cookies, milk, water, a cushion. Twice Amy darted across the street to find Gran peacefully asleep. She beat Paul twice and he beat her once. Amy went to bed with her shoulder and neck muscles fully relaxed.

But at four in the morning she woke, aware of emptiness beside her on the sofa bed. Kaylie had not come home.

Amy had to be at work at eight thirty. She hadn't slept since discovering Kaylie was gone, instead spending her time pacing, calling Kaylie on the cell, cursing under her breath, drinking cup after cup of coffee. Kaylie hadn't answered, the cursing hadn't helped, and the coffee had jangled her nerves.

She left Gran still asleep and ran to the high school. Kaylie had said she had to be in school every day this week in order to qualify for All-City. If Amy used the coins she'd been saving for

Gran's flimsies to catch the number 22 bus at Culver Avenue, she could make sure Kaylie was all right and still arrive at TLN just in time.

Damn her sister! If only she didn't make everything six times harder than it had to be!

The high school looked even worse than when Amy had left it not even a year ago. There was no money to fix anything, so nothing had been fixed. Several windows had boards over them; the rest were barred. The lawn was long since trampled into bare dirt. Kids sat on the steps or milled around the street, waiting for the last bell. Kaylie wasn't among them.

"Student pass, please," said the guard beside the metal detector at the front door.

"I'm not a student. I need to see my sister, Kayla Kent. She may have gone inside already. I'm . . . I'm her guardian."

"Sure you are," he said. "No student pass, no entry."

"But it's really important. Our grandmother is ill, and I have to see Kaylie to—"

"No student pass, no entry. Move off the steps, please."

The last bell sounded and students pushed Amy from behind. She thought of slipping inside in the crush, but a second guard grabbed her arm and firmly propelled her to the side. "Dammit, let me go!"

"Amy?" said a familiar voice.

Mr. Servino! Teachers had appeared in the hallway to try to control the flow of traffic—always futile, as Amy well remembered. Mr. Servino had been Amy's math teacher. He'd hoped she would go on to college, or at least finish long-form high school so that college could be a possibility if the economy improved, but those goals had been impossible after Gran got so sick.

"Mr. Servino, I need to see my sister, Kayla, it's really important! Please help me!"

"It's OK, Javier, I'll escort Amy," Mr. Servino said to the guard. And to Amy, "Do you know what class she's in first period?"

"No."

"Let me check."

He had student schedules on his tablet, which linked to the computer that registered student passes. Slowly the hallway emptied of students. Mr. Servino said, "Kayla's in Ms. Renner's history class. Do you want me to take you there? This is my free period."

"You're sure she's there?"

"Yes."

"Then no, I don't want to see her. Actually, I don't have time before I go to work. I just needed to know she's all right. She . . . she didn't come home last night."

Mr. Servino nodded. Amy recognized the sadness in his eyes. She'd seen it all year when he looked at kids who were throwing away what little chance they had: getting into drugs or getting pregnant at fourteen or joining gangs. Now he was looking at her that way, and she hated it. Her chin came up.

"Amy, you OK?"

"I'm fine. Thanks for checking on Kaylie."

"Wait—you can't leave the building unless I escort you out."

He did. She threw him what she hoped was a confident smile—*See, all good here, on my way to a normal job*—thanked him again, and set off at a brisk walk, ignoring the catcalls of the guys, pathetic or dangerous, who inevitably hung around the school. She was careful to make no eye contact with anyone. Once back on a main avenue, she started to run. Already 7:40 and she'd missed the number 22 bus.

She was out of breath when, at 8:20, she reached Lorimar Street, turned the corner, and ran into a mob.

No, not another scenario, not now!

People marched and chanted, carrying signs that said TIMES BE TOUGH MAN in scarlet lettering. A protest mob, right in her path when she was already late—it had to be a scenario. And there had to be more to it than Amy was seeing—what, holographic tear gas from non-real cops? She wouldn't put it past Myra Townsend. But this time Amy knew she was on camera. She wouldn't be caught passive or frozen or stupid-looking yet again.

Striding up to the nearest protestor, she demanded, "What are you protesting?"

The woman, a faded and tired actor in jeans and shapeless sweater, eyed her warily. Amy saw the moment that the woman pretended to think that Amy was just a mouthy kid. "You don't know there's a Collapse on? We're protesting no jobs, no decent welfare, no hope. Also that those fat-cat bastards just laid off sixty more people with kids to feed." She pointed at the building behind the protestors, which bore the sign LIGNON INDUSTRIES. Amy had never heard of them, but she nodded. No jobs was something she could identify with.

But what did TLN want her to do with this protest?

The woman resumed marching. More people crowded the street, some joining the marchers and some just watching. Amy stood irresolute, and all she could think of was, *That slogan still needs a comma between* TOUGH *and* MAN. Where was the scenario challenge?

Then she saw him.

He was working the crowd, slipping a deft hand into a back pocket, unfastening a purse. Amy saw him leave one wallet, evidently too hard to remove, and take another. He was about her age, dressed in completely unmemorable clothing, a baseball cap pulled down over his eyes. He was big, but so what? This was a setup, she was being filmed by hidden microcameras, and her job was to put on a show.

She pushed through the crowd until she stood beside the pickpocket and said loudly, "Give that woman's wallet back!"

He stopped, startled, and glanced first at her and then around. People turned to look. "That woman there!" Amy said dramatically, pointing at the actress carrying an open purse—another clue that this was a scenario, since who was stupid enough to do that in the city? The woman gasped and felt around in her purse. Amy, hoping her camera angle was good, brought her foot down hard on the pickpocket's instep while raising her knee to kick his balls.

He was too fast for her. She got the instep but before her knee could connect, his fist had slugged her in the jaw.

Women screamed. Amy went down, astonished at the pain. The pickpocket ran, cheetah fast, eluding the two men who chased him. Sirens screamed in the background.

Someone bent over Amy. "Lie still, I'm a doctor." Fingers touched her face.

"Can . . . Myra do . . . *that*?" Amy gasped. Tears sprang to her eyes.

"Jawbone's not broken and your teeth seem intact. You're

very lucky, young lady, he didn't connect square on. What a stupid thing to do."

"Myra . . ."

"What's going on here?" a cop voice asked. Black boots, blue uniform, a holstered gun looming above her. Behind him, the chants resumed: *"Give us back our jobs! Times be tough, man!"*

Times be tough.

"I really can't imagine why you would think that was a scenario of ours, Amy," Myra Townsend said severely. "We don't hurt our participants!"

"I didn't know I was going to be hurt," Amy pointed out, but she knew her position was weak. The cop had taken her and the robbed woman to the precinct to file a police report, then delivered Amy, hours late, to Taunton Life Network. Amy had refused medical services, frantic to get to the station and explain in greater detail than her choked cell call had allowed. At the precinct her jaw had swollen on one side; now it was turning the colors of various types of squash. "Ms. Townsend—"

"Call me Myra. But you know, of course, that TLN assumes no liability for your misjudgments about scenarios. That's covered in your contract. And you weren't even on our premises."

"I don't want you to have any liability. I'm just sorry I'm

so late for work. It won't happen again, I promise you."

The corner of Myra's mouth quirked. A phantom zapped into Amy's mind: *Myra looming huge over tiny circus figures at her feet, clowns and acrobats and a miniature lion tamer with roach-sized lions.* Myra said, "I'm sure you won't be late again. Look, I'm going to have a car take you home for the rest of today. Your pay won't be docked. Just put ice on that jaw and report to work tomorrow."

"Thank you," Amy said. Gratitude flooded her. She'd screwed up, but she was going to get a second chance. Myra's eyes radiated compassionate understanding.

The phantom in her mind vanished, leaving behind an odd, nostril-tickling smell of sawdust.

# Nine

BECAUSE OF THE SWOLLEN jaw, she had to tell Gran the truth about her job. She hadn't lied before, but saying that as a contestant she "solved logic problems" left out a whole lot. Nothing about premises, syllogisms, or the null set usually produced a punch in the jaw.

Sitting on Gran's bed with an ice pack against her face, Amy explained *Who Knows People, Baby—You?*, cheesy title and all. Gran said nothing, her sunken eyes on Amy. When Amy finished, Gran was silent for a long moment and then said, "How edgy?"

Amy smiled. It hurt her mouth. "Not edgy enough to be dangerous. That was just me."

"Amy, do you want to do this TV show?"

She thought of Rafe Torres saying *"I'm here for the money."* She tried to answer Gran frankly. "I don't know yet. The whole thing could be interesting. At first I just went for the salary and benefits, but now . . . I don't know."

"You want to win. Under that sweetness is a deep competitive streak."

"I don't think there are winners or losers among the participants, only the viewers who vote."

"It's television," Gran said flatly. "Eventually there will be winners and losers."

Amy shrugged.

"And when does the first show air?"

"This Saturday, believe it or not." Amy had only just learned this astonishing fact. How could TLN get a show ready that fast? On the other hand, what did Amy know about television production?

Gran said, "That soon? You'll need to tell Kayla about the show before Saturday. And I guess we need to get a TV, don't we?"

Amy had already considered this. Carefully she had divided up the salary she hadn't earned yet: so much for food, so much to get the TV out of hock, so much for cabs to and from Friday night's All-City, so much to be saved in case the whole gig disappeared overnight.

She spent the rest of the day cooking, cleaning, caring for

Gran, and playing two quick games of chess with Paul, both of which she lost. The second Paul saw her swollen jaw he opened his mouth to ask. Amy snapped, "I don't want to talk about it."

"OK."

"Not ever."

"Fine."

"Anyway, it's not as bad as it looks."

"Good. King's pawn to e4."

Sometimes nerds were really restful.


## WEDNESDAY

The next scenario happened Wednesday afternoon.

Amy had spent the morning doing exactly what Myra had said: playing and reviewing a computer game. Even she, no gamer, could do this one, since it was designed to teach four-year-olds to read. Amy used a joystick to move the cat onto the mat, the dog out of the fog, the ball into the hall, and herself into terminal boredom. She counted the minutes until the free lunch that Alex had promised in the company cafeteria but instead was brought a box lunch at her cubicle in the sub-basement. "Just for today," the gofer said airily.

Were the six others doing this, too? Eating a dry sandwich in a cubicle and testing childish games? Somehow Amy couldn't see Waverly spending hours noticing problems with this bug-ridden draft of *I Can Read!* (there was no hall to move the ball into). Nor Rafe nor Violet. But maybe they got more advanced games. Someone should give Waverly a game based on fashion. Oh, if only Amy could afford those kinds of clothes. . . .

"Amy Kent has not made a keystroke in two minutes," the computer announced, and Amy hastily moved the bee into the tree.

At one o'clock the game disappeared and the computer said, "Amy, please report to loading bay number six." A map appeared on her screen.

Thank heavens!

One by one the seven show participants appeared in the loading bay. Myra, looking chic in a gray skirt and fitted Zac Posen jacket that Amy would have given a pinkie finger for, said, "No talking, please. Not just now."

Waverly rolled her eyes. Violet looked amused. When Cai arrived, Amy spent a lot of energy not looking at him, which amused Violet even more. Myra herded them all onto a bus, which deposited them in an alley with a small door. Myra unlocked it and ushered them inside. From the street signs, they were somewhere off Second Avenue, but nothing in the very long corridor that Myra led them through gave her any real clues. Another set of steps, steep and dim; now they were underground. Another long corridor, one more set of steps, and they ended up in a bare, windowless room with thick soundproofing on the walls and seven plastic lawn chairs.

Amy could feel her heart thud. Whatever came next, she had to do well at it, because she certainly hadn't distinguished herself so far.

Myra said, "This scenario you will each do separately. Amy, you're first. Go back through the door we just entered and Alex will escort you. The rest of you, no talking, please."

Violet said, "And I thought I was through with school detention."

Myra said, "*Violet*—"

Violet shrugged and grinned at Amy. But Amy saw the skin pulsing at Violet's temple; she was just as nervous as the rest.

"Amy, go," Myra said.

Alex Everett appeared at the door. He said nothing to Amy as he led her to yet another small door. Now she could hear the muffled noise of people talking loudly. Alex turned to her. "I'm going to open that door, and you're going through it. Whatever happens, you have to last ten minutes. Or else that's it for you on this show."

"Last ten minutes at what?"

He didn't answer. Instead he put his ear to the door, listened for a long, agonizing two minutes, then jerked the door open.

"'Now, by my maidenhead,'" a woman's voice said, "'at twelve year old, I bade her come. What, lamb! what, ladybird! God forbid! Where's this girl? What, Juliet!'"

Alex pushed her through the door and said, "Go."

An old woman bustled across the stage to meet her. The *stage*. Amy was on a stage.

It was everyone's nightmare: being suddenly thrust into a play, the whole matinee audience watching her—she could see them clearly, filling the small theater. Amy had actually been in this theater once, pre-Collapse, when Gran had taken her to see a production of *Death of a Salesman*. Now the audience watched *her* and waited for her next line, and she had absolutely no idea what it was. She could feel the blood rush to her face, turning her crimson with panic and embarrassment. Sweat slimed her forehead.

"'What, Juliet!'" the old woman said again, more loudly. A few titters arose from the audience.

Juliet. This was a modern-clothes production of *Romeo and Juliet*. This woman was the nurse, and the woman standing across the stage was—who? Amy had read the play in short-form high school, but she remembered only the story and not any lines. Wait—"To be or not to be?" No, that was *Hamlet*. Oh, *shit*—

*You must last ten minutes*, Alex had said. Or lose her job.

The nurse's mouth opened to say "What, Juliet!" a third

time. Before the words came out, Amy said, "'Here I am, nurse!'"

More titters from the audience. They were laughing at her. Were they in on this planned humiliation? They must be, or how else could they accept a Juliet played by four different girls: Amy, Violet, Waverly, Lynn.

The woman across the stage said, "'I called, your mother.'"

"I am here!" Amy said.

Laughter from the audience. Amy blinked back tears.

Lady Capulet said, "'This is the matter:—Nurse, give leave awhile, we must talk in secret:—nurse, come back again; I have remember'd me, thou's hear our counsel. Thou know'st my daughter's of a pretty age.'"

The nurse said, "'Faith, I can tell her age unto an hour,'" and Lady Capulet answered that Juliet was not yet fourteen. Then the nurse gave a long speech, which Amy desperately tried to follow. The Shakespearean language was difficult, but apparently it was about Juliet's childhood. Finally the mother told the nurse to "'hold thy peace,'" which she didn't. Another long nurse speech.

Keep talking, nurse! The longer she did, the less Amy had to say.

But eventually the nurse turned to Amy. "'Thou wast the prettiest babe that e'er I nursed. An I might live to see thee married once, I have my wish.'"

"'Marry,'" Lady Capulet said, "'that marry is the very theme I came to talk of. Tell me, daughter Juliet, how stands your disposition to be married?'"

Married. That's right—they wanted her to marry somebody who wasn't Romeo (who?) and Juliet didn't want to. Amy tried to look rebellious and said, "I have no disposition to be married."

More laughter, but not as much. The line wasn't right but evidently the idea was. How many minutes left?

Another long exchange between the mother and the nurse. Amy tried to decode the flowery language. Paris wanted to marry Juliet. The nurse thought that Paris was hot. Finally Lady Capulet put a hand on Juliet's shoulder and said, "'Speak briefly, can you like of Paris' love?'"

Did she? No, not really, or Shakespeare wouldn't have had a play. But had Juliet met Romeo yet? Where in the play was this scene? Better play it safe.

Amy said, "I know not. I hardly know valiant Paris."

More laughter. Amy pressed her lips tightly together. She was growing to hate that sound. A young man entered stage right. Was this Paris? He didn't look all that hot. But no, he knelt before Lady Capulet and said that the guests had come and dinner was served. Lady Capulet said, "'We follow thee,'" and left the stage, tossing over her shoulder, "'Juliet, the county stays.'"

What did that mean? Was Juliet supposed to stay onstage or follow her mother? Then Amy remembered dimly that "the county" referred to Paris, as if he were several square miles instead of a single man. Lady Capulet must mean that she should stay and wait for him.

The nurse said something Amy didn't catch, and they both left the stage. Amy sat down in the chair that Lady Capulet had vacated and waited, facing the audience.

Nothing happened.

She smiled at the audience.

They laughed.

Juliet must have to do something here. But what? Well, she was waiting for Paris; maybe she primped. Amy took a comb from her pocket and combed her hair. The audience roared. She put the comb away. Where the hell was Paris? Was one of the boys supposed to play this part, Cai or Rafe or Tommy? Had they refused?

She was trapped on a stage with nothing to say.

The audience howled.

*Damn them.* Didn't they have any compassion for her? Did they know what was happening? Weren't the ten minutes up?

She rose from the chair and looked toward the wings. Lady Capulet and the nurse stood there, Lady Capulet with her hand over her mouth to keep her laughter quiet, the older nurse with folded arms and a face creased with pity. Amy started toward them but the nurse shook her head, pointed to her watch, and held up three fingers. Three more minutes onstage.

Damn them all. She would tough it out. Amy turned to the audience.

> "Here I stand, with Paris nowhere near
> And my heart sore with waiting. He
> Is not my own true love, but nonetheless
> My mother wishes me to marry. What
> Can I do? I am but a woman
> And these times are hard——"

In her mind she heard the chanting demonstrators: *Times be tough, man.*

> "So I must do as I am bid. Or maybe
> Not. After all, I am neither a borrower nor a lender,
> And even a young girl can have
> A mind of her own. I am a Capulet. I am Juliet.
> Time and tide wait for no man.
> We Capulets can make our own destiny. I will
> Not trust in the stars, but compel them. And may
>   it all
> turn out well that ends well."

Did any of that at all make sense? The laughter still continued, but now Amy also heard scattered applause. She sank into a curtsy, wishing that instead she could kick every laughing hyena out there in the audience right in the balls. Even the women.

"Laugh at me, yea," she cried, raising her eyes to the heavens, "but he who laughs last laughs best!"

The curtain came down.

Amy rushed into the wings. The actress playing Lady Capulet was laughing so hard she sagged against the wall. "Let me see, I counted *Julius Caesar* in that little speech, and *All's Well That Ends Well*, and *Hamlet*. . . . You're certainly an unoriginal original, Amy!"

Amy ignored her. She ran up to Alex and said, "How *could* you . . . made a fool of myself . . ."

"Actually," he said coolly, "you didn't do too badly. It'll make good television."

"You bastards!"

"You can always quit. For now, come with me. I have to get you in a cab before I fetch Violet for the party scene."

Amy said fiercely, "Haven't *you* ever had the nightmare where you're forced onstage in something and don't know your lines?"

"Everyone has that nightmare. Everyone. Which is exactly why you got to live it." He laughed.

Hating him, Amy let herself be put into a cab back to the TV station, where a guard consulted his tablet and sent her back to her cubicle to move the can into the pan, the ant off the plant, the pup by the cup.

# Ten

"WHAT DID YOU DO?" Violet asked Amy the next day at lunch. "Onstage, I mean?"

"I ad-libbed," Amy said.

"You ad-libbed *Shakespeare*?"

Everyone else stopped talking. The seven sat at a cafeteria table. It was the first time they had all been together without Myra or Alex, but each had been sent there from morning duties at the same time so it must be what the producers wanted. Amy didn't like being manipulated, but she was curious to know the others better. Except for Cai, whose effect on her was so strong that she would have preferred to avoid him. She sat as far away from him as she could.

The cafeteria was large, with plain tables, abundant if bland food, and industrial carpeting to hold down noise. This did not work. Amy had to strain to hear people two seats away, but everyone could hear Violet. She added, "What scene was it?"

"The opening scene," Amy said. "I think."

Rafe said, "The opening scene has no women in it. I read the whole play last night."

Amy said, "Then maybe Juliet's first scene. Her mother tells her she wants Juliet to get married to Paris."

Waverly said, "'I'll look to like, if looking liking move; but no more deep will I endart mine eye than your consent gives strength to make it fly.'"

Everyone stared at her. Did Cai's stare hold admiration? Waverly was so very pretty, in her D&G miniskirt and punk jewelry and combat boots. Waverly shrugged disdainfully. "I told you all that I'm an actress."

Lynn demanded, "So you just knew the whole play by heart?"

"Juliet's role, yes. Of course." She took a dainty bite of her sandwich.

Lynn said, "What scene did you get?"

"The balcony scene."

"And you just happened to know it all."

113

Waverly said, "I *killed* in the scene."

Violet did a good imitation of Waverly's usual eye-rolling. Waverly turned on her. "And what scene did *you* get?"

Violet said, "Some lame party. It's when Juliet is supposed to meet Romeo."

Waverly said, "And of course you knew the lines."

"Of course I didn't, bitch. But I know what happens at parties. Romeo came on all smarmy about how hot I am, and I just smiled, grabbed him, and signaled to the musician standing around in the background to play his lute. He did, and I swung Romeo—you never saw such a gay guy in your whole life—into a two-step. When he pulled away, I danced on my own, like Juliet was this narcissistic exhibitionist with great rhythm she wanted to show off."

"Unlike *you*," Lynn said sarcastically.

Violet ignored her. "The musician played along. Well, what else could he do? And I danced the hell out of that scene."

Amy said, "For ten minutes?"

"And a *one* and a *two* and a *three*," Violet said.

"Hardly Shakespeare." Waverly sniffed.

"Hardly matters, bitch."

Cai said, "Didn't the audience laugh at you?"

"Sure, at first. So what? By the end they were clapping the rhythm. I did twenty-two *fouettés en tournant* in a row."

Amy didn't know what a *fouetté en tournant* was, but it sounded impressive.

Rafe said, "I got a scene with Romeo and his friend Mercutio. I didn't know the lines and I didn't pretend to know the lines."

Amy said, "What *did* you do?"

"I went to the front of the stage, held up my hand, and told the techs to bring up a spotlight on me. They did. For ten minutes I talked about how drama fools us into accepting alternate realities as real, which softens us up to accept alternate realities that authorities want us to believe. Pay your taxes because it's a civic duty, look both ways before you cross the street because you might get hit by a bus, obey the cops because they're on your side. It's all bullshit. The authorities want control because that's always what authorities want, and they'll use any means to get it. Drama and fiction and anything else unreal is just one more subtle way of keeping us under someone else's thumb."

Amy said, "Bravo. However, looking both ways before you cross the street . . . You could get hit by a bus. The bus is real enough."

"You'd hear it coming," Rafe said. "Anyway, that's what I did. You asked and I told you."

"And Alex let you?" Amy said. "He didn't bring down the curtain or anything?"

"Of course not. I could have stripped naked and danced a tarantella and that curtain would have stayed up. They wanted a unique response to a humiliating situation, so I gave them one. Without acting humiliated. I'm going to get another cookie. Anybody else want one?"

No one did. Violet said, "Watch out, Rafe, chocolate chips could be a means of government control."

Rafe ignored her. Cai and Lynn declined to say how they reacted to the scenario. Cai merely said wryly, "Let's just say I don't have Rafe's presence of mind. Or his politics." When Violet asked Tommy what he did onstage, he just hung his head and said nothing.

Lynn said, "Well, two more days until the show airs. Then we'll all see who did what, or maybe not in this particular scenario. Does anybody know which episode airs first?" She looked hard at Waverly, who shrugged.

"No idea."

"Really."

"What is that supposed to mean?" Waverly said.

"Just that I saw you hanging around Mark Meyer, looking flirtatious. Trying to exchange information for your cold flesh, Waverly?"

"Actually," Waverly said with poisonous sweetness, "I think you're more his type, and you're probably more used to that exchange. Casting couch and all. Bye, all you sad toads." She took her tray to the bussing table.

On their way out, Amy said to Violet, "Who's Mark Meyer?"

"Techie genius who does their special effects. Wasn't he at your first interview? Young, geeky, leather jacket, tablet always in his hand?"

"He was there, yeah. But how did you know his—"

"Googled the TV station and read all I could. Really, One Two Three, you gotta keep up. Your tablet is your extra brain."

Amy had no tablet. But she nodded, resolving to learn what she could at the library. She was obviously far behind the others.

So was this a competition, like Gran said? If so, who was winning so far? Probably she would find out Saturday night.

Thursday afternoon Amy was "promoted" to production assistant for a soap opera. At first this sounded exciting, but she quickly discovered that it mostly meant fetching coffee from the Starbucks across the street ("I just can't drink that awful stuff they have here"), fetching things from other rooms ("My red scarf, I think I left it either in Makeup or my dressing room or maybe the ladies', the one nearest the green room, or—"), and watching actors emote through overwrought plots

("But . . . Stone . . . Emily swore that Cliff was the father of Madison's twins!"). Amy crossed "television production" off the list of careers she might want someday if she never got to college to study neurology.

Waiting for the unknown, Amy discovered, was worse than facing it. No scenarios occurred on Thursday. But she remained constantly on edge, poised for action she couldn't predict. When an actor came up behind her to complain that she'd gotten his coffee order wrong, she jumped so hard that the coffee sloshed onto his costume. Amy apologized so profusely that finally the actor told her to knock it off, he'd drink the damn coffee the way it was.

When would the next scenario happen? What would it be?

In the evening Amy couldn't concentrate well enough to play decent chess with Paul, who resented it. "That was a really dumb move."

Amy tipped over her king. "Your game."

"I can't believe you had a rating of 1900. Were you lying?"

"No!"

"Then I don't know what's happened to you. It's hardly worth playing you at all."

Amy scowled, but she had no real answer.

The only bright spot was, surprisingly, Kaylie. She had gone to school every day that week, and as she and Amy prepared for bed, Kaylie said abruptly, "I know I've been a bitch lately. I'm sorry."

"It's okay."

"It's just that I'm so keyed up about All-City tomorrow night. This is going to be it, Amy. The band's big break. Tomorrow is the last day I have to sit in that stupid school and listen to stupid teachers drone on about the Council of Trent."

Amy couldn't remember what the Council of Trent was, if she'd ever known. She said, "School is more than that."

"You'd like to go back, wouldn't you?" Kaylie said shrewdly. "Do that summer bridge course to take the college-admit exams. Fuck, I can't imagine anything worse. But when Orange Decision is rich and famous, I'll get it for you. You won't have to work at the boring job anymore. I'll take care of you and Gran both."

"Kaylie," Amy said, because it looked like this might be her only chance, "about my job at the TV station. It isn't exactly . . . I mean, on Saturday night there will be a—"

"Gotta get to sleep," Kaylie said. "I can't be late tomorrow for my last day in hell. But on Saturday there'll be what?"

"Nothing," Amy said. She didn't want to spoil Kaylie's mood. She was glad she hadn't mentioned the show debut when all at once Kaylie flung her arms around Amy, something she hadn't done for at least two years. Into Amy's ear she whispered, "It means the world to me that you and Gran will be there tomorrow night. Really." She whirled away and into the bathroom, singing.

Kaylie really thought her band would win. She really thought this evening would change her life. She really expected to rescue Amy, who at only one year older already had given up such expectations. There was no rescue. There was only what you could scrounge for yourself and yours, through putting up with Myra Townsend and Waverly Balter-Wells. Through yearning for someone not interested in her. Through muscles knotted by tension and a heart clenched against humiliation.

Through not knowing when the next scenario would come.

# Eleven

**FRIDAY**

ON FRIDAY, SHE and Violet sat at a table by themselves. Instantly Lynn Demaris stood by the table. "Myra says we have to all lunch together over there." She pointed to the table where Cai and Tommy already sat.

Violet said, "She didn't tell me that."

"Well, she told me. So come on." Lynn stalked off.

Amy said, "What's her problem? She wasn't like that at lunch yesterday. In fact, she hardly said a word."

Violet shrugged. "Probably screwed up something and is taking it out on us. Stay here, One Two Three, I want to talk to you. How about a shopping expedition sometime after you get paid? No offense, but I think you could use some Violet help with your wardrobe."

Amy smiled. There was no attack mode in Violet's speech, and as always, her exuberance lifted Amy's spirits. With Gran weak, Kaylie often sullen, and Amy's job boring when it wasn't terrifying, Violet was like a bracing wind. It didn't even embarrass her to answer Violet in the way she must.

"Violet, I haven't got any money for clothes. I mean, none. I support my grandmother, who's old and sick, and my little sister. I'm hoping to scrounge enough from this paycheck to get a TV from the pawnshop so I can see our show on Saturday. God, that sounds weird—I can't believe I'd ever be saying a sentence like that!"

"Yeah, I know. But about the clothes—I'm not talking couture. Just, you know, jeans that fit, which yours don't because it looks like you've dropped weight, and tops that don't date from the early Jurassic."

Amy blushed and looked down at her soup. She didn't want it anymore.

"Listen, One Two Three," Violet said gently, "I think you're a saint, taking care of your family like that."

Amy winced, hearing Kaylie's sarcastic *Saint Amy*.

"But this is television and you gotta look as good as you can to keep this job. Now, you probably think this top is expensive—"

"A Carolina Herrera knockoff, three-ply cashmere although the original was six-ply." Violet stared at her. Amy smiled faintly, feeling a little better. "I have an eye, just no money."

Violet hooted. "Who knew? But I'll tell you what, you don't need much money for what I have in mind. You think dancers have money? We're the poorest of the poor. So we all know the thrift shops where rich women donate their castoffs and we all cultivate the shop clerks like we're Farmer Jones and they're prize pumpkins. Cathy at Jeu d'Esprit sets aside things for me. For you we'll try to snag a—oh, hell, here come the spoilers."

Lynn, Cai, Tommy, and Waverly carried their trays to Amy's table and plopped them down. Lynn said, "I told you Myra said that we lunch together! You should listen to me!"

Cai said apologetically, "Myra called our cells."

Violet said, "She didn't call mine," just as it rang. Violet answered, listened, scowled, and moved her chair to make room for Tommy.

Amy hadn't had a cell when she'd interviewed, and she hadn't told Myra that she had one now. She had to save her precious minutes for her family. Tommy sat down beside Violet, with Lynn on her other side. Cai sat between Amy and Waverly.

Instantly every part of her was aware of him: his nearness,

his scent, the heat of his body. He gave her a friendly smile, which she found herself incapable of returning. She could drown in the blue of his eyes. To say something, she blurted out, "Where's Rafe?"

"Rafe!" Lynn cried, so loud that a table of adults turned to look. "Rafe isn't here! I'll find him!" She jumped up and shot off.

"What's her issue?" Waverly said. "She stop taking her meds?"

"Sweet Waverly," Violet muttered. "Everybody's friend."

Tommy said, "I don't like waiting for something bad to happen. It upsets me."

Amy stopped chewing, her sandwich halfway to her mouth. So it wasn't just her; the others were all nodding at what Tommy said. She hadn't slept well last night, which had led to too much coffee this morning, which only made every-thing worse. She said, "It *is* upsetting, Tommy. You're right."

"I don't like it."

"So quit," Waverly said.

"I don't like it."

Waverly rolled her eyes and shifted closer to Cai. Her hand lay provocatively beside his on the table, their fingers almost brushing. Cai moved slightly away. This brought him closer to Amy, which made her take a deep breath. So Waverly wanted

Cai, and it wasn't mutual. But Amy got no vibes from him; his gorgeous body sat beside her as if she were Rafe or Tommy. Or another chair.

Was he gay? No, Amy was good at picking up those particular signals. Cai just wasn't attracted to her.

She focused on Tommy. "Would you like to quit the show, Tommy?"

"Yes. But I can't."

"Why ever not?" Waverly said crossly; she had felt Cai shift away from her. "It's not as if Taunton Life needs a halfwit on the show."

Amy said, "Shut up."

"The mousy one speaks!"

Tommy looked down at the table, blinking back tears. Violet leaned toward Waverly. Her voice was pleasant and casual, as if offering a Tic Tac. "Leave Tommy alone, bitch, or I will cut out your liver and feed it to rabid dogs, who will then shit all over your lifeless corpse. Oh, here come our Rafe and Lynn. Hi, guys."

"Hi," Rafe said. He squeezed in next to Amy, which shoved her even closer to Cai. "Myra decrees that at lunchtime we're an indivisible unit."

"Myra and the Myettes," Violet said.

Amy said, "Or Caesar and the Praetorian Guard."

Rafe looked at her with sudden appreciation. "Dr. Ms. Frankenstein and a bunch of Igors."

Cai said, "I'm thinking Snow Gray and her seven dwarves."

Amy laughed, but not comfortably. Rafe and Cai were both funny, and both smart. It might actually have been easier if Cai had been dumb. Poor Tommy looked bewildered. Waverly gazed at them all with aloof superiority. Lynn chewed her sandwich with a ferocity that surely wasn't normal, then abruptly flung it down, stood up, sat down again, and resumed eating.

Rafe said, "Just another joyous meal here in Point Paradise. Do you think our happy little family is being overheard? Filmed? Of course we are." He picked up the saltshaker and pretended to speak into it. "Hey, Myra, come join us for lunch!"

"Stop that!" Lynn snapped. She sounded almost hysterical.

The weird thing was that at that moment Myra did join them, strolling across the cafeteria in an asymmetrical Karl Lagerfeld jacket. She handed each of them a white envelope.

"A bonus is included for all of you." Myra smiled her kind, motherly smile that by now drew a response from only Tommy. "You've all done well for your first week."

As she walked away, Rafe muttered, "Sweet syrup poured over pure ice." No one replied. They all opened their envelopes, and Amy knew that hers wasn't the only hand that trembled.

Even a small bonus would mean so much to her.

It was more than a small bonus. It dwarfed even the amount withheld from her salary against the advance she'd taken last week.

She sat stunned, staring at the check that meant everything to her and nothing to the vast resources of Taunton Life Network. She knew that, but it didn't affect her gratitude. Money for whatever medicine Gran might need, a new TV instead of an old pawned one, new jeans—

Violet said, "It looks like that shopping expedition might be on after all, One Two Three."

Rafe said, "Golden handcuffs."

Cai said, "Cuff me more, please."

All at once the mood at the table lifted. They rose amiably to go back to their job assignments, and even Lynn was smiling. Amy and Violet made arrangements to meet at ten o'clock the next morning to go shopping. Amy spent the afternoon actually amused by the soap-opera shoot, whose plot now involved a long-lost brother who was possessed by the ghost of a man killed by the heroine's cousin, with whom she had a child kidnapped by the hero's first ex-wife, who had fled to Dubai with an Arab oil mogul. *Shakespeare it ain't*, Amy thought, stepping carefully over snaking cables backstage to bring another order of coffee from Starbucks.

On the street there was another protest march, two dozen tired people plodding in a circle, their homemade signs scarlet with TIMES BE TOUGH MAN. She avoided them, again squelching the impulse to tell someone, anyone, that the slogan needed a comma. Back inside, Amy stood around while the lighting was changed for the next shot. She planned six different ways to spend her bonus, until her cell rang.

"All cells silenced on the set!" the director roared, glaring at her even though nobody else was silent during setups. Amy scurried into the corridor, her heart thudding. Nobody but Kaylie and Gran had this number. . . .

She was wrong. "Mark Meyer here," the caller said. The show's tech guy, whom Amy had hardly seen. "Myra wants everybody in a meeting at five thirty in her office, 29-C. Be there."

"How did you get this—" But he had already disconnected.

It was 4:50. Amy had hoped to leave work early. The All-City Youth Talent Show started at Bentley Arena at seven thirty, and Amy had to get home, order a taxi for Gran, and get to the arena early enough to get Gran settled in a safe place by six thirty, before any huge jostling mob could arrive. Amy had planned to bring sandwiches to eat while they waited, along with enough pillows and blankets to make her grandmother comfortable. It could all work because Gran had had a really good week. But now this meeting—

She called back the number on her cell. "Mark? This is Amy Kent. I'm afraid I can't make the—"

"You don't have any choice," he said brusquely. "It's a requirement. Be there or else."

Her temper rose. "Or else what?"

He disconnected.

At 5:20 Amy told the director she'd had a summons from her boss. He nodded, not caring. It wasn't as if she was doing anything that mattered. Amy stomped from the studio to the elevators and took one to the twenty-ninth floor.

She'd never been up here before. Under any other circumstances, she might have felt intimidated, but now she was too angry. Well, all right, maybe still a little intimidated. The elevator opened onto a big carpeted lobby. It had no windows, but the luxury more than compensated. Deep leather chairs and sofas, little marble tables, paintings on the wall in severe, elegant frames. One whole wall was taken up by five TVs, each turned to a different channel, all on mute. A receptionist sat behind a low marble counter. She was in the same glossy good taste as the room, and looked just as expensive. Amy wanted to hitch up her too-big jeans, but she resisted.

"May I help you?" the receptionist said doubtfully.

"I'm Amy Kent. I have a meeting with Myra Townsend. I'm a little early."

"Oh, yes! Go right in, Ms. Kent. Ms. Townsend will be with you shortly."

Myra's vast office was even barer than the lobby, with an entire wall of glass that looked over the city to the bay. One end held a huge teak desk and a wall of TVs. At the other end a few leather chairs ringed a low glass table. That was it. The room was big enough to echo, Amy thought, if it hadn't been for the thick beige carpeting. Lynn Demaris perched uneasily on the edge of one chair.

"Hi, Lynn," Amy said.

Lynn sprang up as if shot, whirled around, and then re-laxed. Marginally, anyway. "Oh, it's you, Amy."

Who had she been expecting? Lynn's sharp features all looked twitchy, like a nervous rabbit's. She kept curling and uncurling her fingers, not quite making fists but close. Amy got a sudden phantom in her mind: *a dark tornado, with tiny figures whirling endlessly inside.*

Chilled, Amy said, "I'm sorry I startled you. Do you know what this meeting is about?"

"Why should they tell me? Or any of us? I just know it bet-ter be short."

Amy shared that sentiment. However, she couldn't think of anything else to say to Lynn, so she walked over to the win-dow and watched the traffic far below. Over the bay, clouds rose in the high, dark, anvil shape that promised thunder.

Cai entered with Tommy. They spoke in low tones. Tommy seemed very upset, with Cai soothing him. Amy was glad for the excuse to not make chitchat with Cai. Even the sight of him with his sleeves rolled up, exposing muscular forearms, made her breath come faster.

Violet's explosion into the room, with Rafe in tow, was welcome. Both of them seemed to still be in a great mood.

"You're full of shit, Rafe," Violet teased, "and what's more, you know it. John Milsom!"

"Milton," Rafe corrected, grinning, "and if you ever read anything besides *Dance* magazine, you'd recognize the quote. Also its aptness to the current culture in this country."

"Rafey, nobody but you would recognize that quotation. Here, I'll prove it! Amy, Cai, Lynn, listen to this! Did you ever hear such bullshit in your life?"

Rafe struck a pose and declaimed dramatically:

But what more oft, in nations gone corrupt,
And by their vices brought to servitude,
Than to love bondage more than liberty—
Bondage with ease than strenuous liberty.

Cai said, "Never heard it before. Do you really think our civilization is corrupt?"

"Rotten at the core," Rafe said. "Amy?"

"I don't know the quote. But—"

"I have fallen in with uneducated idiots. Lynn?"

"*But*," Amy insisted, "I don't think people have chosen bondage. It's just that times be tough, man. With a comma."

Rafe laughed. "Shut up," Lynn said, and at her tone they all did. Her fists were clenched for real now, and her eyes wild. Amy couldn't imagine what was wrong with her.

Cai said, "Lynn?"

She didn't answer, merely stomped over to the window and stared down at the traffic.

Rafe and Violet's exuberant alliance broke. Rafe slouched in a leather chair. Violet went to stand by Amy, but her gaze was on Lynn. She whispered, "Somebody needs a nap."

"Or something," Amy whispered back.

Waverly came in, spoke to nobody, and sat on an empty sofa. Envy of Waverly's outfit swamped Amy. She didn't recognize the designer, but Waverly's high leather boots, asymmetrical skirt, and scoop-neck top in rich chocolate perfectly set off the blonde's dramatic coloring, made more dramatic by gold eye makeup.

Amy noticed a coffee stain on her jeans.

By five forty-five, Amy's concern had grown. Where was Myra? If she had trouble finding a cab for Gran, they might not make the arena before long lines formed. Gran couldn't stay on her feet too long. Damn, Amy should have rented a wheelchair or something . . . except that until she got paid today, she'd had no money for a wheelchair. As it was, she was going to have to find the bank that TLN's check was drawn on to cash it there, plus open a checking account. . . . No, that would mean fees. TLN was supposed to have opened an account for her, but somehow that hadn't happened. Better to carry large amounts of cash home and hide it?

Myra's desk clock chimed six soft musical notes like a caress.

At six fifteen Violet said, "Well, it's been very nice but I have to run along. But do let's stay in touch and do this waiting-in-silence thing again real soon."

"Violet, you can't," Amy said. "It's your job!"

"And Myra's rudeness. Ciao."

Violet waved two fingers and walked to the office door. She said, "It's locked!"

"What?" said Cai, sounding more startled than alarmed. He tried the door, rattling it hard, then turned to face the rest of them. "Locked. It's a scenario."

Panic swept Amy. How long were they going to be kept in here? Doing what? She pulled out her cell. "I have the number for building security!"

Rafe said, "If it's a scenario, do you really think they'll answer?"

They didn't. All of them had Myra's number; she didn't

answer either. Violet blew a raspberry into Myra's voice mail.

"Well," Cai said, "we better——" Before he could finish, Lynn went batshit.

There was no cell in her hand. She raced to the door, rattled the knob, and started screaming. There were no words in the scream, which made it all the more horrible, like the high-pitched shrieks of an animal with its leg broken by an iron-clawed trap. Lynn kicked the door, pounded on it, threw her small body against it, all the while screaming.

Amy ran toward her. "Lynn, don't, it won't help, you'll only hurt yourself or——"

Lynn whirled around and slugged her.

Amy's jaw, still slightly swollen and more than slightly discolored from the pickpocket's blow on Tuesday, exploded into fresh pain. She staggered backward. Cai caught her before she fell. Despite the pain in her jaw, an electric jolt ran through Amy as Cai's arms closed to support her. So strong was the feeling that Amy hardly noticed what was happening to the room until Violet cried, "Oh my God!"

Trees were growing from the carpet in Myra's office.

Brown trunks, as thick around as laundry hampers, pushed up from the carpet. Halfway to the high ceiling, branches sprouted, bearing dense green leaves. Cai released Amy, who put one hand to her sore face and extended the other at full arm's length to touch one of the trees. Her hand went through it. "A hologram!"

But like the dog in the maple and the rats in the shopping mall, these trees looked completely solid and totally real. Amy could no longer see Violet or Rafe or Waverly through the dense forest. The lights went out.

Immediately a glow from the ceiling replaced them—stars. The ceiling shone with stars so realistic that for a crazy second Amy thought they had somehow been transported to a mythical forest—she could hear leaves rustling in the breeze! She could smell the night air! But no, it was only special effects in Myra Townsend's office.

"Wow," Violet said, inadequately.

Cai said to Amy, "Are you all right?"

"Yes," she lied. Her jaw ached where Lynn had hit her. Worse, her knees trembled; that was due to Cai. It was both relief and desolation when he moved away from her and said, "Tommy?"

"Don't come near me!" Lynn shrieked.

"Where is Tommy?" Cai said. "He gets frightened. . . . Tommy!"

A howl came from somewhere in the darkness, a cry of pure fear: Tommy. He came barreling toward Cai through—literally—the dark, rustling trees. Amy, now slumped against the door, fully recognized for the first time the extent of Tommy's mental disability. Why had Myra and Alex put him on the show? Anything new to him was upsetting.

Tommy was also six-foot-three and 250 pounds. As he ran toward the safety of Cai's voice, he was running in Lynn's direction. Her shriek rose to inhuman levels. "Stay away from me!"

Cai led Tommy away. Lynn, muttering, subsided and disappeared among the trees. Amy tried to call Kaylie and then Gran, but both calls failed. So did every call from Violet's and Rafe's cells. "Locked in electronically as well as literally," Rafe said. "I guess we wait for whatever comes next."

But for a long while, nothing did. The three of them wandered between the trees. Unease gripped Amy: Would real animals run through the fake forest? But nothing happened, and eventually she, Violet, Rafe, and Waverly settled into the leather chairs around the glass table, which now sat in a forest clearing. Cai and Tommy had camped near the door, where Tommy seemed to feel more secure. Cai was engaged in calming him down.

"Cai had a brother like Tommy," Waverly volunteered. "He died."

"How do you know?" Amy wondered why Waverly was bothering to talk to them. Then she realized: this must all be being filmed. She sat up straighter.

"Cai told me," Waverly said. "He was good to his brother and he's good to Tommy. I like that."

Violet murmured, very low, "Trying to change your image, Waverly?"

Rafe said, "Well, here we all are. Somebody think of something camera-worthy to do."

Violet got up and began to dance, something modern. Her long body bent and swayed, passing through trees as if they weren't there—which, of course, they weren't. Still, it gave her dance an eerie, mythical feel.

Rafe said, "You look like a dryad, except that they were never so tall." He began to sing, an old folk song about lovers meeting early one morning when the buds were all "a-green-o." His voice was surprisingly tuneful and sweet. Waverly made a sound of disgust, rose, and stalked off.

Violet danced until sweat poured off her. Her long legs curved and rose, her arms swayed, her supple back arched. She finally stopped, only because Rafe had stopped singing. He said, "Not bad."

"God, I miss that. During this show, I have to take class in the evening, and I really prefer morning."

Amy said, 'You're wonderful."

Rafe said, "How long have you been dancing?"

"Eight years, since I was ten. The last two professionally. The stories I could tell you!"

"Tell one now," Amy said. The more Violet talked, the less Amy would have to. It was now nearly seven o'clock. No time to get Gran to Bentley Arena; Amy would just have to get a cab and see Kaylie in All-City without her. The second this stupid scenario ended, if it ever did.

Violet said, "Well, last year I was in a production of Lane Carstairs's *Tripos*. Only as a background dancer. But after the first act, the principal dancer got greedy. She stayed out in front taking curtain call after curtain call, like it was the end of the whole show. It was Carlotta Neiman, of course."

The names meant nothing to Amy.

"So," Violet continued, "the stage manager signaled to have the curtain dropped in front of her, just so we could all get on with it. But just as the curtain falls, Carlotta steps forward to do one more egomaniacal curtsy, even closer to the audience. She has this signature deep balletic reverence, where she looks up through her lashes and smiles, like she's Anna Pavlova crossed with a *Vogue* model. Anyway, the curtain falls and whacks her. Those things are *heavy*. She stumbles and collapses on the stage and breaks her leg. Shouting, yelling, threats to sue. Finally the understudy dances the second two acts, and then *she's* so leery about the curtain that she won't take a curtain call at all. The stage manager's begging and pleading with her. The whole production's a shambles anyway, so the lead male dancer, whose nose had been out of joint because *Tripos* is all bravura female dancing and the men get to do practically nothing, ties a practice skirt around his hips, goes out on stage, and does a perfect imitation of Carlotta's famous curtsy. And the audience goes wild."

Rafe said, "Was he fired?"

"Are you kidding? He was mentioned positively in every single review!"

Violet told story after story about the dance world. Rafe countered with stories about working summers and after school as an apprentice refrigerator repairman, which Amy would not have thought a particularly humorous occupation. But Rafe's stories were hilarious. Cai and Tommy came to sit and listen. Lynn did not reappear, but Waverly did, lurking between the false trees. Tommy was smiling now. He even volunteered, "There are no spiders on these trees. Not even fake ones."

"Good," Violet said. "We already have Myra."

However, Amy couldn't really enjoy the camaraderie; she was too aware of time passing. Seven thirty—All-City was starting. When was Orange Decision scheduled to go on? Kaylie hadn't said. If this stupid scenario ended right now and Amy caught a cab almost instantly, maybe she could—

The "sky" brightened to a strange glow, and beams of light

shot down from the ceiling. The beams were so sudden, so bright, and so red that Amy was momentarily blinded. Tommy cried out. When sight returned, Lynn came tearing through the trees.

"They're coming for me! They're coming for me!"

"Who?" Cai said.

"Them! Them!" Lynn's voice rose to a shriek. Standing in a red beam, she looked demented, her face twisted with fear and her hands curved into claws. "They're after me and you all knew about it! You're in on it!"

"Who?" Cai asked again.

"You know who! The aliens!"

Rafe began to whistle the theme from *The Twilight Zone*. Waverly gave a snort of disgust. Tommy said, "I don't like this! Lynn, stop making that noise!"

She didn't. Tommy took a step toward her. He looked more confused than menacing, but Lynn screamed, "Stay away from me! You're one of them!"

Amy managed to get out, "He's not—" That was all the time she had before Lynn, running backward through the trees, yanked something small and dark from her pocket, aimed at Tommy, and fired.

In the dark office the shot sounded like an explosion. Waverly screamed; Cai gasped. Tommy fell to his knees and put his hands over his ears. By the eerie glow of the overhead "stars" Amy saw tears roll down his face.

Lynn fired again. Cai ran toward her but she eluded him, a small darting figure, and jumped up onto Myra's desk. The clock thudded to the carpet. Lynn shouted, "Don't anybody come near me or I'll shoot you! I will!"

Violet said, her voice shockingly clear and shockingly quavery in the sudden silence, "This isn't part of the scenario. She's really lost it."

*No. She hasn't.*

The phantom jumped whole into Amy's mind, and she realized that she'd seen it before: *the empty cardboard box.* Lynn wasn't really having a psychotic break. She was part of the scenario arranged by Myra. The gun wasn't real.

Cai, who evidently thought differently, said shakily, "Lynn, give me the gun. You don't want to shoot anybody here."

"Keep away!"

"I will, I promise." It was the same soothing voice he used with Tommy. "Just give me the gun."

"No!" She fired again and Cai dropped to the floor. For a heart-stopping moment Amy thought she'd been wrong and Cai had been hit, but he had merely ducked. Tommy clutched at Cai, who put one arm around Tommy's shoulders. In the glow of "starlight" Amy could see that Cai's arm shook.

Waverly and Violet had disappeared, probably crouching behind the real chairs or even the fake trees. But Rafe crept across the carpet on his belly, staying in shadows, toward the desk. He was going to try to disarm Lynn.

Had Rafe guessed that Lynn was an actor? Rafe was smart, the smartest of all of them. But he didn't have Amy's phantoms, and she guessed that he was, at best, uncertain about Lynn. That made him heroic, but all at once Amy wanted the heroism for herself. This was her chance to redeem herself for freezing in front of the rats, for not knowing *Romeo and Juliet*, for doing nothing in the ersatz lobby attack. This was Amy's chance to shine on camera and keep her job, and she was taking it.

"Lynn!" she said, moving toward the desk into a "clearing" where Lynn could see her plainly.

"Don't come closer!" The gun swung in Amy's direction. Which was also Rafe's direction and he stopped creeping forward, motionless below the eerily realistic trees.

"I won't," Amy said. She had to fight to keep her voice steady, even though there was no real danger—was there? If she was wrong . . .

"I won't come closer, Lynn. I just want to ask you a question. About the . . . the aliens. How do you know that these trees are their doing?"

"I know!" Lynn snapped. "None of you understands the situation the way I do!"

"Well, *I* certainly don't understand it," Amy said. "Could you . . . will you explain it to me? Please?"

In the gloom Amy couldn't see Lynn's expression. Did Lynn suspect that Amy knew she was acting? If Lynn was suspicious, would she go along anyway, because it would "make good television"? Those must be blanks in Lynn's gun, but if Lynn chose to fire directly at Amy, then what? Amy was not going to pretend she had been shot. Lynn must know that. And it was in Lynn's best interest to keep this confrontation looking "real" for the audience.

*Damn you, Myra!*

Lynn said, "The situation is desperate! The aliens are going to take over Earth. They've been closing in for two years now, choosing their contacts, trying to take over our minds . . . but I won't! I *won't!*" Her voice rose to a shriek.

"Of course you won't," Amy said gently. "But you know that we're not aliens. We're just people who don't want to be taken over. Like you."

"I *don't* know that," Lynn said. "I don't know who they've already taken over! Don't come any closer, I'm warning you!"

Amy hadn't moved, but Rafe had. While Lynn's attention was focused on Amy, Rafe had crept closer to the desk, angling toward its base. Amy guessed he would circle to one side and try to take Lynn by surprise. She wanted to get there first. Carefully she measured the distance to the desk. A little too far.

Amy took a step closer. "Lynn, I'm really interested in what you're saying. Sometimes things have happened, in my mind, I mean. Like . . . presences. Maybe you're the answer to what I've been wondering about and struggling with!"

Lynn said, "They tried to get to you?" Her voice held wonder, fear, longing for someone to understand—she was a good actor. Too bad the Oscars didn't include a category for Best Supporting Actress in a Mind-Fucking Manufactured Scenario.

"They don't have me," Amy said. "But I think they're trying. Can you help me?"

"I don't know," Lynn said uncertainly.

"At least tell me where the aliens come from." She took a step forward.

"Stop!" Lynn screamed. "I don't know about you and if—"

Rafe had nearly reached the desk. Amy couldn't wait any longer. She launched herself forward, into a handspring. Her muscles weren't warmed up enough and she was out of practice, but the spring took her halfway to the desk, just as Lynn fired. Amy's second handspring, pushed into with all her strength, flipped her up onto the edge of the desk, where she grabbed at Lynn. The small girl hadn't expected that. She yelled and lunged, throwing Amy off balance. Both girls crashed together off the desk and onto the floor. Amy rolled on top of Lynn and pinned her arms, but there was no need; Lynn had gone limp and unconscious.

"Get off her!" Rafe said, the first to reach them. "Is she breathing?" He picked up the gun from the carpet.

"She's breathing," Amy said grimly.

Rafe said, "I think she hit her head on the edge of the desk."

His words jolted Amy. What if Lynn wasn't acting, if Amy really had injured her? All at once Amy felt shaky, and as if she wanted to cry. *Stop it!* She told herself fiercely. It was just the backlash from adrenaline, she was fine—

Rafe peeled back Lynn's eyelids and peered at them. Lynn didn't move. Others came rushing up. Violet said, "My God, Amy, are you all right?"

"Just . . . just shaken."

"Your head is bleeding!"

Rafe looked up. "Head wounds produce a lot of blood relative to their seriousness. Is your vision blurry?"

"No," Amy said. She forced herself to breathe naturally.

Lynn stirred, opened her eyes, and began to cry.

Rafe, unsentimental, moved away from her. Cai moved in and put his arms around Lynn. It wasn't clear to Amy whether he was restraining her or comforting her: maybe both. But the sight of Cai holding someone else sent an irrational spear of jealousy through Amy. She looked away, knowing herself to be an idiot.

"Wow," Violet said breathlessly. "You're brave! Come away from that nutcase, One Two Three." She pulled Amy to her feet and led her through the "forest" to one of the leather chairs. Violet pushed her down into it and knelt beside the chair. She ripped the bottom off her own T-shirt, exposing perfect abs, wadded up the material, and held it to Amy's head. "Where did you learn to do those backflips?"

"I used to do gymnastics. Don't fuss over me, Violet, I'm fine." She pushed Violet's hand away and pressed the cloth to her head.

"Well, it was pretty fucking heroic, what you did. She could have killed you."

"I doubt it," Amy said truthfully. Then Rafe was beside her, peeling back the cloth and examining her wound. Amy remembered that he wanted to be a doctor.

He said, "Superficial, just like I thought. Any headache?"

"No. I'm fine, Rafe."

"Uh-huh." His eyes met hers. They were brown, with gold flecks—Amy hadn't noticed before. She saw that he knew Lynn had been acting, that he was going to go along with the pretense, and that he wanted her to do the same. She gave a tiny nod.

Violet, oblivious, said, "Well, *I* think you're both heroes. Looks like I underestimated you, Rafe. You're not just a nerdy brain after all."

"No," he said dryly, "I've got the same number of balls as Cai. They're just not as pretty."

Violet laughed. Amy turned her head—where was Cai? And Tommy and Waverly?

Rafe said, "Cai has Lynn under control. He took her over to a corner and he'll just listen to her or talk to her or whatever it is he does so well. Tommy—"

Violet said, "*Is* help coming?"

"Oh, yeah. A scenario gone this 'wrong'"—only Amy heard the quotation marks—"has to be ended. Should be any second now."

Amy said, "Where are Tommy and Waverly?"

Before Rafe could answer, the trees disappeared and the doors were flung open. Three men ran in, faces creased in concern. "Anybody hurt?"

"Amy and Lynn are," Violet said.

"I am not," Amy said crossly. "I'm fine!"

"Let me see," one of the men said. "I'm a paramedic."

Another man demanded, "What happened here?"

Violet began to explain. Rafe again caught Amy's gaze. They smiled faintly at each other, co-conspirators. Amy knew it would be her last smile for a long time. It was eight thirty; she and Gran had missed Kaylie's band at All-City.

Myra Townsend rushed into her office. "Oh, everybody, I'm so sorry, we had no idea—"

*Sure you didn't.*

Amy demanded, "Do our cell phones work yet?"

Myra looked at her. For a brief flash the kind, motherly concern was replaced by shrewd speculation; Myra guessed that Amy had seen through Lynn's act. No phantom told Amy that, but she didn't need one. Myra knew.

But all she said was, "Yes, of course, dear, your cells work now. Go ahead and phone whomever."

Amy stood, walked away from everyone, over to the glass wall, and called Gran, who was frantic. Amy told her that she'd had to work overtime under circumstances where she couldn't call, and would explain more later. Gran, never slow on the uptake, said only, "I'm sorry, Amy. And Kayla will be too. But the important thing is that you're all right."

"I'll be home when I can," Amy said. "Love you." *Sorry* did not describe what Kaylie was going to be.

When Amy turned, she was surprised to find Rafe, not Violet, at her elbow. Waverly and Violet stood on opposite sides of the vast room, talking into cells. Everyone else had gone.

Rafe said, "Myra and two security guards took Lynn to a 'hospital.' Cai took Tommy home."

"Oh," Amy said. She suddenly had no energy to think about Cai, about Tommy, about TLN, about anything except Kaylie. Across the room Violet, frowning, snapped shut her cell, waved briefly at Amy, and stalked out. Apparently Violet had her personal-life problems, too.

Amy said dully, "I have to go home."

"Sure."

They walked out, Waverly trailing behind, ending her phone conversation. In the elevator the three of them said nothing. Amy was glad the lobby was nearly empty; few people to see her holding the bloody wad of cloth to her head. They reached the street just as a black car pulled up. A uniformed chauffeur jumped out and opened the door for Waverly, who got in without so much as a glance at either Rafe or Amy. The car pulled away.

"Never thought of offering us a ride," Rafe said. "No, that's not correct—she probably did think of it and took pleasure in not doing it. Taxi!"

A cab stopped. Rafe opened the door and gently pushed Amy toward it.

"I can't," she said. Until she cashed her paycheck, she had

exactly twenty-seven cents in her jeans. The thought of walking all the way home, bleeding from the head and dizzy with hunger, nearly started tears, but there was no help for it.

"My treat," Rafe said. "Get in."

"But you—"

"Get in!"

She did. Nonetheless, she finished her sentence. "—don't have much money either."

"No," Rafe agreed, "but I'm spending some of what I do have on this. Give him your address, Amy."

She did, then leaned back against the seat and closed her eyes. Rafe said quietly, "The scenarios are getting rougher."

"Yes."

"How far are you prepared to go?"

"How far do you think Myra is prepared to go?"

"All the way."

Amy's eyes flew open. Rafe's face was grim. He said, "Depending, of course, on the ratings. If they're good—and I think they will be—eventually TLN will create scenarios that are both dangerous and illegal, in—"

"They can't do that!"

"In ways that have plausible deniability. Lynn was just the first. They'll present this as if she was a legitimate contestant who just happened to go bonkers—just watch. The next thing we'll hear is that her 'family' has taken her away to get her some help. But for the rest of us, things could get really rough. What I want to know is, are you willing to ally with me, to meet any scenarios as a team? You were impressive back there."

"Thanks. I think. But it doesn't . . . I don't see how TLN could dare do anything really illegal."

"Then I'll be wrong. But I don't think I am. What about the alliance?"

Amy said, "OK. Yes. Only I already promised Violet the same thing."

"Violet? She said that things might get rough?"

"No. Only that we should be allies. We're friends."

Rafe chewed on his lip. Amy had never seen anyone actually do that, but Rafe did: the entire left side of his bottom lip disappeared between his teeth, reappearing red and slightly swollen. It looked painful, but Rafe didn't seem to even notice. He said, "Do you think Violet could be another of Myra's plants?"

"Violet? No."

"How do you know?"

"I don't *know*," Amy said. "I mean, you could be one too, and this whole conversation scripted. But I don't think so."

"How did you know about Lynn?"

"How did *you* know?" Amy countered. She wasn't about to tell Rafe about her phantoms.

"She was acting out paranoid delusions, but some of her

behavior didn't fit the template. I've read up on this. I think I told you I want to be a doctor."

"You did, yes. I just had a gut intuition about Lynn. And I do about Violet, too. She's not a plant."

"OK, I'll accept that. See if she'll accept a three-way alliance. What about Cai?"

"What about him?" Amy hoped that in the half-light of the cab Rafe couldn't see the blood creep into her face at Cai's name. God, she was pathetic.

"Do you think he's a plant too?"

"No," Amy said, "but I don't know for sure."

"Well, Tommy's not, poor guy. Not bright enough. Waverly?"

"I don't know."

"I don't think so. She's just an ambitious rich bitch who desperately wants a TV career. So that's six of us still in, all legitimate. With us three against the others, if necessary."

Against Cai? Amy hadn't realized that. But it didn't matter, because she still thought Rafe was wrong. Myra's scenarios might be frightening and/or humiliating—especially if Amy didn't do well at them—but she didn't believe they would be actually dangerous. It would just be playacting, as with Lynn. Rafe had a touch of paranoia himself.

The cab stopped at her apartment building and Amy got out. "Thank you, Rafe. I really appreciate this."

"Get some rest over the weekend. Unless, of course, Myra decides to spring Lynn's aliens on us."

Amy laughed, but weakly. She almost hoped that Kaylie wouldn't come home after All-City, that she would sleep wherever she had before. But Amy didn't really believe that would happen.

She let herself into the building, heard Buddy snarl and bark behind Mrs. Raduski's locked door, and trudged upstairs. Gran lay heavily asleep. Probably she had struggled to stay awake until she heard from Amy and then, worn out with tension for both her granddaughters, had slipped into this stone-like sleep. Well, most likely it was good for her.

Amy made herself a sandwich, cleaned up the kitchen, and changed into her old blue bathrobe, all the while tensed for Kaylie's phone call or arrival. In the bathroom, brushing her teeth, she studied herself in the mirror. Exactly what a television star should look like:

Jaw swollen and bluish from being punched—check.

Temple scabbing over with dried blood—check.

Under-eye sag from worry and lack of sleep—check.

Hair wildly in need of washing and cutting—check.

She showered and shampooed. It didn't help much. She pulled out the sofa bed. Then there was nothing to do but wait for Kaylie.

# Twelve

SOMETIME AFTER MIDNIGHT the door burst open and Kaylie exploded into the apartment. "You weren't there!"

"Kaylie, let me explain what happened. It—"

"One fucking thing I want from you and you wouldn't do it! The most important night of my life and you couldn't bother to show up!"

"I couldn't! I had to work late and—"

"Oh, right—they locked you in a room and cut off phone contact and *made* you stay at work!"

"Yes!" Amy shouted back. "They did!"

Kaylie went icy. In a low, dangerous voice she said, "You never lied to me before."

Amy had, of course she had, and what kind of universe was it when she got away with lying but was punished for telling the truth? "Listen, Kaylie, it's true. My job—I'm going to be in a TV show. It starts tomorrow night, in fact, on TLN. It's a weird show, I never know when they're going to film, and today they—"

"*You* are going to be on a TV show? What can *you* do? Is it some sort of nerdy chess show?"

"No, it's more like . . . it's hard to explain what it—"

"You can't play or sing or dance or act! You're still lying to me!"

"I'm not!" Amy cried, finally losing her temper. "God, I'm only trying to take care of this family! I hate this TV show and I wanted to be at All-City and they literally locked us in to film! Why don't you ever cut me any slack when I'm doing the best I can!"

"Saint Amy. Yeah, we all know about her. Amy the Angelic and Kaylie the Satanic—that's always the way it's been, isn't it? And tonight I finally had a chance to shine in front of you and Gran, only you—"

"Kaylie," Amy said, suddenly breathless, "did you win?"

The second she said it, Amy saw it was wrong. If Kaylie had won, she wouldn't be so furious now. Amy's question had only jabbed at the wound and, like any tormented creature, Kaylie bit back.

"We came in twenty-third! There, are you happy now? You're going to be a TV star and your little sister failed again. Enjoy your victory!" She whirled toward the door.

Amy grabbed at Kaylie to stop her from leaving. Her hand closed on Kaylie's shirt. Kaylie yanked herself free and the light material tore. With a curse so filthy that Amy's eyes widened, Kaylie slammed out of the apartment.

Amy stood still a long moment, then threw open the window. "Wait! It's too dangerous this late at—"

Kaylie appeared on the street two stories below. Without looking up, she yanked open the passenger door of a waiting car and jumped in. Light from Amy's window gleamed briefly on the shoulder left bare where Amy had torn away Kaylie's shirt. The car sped off.

Amy was left with the cloth in her hand, an exquisite gauzy silk, light as spiderwebs. The color shaded from green to blue, changing under the light as she turned it in her hands. A tiny label was sewn into the seam: Carolina Herrera. Amy had last seen this blouse in a window downtown, at one of the city's most expensive boutiques.

She groaned and cracked open Gran's door. Amazingly, she still lay asleep. Either that was good because she'd missed the fighting, or it was bad because she was so sick that noise couldn't rouse her. Amy didn't know; she was too tired to think about it anymore. As she staggered to the sleep sofa, a phantom came to her mind. No, not a phantom: a memory, one of the few she had of her mother. The memory was of a blurry, sweet-smelling presence leaning over Amy's bed and saying, "It will all be better in the morning."

*Right, Ma. Good one.*

But it was better.

Amy woke to sunlight streaming through the window, the smell of fresh toast, and Gran at the stove. "Good morning, sweetie. Kayla gone out already?"

"No, she—what time is it?! I was supposed to meet a friend at—"

"Your friend called on your cell and you didn't even hear it, so I answered. She said she wants to meet you later than you'd planned and you should call her when you're awake. Where's Kaylie?"

"She came home last night and left again. With friends."

"I see," said Gran, who probably did. She sighed and buttered the toast.

Amy leaped up. "Let me do that."

"I think I will." Gran sat down heavily at the table, clearly worn out from getting herself up, dressed, and into the kitchen. "What happened to your head?"

"Nothing important. Kaylie was mad because we didn't make All-City."

"I figured." And then, in a rare lapse into the past, "Your father was a fiery, impulsive man. Kayla is like him, even though she looks like Carolyn. Genetics count for more than we like to think. Is she going to stay with these friends until she calms down?"

"Yes."

"Who are they?"

"I don't know them very well—"

"You don't know them at all."

Amy gave up. "No."

Gran sighed. Her lips trembled, but all she said was, "She'll come home when she's good and ready and not before, and there's nothing you can do about it. Even in my day, the police were too busy to track a fifteen-year-old runaway, and now they'd just laugh if you called them. A sour laugh. Did you hear that three protestors died in that big march last night in DC?"

Amy shook her head. She hadn't even known there'd been a march in DC last night. But then, there so often was. People were scared and angry. TIMES BE TOUGH MAN.

Gran said, "But what can we do except muddle on through? Oh—I made accidental verse. Amy, what's on your agenda today? And don't say stay with me. Because I feel pretty good."

She didn't look pretty good, but neither did she look as bad as she sometimes did. Before Amy could answer, Gran said in the tone that allowed no argument, "Go shopping with your friend. And buy a TV. Your show premieres tonight, doesn't it?"

"Yes." A strange mixture of anticipation and dread settled into Amy's mind, thick as fog. She didn't even know which scenario would be first. Or how Myra would have edited it.

"Well, I'm going to take a long nap so that I'm awake for it. Bring me back a flimsie, will you, Amy?"

"Of course," Violet said.

Amy called Violet. "Hey, One Two Three. Change of plan. Meet me at Fourth and Leland at two o'clock. Do you know where that is?"

"I can find it. But why?"

"It's a surprise," Violet said. "Just don't be late."

"Violet—this isn't another of Myra's scenarios, is it?" Amy didn't think she could take another one so soon.

"Of course not—this is *me*. Don't get as paranoid as poor departed Lynn. Who's probably in some loony asylum right now."

*No, she's not.* "Two o'clock on the corner of Fourth and Leland."

"See you then."

Amy walked through a glorious spring day to a branch of TLN's bank and cashed her paycheck. She put the cash in her bra and scurried home, keeping to main thoroughfares, relying on the crowds of people out in the bright sunlight to deter muggers. Not that she looked like a person with anything to mug for. At home, Gran was asleep. Amy laid the flimsie she'd bought her on the nightstand, divided her money, and thought about a good place to hide the bulk of it. From burglars, from Mrs. Raduski, from Kaylie, if Kaylie ever came home again.

She would. Eventually, she must.

In the back of the low cupboard holding pots and pans was a chink out of the rotting wood. Feeling with her fingers, hoping it wasn't a rat hole, Amy encountered a shallow depression. She put the bills in there and then wedged another piece of wood, ripped from a splintered floorboard, over the depression. Perfect. Gran couldn't bend down that low, and Kaylie cooked an actual meal only once a century. That stew she'd made had been it for the next ninety-nine years.

With some of her remaining money, Amy bought a TV from the pawnshop three blocks over. Their own had been sold to somebody else when the ticket expired, but this one was cheaper. It was also small and ancient. Amy made the clerk turn it on to be sure it worked. The picture was slightly blurry but there. Good thing TLN wasn't sub-stat, a subscription station, or Amy would miss her own show.

Although even thinking about watching it made her stomach churn.

She carried the TV home and set it up for Gran, who was delighted to once again get a news channel. Amy put a pot roast in the oven at a low temperature, left Gran sitting up in bed watching congressmen yell at each other, and went to meet Violet.

"Hey, One Two Three. Well, *you* look better than yesterday. Not that that would be hard."

"I got some sleep," Amy said. Violet looked wonderful. Her long black hair gleamed in the sunlight; her makeup was perfect. Amy envied the low-cut black top—not designer, but good quality—and tight white jeans on Violet's long, long legs. "So tell me—what's the big mystery?"

Violet pointed down the street. "See that café there? The one with the green awning?"

"Yeah, so? I already ate lunch."

"We're not going in there. We're waiting for someone to come out."

"Who?" Cai? Amy's throat tightened.

"Mark Meyer."

It took Amy a moment to remember who that was. "The tech guy on the show?"

"Bingo."

"Why?"

"Don't give me that sour face, One Two Three. Or that much innocence, either. Don't you get it? Mark undoubtedly knows the next scenario. Probably he planned the next scenario. If we know too, we'll have a leg up on everyone else."

"And why should he tell us?"

Violet dropped her lashes, looked up at Amy through them, and moved her luscious body provocatively. Two men across the street immediately went on high alert.

"Violet," Amy said, "you can't mean it."

"Just watch me."

"But . . . you wouldn't . . . I mean, if you're planning on seducing Mark, you don't want me along!"

"Two look less like a setup than one," Violet said, abandoning her pose and scowling at the guys across the street. "Besides, I'm not positive I'm his type. He's a tech nerd, after all. Probably plays chess. You might be more his style, although I do wish I'd arranged this so we buy you new clothes first instead of second."

Amy said, "I am *not* going to—"

"Oh, no heavy stuff, just flirting. You can flirt, can't you?"

"No."

"Pretend he's Cai." Violet grabbed Amy's arm and dragged her down the street. "Come on, we don't have much time. He's at some tech group that meets here every Saturday."

"How do you know that—let me go! I'm not doing this!"

"I know because I made it my business to know; no I won't; and yes you are."

Violet's grip was a vise. Amy was outside the café door before she wrenched herself free. The memory of Kaylie tearing herself from Amy's grip last night flooded her mind. At least her own shirt didn't tear.

"Violet, I am *not* doing this. It's pathetic and sneaky. And—"

"Hello, Mark," Violet said.

He had just emerged from the café, blinking in the sudden sunshine, and then blinking in surprise at finding them there. Dressed in jeans and a leather jacket too warm for the day, he was shorter than Violet, taller than Amy. She felt herself flush in embarrassment.

Violet went into seductive mode. "What are you doing here? Amy and I are going shopping for clothes."

Mark said nothing. But his eyes flickered to Violet's perfect, half-exposed breasts in the low-cut top. She smiled.

"We're going to look at shirts and shoes and maybe night things. But can we buy you a cup of coffee first? I promise not to ask anything about the show, if you're not allowed to talk about it."

Mark said flatly, "Waverly already tried this."

"I don't know what you—"

"Yes, you do. You think if you play girly with me, I'll tell you about upcoming scenarios. Not going to work."

Violet snapped, "Are you gay, then? Should Cai try?"

Mark looked at Amy, who was scarlet with embarrassment. He said, "I thought *you* would be above this. But you are, aren't you? This wasn't your idea."

Amy stayed mute. She would not throw Violet under the bus.

Mark smiled faintly and strode away.

Amy turned on Violet. "Well, *that* certainly went well!"

Violet shrugged. "You win some, you lose some, sometimes the avalanche rolls right over you. Stop glaring at me, One Two Three, it was worth a shot. Besides, you're not the type that stays mad long. Let's go shopping."

"Violet, that was really embarrassing!"

"Like being on this whole show isn't embarrassing?"

She had a point.

Violet continued, for once dropping her wise-guy persona. "Do you know what a dancer's life is like in this economy? I live in a crappy one-room apartment with two other girls. We sleep on air mattresses and do pick-up waitressing at night—when we can get it—so we can have money to take class every day and buy practice clothes. When there's an audition, over a thousand girls show up, and they take maybe two. Some days I didn't eat. My family back in Tulsa can't help me, they're sinking, themselves. This job is the rainbow pot of gold for me, and I'll do anything to keep it. And don't tell me you're not the same, you standing there with your jaw bashed and your head bashed and your willingness to risk your life to take on a gun-waving psychotic standing on her producer's desk."

Honesty spawned honesty. Amy, no longer angry, said, "She was a plant."

"What?"

"Lynn. I guessed that she was a plant, an actor hired to create some pretend danger. I wasn't really risking much."

Violet stared, then broke into a raucous laugh. "Amy, I'm glad we're friends. And allies on the show."

"With Rafe," Amy said. She explained the new three-way alliance, and Violet nodded.

"OK. He's really smart. Now—can we please go shopping? Maybe if you looked better, you *could* have gotten to Mark."

Violet was Violet. For the next three hours Amy let herself be led to stores she never knew existed. Tiny vintage shops, up-scale consignment shops on deep clearance, wholesale irregu-lars—Violet knew them all, and she could haggle on prices in a way that never would have occurred to Amy. By evening, Amy, who had been firm about buying only three items although she lusted after a dozen more, hardly knew herself. She stood in front of a scratched dressing-room mirror in a blue ("Defi-nitely your color as long as you don't go pastel") Marc Jacobs top with a small tear in a mostly unnoticeable place, and per-fectly fitting dark-wash jeans ("Your waist is good but you might want to play down that swell of hips just a little"). Violet had just finished snipping wispy bangs into Amy's unmanageable hair, plus long side layers that framed her face. The rest she'd twisted into a high chignon, held with a pencil borrowed from the clerk. In a plastic bag at Amy's feet was a secondhand charcoal Zac Posen sweater that somehow made her skin look like cream.

"See," Violet said triumphantly, "I told you I had great taste."

"I already knew that. *Thank you*, Violet."

"Now all you need is a plastic hair stick to replace that pencil, although I'd hoped we could find an old tortoiseshell one. Still, you can't have everything. However, you cannot wear those ratty sneakers with these clothes. Here, these are a gift from me." She handed Amy a pair of the new stretchable flats, black with tiny mirrors sewn in the sides, last year's runway sensation that now appeared in knockoffs all over the city.

"Violet, I can't——"

"Sure you can. They're as flexible as sneakers, see—you can still do backflips or pole-vaulting or whatever comes up next."

"You told me you don't have any money and——"

"And I can't bear to see anyone wear those jeans with holey sneakers. It completely offends my sensibilities. Which, I know, nobody believes I even have. Take the shoes. And now don't you have to get home to that grandmother you told me about?"

"Yes. I can't thank you enough for—"

"Sure you can. Take me home with you."

Amy blinked. "What?"

"You have a TV, right? My little dancers' hellhole doesn't. I was going to watch the show tonight at some bar, but I'd rather watch it with you. Can I do that?"

Amy grinned. "Of course!"

"And will you give me dinner? I don't eat much."

"Pot roast with potatoes and carrots."

"I take it back. I eat like a horse."

They walked home, Violet's bargain hunting having brought them within ten or twelve blocks of Amy's apartment. Twilight had turned the air colder. Still, Amy was warmed by the admiring glances she got in her new outfit and hairdo. The glances were worth the gooseflesh. Violet chattered away, making Amy laugh with more outrageous stories of a dancer's life. Mrs. Raduski must be out walking Buddy, because no snarling or growling greeted them in the vestibule. The delicious smell of pot roast drifted from the apartment. Life was good.

Except for Kaylie, and the TV show starting in less than two hours.

# Thirteen

**SATURDAY**

MUSIC STARTED LOW, gradually becoming more audible: rap set to keyboards performing atonal music. The rap words were indistinguishable and stayed so, but the strange music sounded both energizing and slightly menacing. "Catchy," Violet said, "but hardly danceable."

Amy, Gran, and Violet sat on the sofa, facing the small television. Reception had improved after Gran fiddled with the TV. Amy's palms were slick with nervous sweat. Gran looked tired but interested, and she seemed to like Violet.

On screen two teenage actors described the show and how audience voting worked, finishing with "Each week: seven participants, five possible responses, seventy-eight thousand one hundred twenty-five chances to get it completely right. Way better odds than the lottery! And if you're one of those that do, within the first two hours after the show ends, you split five million dollars with the other winner!" The music rose to deafening levels, eerie and menacing and the title came up in scarlet:

WHO KNOWS PEOPLE, BABY—YOU?

Abruptly the music ceased. Total quiet. Brick-or-concrete walls narrowly set apart from each other, lined with blue Dumpsters. Myra wasn't going to use any of the four scenarios since Amy had been hired; she was going to use the audition in the alley.

"Huh," Violet said. "Maybe that's the only one they had time to edit so far."

That made sense. Amy's hands twisted together so hard that the tips of her fingers went bloodless.

Waverly was thrust out of a door into the alley lined with blue Dumpsters and encountered the "dying" actor bleeding and gasping on the ground.

"Well, well," Violet said, "look who's first. Our little rich bitch. Oh, sorry, Mrs. Whitcomb."

Gran merely shot Violet an amused glance; Gran wasn't

that easy to shock. Amy decided that Myra and Alex had put Waverly out there first because she was the best dressed. The contrast with the "homeless" guy in the alley would be all the greater. Waverly strolled along, scowling at where she found herself—obviously she didn't know she was being filmed any more than Amy had known.

Waverly reached the homeless man gasping and bleeding on the ground. She didn't even slow down. Her path altered to move as far away from him as possible, and she kept on going.

"Such a sweetheart," Violet said.

"A heart soft as butter," Amy said. "Didn't even call for help."

The injured man stopped being injured. He leaped up, ran after Waverly, and caught her easily. The camera zoomed in to her face, outraged and terrified, and then to his, predatory and evil. Waverly screamed and started to struggle. The screen went black. A voice-over said, "How did Waverly react? Do *you* know?" Then a list appeared, accompanied by pulsing music, with Waverly's picture above it:

WAVERLY:
1.  Fights—and wins!
2.  Tries to run—and escapes!
3.  Tries to run—and is caught!

4.  Strikes a bargain with the attacker!
5.  Freezes and cries!

Violet said, "Well, we know her and the viewers don't. I'm guessing she freezes and cries, hoping for his sympathy 'cause she's so hot."

"No," Amy said, "don't underestimate her. She's not stupid. She'll try to strike a bargain, buying her way out. She—oh my God, Violet, we're sucked into playing!"

Gran said quietly, "This is going to be a very successful show, girls. You both need to be prepared for that."

Amy said nothing. She stared at the screen as the show ran through the other six participants grabbed by the predator. The same list appeared after each name. Then the hosts were back, hyping up the need to vote and the promise that on Wednesday night the show would reveal exactly how Waverly, Cai, Rafe, Amy, Lynn, Tommy, and Violet reacted! The actual film! You'll be amazed and amused and affected! And someone will win a share of five million dollars—maybe you! So vote now! The whole list and all the names, identified by small head shots, stayed on the screen while the music pulsed and, presumably, watchers texted their predictions.

Violet snorted. "Well, that's helpful—like they can tell from a head shot who will do what."

Amy said, "Each week they'll learn more about us."

"Too bad we can't vote. I could make a fortune."

"Amy," Gran said, "which of those five behaviors was yours?"

Amy said, "I jumped onto the Dumpsters and evaded that guy as long as I could, but eventually he cornered me. So I guess I'm 'tries to run and gets caught.'"

Violet said, "I bet you put up a good show, though. I'm 'strikes a bargain with the attacker.' But I'm not saying what I offered him."

After Violet's performance with Mark Meyer that afternoon, Amy could guess. "Good thing it was only an actor and not—Gran!"

"I'm all right, just tired. Will you excuse me, Violet?"

She had slumped sideways against Amy. Amy helped Gran sit upright, then pulled her to her feet and walked her into the bedroom. Gran kept reassuring her, but fear squeezed Amy's chest; Gran's attack of weakness had come over her all at once, in a way Amy hadn't seen before. She could barely stand. Amy said, even though she already knew the answer, "When are your test results due back?"

"Next week."

Amy helped her into her nightdress, to the bathroom, back to bed. Violet tactfully kept her eyes on the TV, now airing some stupid show she couldn't possibly be interested in. When Amy had Gran settled, Gran fell asleep almost immediately. Amy sat beside her for a few minutes, remembering so much: Gran singing Amy and Kaylie asleep every night after Mommy died. Gran already old but not yet infirm, explaining Mendelian inheritance diagrams to Amy's sixth-grade class. Gran creating elaborate birthday cakes in any shape Amy or Kaylie chose. Only in the last few years had Amy really appreciated how much sacrifice must have been involved for a woman nearing seventy to take on two small girls to raise. Kaylie still didn't appreciate it.

Amy left the bedroom, closing the door softly behind her. Violet had turned off the TV. She said, "Well, One Two Three, I think I'll take off now. Thanks for dinner and the show preview, I think it—"

The apartment door burst open. Kaylie barreled in.

She stopped short when she saw Violet, and her eyes widened. She blurted, "You're one of the other people on the show!"

Amy's stomach churned. If Kaylie was going to throw a nasty tantrum in front of Violet—

She didn't. Kaylie flashed an enchanting smile, dark curls bobbing, and held out her hand. "I'm Kaylie Kent, Amy's sister. I'm so glad to meet you! I'm sure you'll be great on TV—although not as great as Amy, of course!"

Amy blinked. Kaylie turned and hugged her. "I'm so proud of you! The show will be a big success, I just know it!"

A phantom in Amy's mind: *a tiny furious figure beating on a closed door, trying to get in.* Like Amy needed that to understand Kaylie's sudden sweetness! But it didn't matter where the sweetness came from, as long as it defanged her sister.

"Thanks," Amy said.

Kaylie said, "I want to hear all about it!"

Violet left, raising one eyebrow at Kaylie and whispering to Amy, "Your little sis is gorgeous." Then Kaylie questioned Amy relentlessly about the show: what Amy had done, what the others had done, what they were like, what happened after that, and then what? If Amy hadn't suspected Kaylie's motives, she would have been delighted; the talk almost felt like the ones they used to have, years ago. But when Amy tried to ask Kaylie what was going on in her life, Kaylie yawned.

"I'm really tired. Late night last night. Let's sleep now and talk tomorrow, OK?"

"OK," Amy said, because she didn't see any other choice. And at least Kaylie was safe at home.

For now, anyway.

✳ ✳ ✳

Late evening, and lights still burned in the Taunton Life Network building downtown. James Taunton sat in a deep chair, facing a bank of computers where two techs monitored incoming data. Myra Townsend and Alex Everett stood beside the chair. Myra's temple pulsed with tension. Alex slouched, too relaxed.

A tech said, "We have a winner. In Raleigh, North Carolina."

"Great!" Alex said. "We get to give away five million dollars."

The tech said, "The data is still coming in. There might be more than one winner."

The second tech said, "Here comes the West Coast now. . . . Hey, that's really good for a pilot! A two point six rating and eight percent share!"

The first tech said, "Another winner. In Des Moines."

Alex straightened, underscoring how fake his relaxation had been.

James Taunton rose, walked over to the screens, studied them. The techs leaned respectfully aside. Everyone held their breath. Finally Taunton turned to the two producers.

"It's a go. Nice work, Myra, Alex. Keep it up." He left the room.

Everyone breathed again.

Myra said, "Alex—tomorrow. For the next scenario."

Alex looked doubtful. "Tomorrow? They just had the Lynn thing last night."

"That's why they won't be expecting it tomorrow. And we've got to do it before everyone starts recognizing them on the street and we have to move them. All six of them could go viral on the Internet." Then, more sharply, "You're not going to tell me it's not ready?"

"Of course it's ready," Alex said, offended. "It's just that doing another scenario so soon is being a little rough on them, don't you think?"

"That's not really the point, is it? They signed up for it. The real point is to keep Taunton impressed. Mark has everything in place?"

"Yes."

"Then call him. Now." Her eyes went back to the screens.

Not until after Alex left the room did Myra permit herself to sit down. She had been clenching her butt cheeks to keep her legs from trembling, an old trick. No one understood how important the success of this show was to her—not Alex, not Taunton, not Mark, and certainly not the talent. Those kids thought they understood economic hardship. But they had barely reached adolescence when the Collapse happened. They didn't know what it was like to see the future you'd so carefully built crumble overnight into so much rubble.

Myra had lost well over a million dollars in the stock market. Her previous job had disappeared during a panicky corporate reorganization, and she'd lost her beautiful house. Nor was Amy Kent the only person with relatives dependent on her salary.

Myra Townsend was going to make this TV show work no matter what that took.

"Looking good," a tech said, gazing at the screens.

"Yes," Myra answered, unsmiling, as she watched the numbers climb and climb.

# Fourteen

AMY WOKE ON Sunday morning to knocking at the front door. She sat up on the sofa bed as Gran rose from the little table.

"Good morning, Amy." Gran, dressed in slacks and a sweater that both hung too loosely on her, hobbled painfully toward the door. "I'll get it."

"No, let me! Sit down again, Gran. Where's Kaylie?"

"Gone out. It's nearly noon."

Noon! Amy had slept as if she were part of the bed. Gran peered through the peephole. "It's a boy on crutches."

Paul. How had he managed two flights of stairs? Amy said, "That's my chess partner!" Gran unlocked the door and Amy, heedless of her pajamas, leaped from bed and flew over.

Paul leaned against the wall, panting and scowling. At the sight of Amy, he scowled harder. "Well, at least you're alive."

"Why wouldn't I be alive? How did you get upstairs?"

"I managed." His face had gone so pale that Amy darted forward to put an arm under his, and was even more alarmed when he didn't protest. She got him inside and seated at the table.

Gran said quietly, "Would you like some coffee?"

"Yes," Paul gasped.

The hot coffee seemed to revive him. He said coldly to Amy, "You didn't come over. You don't have a phone. We were supposed to play chess yesterday afternoon. I thought maybe you were sick, or moved away, or dead."

Chess. Now Amy remembered the tentative date, lost in Violet's reshuffling of the shopping schedule and in everything that had happened since. She said, "I'm sorry, Paul. Stuff happened. Did you . . . did you happen to watch TV last night?"

"I never watch TV," he said scornfully. His gaze fell on Amy's cell, recharging by the sofa bed. "So you do have a phone. Could have saved me the trip over. But since I'm—"

Amy said, exasperated, "Why didn't you just send your mother?"

"She's gone on Sundays." He didn't explain where, or why.

"But as I was saying, since I'm here, let's play some chess."

It didn't seem to register with Paul that Amy was still in her pajamas, that Gran sat with her eyes closed in the easy chair, or that Amy might have other things to do. On the other hand, chess suddenly sounded soothing. Normal. Paul, too, sounded soothing, in that he had no idea of yesterday's events, and wouldn't have cared anyway.

OK, Kaylie was right—Amy was nerdy. So what? She got out the chess set.

"Here, set this up while I get Gran to bed and I get dressed."

They played two games and Amy won both. She felt curiously sharp and focused. Paul kept looking at his watch, but he was a good loser; after the second game he looked at her with admiration. "Nice play. I'm going home now. Will you help me down the stairs? Going down is trickier than coming up. Just go first to stop me if I slip."

"Sure." Gran was still asleep. Kaylie had called to say, with suspicious sweetness, that she was practicing with the band but would be home to fix dinner. If she really did it, that would make twice in the same century.

Amy and Paul left the apartment. He seemed to move even more slowly than usual, but when she asked him if anything hurt, he scowled and waved away her question. Well, some people were prickly about anything that looked like pity. Slowly they made their way downstairs. There were two flights, each with a turn halfway down, at a cramped landing no more than a yard square.

At the first landing Paul gasped, "Wait here a minute. Let me . . . just wait."

"OK," Amy said. The wait seemed long. Amy began to feel very strange.

All her sharp focus drained away, as if someone had turned on a vacuum cleaner and gently, silently, sucked it all out of her. A dreamy lassitude took her. Paul, a step above her, had turned his face to the wall and seemed to be breathing into his shirt collar. Amy had to fight a powerful urge to sink bone-lessly to her knees.

"Let's go," Paul said after a timeless pause, and she forced herself to move.

Another step, then another. Seven steps to the tiny land-ing next to the Chans' second-floor apartment. Paul's face was still turned away from her.

Amy felt so disoriented, so strange. . . . The feeling was even stronger here than on the landing above.

Mist began to form before her eyes.

"Amy?" Paul's voice said, as if from a great distance. "Are you all right?"

No words would form. *How odd*, thought the last part of

her brain that still seemed to work, *I always have words*. But not now. Language slipped away. Amy didn't miss it. It was pleasant, so pleasant, to stand there dreamily in the mist, her mind empty, the mist so pretty as it swirled and then took on pale colors and then came together somehow . . . why, it *was* coming together, into something, into a form, a person . . .

"Hello, Amy," whispered the shifting, pale form.

"Mama," Amy said, and smiled, reaching out her hand. Her mother was back, come to visit just as Amy had always secretly hoped, back from the dead——

*Back from the dead.*

Amy's eyes widened. She couldn't move, couldn't think, but there was her mother, or her mother's ghost. . . . The universe tilted and spun.

Then Paul was running down the stairs, leaving his crutches behind, and somehow this didn't seem at all odd. It didn't even matter. Nothing mattered but Amy's mother, back again. And that meant there really was life after . . . no, that wasn't it . . . she couldn't think. But here was her mother, smiling at her, dressed in something white and floaty, and . . . *her mother . . .*

"Mama!" Amy burst into tears. She put out her hand to touch her mother, to embrace her one more time, just as she had longed to do for more than a decade. Amy's hand went right through her. Just as if . . . as if she were . . .

"No!"

But her mother was fading, the mist swirling apart, going away. Another second, two, three, a lifetime of seconds spent in longing and fear of yet another loss, and her mother disappeared. Amy, crying, fell to the floor.

But only for a moment. Her head began to clear.

Not really her mother. And not an illusion in Amy's mind, either, despite the drug that Amy could still smell dissipating on the air.

Mrs. Raduski came out of her apartment below and called up the stairs, "What was that thumping? What's going on up there? I'll set my dog on you, I will!"

Amy's head cleared. Not an illusion, a *hologram*. Like the dog in the tree, the rats in the parking lot—

"You here, where are you running to?" Mrs. Raduski called. "You, boy, stop!"

Amy's head cleared. *Paul, clattering down the stairs, not crippled at all—*

Barking, snarling, a cry of pain. Paul.

Amy's head cleared completely and she staggered to her feet, raced down the stairs, and caught up to Paul. He lay on the sidewalk, screaming, Buddy's teeth fastened on his leg. Mrs. Raduski was yelling into her phone, "Come quick! Come quick, I caught a thief! My dog got him, come quick!"

"He's not a thief!" Amy cried. She was so furious she could

barely see straight. The second that Mrs. Raduski reluctantly called off Buddy, Amy was on Paul, kneeling beside him and beating him with her fists.

"You were in on it! You're a plant from the show! You bastard, you fucker, I trusted you!"

Paul looked at her coldly. His leg bled freely. He snarled at her, "Hey, you signed up for this! I didn't sign up for dog bites! Get a fucking ambulance here!"

"You're not even crippled, are you? And you . . . drugs in the air on the stairs . . . my mother!"

Mrs. Raduski demanded, "What's she babbling about? Where are them cops?"

Amy stalked off. Let Paul bleed to death. Let Mrs. Raduski's cops arrest him. A plant, just like Lynn had been a plant. . . .

The full extent of what Myra Townsend had done hit Amy. Myra had hired Paul and his mother, moved them into an apartment across the street, made sure she got an actor who played very good chess, rigged the hallway with breathable mind-altering drugs and unseen cameras and Mark Meyer's tech equipment to create a hologram that Amy had believed in . . .

Hatred of them all swept through her, along with a renewed sense of loss and bereavement. Her *mother* . . . How dare they—

She raced back upstairs, grabbed her cell, punched in Myra's number. Straight to voice mail.

"This is Myra Townsend. I—"

Amy screamed into the phone, "I quit! Do you hear me, Myra? I quit!"

"—cannot receive messages on this phone until Tuesday. Please call my other number. Thank you."

Amy didn't have Myra's other number. She threw the cell phone across the room. Just as she was about to pound with her fists on the wall, she stopped herself; it would wake Gran.

Gran. She mustn't know that Amy thought she'd seen her dead mother. Amy could at least spare Gran, if not herself. Even if that meant pretending that nothing had happened, that Paul and she had just played chess like normal human beings.

The people at TLN were not normal. Not Myra, not Alex, not Lynn, not Mark. Normal people did not do things like this, did not reach into your chest and tear out your heart just so they could film you bleeding. Myra was a monster, and first thing tomorrow morning Amy was going to march into Myra's office, curse her out, and quit.

"Amy?" Gran called from the bedroom. "I hear sirens!"

"Yes," Amy called back, fiercely mastering her voice. "I'm looking out the window now. I think Buddy bit somebody down on the sidewalk."

# Fifteen

**MONDAY**

"I QUIT!" AMY SAID. "What you did was manipulative and despicable and just plain sick, and I quit!"

Myra Townsend gazed at her calmly. "Are you sure, Amy?"

"Yes, I'm sure! What did you make the others see—their dead parents too? Or grandparents? Or friends? Violet lost a dancer friend to cancer—did you make her see him? Talk to him? And you swore to me that there would be no filming in my apartment!"

"You weren't in your apartment," Myra said. "You were in the stairwell."

"Same thing!"

"It is not. Now, I know you're upset, Amy dear, but—"

"Don't call me dear!"

"Then I'll call you hasty, to say the least. You need to think this through. Were you harmed in any way? Has your contract been violated in the smallest clause?"

"I'm not talking about my contract, I'm—"

"You should be talking about your contract. It's legally binding. And yes, it says you may quit. But if you do, you lose your salary, all medical benefits for your family, and a chance at real money beyond that. The pilot was a success, and soon you'll be a TV star."

"I don't care!"

"Maybe not, but possibly you care about treatment for your grandmother. You told Paul's 'mother' that she is very ill, possibly terminal. Is it worth a little emotional upset on your part to let your grandmother live her last days in pain-free comfort, someplace better than your—forgive me—seedy apartment? We can make that happen, and we will. But not if you quit."

Amy stared at her, at Myra's perfect makeup, belted Tom Ford suit, artfully tousled hair. In the opulent office that on Friday night had been full of fake trees and real fear. Myra's face was serene, and utterly cold.

Amy said softly, "I despise you."

"I know, dear. But that's a producer's lot. Now, I'll promise you this, just so you can calm down: Today there will be no scenarios. You have my word."

"I don't think your word is worth much."

"Oh, but it is. Think, Amy—have I ever actually lied to you? Withheld information, maybe, but not lied. If I say there is no scenario today, then there is not. You look very nice, by the way. You've been shopping."

Amy wore the jeans and Marc Jacobs sweater that Violet had helped her find. Myra's flattery was contemptible. Amy glared at her—as if a glare would affect Myra Townsend!—turned, and left the office before tears of anger could start. Sometime this week Gran would receive her test results from the doctor.

Amy was assigned to more children's-game review in the deep basement, and so worked alone all morning. This game was supposed to teach small children about big-bigger-biggest, small-smaller-smallest, hot-hotter-hottest. Amy moved a nose-twitching rabbit around the screen. Several times the rabbit would not move into the right position; this was an early version of the program and it had bugs. She made notes of these on forms stamped PROPERTY OF TAUNTON LIFE NETWORK.

At lunchtime she nearly ran to the cafeteria. What had Violet been made to endure? Rafe? Poor Tommy? How low had Myra gone?

*Slimy, slimier, slimiest.*

\* \* \*

"It was no big deal," Waverly said, picking up a forkful of salad. "I never liked my cousin all that much anyway."

"Such sweet family loyalty," Violet said. "It's downright touching." Violet seemed unusually subdued, but there was a dangerous look in her eyes that made Amy hold back her questions.

She, Waverly, Violet, and Rafe were the first to reach the lunch table with their trays. Around them sat tables of adults, many of whom glanced frequently in their direction. Either they had seen the show on Saturday or they had already heard that it was a success. Amy didn't care. She said, "Rafe? Did you see a fake ghost too?"

"Yes, but I knew it was fake right from the beginning."

"How? The drug in the air——"

"I recognized that drug. I've smelled it before." His face was stony. Amy shut up, but not Waverly.

She said distastefully, "You use?"

"No. But my brother did."

*Overdose*, Amy guessed.

Rafe said, "You should see your face, Amy. No, you weren't in any danger from that particular drug, not from one exposure. I only meant that I'd smelled it when my older brother was using everything under the sun. At the first whiff I held my breath, and when I couldn't hold it anymore, I ran."

Violet said, with more gentleness than Amy had ever seen from her, "But you didn't run right away."

Rafe shrugged. "I wanted to see what the gig was."

Waverly said, "And what was it?"

Rafe shot her a contemptuous look. *His dead brother*, Amy guessed. She said quickly, "Myra promised me no new scenario today. Let's see if she keeps her word."

Rafe snorted. Tommy rushed over to their table, his soup sloshing over the bowl onto the tray. His broad face glowed.

"Guess what, guys! I saw a ghost yesterday! And it spoke to me!"

Silence around the table.

Was it possible, Amy thought wildly, that Tommy *believed* in Myra's illusion? She'd known his IQ was low—but how low?

"It said my name," Tommy said proudly. "'Tommy.'"

Very low. Oh, you *bitch*, Myra, putting him on the show to be laughed at.

Violet said cautiously, "Was the ghost anyone you knew?"

Tommy looked puzzled. "I never met any ghosts before."

Waverly smothered a laugh. Amy glared at her and said to Tommy, "Well, then, that was quite an experience. What . . . what did you do?"

"I tried to talk to it, but it went away too soon."

Rafe said, "Tom, we all saw ghosts. We think they were illusions created by the show. You know, like the trees in Myra's office."

Tommy's face clouded. "Not real?"

"No."

Tommy shook his head. "No, mine was real. It said my name."

Amy said, "You should talk to Cai about it."

He nodded vigorously. "Yes. Cai knows."

But when Cai approached the table, it was clear he didn't want to talk to anyone. Amy knew he would make an exception for Tommy, but right now his dark brows pinched together and his mouth was a thin straight line. It didn't matter; Amy's palms still grew moist when she was around him, and she felt every nerve in her body spring to high alert. *Stupid, stupid.* He wasn't interested. Evolution really screwed up on this one, she thought—one-way attraction benefited nobody.

Rafe said cynically, "So I see that nobody actually quit the show."

Amy looked down at her bowl of clam chowder. She didn't want it.

Waverly said, "Really, Rafe—anybody who gives up that easily doesn't deserve a career in television. Have you seen how everyone is looking at us for the— Here comes one now."

A girl, not much older than them, approached their table.

*Intern*, Amy guessed, or possibly a newish secretary. She smiled at Cai. "I saw the show last night. Can I have your autograph?"

Cai looked startled, then scrawled his name. The girl thanked him, blushed, and bounded off. She didn't ask for anyone else's autograph. Waverly looked deeply annoyed, and Amy grinned at Violet. Mean of her, but Waverly's annoyance was the first thing to make her smile in nearly twenty-four hours.

Violet grinned back.


Myra Townsend kept her word. There was no new scenario on Monday. But when Amy arrived home after work, a brightly painted van stood in front of her building: WKZZ TV. A woman jumped out, a man behind her with a camcorder up to his eye.

"Amy! I think we're the first to track down one of TLN's newest stars! How do you think you did in the first scenario on *Who Knows People?*" The woman smiled hugely; she seemed to have too many teeth. "Amy?"

"I—how did you find out where I live?" The TV show had included no last names.

The teeth, astonishingly, multiplied. "Oh, we have our methods. But tell your fans, Amy—are you pleased with whatever you did in that alley? Give our viewers just a hint!"

"I can't talk about it."

"Sure you can—the voting period ended. Just a hint! Did you escape the rapist that grabbed you?"

Amy walked past the van toward her door. Both the reporter and the cameraman followed.

"What about the others, Amy? Who do you think did the best?"

Say nothing. If she said nothing they would go away. Wouldn't they?

"How did Cai perform? He's gorgeous, isn't he? Are you two dating, hmmmm?"

Amy darted inside and slammed the door.

Mrs. Raduski stood in the vestibule, Buddy snarling on his leash. "Well," she said.

You could never tell about Mrs. Raduski. She might decide Amy's new celebrity was a thing to be fawned over because it was *television*. Or she might decide that Amy was "getting above herself," which really meant getting above Mrs. Raduski. Or she might, because she intermittently liked Amy, decide something else entirely.

Mrs. Raduski said, "Aren't we getting pretty big for our britches."

Option number two. Amy said, "Hi, Mrs. Raduski," and escaped up the stairs.

Gran sat in the chair by the window, looking down at the TV van. "Good day at work, honey?"

"Quiet day," Amy said. "That van will go away soon, won't it?"

"We can only hope. With all the real news in the world, most of it reaching a critical point, you think those people would find better things to do than harass you. Especially today."

"They weren't exactly harassing me," Amy said. "Why 'especially today'?"

Gran looked surprised. "You didn't hear at your job?"

"Hear what?"

"About the merger?"

Amy shook her head. She moved to Gran's chair; her grandmother looked tired and very pale. "Are you all right?"

"Taunton Life Network was acquired this morning by Pylon Global, the mega-conglomerate based in Dubai. They also own Cameron Enterprises, the nuclear-power-plant builders, and a major chemical-and-fertilizer company that's transnational. TLN is their first venture into communications, but it won't be their last. Amy, Pylon attracts major protest demonstrations everywhere, from all sorts of groups. Environmental, human rights—that's because of that mess they created in Africa—as well as wage protesters. The TLN building could be besieged."

Amy didn't know what mess Pylon had created in Africa, and she didn't ask. She was more concerned with Gran.

A phantom leaped into her mind: *a rain of pellets, each one a piece of paper rolled into such a tight little ball that the pellets were hard as stones.*

She said slowly, "Your medical tests came back."

Gran didn't ask how Amy knew. She just put out one thin, blue-veined hand to grasp Amy's. "Amy, you're going to have to be very strong."

"Tell me. Don't sugarcoat, Gran—just tell me."

For a long moment Gran said nothing. Amy knelt by her chair, face upturned, waiting. Time seemed to stop.

Finally Gran said, "No need to tell you to be strong; you always are. My tumor is inoperable, Amy, and very aggressive. I have only a few months left, at best."

Amy choked out, "With better medical . . . with money . . ."

"It wouldn't make any difference, except in comfort level. But I'm not frightened. I've had a long run and a good one, and to tell the truth, I've always been curious about what comes next. I'm desperately sorry to leave you and Kayla, but you mustn't grieve too hard."

"I—"

"Ah, don't cry, honey. It's providential that you have this good job. You'll not only survive, you'll flourish, I *know* it. And you can take care of Kaylie. Now, would you mind bringing me a cup of that herbal tea? It's so soothing."

Amy stumbled into the little galley kitchen. She knew

Gran wanted the tea mostly to give Amy something to do with her hands, and with her stunned grief. As the water boiled on the stove, Amy warmed her suddenly cold fingers over the steam and willed herself not to cry. Gran, never given to displays of emotion even when her feelings ran strong, was meeting this thing with stoic courage. Amy would do the same. For Gran's sake.

But her hands shook as she opened the tin box where they kept tea bags. Peppermint? Lemon? It didn't matter. Nothing mattered anymore.

No, that wasn't right. That kind of easy cynicism wasn't *right*. Things mattered. So much mattered to Gran, not just Amy and Kaylie but the country, the world, the science she had practiced until the Collapse cut off nearly all research funding. Things mattered to Gran, and that was why she wasn't afraid now. She could look beyond herself.

As Amy poured the hot water over the tea, she thought: *But Gran must be a little bit afraid.* Wasn't everyone, of dying? If so, Gran would never let it show.

Carefully she carried the two cups out of the kitchen. "Here's your tea. I made myself some too." They sipped in silence until Amy said, "What can be done for you in the . . . the meantime?"

"Nothing right now. When I need it, an in-home nurse,

which your splendid new medical benefits will pay for. I'm very grateful, Amy. Then perhaps a hospice, depending on how it goes. I meant what I said before, you know. I'm not afraid, and I'm curious about what comes next. Since of course I have no idea and neither does anyone else, despite what some think."

Amy, to her own astonishment, managed a small smile. "Amelia Whitcomb, scientist to the end."

"You betcha." Gran looked at her with admiration and Amy knew she'd made the right decision to keep her emotions under control. That was Gran's way, and Amy was going to do everything she could to make sure Gran got her every wish for whatever time was left. Even if she had to fight Kaylie, Myra Townsend, TLN, and the rest of the world to make that happen.

Amy's cell rang. "Hello?"

"One Two Three!" Violet sang out. "Guess what? I just got a call from a dance troupe to fill a guest spot. They saw me on the show. Well, OK, it's only a sub because a dancer fell and can't work, but I think it's an omen of things to come."

"Are you leaving the show?"

"Of course not. I'm waiting for the real offers to come in. But I think that eventually they will. You know what? I think that bitch Myra Townsend will pull this off. I think we're all going to be stars!"

# Sixteen

**TUESDAY**

THERE WAS NO sign of stardom on Tuesday morning. The 6:30 a.m. news, which Amy watched with Gran, focused on the TLN merger. A Pylon executive, sounding rehearsed, said, how glad he was for TLN to be "joining the Pylon family," and that TLN would be run as an independent division, with James Taunton remaining in charge. "Nothing at TLN will change," he said.

Not quite.

Outside, cold rain drenched Amy as she waited for a bus that never came. More trouble with the citywide transport system. No one in the wet huddle of commuters at the bus stop recognized her, or even glanced at her. Eventually they all gave up on the bus and began to walk, and so did Amy. The few cabs sped past, full of luckier people, and anyway Amy didn't want to spend money on a cab. She wanted to save all she could for whatever Gran needed.

By the time she reached downtown, the rain had stopped but she was running to not be late. But then she couldn't get anywhere near the building.

A vast mob of people surrounded TLN. They formed a human chain, arms interlocked, at the bottom of the broad, shallow steps leading to the glass doors. The chain extended around the corners, and more protesters blocked the street, surging forward as yet more rushed to join them. All traffic was stopped. This was not a crowd of polite, sign-carrying demonstrators. There were signs, but they were being waved as if in a hurricane, and many were splashed with red to resemble blood. People shouted and screamed. A man with a bullhorn stood on a makeshift platform, although there was no way to hear what he might be saying over the ear-hammering noise. The signs were violent:

NUKE PYLON, NOT US

DEATH TO CHEMICAL-DEATH MERCHANTS

HOW MANY DEFORMED BABIES ARE TOO MANY?

KEEP PYLON IN DUBAI!

BLOW UP CAMERON BEFORE IT BLOWS UP US

Amy paused across the street from the TLN building, at the far edge of the crowd, uncertain what to do. The building behind her was fronted by a small plaza, decorated with little ornamental trees in pots. Waist-high concrete barriers, disguised as natural-stone gateposts although without gates, ringed the plaza to prevent traffic from leaping the curb and plowing into the flimsy trees. Amy climbed on top of one of the stone posts for a better view.

Police sirens wailed a few blocks away, then stopped, unable to get any closer.

Amy saw Waverly a block away in the other direction, standing beside a long dark car and scowling. A few minutes later Cai and Tommy appeared. They began to push their way through the crowd toward the TLN building, Cai in the lead, both their wide shoulders opening a path forward. Could they cross the protest line safely and get into work? Should Amy try to follow them?

Cops in full-body armor began to penetrate the crowd from the opposite side of the building. Some protestors gave way before them, some did not. The police presence seemed to galvanize the crowd. All at once the man with the bullhorn succeeded in welding their noise into a single chant, which spread throughout the mob: *"No Pylon python! No Pylon python! No Pylon python!"*

A huge banner suddenly dropped from a fourth-story window of the building beside TLN: a vicious coiled snake squeezing to death two helpless children. At the sight of the banner the crowd let out a huge roar. More people surged from side streets, pushing up against those already present, knocking over the potted trees in the little plaza behind Amy. Some of these were carrying TIMES BE TOUGH MAN signs— evidently another demonstration had heard about this one and joined it.

"*No Pylon python! No Pylon python!*"

Amy grew frightened. She co10uldn't get down from the stone post; there was no room to stand. The cops shouldered forward, trying to reach the steps in front of TLN. Amy spied Rafe in the crowd; he was holding a TIMES BE TOUGH MAN sign and shouting something incomprehensible. She could no longer see Tommy or Cai.

Still more people poured from side streets, forcing forward those already there. People closest to the buildings tried to go into them, but many doors were locked against the mob. A second bullhorn, this one electronically amplified and belonging to the cops, screamed for the crowd to disperse. The crowd gave an answering roar, so deep and loud that Amy's ears rang.

Someone threw a rock at a cop who had reached the steps

of TLN. It missed, but the cop pulled a canister from his belt—tear gas?

"Let me down!" Amy yelled. The tsunami of people washed forward—people in the front must be getting crushed! But the chanting went on—*"No Pylon python!"*—and the banners waved and it seemed that the streets were made of people, were tiled with them, packed together with shouting, contorted, furious faces and shaking fists.

Someone knocked Amy off her perch. She fell sideways, clutching at air, but the people were so close together that she could not fall between them. She rode the tops of their shoulders, flailing helplessly, afraid that if she did slip between them, she would be trampled. She was a piece of flotsam on a shifting, angry sea.

Cops pulled the leader off the rickety platform and carried him away, struggling and shouting. The crowd surged this way and that. To her horror, Amy glimpsed something through a sudden brief gap between the people she rode on: *a body*. There was a person down there beneath everyone's feet, a person unable to get up, a person being trampled to death.

All at once the noise lessened. A man tried to throw Amy off his head and she was turned like a flipped burger so that she now faced the platform. Kaylie stood there, taking off her clothes.

Kaylie ripped off her blouse and bra, and the momentary startled reaction among enough people below—especially men—created a brief abatement of noise. A person could finally be heard. A man leaped up beside Kaylie and shouted, "Freeze! Everyone stand still before more of us get hurt! Just freeze and you'll be safe! We can get out of here slowly and no one will die!"

Not everyone stopped shouting and pushing, but enough did. Kaylie unzipped her pants. Her perfect breasts caught the sunlight and gleamed. The man kept shouting, "Just don't move! Just don't move!"

Kaylie tore off her pants. She stood in black lace panties—stolen from where?—and raised her arms above her head. Enough people had stopped moving so that the terrifying surges were arrested.

"Just don't move! Just don't move! Now, the people at the crowd edges, move back to let others breathe! That's it, just move back at the edges!"

The platform wobbled and the man caught Kaylie, steadying her. Her pale, gorgeous body was a beacon, a focal point as the man shouted directions for safe dispersal. Some counter-shouting from the people holding the violent signs was, for the most part, ignored. Most of these people wanted to protest Pylon Global, but not at the cost of dying.

The bodies below Amy moved slightly apart, and she felt herself start to fall. But then strong arms grasped her. A voice said, "Steady, Amy, I've got you—"

Cai.

In another moment he had her on her feet, crushed between him and Tommy, but with enough room to breathe. His right arm kept her upright. She could feel his muscles stand out like cords. The crowd loosened a little more, and then still more. No tear gas was released. Eventually Cai, Tommy, and Amy were able to wiggle to the edge of the mob and then into a side street.

"Kaylie!" Amy gasped, slumping against a concrete wall. "Is she . . . Kaylie . . ."

"Who's Kaylie?" Cai said. "Are you all right?"

"Kaylie! The girl on the platform . . . taking off her clothes . . ."

Tommy peered around the corner. "She's gone. No, she's OK—a cop has her."

"Will they arrest her?" Amy said.

Cai said, "They shouldn't. She kept a bad situation from being a tragedy. I don't think anyone was actually trampled."

"Yes, there was," Amy said. Again she saw the body beneath panicked feet, a human being treated as if he or she was no more than a rug.

Tommy said, "Do you know that girl?"

"She's my sister."

"Your sister!" Cai said.

At his tone, Amy looked up. He said, "She was incredibly brave. And unbelievably gorgeous." Cai's face glowed as it had never glowed for Amy. His blue eyes held excitement and longing. All at once, he blushed. "Will you introduce me?"

Amy could only nod while people surged past her, shouting words she didn't understand.

Amy took a cab back home. Alex had called all of them on their cells, asking if they were all right. The moment her cell rang, Amy had a phantom: *Alex dressed as a knight in black armor, seated on a horse and waving a sword.* She was too shaken and too dispirited to think about the phantom. "Amy! Are you all right?"

"Yes. I was . . . yes."

"Where are you?" Alex demanded.

"A side street, I don't know the name. With Cai and Tommy."

"Out of the crowd?"

"Yes." Around the corner and down the street she could still hear shouting, sirens, chaos. People ran past her, but not in those frightful surges of packed humanity. That nightmare of being tossed on the top of the crowd, that glimpse of the body trampled beneath . . . A shudder ran over her from neck to knees.

Alex said, "Go home. Take a cab if you can find one—TLN will reimburse you. None of the three of you is hurt?"

"No."

"Stay at home until you hear from me. I have to call the others." He clicked off.

Tommy said, "Who was that?"

"Alex. He said for all of us to go home and stay there until he calls. But I can't. Kaylie—I have to find Kaylie."

Her cell rang again—Kaylie. Amy clutched the phone hard. "Where are you? Are you all right?"

"I'm fine," Kaylie said. "I'm inside your building with a cop. He—"

"Are you under arrest?"

"No, no. They just want me to stay inside until it's safe. And until I get some clothes." She actually giggled.

Anger washed over Amy, so strong that she knew it wasn't caused only by Kaylie but by Amy's own helplessness. But Kaylie was the immediate target. "This isn't a joke!"

"Not to me," Kaylie said in a different tone, and hung up.

Cai said, "Is she—"

"She's fine," Amy snapped. "*She's* always fine."

Cai's eyes widened at Amy's anger, but he said nothing more. Tommy fastened on the point that mattered to him. "Alex says to go home? For all day?"

Cai said, "I'll take you, Tommy. But I think the chance of getting a cab is zero. Amy, we'll walk you home."

"I don't—"

"Just shut up for once," Cai said wearily, "and let somebody else make some decisions, OK? Come on."

The three of them walked uptown in unpleasant silence. People still pushed past them, but not dangerously. Ten blocks away, a cab stopped to let someone off, and Cai leaped forward to yank open the door. "Hey!" The cabbie said, "I already got a fare waiting!"

"Yeah, us," Cai said. "Amy, give him your address."

The cabbie scowled, measured the size of Cai and Tommy, and shrugged. He pulled away from the curb.

Amy said, "I don't have any money."

"I got it," Cai said curtly.

She knew that he didn't have much money either, and that neither he nor Tommy lived anywhere near Amy. But she said nothing and just stared out the window at the city, still wet and soggy from the morning rain, until she could no longer hear the sirens behind her downtown.

Myra leaned forward in her leather chair in the screening room. "Stop right there—no, back up—yes, there. Can you enlarge the lower left quadrant?"

The tech sitting at the computer keyed rapidly. On-screen, a section of the crowd zoomed forward. Rafe came into view, holding a bullhorn and shouting.

Myra frowned. "It's pretty grainy."

"Well, after all," the cameraman sitting next to her said petulantly, "it wasn't like we had setups. This isn't bad for footage we got just by chance."

Alex, on Myra's other side, said quietly, "You can't use it, Myra."

"That's not your decision."

"It doesn't have to be. Just *think* for a minute. Putting this on the show would be exploiting a civic tragedy. A woman died in that mob, Myra. Trampled underfoot. And there are a dozen other people in the hospital. You can't use this as a scenario even if you find clear footage of all six of them. First, it would be ghoulish. Second, it's hardly good PR for TLN, seeing as those protestors were objecting to our merger with Pylon. Third, it would cause a national outrage."

Myra said, "First, ghoulish is good for ratings in this show's demographic. Second, the protestors are the villains here— *they* trampled that woman, we didn't. Third, outrage is what this network does. Or have you forgotten that in your sudden moral superiority? You, who used to produce porn?"

On-screen, Kaylie climbed onto the rickety platform from

which a cop had pulled the protest leader. The cameraman said, "There, bottom left edge—is that Violet?"

"Don't zoom in yet," Myra said. "We'll look later." Her gaze stayed on Kaylie, who ripped off first her top and then her lacy black bra. "That one knows how to command attention."

Alex said quietly, "Porn has nothing to do with this. On my old show nobody died."

Myra wasn't listening. She watched Kaylie as half the crowd swung their gaze to her voluptuous nakedness, allowing the man with the bullhorn to seize their attention long enough to prevent more deaths.

Myra said, "Too bad she's not a player on the show."

Alex said with sudden harshness, "You know about her— she's been phoning both of us nonstop. She's fifteen. Underage."

"A shame," Myra said. She drummed her long manicured fingernails on the tabletop. "Really a shame. I think we might have auditioned the wrong sister."

# Seventeen

WHEN AMY REPORTED to work on Wednesday, the front of the TLN building showed no sign of yesterday's mob. Amy felt heavy-eyed, having watched TV news far into the night. Over and over again came grainy shots of Kaylie, captured on a hundred cell phones held up in windows or on the edges of the crowd. Kaylie herself had not come home, phoning to say excitedly that "some people from the protest" were putting her up for the night. Before Amy could object, Kaylie had clicked off.

Violet met Amy by the employees' entrance to TLN. "Hey, you don't look so good, One Two Three."

"I'm fine."

"If you say so." Violet offered no comment about Kaylie, for which Amy was grateful. Instead Violet said, "So tonight's the second half of our great debut. Can I watch again at your place?"

"Sure."

Inside, the security guard consulted a tablet. "Ms. Kent, Ms. Sanderson—you report this morning to Room Five-forty-six."

Amy said, "What's Room Five-forty-six?"

"Fifth is a studio floor," the guard said. "I don't know what the room is."

It turned out to be Hair and Makeup.

"Well, well," Violet said. "Are we under orders to get makeovers? Just so long as nobody cuts my hair."

The room was full of actresses being worked on for various shows. Amy recognized none of them, but then she didn't watch the melodramas that were TLN's staples. A small man with a head as bald as an egg rushed up to them.

"Ah, yes, Amy and Violet. I'm Enrique. Let me see. . . ." Experimentally he lifted a hank of Amy's barely combed hair. "Tragic, really tragic. When were you last shaped?"

Amy demanded, "Did Myra order a haircut for me?"

"That and more. Much more. You will leave here a different person, my dear. And a far prettier one. You, Violet— you're not doing too badly already but those brows—no, no."

"Bring it on," Violet said. "Just don't touch the hair."

Enrique called an assistant, who led Violet away. Enrique said to Amy, "I will do you myself—you practically need an *intervention*. This way. I see hours of work ahead of us. Can I get you some tea? Mineral water?"

"Coffee, please." She felt resigned, even though she didn't really like being fussed over. This was what Myra had ordered. And it was better than reviewing more children's learning games. *Put the bug on the rug.*

"Coffee—no, no. Bad for both the complexion and the teeth. Perhaps that is why yours so badly need whitening."

Amy, who thought her teeth were sufficiently white, settled for mineral water. Then she settled in for eight hours of being fussed over.

The first five hours were the worst. Amy's hair was washed, colored, frosted, cut, blown out, all of which involved multiple products with multiple odors both good and bad.

*Put the messes on the tresses.*

Her brows were waxed, her legs were waxed, and only because she adamantly refused was she spared a bikini wax. Her teeth were whitened. A facial mask was troweled onto her skin and the greenish stuff, which smelled of some sort of vegetable, hardened and tightened until it was ripped off.

*Pull all trace from the face.*

"Aaahhh," breathed Enrique. "See how much better!"

To Amy her skin didn't look all that different from before, but she smiled obligingly at Enrique.

He said, "You begin to look presentable. Now, makeup. Clothilde!"

A woman rushed over. Heavyset and dressed in shapeless black, she had the most penetrating gaze that Amy had ever seen. Clothilde took Amy's face in her hand, forcefully turned it this way and that, and said doubtfully, "Well . . ."

What did that mean? Amy said, "I don't really wear very much makeup except maybe a little——"

Clothilde ignored her. She and Enrique launched into a product discussion, most of which sounded unintelligible. Amy resigned herself anew, except for the occasional frown when Clothilde applied yet another layer of something.

"Face still!" Clothilde said. "Did the ceiling twist around like that while Michelangelo was painting? No, don't you laugh, either! You are a marble statue—you hear me? You are the *Venus de Milo!*"

*Who didn't wear makeup*, Amy thought. She kept her face still.

When Clothilde was done, Amy was allowed to stand up. Enrique rushed over—nobody here seemed capable of moving at less than a run—and he and Clothilde walked around Amy, regarding their results from every angle while she gazed at her reflection in the mirror.

She both was and was not herself. Prettier, yes—that

couldn't be questioned. Her heavy, honey-colored hair now waved in artful, tousled layers to her shoulders, with side-swept bangs and more volume on the top. Her skin, which was not flawless, appeared to be so, and her eyes looked much larger, framed by twice as many lashes as before. The lids shaded from taupe to a subtle blue, deepening the color of her irises. Her teeth gleamed between lips colored rose. Prettier—but a little like a doll.

"I—" she began, not sure what she was going to say. It didn't matter; Enrique interrupted her.

"Now wash it all off."

"Wash it off?"

"Yes, of course. For the lessons. You must learn to do this yourself, my dear. I cannot attend to you every morning. I have everyone to do!" His arm swept grandly to encompass the rest of the room, in which no one else remained. Violet and Waverly had left long ago, apparently needing less correction than Amy.

She took off her makeup, put it on, took it off, put it on, while Enrique despaired and Clothilde told her to be Georges Seurat, not Jackson Pollock. "Small brush strokes! Small! Do not just pour the product on!"

When they were satisfied—or possibly just exhausted—Amy was released. She got up from the makeup chair with profound relief.

"Now, do it that way every morning," Enrique said. "Here is your tote of product and tools. And here comes Serena."

Serena was a six-foot-tall black woman, the most elegant creature that Amy had ever seen. Amy's eyes went hungrily over the Prada skirt, top by a designer so "now" that Amy couldn't even name him, and Christian Louboutin gladiator sandals whose heels added another two inches to Serena's height. Thin as a model but several decades older, Serena studied Amy and then said, "Size six petite, thirty-four B, twenty-nine inseam, five and a half shoe?"

Amy stood speechless.

"What you're wearing isn't too bad"—the jeans and sweater that Violet had picked out—"but we can do better. Follow me."

For the next two hours Serena had Amy try on clothes in what looked like a vast department store on the eighth floor. Each time anything was pulled over her head, Amy's entire face was swaddled like a mummy to avoid getting makeup stains on any cloth. Serena did not permit talking, so Amy longed in silence as one gorgeous, expensive outfit succeeded another on her body. Serena sat in a chair and made notes on a tablet as assistants sprang forward to swaddle Amy, clothe Amy, reswaddle Amy, unclothe Amy, rush to and fro with thousands of dollars' worth of clothing in their arms. The labels went by like a parade of fireworks: Dolce & Gabbana, Zac Posen, Gary

Graham, Isabel Marant, Christopher Kane, Ludie Barzak.

Finally, just as Amy didn't think her legs could support her motionless posture any longer, Serena stood. "All right," she said in the cool voice that Amy had hardly heard for three hours. "You can dress and go home."

"And the clothes—"

"Will be delivered to your home tomorrow morning, of course. Here is the list I've chosen for you, with the combinations you are to wear to work for the rest of the week. Do not soil them; dry-cleaning is picked up only on Fridays, delivered back Sunday afternoon. Make sure your doorman expects all deliveries and gets them to you promptly, unless your bodyguard has that duty. Good-bye. It would be well if you lost four pounds." Serena walked out, leaving Amy openmouthed.

Doorman? Bodyguard? What universe did Serena live in?

On the bus home she studied the list. She was apparently receiving eight pieces, which could be mixed and matched. Amy could hardly read Serena's spidery handwriting without being swamped by disbelief:

Layered silk top (Gary Graham)
Basic white tee (Alexander Wang)
Shirred top (Escada)
Sweater in dull bronze (Vince)

Mosaic-print miniskirt (D&G)

Black denim jeans (7 For All Mankind)

Silk charmeuse pleated pants (Chloé)

Cropped leather jacket (Fendi)

Calfskin sandals (Miu Miu), Manolo B. heels, Prada
  boots

Could this be true? Would she get to keep the clothes? What if she tore or otherwise damaged any of them? Who would receive the package—Mrs. Raduski hardly qualified as a "doorman." Had Violet and Waverly received outfits, too? And the boys?

In the midst of all her questions, Amy had only one sure answer: Myra Townsend must expect the show tonight to be a success. And if it wasn't?

Well, the clothes weren't here yet.

At eight p.m. Amy, Violet, and Kaylie lined up on the sofa. Gran sat in the old easy chair. Amy had made popcorn, which no one was eating.

"Well," Violet said, "here goes nothing."

Kaylie shot Violet a look of dislike. The two had not hit it off well. Kaylie, however, had behaved herself, which seemed to Amy almost as ominous as her refusal to explain where she had spent last night, or with whom, or how she had gotten involved with the anti-merger protestors in the first place. Neither had she said anything about Amy's makeover beyond a single "Wow." Violet, to Amy's eyes, looked exactly the same; either she had resisted being transformed or else had washed everything off her strong-featured face.

Gran, looking drawn but bright-eyed, said, "I hardly know what to expect."

Neither did Amy. Her chest tightened around her lungs. The show's atonal music began, strange and menacing, building to the title:

## WHO KNOWS PEOPLE, BABY—YOU?

The teenage hosts appeared, briefly reexplained the show's setup, and then reran the clips of the seven encountering the "homeless" predator in the alley. The girl kept up a running patter that mostly came down to "What did she do?" "What did he do?"

"Annoying," Violet said.

The list of possible actions flashed onto the screen:

1.  Fights—and wins!
2.  Tries to run—and escapes!

3. Tries to run—and is caught!
4. Strikes a bargain with the attacker!
5. Freezes and cries!

"So," the girl said, somehow making it sound like a threat, "who knows people? You, baby? Let's see how each of these people *really* behaved."

Waverly, in a body-hugging silk dress, was thrust out of a door into the alley lined with blue Dumpsters and encountered the "dying" actor bleeding and gasping on the ground. She took a path as far away from him as possible and kept on going. When he leaped up and caught her, she screamed and struggled. Amy felt her breath come faster, remembering her own terror in the alley. But then Waverly stopped fighting and said levelly, "Let me go and I can get you money. A lot of money. A very lot—my father is a rich man!"

The actor paused. "How much?"

Kaylie laughed sourly. "She's going to buy her way out!"

And she did. Deftly Waverly negotiated an amount and a "safe" way to convey the money. The man negotiated guarantees that she would not call the police: "I know your name, your address, your schedule, and I have friends—screw me now and you'll never be safe again." They came to an agreement, and Waverly ran from the alley, graceful even in her Ferragamo heels. The screen flashed: "WAVERLY: Strikes a bargain with the attacker!"

Violet said, "Good thing she's got such a rich daddy."

Gran said, "She's smart but heartless," which seemed to Amy dead accurate.

Cai was next. Kaylie leaned forward, absorbed, her full lips parted a little. Cai tried to call for help on his cell, which of course had its signal jammed. When the man attacked, Cai, bigger and stronger, easily fought him off, got him in a headlock, dragged him from the alley, and started to call the police as the clip ended. The screen showed "CAI: Fights—and wins!"

"Our do-good hero," Violet said.

Lynn was up. While the actor still pretended to lie helpless and bleeding on the ground, Lynn went through his pockets and stole his wallet and keys. When he grabbed her, she used her keys on his face and the clip ended with "LYNN: Fights—and wins!"

Kaylie said, "That clip was short. I bet she really maimed him."

Rafe first tried to assess the man's medical condition, asking questions and taking vital signs. When the man attacked, Rafe reacted instantly. He was shorter and lighter than the attacker, but much faster. Slipping out from his grasp, he dodged and feinted until he escaped the alley. "RAFE: Tries to run—and escapes!"

Amy watched herself appear on-screen. It was excruciating. She jumped on the Dumpsters, ran over them, almost got away but chose a wrong turn and ended up trapped against the building. "AMY: Tries to run—and is caught!"

Kaylie said, "Well—maybe not your most shining hour, sis. Although that Dumpster trick was pretty good."

"Shut up," Violet said sweetly.

Amy glanced at Gran. She lay still, her mouth open. For a horrifying second Amy thought she was dead, but of course she had only fallen into the unpredictable sleep of the sick and old. Just as well. She didn't need to see Amy make a fool of herself. So far, Amy had been the only one to not escape.

Tommy didn't either. He spied the bleeding man, looked confused, walked toward him, backed away, rushed forward again, and knelt helplessly beside the man. When the actor grabbed him, Tommy let out a howl of anguish and curled into a fetal position, tears running down his face. The camera lingered on the sight before giving way to "TOMMY: Freezes and cries!"

"The bastards," Amy said softly.

Kaylie said, "What's wrong with him? He's as big as Cai, he could have taken that guy easy!"

"He's mentally challenged," Violet said, "and Myra's even more of a bitch than I thought."

Violet was the last participant, and hers was the longest segment, with the most close-ups and dialogue. When she was grabbed, Violet pretended she was panting for sex with this "hunky thug, the kind that have always turned me on," until he released his grip in bewilderment and she ran on those long, long legs. "VIOLET: Strikes a bargain with the attacker!"

"Huh," Kaylie said, a complex syllable carrying satisfaction, envy, and scorn.

Amy didn't know what to say. She couldn't look at Violet, for whom she felt a deep embarrassment that Violet apparently didn't feel for herself. Amy was doubly glad that Gran was asleep.

The rest of the show consisted of identifying the winners who had voted correctly: "Against odds of 78,125 to one!" There were three winners, each of whom was brought onto the show and presented with a check for $3,333,333.333. The payout was one penny short.

"How did they know how to vote?" Kaylie said. "They didn't know yet what you guys are each like."

"Random chance," Amy said, but she didn't bother to explain the math. All at once she felt exhausted and dispirited. What had she gotten herself into?

The feeling didn't go away after Violet left, Amy woke Gran, and she and Kaylie helped her to bed. Kaylie looked thoughtful and said little until they had opened the sofa bed. Then Kaylie looked straight at Amy and demanded, "Why you and not me?"

"Random chance," Amy said, aware that she was echoing herself. She expected more argument from Kaylie, or more *something,* anyway, but it didn't happen. Kaylie slipped out of the apartment while Amy was in the bathroom, and Amy went to sleep.

Only to wake to chaos.

# Eighteen

**THURSDAY**

## "AMY!" BELLOWED MRS. RADUSKI

outside the apartment door. "Get your ass out here!"

Amy woke from vague, unpleasant dreams. Daylight streamed in the window. Mrs. Raduski pounded on the door and Buddy snarled. Amy bolted upright. Gran called feebly from the bedroom, "Amy? What is it?" and Amy jumped out of bed and unlocked the apartment door.

"Mrs. Raduski! What's wrong?"

"What's wrong? I'll tell you what's wrong, Little Miss Trouble. All them vans blocking the street and banging on my door and upsetting my tenants! Nobody can't even go out on the public sidewalk without being set on! You just go down there and make them move!"

Buddy lunged and tried to bite Amy. She eluded him with the deftness of long practice. She went to the window, calling over her shoulder, "It's all right, Gran, it's just Mrs. Raduski."

"No, it *ain't* just me!" Mrs. Raduski said. "See down there?"

Five vans crowded the street, each with the bright logo of a TV station or Internet news link. Around them pressed a crowd of people, mostly young, some of whom certainly should have been in school. One looked up and cried, "There she is!" Cameras and cell phones clicked as Amy closed the curtain, but not before she heard someone else scream, "How do you feel about the attack on Tommy?"

Attack? On Tommy? What was— Her cell rang. Mrs. Raduski snapped, "I mean get them people out *now*!" and slammed the door. Gran called again, "Amy?"

"Coming, Gran! It's all right, Mrs. Raduski is just upset about— Hello?"

"Amy," said Myra's cool voice, "TLN will move you in one hour. Please be ready with just what you can carry. A car will arrive and the driver will have TLN identification."

"What are you talking about?"

"Haven't you seen the news? By the bye, in the normal way you would have needed to be at work in fifteen minutes, which means you've overslept. One hour, dear."

It was the "dear" that did it. Myra Townsend's condescension, her calm assumption that she could reorder Amy's life whenever and however she wanted—Amy might even have put up with those as part of the price she'd decided to pay for Gran's medical help. She had made that bargain, and she would keep it. But Myra's pretense that she was motherly and kind, acting in dear Amy's best interests—it was no part of the bargain to accept that. Cold fury, so much more useful than the hot variety, infused her voice.

"We're not moving, Myra. Here is where I live and here is where I intend to go on living. Nothing in my contract allows you to shuffle me around like a pawn on a chessboard."

"Turn on the news, dear," was all Myra said, and clicked off.

Amy didn't care if the news showed earthquakes and supernovas. She wasn't going. Myra did not control her private life. There were limits!

She turned on the news.

". . . wildfire under control in Colorado after aid from local smoke jumpers and the combined resources of three states' firefighters. Meanwhile, in local news, one of Taunton Life Network's newest stars was attacked this morning as he walked in Lincoln Park. Thomas 'Tommy' Wimmer, eighteen, was gathering spiders as part of his hobby when he was hit with a tire iron by an unknown assailant. Wimmer appeared last night on the new TLN show *Who Knows People, Baby—You?* and unconfirmed reports from eyewitnesses to the incident say that the attacker was a viewer who would have won over a million dollars except for guessing wrong about Wimmer's show participation. Stay with us as we cover this breaking story. Also this morning, the mayor's Budget Advisory Committee—"

Tommy. A tire iron. How badly was he hurt?

Gran stood in the bedroom doorway, leaning heavily against the jamb. One look and Amy knew it was one of Gran's bad days. She rushed to support her to the table even as her cell rang again.

Gran managed a weak smile. "Grand Central Station around here."

"I—just let me get this."

She eased Gran into the upholstered chair and grabbed for her cell. Violet.

"Did you see the news?"

"I just did. Violet, what's happening?"

"A bunch of different things. First, we're a success, or rather the show is. Second, the crazies are coming out. Myra announced that the prize money is being upped to ten million dollars. Third, we're all being moved to 'a secure location.' Don't you love it? I feel like the president."

"You're going?"

"Of course I'm going! Weren't you listening when I told you

about the hellhole I share with two other out-of-work dancers? It makes your place look like the Taj Mahal. My roommates are teal with jealousy—that's a shade deeper than green. You don't mean to say you're not—Amy! What is it?"

Amy screamed. From where she stood in the living room, she could see past the pulled-out sofa bed and into the dimly lit kitchen. A rat stood on the counter, eating last night's popcorn that, in the rush of television and emotion, no one had put away.

The rat raised its head and stared unmoving at Amy.

For a crazy minute she thought that the rat was unreal, another of Mark Meyer's tech tricks like the rats in the plaza outside the doctor's office. If she moved toward it, it would dissolve. She couldn't move toward it, couldn't move at all. Gran called to her, Violet called to her over her cell, and neither of them equaled the message coming from that silent rat with its monstrous flat black eyes and naked tail.

A long moment spun itself out.

Then the rat jumped off the corner and disappeared behind the refrigerator, its ugly tail the last to disappear. Amy put out a shaky arm in Gran's direction, which was supposed to indicate she was all right. Into the cell she said, "Yes. Yes, Violet, yes. We're moving."

**\* \* \***

The car, a black Chrysler with opaque windows and a chassis that looked sturdy enough to withstand ballistic missiles, arrived promptly. All but one of the press vans had given up, and most of the fans—if that's what they'd been—had presumably gone to jobs or school. Only a few cameras flashed as two men in dark suits helped Gran down the stairs and into the car. She sank back against the seat and closed her eyes. Neither of the men questioned her state or spoke more than bare necessities to Amy. Their impersonal efficiency was a little frightening, as if Amy were being aided by machines with their own agenda.

Kaylie's cell was off, but that problem was addressed by the man who met them at what seemed to be the loading dock of a large building. More alleys, more Dumpsters. Amy had a sharp sense of déjà vu, which then became a phantom in her mind: *a vast brick pile, grimy with centuries of dirt, its windows barred.* Amy had seen that image somewhere before, but where?

Not here. The loading dock led to a concrete room stacked with crates, one wall of which was lined with locked doors. The men, one nearly carrying Gran and the other Amy's two pathetic suitcases, unlocked one and led them through. An elevator took them to the seventeenth floor, where they emerged into a hallway with thick gray carpet and bronze-colored walls.

"Hello, Amy," Alex Everett said. "We're glad to have you

here. And this is your grandmother? Ma'am, would you like to see a doctor? I can summon one to your suite."

Amy thought of all the painful bus rides, all the scrounging for cab money, all the times she'd been told, "No insurance? Well, then, I'm afraid there's nothing we can do." And now: *I can summon a doctor to your suite.* Just like that. The profound unfairness of the world flooded her all over again.

Gran quavered, "Yes, please."

The suite was quietly luxurious without being ostentatious. Two bedrooms with full baths plus a half bath, a main room with two sofas, a chair, and a table that sat six. TV and a desk with a computer. Amy saw Gran settled into bed and then returned to Alex.

"We've called your sister and told her to come here," Alex said. "Any other names you want placed on the visiting list can pass security if they have photo IDs the first time, matching retinal scans after that. You need to get your own retinal scan on file at the security office behind the concierge's desk as soon as possible. Also tell them what alias you choose to be registered under; only calls addressed to the alias will be allowed through the land line. The clothes Serena chose for you are in your bedroom. You don't need to report to work today—Myra will call you. Order your meals from room service. Don't say anything on the phone or online that gives away where you are, and above all, do not leave the hotel for any reason. Any questions?"

"Yes. Where am I?"

"The Fairwood Hotel on Sixth Avenue."

"How is Tommy?"

"In good condition. The tire iron hit his arm but without breaking any bones, God knows how."

"Did you or Myra order that attack?"

Alex stared at her. "Don't be ridiculous, Amy."

She believed him, and felt a little ashamed. Shame blunted her next question. "How did you get my sister's cell number? I never gave it to you."

"She called us."

"Kaylie did? When?"

"Which time?"

*Which time?* Did that mean Kaylie had been calling Alex or Myra regularly? Why?

But Amy knew why. Kaylie wanted to be on the show too. That was why she'd been so nice to Amy lately. And Kaylie could easily have gotten Myra's number off Amy's cell while Amy slept, going behind Amy's back to make her case to TLN. That tactic seemed to have failed, but Amy was pretty sure she knew what Kaylie would try next.

Alex said no more. After he left, Amy went into her new

bedroom and sat on the bed, staring at the packages that held all the clothes TLN had picked out for her. Just as they had picked the Fairwood Hotel, had picked Gran's new doctor, had picked Amy herself.

But not the rat. That had been in the old apartment already.

The doctor had Gran sign some transfer-of-records forms, gave her some pills "to make you more comfortable," and promised to return. Amy, who had never seen a doctor make a house call before (all right, "hotel call"), didn't think he'd helped much. But Gran did seem to be resting easier when Amy finally left her to explore the hotel. The first person she saw in the hallway was Rafe.

He said in his abrupt way, "You've seen the clip of you on the Internet?"

"I haven't even turned on the computer yet."

"It's you jumping onto the Dumpsters, Lynn robbing the actor's pockets, and Violet offering sex," Rafe said flatly. "Those are the three that went viral. Looks like you girls are winning."

"I didn't know it was a competition."

He grinned, but without mirth. "Everything's a competition, Amy. All of life. Come on, I'm going to have a late breakfast with Violet. She didn't know when you'd get here and your cell isn't answering anymore."

"I ran out of minutes." Somehow it was all right to expose her poverty to Rafe, in a way that it wasn't to, for instance, Cai. Rafe hadn't even noticed her new clothes, the black jeans and layered silk top, neither of which was what Serena had dictated that Amy wear today.

He said, "Ask Myra for a new cell. I think we can ask for pretty much anything we want. Temporarily, anyway." He started down the corridor and motioned for her to follow.

"What do you want, Rafe?"

"A medical education. *That* Myra is not going to give me. I might run an EKG and detect her lack of a heart."

Amy laughed. Violet's room, large but not a suite, was littered with suitcases and ripped packaging and clothes; it looked like an explosion in Neiman Marcus. Violet, looking great in skinny jeans and a one-shouldered top, shoved everything into a corner. Amy was suddenly ravenous. Their room-service orders appeared with amazing promptness and they ate them on a round table of some silvery material that reflected Amy back to herself.

Rafe raised a glass of fresh-squeezed orange juice toward the ceiling. "Thank you, Myra."

Violet stopped a spoonful of yogurt halfway to her mouth. "You think we're being filmed?"

"I think everything we do from now on is being filmed. And that we should remember that."

Amy said, "I think that might be a little paranoid. After all, we weren't filmed in our apartments, before."

"We weren't TV stars, before. And the second ratings fall, we won't be filmed again. But right now, we're lab rats—poke them in their cages to see what they do and carefully record the results."

Amy considered this. "OK, maybe filming in the living room of my suite—I have a suite, guys, see the advantage of having actual relatives—but not in the bedroom. I don't believe it. And do you see any cameras?"

Violet said, "Don't you think Mark Meyer is capable of hiding them? He produced an entire forest in a high-rise office, for chrissake. And microcams are easy to disguise these days. But actually, One Two Three, I think you're right. No filming in bedrooms. Too many potential lawsuits."

Rafe just shook his head and chewed another forkful of eggs Benedict.

A knock on the door, which Violet opened. "Hey, Cai, come on in and . . . oh."

Amy's stomach tightened. She caught Rafe studying her a

second before her gaze moved, as if pulled by a tractor beam, to Cai. With him was Kaylie.

"Hey, sis," Kaylie said casually, just as if she were expected to be there. "Is that breakfast? Oh, we're starving!"

*We.* Amy sat utterly still. *We.*

Where had Kaylie spent the night?

Violet broke the long, awkward pause, which seemed to bewilder Cai, by speaking directly to him. "How's Tommy?"

"Doing well. They'll release him later today. I just came from the hospital. Kaylie was already there, trying to get information about him." He looked at Kaylie with adoring eyes, clearly considering her an angel of mercy. Kaylie smiled modestly.

She looked fantastic. Her dark curls shone and bounced. She wore the green silk sweater that had once represented the height of quality to both her and Amy, and next to the way it darkened her eyes to emerald, Amy's new top faded into a pile of gray cloth.

Rafe said coldly, "I'm Rafael Torres."

"Hi," Kaylie said, clearly uninterested. "Cai, are you hungry? Maybe we can order breakfast, too?" She touched his cheek.

Violet said, "Sorry, we're all done, and I need to clean up here."

"Oh, that's all right," Kaylie said, "I should check on Gran, anyway. Cai, we can order and eat in our suite. Mine and Amy's, I mean."

"Well . . . OK." Cai seemed to sense that more was going on here, but he didn't know what. However, from the look he gave Kaylie when she touched his cheek, Amy could see what would be going on eventually. Her breakfast curdled in her stomach. And now she couldn't even go back to her own suite without seeing them.

"Well, bye-bye," Violet said. "Gotta get organized now."

Cai and Kaylie left. Violet glanced from Amy to Rafe, clearly unsure what he guessed, or what Amy wanted said in front of him.

Amy didn't want anything said, not with anyone. She wanted to go somewhere and get herself under control. After all, how stupid was she being? Pretty damned stupid. She had no claim on Cai, and he had never shown any interest in her. This was just pheromones, just a silly crush, just nothing. That it hurt so much was the ultimate stupidity. *"You feel too much, Amy."* Stupid.

So why didn't telling herself any of this actually help?

Then Rafe said the perfect thing. "Amy—want to play some chess?"

Violet said scornfully, "She doesn't—"

"Yes, I do! Do you have a set with you? I brought mine

but—" But she didn't want to have to go to her room to get it.

"I have one," Rafe said. "What I don't have is an official FIDE rating, and yours is pretty high."

"But when we first had general introductions and I asked if anyone played, you didn't volunteer that you—"

"I don't tell everybody everything. Come on."

Rafe's room, two doors down from Violet's, was identical to it but much neater. On the polished table Rafe set up a cheap plastic chess set. He didn't talk, which Amy appreciated. She beat him, but not so easily that it didn't keep her mind occupied. As always, absorption in the game, both logical and intuitive, soothed her. Violet might not understand, but Amy was not Violet.

"Did you know," Rafe said after he lost the second game, "that Benjamin Franklin loved chess?"

"I do know that," Amy said. "He was the best player in the colonies, and considered chess good training for life. Rafe, I think the next scenario will come soon."

"I think you're right. And meanwhile, we'll get more busywork—oh, sorry, Myra—more game reviews to keep us occupied while we're sequestered here. And, I guess, selected interviews. To keep us in the public eye and show off those glamorous clothes you're wearing."

So he had noticed. Rafe wore his old jeans and a sweater stretched out at the neck. Amy raised an eyebrow and gestured at the sweater, and Rafe grinned. "I'll wear the new stuff when Myra gives me a reason to."

His cell rang. Rafe answered, listened, and said to Amy, "Credit me with telepathy. That was Myra. All hands on deck in the hotel ballroom an hour from now. It's interview time."

Amy put three pawns in their cardboard box. "What do you think they'll ask us?"

"Drivel. Then they'll write entirely different drivel and attribute it to us. Why are you picking those up? An hour is time for another game."

"I have to put on makeup. And the outfit Serena told me to wear. And do my hair. It takes longer than you—I'm a *girl*, Rafe."

"I know," he said, putting away a clutch of pawns, his head bent so that Amy couldn't see his face.

The interview at first looked intimidating—cameras, reporters, lighting equipment filling the hotel ballroom—but turned out to be easy because no one but Myra got to do much talking. She controlled the whole thing so completely that not even Waverly got to say more than a few bland sentences. Afterward all six of the "Lab Rats"—Rafe's nickname had stuck, although Amy wished he'd picked some other rodent—went to the TLN suite for "debriefing." Myra reminded them, "No blogging, posting, Tweeting, or Facebook until we say so, but you can surf the Internet and e-mail each other. You each have an AOL account under the alias you used to register with the hotel."

"AOL," Violet muttered. "ISP for the half-dead." Amy stifled a laugh.

The evening was spent in Amy's suite with Violet, Rafe, and even Waverly checking out their own images on TV and the Internet. Cai and Kaylie had not appeared, to Amy's relief. Kaylie slipped into her own bed sometime during the night, although that relief Amy didn't want to admit even to herself.

Alex Everett keyed a number into his cell. He wasted no time on preliminaries. "Myra, did you order that attack on Tommy Wimmer?"

"Don't be ridiculous," Myra said, and hung up.

Frowning, Alex slowly lowered the dead phone.

# Nineteen

THE NEXT MORNING Myra startled them all.
"Time for your next scenario," she said.

Glances among the Lab Rats. Cai said cautiously, "You're
telling us beforehand that it's a scenario?"

"Yes." Big smile from Myra, which no one returned.
"You've all had breakfast? Good. Change into jeans and meet
me at the loading dock in ten minutes."

At the loading dock Amy touched the heavy bandage on
Tommy's arm. "Hey, you all right?"

"Somebody hit me."

"I know. Are you all right now?"

"Yes." Tommy gave her his sweet smile.

240

They piled into a stretch limo. No one spoke much. The ride took them deep into the suburbs, where the car stopped in an industrial park. Its sign said PYLON RESEARCH & DEVELOPMENT. Amy blinked. Pylon, newly merged with TLN, the target of the protestors who'd objected to its holdings in chemicals and in nuclear power. Pylon the python.

"Mushroom cloud, here we come," Rafe said.

Waverly said, "Shut up."

Myra, who had traveled in a second car, met them in a conference room containing a table with four computers and a pile of neatly stacked boxes of sneakers. "All of you, find the box with your size and put on the sneakers. You all wore the jeans that Serena chose, good. Now, you'll do this scenario in teams of two. The teams are Cai and Violet, Amy and Rafe, Waverly and Tommy."

"No," Waverly said instantly.

Myra gazed at her.

"I won't work with Tommy. You just want to make me look bad, like I did on the show on Wednesday. It's not fair!"

If Waverly had looked bad on Wednesday, it hadn't been Myra's fault. Waverly had walked past a bleeding man and then bribed her way out of trouble with her father's money. Amy expected Myra to ignore Waverly's outburst, but instead she looked thoughtful.

"Perhaps you're right, Waverly. Your responses to Tommy might be all too predictable. All right, the teams are Cai and Violet, Amy and Tommy, Waverly and Rafe."

Waverly smiled, as well she should: Rafe would make a good teammate. But what if this unknown scenario required brute strength instead of brains? Then Amy would be lucky to team with Tommy—maybe. Tommy's left arm was bandaged. Was he right- or left-handed? Amy couldn't remember. Her chest tightened.

"Because there is only one venue for this scenario," Myra continued, "you need to take turns. Tommy and Amy are first. The rest of you are free to use the computers or to talk or to send out for coffee if you like. But you may not leave this room. Amy and Tommy, follow me."

They were led through corridors and down an elevator to a basement room with nothing in it except a huge windowless white box and a bank of computers staffed with technicians. The techs regarded Amy and Tommy curiously. She was reminded of the hospital room where Gran was slid into an MRI while doctors monitored the results from the outside. Amy felt a shudder run through Tommy's body.

Myra said, "This is the prototype for a new virtual reality game being developed by one of TLN's new affiliate companies. You will recall that the contract you signed prohibits any discussion of the tech you see at TLN, and I want to emphasize that we can prosecute if you violate nondisclosure. And we will. Tommy, that means you can't tell anybody what happens inside this box, not *anybody*, or you will get in big trouble. Do you understand?"

Tommy nodded, wide-eyed with fear. Amy took his hand.

"All right, then," Myra said pleasantly. "This game is called Frustration Box. The object is to make the door open to let you out. And here is your only clue: 'red yellow.' Did you get that?"

"Red yellow," Amy repeated. "What does——"

"Good luck," Myra said. Abruptly a narrow door opened in the box and Myra nudged them through. With amazing speed the door sealed behind them.

Amy and Tommy stood in a featureless white room about twelve feet square: white plastic-looking walls, ceiling, floor. No windows. The only hint of cameras was a line of translucent ceiling panels down the center of the room, set flush with the rest of the ceiling. Amy waited, but nothing happened.

"What . . . what are we supposed to do?" Tommy said.

"I don't know yet. We wait, I guess."

A voice from the ceiling said, "Game on. Twelve minutes." Dots appeared on the walls.

Amy spun around, surveying them. Three yellow, three red, three blue, scattered among the four walls. But what was she to do with them? As she wondered, the dots disappeared and then reappeared in different places, on different walls. Tommy trembled.

"It's OK, Tommy, it's a game!" Amy said as cheerfully as she could. "Remember that Myra said 'red yellow'? Let's press first a red dot and then a yellow one and see what happens."

Nothing happened. The dots kept disappearing and re-appearing. Amy and Tommy each pressed a red one and then raced to press a yellow one; the dots never seemed to appear close together. Nothing made the door open.

After a few minutes of this, the ceiling voice said, "Ten minutes." And the *walls shifted*.

Amy gasped. The length of room stretching away from the locked door was still about twelve feet, but now the width was only ten feet. Would it become narrower and narrower until they were crushed? No, that couldn't happen, this was a *game*, it had to be safe. . . . Didn't it?

"The wall moved!" Tommy cried.

"Yes, isn't that fun?" Amy choked out. "It's to make us think faster! Tommy, you press a red dot at the same time I press a yellow one. Ready? Go!"

It didn't open the door. They tried pressing two red ones and two yellow ones at the same time, Amy stretching her body full length against one wall and Tommy contorting himself to use both his bandaged arm and his good one at the same time. That didn't work either.

"Eight minutes," the ceiling said, and the wall moved forward another two feet.

Tommy gave a great cry and curled up on the floor in the fetal position, as he had during the alley scenario. Amy, hating Myra Townsend and Alex Everett all over again, knelt beside him. "Tommy, you have to get up. We can do this, we *can*."

"No we can't! The walls will squish us!"

"I promise you they won't. It's just a game. Nothing will hurt you—Tommy, I promise!"

He didn't move. Amy glanced at the ceiling. Was this being filmed? Of course it was: film for the cruel and insensitive to laugh at when it aired on TLN. Last night on the Internet, Amy had read hundreds of comments about the show, from reviewers and bloggers and YouTube commentators. Many had been outraged at putting Tommy's mental disabilities on display, but more had been either amused or falsely judicious, saying that Tommy must have chosen this and anyway he was making a pile of money off it.

Why had Tommy chosen this public humiliation? Why didn't he un-choose it?

Now was not the time to ask. Amy went on pleading with him to get up until the ceiling said, "Six minutes," and the wall moved again. Now the walls were only six feet apart. Amy gave up on Tommy and studied the dots, which seemed to be appearing and reappearing faster than before. *Red yellow, red yellow, red yellow. . . .* No help in Myra's "clue." What else did she notice about the pattern of the dots? Were they somehow connected to mathematical progressions: prime numbers or doubling or Fibonacci sequences or—

No. No connection that she could see. Besides, this had to be a problem that the game company could market to ordinary people, not just to nerds with a weird taste for mathematics. Unless this particular game set had been programmed just for the Lab Rats, which it probably had been to make it difficult enough for the show.

*Programmed just for the Lab Rats.*

"Tommy, get up!" Amy said. "I have an idea!"

Tommy didn't move. Amy wanted to kick him, to cradle him, to get him away from a place he found so humiliating and terrifying. Then she had a second idea.

She knelt by Tommy and put her mouth directly over his ear. "Tommy, this is what you have to do. It's what Cai wants you to do. He told me. You trust Cai, don't you?"

"Cai," Tommy murmured.

"Yes, Cai, who takes care of you. This is what Cai wants you to do. Count to ten very slowly—you can do that, can't you?"

A slight nod of the head.

"Count to ten. Then jump up and say, 'I got an idea!' Then put your eyeball right up to a red dot. Right up to it. Can you do those three things? Count to ten, say 'I got an idea!' and put your eye up to a red dot. For Cai!"

Another nod. Amy jumped up and said with disgust, "Then I'll try my idea alone!" She raced over to a wall of dots and waited. When the wall moved again, she touched a red dot then a yellow at the exact time the walls moved. And wouldn't it be weird if that really was the key?

It wasn't. The ceiling said, "Four minutes," and the wall moved to four feet away from its opposite side, barely providing enough room for Tommy's huddled bulk. Amy held her breath. Would he do it? He had to remember the three instructions, he had to overcome his fear, he had to trust her, or at least trust that she really did represent Cai . . . which of course she didn't. Poor Tommy, everybody lied to him—

"I got an idea!" Tommy yelled, jumping up and smashing into one of the walls. His injured arm hit the hard plastic, he cried out in pain, and Amy grimaced. So much for her plan—

But Tommy turned himself in the narrow space and jammed his eye against a red dot just before it disappeared. Amy immediately did the same to the closest yellow dot. And the door to the Frustration Box swung open just as the ceiling announced "Two minutes" and the wall slid again.

Red yellow. Programmed just for the Lab Rats. And Myra's insistence that "for security reasons" all their retina scans be on file. Not their fingerprints—just their retina scans.

Tommy whooped and squeezed through the two feet of space to the door. Amy followed, fighting claustrophobia and triumph. She still had to face Myra.

Myra stood just outside the door to the Frustration Box. She looked sour. "So that was Tommy's idea."

"Yes. You got it on film," Amy said innocently. There—let *that* shut the mouths of all those cruel jerks laughing at Tommy on the Internet.

"Sebastian will take you to the limo." Myra gestured to one of her flunkies, who led Tommy and Amy out. Amy went with her head high, thinking that at least this episode of the show was one she wouldn't cringe while watching. Tommy would look like a winner even if, once again, she would not. There were public winners and there were private winners.

Something Myra would never know anything about.

The limo took Tommy and Amy back to the Fairwood Hotel without waiting for the others. Amy, not knowing if they were being filmed while in the car, waited until she and Tommy were on their floor. Then she led him to a small sitting area she'd discovered on the floor above, an alcove at the end of a hallway with two chairs, a small table, and a spectacular view of the city eighteen stories below.

"Why are we here, Amy? Is it another game?" Tommy looked apprehensive.

"No, no. I just want to talk to you."

"Did Cai say it was OK?"

"Yes." Another lie, but Amy didn't think Cai would object. "Is Cai related to you? Your cousin or something?"

"Cai is my guardian."

For a moment Amy thought he meant "legal guardian," but then Tommy burst out, "A real guardian, not like my fucking uncle Sam!"

It was the first time she'd ever heard Tommy curse. His face distorted into fury, and an involuntary jolt of fight-or-flight shot through Amy. Tommy looked scary when angry. And he was so big!

"Sorry," he said, flushed, and looked like Tommy again.

She pushed on. If she and Tommy were ever teamed again, she needed to know this stuff. "So Cai is your 'real guardian' because he takes care of you, right?"

"People are mean sometimes."

"I know. Tommy, was your uncle Sam mean to you?"

Tommy panicked. His eyes darted around, and he shoved his fist—practically the whole thing—into his mouth. Around the fingers he mumbled, "I can't tell!"

She put a hand on his arm. "It's OK, you don't have to tell me. But . . . did you tell Cai?"

"I can't tell anybody!" Tommy looked ready to bolt.

"You don't have to. You don't have to tell anybody any-thing. And Cai is your guardian and I'm your friend, OK?"

Slowly he calmed down. Amy stroked his sleeve, thinking of all that strength coupled with all that fear. What had been done to this poor boy? Then she got a sickening clue.

Tommy said, "I don't like tiny little places like that game!"

"No, no. But we won, Tommy. You and I won."

That calmed him a little. He said, with a sudden flash of shrewdness, "But it was your idea, Amy. Not my idea."

She smiled. "True. But that will be our secret."

"OK." Tommy's smile vanished. "Cai's brother died."

"Oh." She couldn't think what else to say.

"Cai was his guardian, too. His name was Josh. But Josh couldn't even read and I can."

Waverly had said that Cai had a mentally challenged brother who died. And now Cai had taken over protecting and guiding Tommy. Amy's heart ached. Cai was such a good guy—far too good for Kaylie.

*That's just jealousy talking.*

Ashamed of herself, Amy stood. Tommy followed her lead. "Where are we going now?"

"I have to check on my grandmother. She's sick."

"Is she going to die? Like Cai's brother?"

Amy looked at Tommy. He didn't know to not ask stark questions; neither Rafe nor Violet had actually asked her that. Amy said, "Yes. She's going to die."

"I'm sorry," Tommy said simply. "That's sad."

"Yes, it is. Let's go back to our rooms, Tommy."

"I'll wait in my room for Cai."

"Good plan." And Kaylie had better be with Gran, as she'd promised.

She was, watching music videos on TV. The sisters smiled falsely at each other. Kaylie said, "Monday I need to start back to school, so you'll have to get a nurse or something to watch Gran."

"OK." And then, out of doubt or concern or malice or some unknowable combination of the them all, Amy said in a tone she knew was nasty, "Are you really going to school? Or just getting out of here because it's boring?"

Kaylie refused to rise to the bait. "To school." And then, "Cai wants me to."

"Oh," Amy said, and went in to check on Gran.


"We might need to replace Tommy," Myra said, pushing back a strand of hair that had fallen forward as she peered into the editing machine. "His responses are too predictable. They'll skew the voting."

"He wasn't predictable in today's Frustration Box scenario."

"That was Amy's doing and you know it."

Alex said, "He doesn't like being here. Myra, you hired him outside of our audition process—how exactly did that happen? You've never told me."

Myra shrugged.

"He clearly doesn't want to be here. What's our hold on him? Because if you—"

Mark Meyer burst into the room. "Who the fuck set up that lame Frustration Box scenario?"

Myra said levelly, "I did."

"I do tech around here! I thought that was understood! Christ, a lame video parlor prototype—what's next, we have them play Monopoly?"

"Mr. Taunton likes it."

"Mr. Taunton hardly falls into our target demographic, Myra. And he won't like it when he sees the ratings. *And* he knows jack shit about tech! You're treading on my territory!"

She said pleasantly, "I think you should remember your manners, Mark. This show is my territory, mine and Alex's, and you create the tech we agree on. You do it superbly, but the responsibility for this show is mine, and I will use whatever scenarios make it a success."

"I'm going to Taunton with this!"

Myra looked at Mark, running her gaze deliberately and distastefully over his artfully torn jeans, running shoes, and tee that said THINK OUTSIDE THE QUADRILATERAL PARALLELOGRAM. Taunton liked old-school polish. But he also had his unpredictable side; after all, he'd insisted on that little bitch Amy Kent. Sudden doubt flickered in Myra's eyes. Alex saw it; Mark did not.

But all she said, still in that pleasant calm voice, was, "All right, Mark. Take your objection to Mr. Taunton."

Mark slammed out of the room with the same force he'd exploded into it, and Alex rubbed his chin, thoughtfully eyeing Myra.

# Twenty

SATURDAY NIGHT THE second scenario played on *Who Knows People, Baby—You?*, now referred to on the Internet as *Who–You*. Gran, who seemed to have had a bad day although she wouldn't say so, had fallen heavily asleep just after dinner and Amy didn't wanted to wake her. A nursing aide now stayed with Gran full-time, sleeping on the second bed in the larger of the hotel suite's bedrooms. That left Amy and Kaylie sharing the smaller room, but Kaylie hadn't come to bed last night. Amy knew she was with Cai, and tried not to think about that, and couldn't help thinking about it.

To avoid waking Gran, the six Lab Rats plus Kaylie crowded into Rafe's room. Even Waverly joined them, probably bored with being sequestered in the hotel. She wore clothes that, Amy would have bet, Serena had *not* picked out: an all-but-transparent calf-length skirt, a top made mostly of intricately woven chains, and combat boots. Amy didn't like the outfit, but on Waverly it looked spectacular. Kaylie eyed it enviously.

All of them had spent hours reading the endless comments about the show in the blogosphere. The hype was building, and Myra was feeding it by deliberately granting no more access to the participants. Or maybe she just wanted the misinformation to build so that it would be harder to vote correctly. However, the lack of facts deterred none of the loonier fans. Various sites on the Internet said that:

- Waverly was a lesbian in love with Violet.
- Violet was transgendered.
- Cai, with his unplaceable dark good looks, was a terrorist recruited in Afghanistan.
- Waverly was a lesbian in love with Amy.
- Tommy had run away from a circus, where he had performed as Silas the Strongman.
- Amy had a criminal record that had disqualified her from the Olympics in gymnastics.
- Lynn was a renegade nun from the order of the Poor Clares.

- Rafe was "really" a thirty-year-old genius dropout from Harvard.
- Waverly was a lesbian in love with Lynn.
- Amy had been raised on an elephant farm.

Was there even such a thing as an elephant farm? Amy pondered this as she settled into a chair as far from Cai and Kaylie as possible. They were holding hands. The very air in the hotel room felt thick, clogged with anticipation and dread.

Violet said, "So which scenario will they use? I'm betting on the trees in Myra's office. I mean, I'm really betting—here." She tossed a dollar bill onto the floor in front of the TV.

"No," Rafe said, "they'll save that one for later. Myra will want the drama to build—won't you, Myra?" he shouted at the ceiling. "It'll be Mark Meyer's fake rats."

Tommy said, "I don't have a dollar."

"I've got you covered," Cai said, tossing two dollars onto the heap. "Which scenario do you think will be next?"

Tommy screwed up his face. "That box with dots."

Amy said, "I pick the lobby attack."

Rafe said, "Too much like the predator in the alley. TV feeds on variety."

He was right. After the initial hyped explanations, the screen showed Cai coming out of what must be his apartment building. It looked even worse than Amy's. Cai took a short-cut through an alley, and all at once rats swarmed toward him from both ends. A close-up of his horrified face and then back to the raucous music and overexcited hosts presenting this week's list of options:

CAI:
1. Fights off the rats!
2. Tries to run—and escapes the rats!
3. Picks up a rat to eat it!
4. Is saved by someone else!
5. Freezes and cries!

Violet said, "'Picks up a rat and eats it'? Who are they kidding?"

Rafe grinned at her.

Amy said, "You didn't." Then it dawned on her. "You knew right away they were fake."

"Guilty," Rafe said.

"And that means that by then you'd guessed that these are faked scenarios."

"Guilty twice."

He was so smart. But in turning to look at Rafe, Amy had caught a glimpse of Cai. His face had gone white; his dark eyes looked huge; his hand had gone limp in Kaylie's. All at once, and without the aid of any phantom, Amy knew that he was even more terrified of rats than she was, and that he'd frozen and cried. It hurt her to even picture it. She turned back to the TV.

Each of them encountered the rats in a different place, and each but Cai was with another person, making possible the option "Is saved by somebody else!" Which described Amy's behavior. When the second half of this scenario aired on Wednesday night, Kaylie was going to be the hero. That would make the second time in a row that Amy had ended up looking like a wimp.

All at once she didn't want to watch any longer. The rest of the show was going to be filler anyway; the Wednesday-night segments, which revealed both how people behaved and the winners, were stronger. She said, "I'm going to check on Gran."

The nursing aide was watching the show in the suite's main room, texting her votes on her cell. She said guiltily, "Mrs. Whitcomb is asleep."

"That's good," Amy said, going into Gran's bedroom and shutting the door. Her face slack in sleep, Gran looked older than ever. She breathed heavily, as if the effort cost her, but she didn't seem to be in pain.

The doctor Myra had sent had said that Gran could take as many pain pills as she needed, and Gran was balancing the desire to stay comfortable with the desire to stay lucid. The doctor had refused to say when the end might come, but he had visited every day—and what did *that* cost? Without Myra,

Gran's end-of-life might have been intolerable. Amy should be grateful to Myra. Especially since Amy sensed that Myra was sincere when she'd told Amy, "I lost my own mother a few years ago. I know how hard this is." And yet Myra had the cruelty to somehow force Tommy onto the show, where he was frightened and bewildered and humiliated. How could one woman be so complicated?

When Amy emerged from Gran's room, Rafe stood in the living room. She said, "Is the show over?"

"Not quite. Come on, Amy, let's take a walk."

"Where?" She was tired of the hotel, tired of everything.

"You'll see."

They took an elevator to the basement. At the end of a dim corridor Rafe produced a key and unlocked a door marked AUTHORIZED EMPLOYEES ONLY. Amy said, "Where did you get the key?"

He didn't answer until they were on the other side of the door. "Bribery. It took a big part of last week's salary. But maintenance staff always has at least one person who feels victimized, and you never know when you might need an escape hatch."

It didn't look like an escape hatch; the dim, cavernous room was filled with unopened crates, broken furniture, stained mattresses, and a wall of equipment on metal shelves bolted to the wall. But Rafe led her through an unlocked door on the other side of the room, through a long, low tunnel with pipes overhead, and up a rickety flight of wooden steps. A door at the top said DOOR WILL LOCK AUTOMATICALLY BEHIND YOU. Then they were outside, standing in a clean alley with a bustling street at the far end.

Amy peered down the alley. "That's Fenton Street!"

"With all its classy shops and all its armed guards to keep the peace for rich folk. Come on, you can pass. You look the part."

Amy wore her jeans, bronze-colored Vince sweater, and new calfskin sandals. For the first time she noticed that Rafe had shed his usual grubbies for jeans, a shirt, and boots that presumably Serena had picked out. Had he planned this even before the TV show came on?

Fenton Street stood out in the economically desperate city like a diamond on a mangy dog. Luxurious shops, expensive restaurants, well-dressed people carrying shopping bags with bright logos. The April night was warm and sweet. Amy and Rafe peered into store windows, mock-arguing over the merits of antique desks, emerald necklaces, handbags of Komodo dragon hide. Nang's Electronics had state-of-the-art electronics that did everything but take out the trash. Gradually Amy's mood improved. Rafe bought them lattes at a little sidewalk café where the coffee was priced like fine wine, and Amy knew that, too, was a sacrifice.

"So," Rafe said, sipping his coffee as they watched people

stroll by, "what's your story, Amy? Are your parents gone?"

"Yes. My father disappeared right after Kaylie was born, and my mother died in a car crash when I was four."

"My father abandoned us, too."

"That isn't what I meant by 'disappeared.' I mean, literally. He was a war correspondent and he disappeared somewhere in Afghanistan. Nobody ever learned what had happened to him. Or if the government did, they didn't tell my mother. Eventually he was declared legally dead, but no one really knows."

"I'm sorry," Rafe said.

Amy shrugged. "I don't remember him at all. I remember my mother, but not very well. Gran raised us."

"And you had a happy, middle-class childhood."

She smiled. "How do you know that?"

"All I have to do is look at you."

Amy wasn't sure what he meant, or if she liked it. Was she really that transparent? Did he consider "middle-class" the same as "boring"? She said, "I did have a happy childhood, pre-Collapse. Gran was a scientist, working in a biotech lab. We had a nanny who took care of us while she was at work, Rosa Cortez. She was wonderful, too."

He stiffened slightly at the Latino name. "An illegal alien?"

"No, of course not."

"What happened to her?"

"She went back to the Dominican Republic when I was

twelve. When the Collapse came, she lost all hope of getting the rest of her family here, so she went home."

"And your grandmother lost her job?"

"And her investments, which had mostly been in the biotech company she worked for. Gran believed in green. What about you? Same story?"

But Rafe didn't answer her. Instead he pointed discreetly to a girl passing on the sidewalk, dressed in miniskirt, combat boots, and poncho. "That's something Waverly would wear."

"No, it's not. The miniskirt is from Walmart and the poncho is ethnic from someplace in South America. Waverly doesn't do ethnic."

He stared at her. "How do you know the skirt is from Walmart?"

"Well, maybe not literally, but it's rayon and badly made."

"You can tell that?"

She grinned. "Rafe, anybody could tell that."

"Anyone female, you mean. If her clothes are so cheap, why wasn't she being hassled for being on Fenton Street?"

"Because that thick gold necklace she had on was genuine. A gift from a boyfriend, maybe."

"OK, Miss Fashionista, what about that woman? Her clothes, I mean?"

"Vintage Chanel—1950s."

They fell into a game, with Rafe making up preposterous

stories about passersby based on what Amy said about their clothes. That one was Marie Antoinette reincarnated; this one had escaped from Russian pirates; an innocuous-looking man was a robot designed not to be noticed. Amy giggled and egged him on. It was the best time she'd had since the shopping expedition with Violet.

Rafe turned serious. "What's your ambition, Amy? If the Collapse hadn't happened, what would you do?"

"Go to college and study neurology." Should she tell Rafe about her phantoms? No. She'd never told anyone but Gran. Instead she said, "How the brain processes information—that fascinates me. Do you know about the new experiments on time perception?"

"No. Tell me about it."

She did, explaining the research she'd read about in Gran's flimsies. When the waiter came by for the second time to ask if they wanted anything else, Amy realized how long she'd been talking, and she blushed. "I'm sorry. I've been blathering."

"It was interesting," Rafe said, and actually seemed to mean it. "You're smart as well as pretty."

He said it awkwardly, like a person not used to paying compliments, and he didn't seem to realize it was a cliché. Before Amy could answer, a man plopped down on the chair next to her. Amy could smell him: unwashed, unshaven, thin and ragged, he slumped in the elegant little wrought-iron chair for all of five seconds before security was on him. "Sir? You need to leave."

"I can pay!" he said, and began pulling dirty one-dollar bills from his pockets. People turned to look.

Without any discussion, the security man had the guy on his feet, his arm behind him, escorted toward a waiting closed car. Amy looked at the greasy bills on the table.

"But he has enough for coffee!"

Rafe said, "Spoiling the ambience."

Amy darted forward, grabbed the money, and ran to the car just as the man was being shoved in. The inside of the car was nothing but an empty space, seats removed, with a steel grill behind the driver. Three other ragged people already huddled on the floor. Amy pushed the bills at the ousted man and stared defiantly at the security officer. She saw him take in her clothes, her shining hair, her makeup, and make his decision.

"Thank you, miss. Appreciate it." The car door slammed, the vehicle pulled away, and the security officer strolled off.

Rafe was by her side. "You shouldn't have done that, Amy."

"It's not fair!"

"None of it is fair. But don't endanger yourself."

"Like you did joining that protest against Pylon outside the TLN Building? I saw you with a TIMES BE TOUGH MAN sign!"

"You did? I didn't see you."

She didn't want to tell him about being nearly trampled, if it hadn't been for Cai and Tommy. Instead she said, "Gran says the depression is starting to lift."

"I think she's right. But a lot of people have slipped too far down the economic scale to ever recover."

"'Ever' is a long time."

"You're right. I stand corrected. Amy, I've wanted to tell you that—"

A car screeched to the curb, even more shocking in that cultured, cheerful, well-mannered place than the homeless man had been. Alex Everett opened the door. "Get in, please. Now."

Rafe didn't look surprised, and after a moment neither was Amy. They'd been tracked through their cells, of course. She gave Alex her sweetest smile. "I think we're not ready to go back yet."

"I think you are," Alex said, and a certain quality of weariness about him caught Amy's attention. A phantom leaped into her mind: *a squirrel clinging desperately to a branch, trying to not fall.* But . . . Alex Everett? A squirrel?

Rafe said slowly, "Something has happened."

"Yes. Get in. No, Amy, it's not your grandmother. . . . I'm sorry, I should have said that right away. No one is hurt. But you must come back now."

They got into the car and it sped back to the hotel.

\* \* \*

"I thought the contractual rules were very clear," Myra said. Only a throbbing of the skin at her temple belied her calm, set face. "Clear enough that half of the cast would not betray them. Plus one hanger-on."

Amy and Rafe had not been the only ones who had left the hotel. Across the table from Myra and Alex, in what was evidently the TLN suite, sat Rafe, Amy, Cai, and Kaylie. How had Cai and Kaylie got out? Amy didn't know, but what mattered was not so much their escape as their destination.

"A dance club!" Myra said, and her tone might as well have said "a circle of hell!" "Cai, how could you be so stupid? You must have known you'd be recognized instantly."

No one had recognized Rafe and Amy. But the people on Fenton Street hadn't been in the show's demographic; Fenton Street was mostly older, richer, more sedate people who probably found Taunton Life Network vulgar and sleazy. Well, it was. Besides, Rafe and Amy didn't look like Cai. At least half of the Internet furor was over him, mostly from girls.

Kaylie said meekly, "It was my idea, Ms. Townsend, not Cai's. Blame me."

Amy looked sharply at her sister. Meekness was not part of Kaylie's character. But neither was stupidity. If Kaylie had talked a reluctant, infatuated Cai into a dance club, it was because Kaylie had wanted to be seen there with him.

Amy said, "But what actually happened, Myra? Isn't this just more PR for the show?"

"What 'actually happened' was a riot. Cai was mobbed, the cops were called, the club ended up trashed, to the tune of hundreds of thousands of dollars. But you're right, Amy, all of that might just have been PR except for the fact that the mayor's daughter was there, she got injured in the fight, and the mayor called Mr. Taunton."

*Aha*, thought Amy, just as the phantom leapt into her mind: *the squirrel hanging from a tree branch.* But she never got two phantoms so close together, and never the same one repeated. And Myra, helplessly hanging without a net? Myra Townsend? Myra didn't care that the mayor's daughter had been injured. She cared that Mr. Taunton was unhappy with her.

Kaylie repeated, "I'm sorry." Her big green eyes filled with tears. Amy could have told her that was a futile tactic with Myra.

"I think, Miss Kent, that you should not visit Cai again until the season's filming has ended."

Rafe said easily, "And when might that be, Myra? Three more episodes, right?"

"Yes," Myra said, evidently too angry to remember that she had refused to give out this information earlier. "Surely even young love can wait another few weeks."

"Cai won't wait," Kaylie said confidently, dropping her

meekness and meeting Myra glare for glare. "He wants me here. Besides, I live here. My grandmother and sister are here."

"If I say you cannot be here, then you will not be here. We'll locate you in another hotel, at our expense, of course. With a chaperone. I'm sure your grandmother will agree."

"She won't!"

"Then we will have to relocate her, too. Which may not be good for her precarious health."

"You wouldn't dare!"

"I will do what is best for the show, for you, and for your grandmother. After discussing it fully with her, of course, including the need for your safety."

Kaylie glared at Myra. "OK, I'll move. But Cai and I will just see each other outside the hotel!"

Myra smiled and said nothing. After a moment of uncertainty, Kaylie smiled, too. Neither smile conveyed pleasure. Amy looked at Cai. She had no phantom in her mind, but he sure looked like a hanging squirrel to her.

# Twenty-one

THE NEXT AFTERNOON Waverly said to Amy, "So you and Rafe are a couple now?"

Amy stepped up the speed on her treadmill. She and Waverly were the only ones in the hotel gym, Waverly dressed in a lululemon workout outfit that Amy had priced online at several hundred dollars. Waverly's blonde hair was pulled into a ponytail and she wore no makeup. She looked beautiful even while sweaty. Amy wore her old yoga pants with a hole in one knee and a tank top that could have been a lot cleaner. For ten minutes the girls had worked out in silence, with Waverly impressive on the Stairmaster and Amy trying to not notice.

"Rafe and I are just friends," she said over the sound of the treadmill, which was louder than it should be. You'd think that a classy hotel like this would have quieter equipment.

"That's not what I heard."

Amy turned off the treadmill. It slowed and stopped with a malfunctional whine. She wiped sweat off her face. "What *did* you hear, Waverly?"

"That you and Rafe escaped last night for a little couple time while everyone else was watching your sister's riot on the Internet."

"It was not 'couple time,'" Amy said, irritated, "and it was not 'my sister's riot.' How did you hear that Rafe and I left the Fairwood anyway?"

"There are precious few secrets in this place," Waverly said, and that at least was true. "OK, so you and Rafe are 'just friends.' Despite the way he looks at you. So tell me something else: What's eating Violet?"

"What do you mean? Violet's fine."

"Have you seen her this morning?"

"No." Myra had given Amy the day off. Amy had woken when Gran did at four a.m. Gran had been in so much pain that Amy, after frantic calls to the doctor and to Myra, had increased her pain medication. That helped, but Amy had found it hard to go back to sleep. When she did, she slept until noon. She left Gran, who was feeling much better, with the nursing aide and came down to the gym, hoping a workout would restore some energy. So far this had not happened.

Waverly said, "Well, I saw Violet at breakfast. She alternated between gloomy and nasty. I thought you might know what happened with her."

"Like you care," Amy said.

"You're right, I don't." Waverly lay down on a mat and began push-ups. "I don't like weaklings."

"Violet is not a weakling!"

"Yes, she is, and you're just too trusting to see it. But I'll tell you something I've learned: You're not."

Amy grimaced. She was not going to be taken in by flattery from Waverly.

"I misjudged you," Waverly said, not even breathing hard. Five, six, seven push-ups—she was strong. "You're actually a formidable opponent."

"We're not each other's opponents."

"The hell we're not. But let me tell you—no, not here."

Waverly stood up—still not breathing hard—and took Amy's arm. Amy followed her out of the gym and into the locker room, where it would have been suicide to record anything; other hotel guests stripped here. Nonetheless, Waverly breathed her words into Amy's ear.

"My father has a lot of money—I'm sure you know that. He also has considerable resources of other kinds. I had his security people run deep backgrounds on all of you. Violet is not what she seems. For one thing, she's not eighteen."

"So she turned nineteen recently? Big deal!"

"She's twenty-six. With a criminal record. And 'Violet Sanderson' is not her real name."

"You're lying!" Amy pulled away from Waverly. But despite herself, small things that had nagged at her mind before now sprang into it. Violet's seemingly long dance history, filled with so many stories—would an eighteen-year-old have had time for all that? Violet's saying she'd planned on watching the show's debut on a TV in a bar, when the drinking age in this state was twenty-one. Violet's one, offhand reference to trying out for the chorus of the musical *Great Day in the Morning*, which Amy vaguely remembered as having opened and closed, a failure, while Amy was in the sixth grade. At the time she'd thought she must have been wrong about the date—but what if she wasn't?

Waverly said, "No, I'm not lying. You're too trusting."

Like Amy hadn't heard that before. She scowled at Waverly. "I don't trust *you*. Why are you even telling me all this?"

"I can be trustworthy, but I'm out for myself first. So is everybody else, but most people don't admit it. I do. That makes me honest. And I'm telling you 'all this' because I think that you and Rafe are my best potential allies here. Tommy is ludicrous, Violet deceptive without my knowing what she's really after, and Cai is being led around by the nose by your little sister, who nobody in their right mind would trust. I'd like to form a mutual-help pact with you and Rafe."

"No." Amy already had a pact with Rafe and Violet—not that it had yet done any of them much good.

"There's another reason, too." Waverly's face suddenly softened. Amy didn't trust that and her own face probably showed it, but then a phantom sprang into her mind: *a beating heart, bloody and exposed.* It looked like the one she'd seen during an online open-heart surgery in her science-class software.

Waverly, sounding unlike herself, said abruptly, "My grandmother was the only person in my entire family who was ever kind to me. She died last year."

"I'm so—"

Waverly's face hardened. "No false condolences, please. I'm sorry I even told you. Just consider everything I said, including my offer. Or don't. It's up to you." She walked away, ponytail swinging.

Amy called after her, "You're wrong about Violet. Also about Kaylie!"

"Really?" Waverly said without breaking stride or turning around. "Have you had the TV on this morning? On the Celeb! Channel?" She left the locker room.

No chance of finishing her workout now. Amy took the elevator to her suite. The nursing aide was bathing Gran. Amy called, "I'll be in when you're done!" and turned on the television.

*Celeb!* ran through a story about one star's adorable twins, followed by a story about another star's bad behavior, and then the screen flashed to Kaylie in front of a thicket of microphones.

"In case you missed it," said the announcer in an awed tone that implied a presidential death or a UFO arrival, "Kayla Kent, sister of a participant on the mega-hit *Who Knows People, Baby—You?* gave a press conference earlier this morning. The fourteen-year-old has—we can hardly believe it ourselves!—been forced by rival station Taunton Life Network into separation from her family, including her dying grandmother. Yesterday evening—"

Kaylie—who was fifteen, not fourteen—wore a babydoll dress, white tights, and flat shoes that made her look innocent and helpless. No makeup. Her dark curls straggled pathetically as she blinked back tears, explaining to reporters that she had been forced to move alone to a different hotel, away from the only family she had left since the death of her mother, when all she wanted was to nurse her dying grandmother: "The person who raised me! Oh, I just want to be with my granny and sister!"

Myra had been outplayed.

"Amy?" Gran called from her room.

She lay in bed, her barely touched breakfast on the side table. The nursing aide sat beside her. Amy saw immediately that the painkillers had not yet worn off. Gran's eyes were wide and shiny, and her old face wore a drifty expression foreign to its usual serious control.

But there was nothing drifty about her words. "Sit down. Thank you, Solange, you can go. Where's Kayla?"

"Out," Amy said. Although probably not for long.

"As I will be soon. I think the tide will go out easy, Amy. No, don't look like that—we already had this discussion. What I want to talk about is your future. Has this TV show given you a raise?"

"Not yet."

"Then ask for one. Demand one. Solange was just telling me what a big success it is. But media successes don't last. Actually, no kind of success lasts forever. I had Solange write down a name on that paper there. It's a lawyer. I want you to call him today about representing you for your next contract, and about insisting it be negotiated right now."

"Next contract?" Amy was counting the episodes until she was out of this one!

Gran's gaze sharpened. "You don't want to do this more than one season?"

"No. But I will if—" She stopped and looked away.

"I won't need your money much longer, honey," Gran said gently. "But you will. You have a good brain, Amy. You *must* get a good education. Kayla, too, although probably not in anything academic. That's my greatest wish: that you girls get good educations. At least ask TLN for a big bonus. Now, while the show is hot and you have bargaining power."

"OK."

"Promise me you'll try for college."

"I promise."

"I mean it when I say that success doesn't last forever. And neither does despair. Are you watching the news?"

"No," Amy admitted. Gran thought news, keeping up with the world, was very important. But then, Gran wasn't dealing with Myra Townsend, Kaylie, Waverly, Cai, or Violet.

"Things reach a flash point, Amy. In 1936."

"What?" Gran seemed to be wandering—1936 was eighty years ago.

"It could have gone two ways. The height of the Depression, unemployment at twenty-five percent, financial institutions failing, people hungry and displaced—a lot like now. In Michigan, auto workers seized several General Motors plants and held them for forty days. The National Guard was mobilized and we could have gone into revolution—also like now. Cities burning, violence. But we went the other way, with government policies under Roosevelt to get people eating and working. A flash point, Amy. We're nearly there now. It could go either way."

Gran's voice had gone hoarse and weak. Amy was more concerned with that than with whatever had happened in

1936, although she knew better than to say so. Taking Gran's hand, she said, "Can I bring you anything?"

"One more pain pill."

"If you first eat a few more bites of oatmeal."

Gran smiled, eyes closed, and Amy knew she was remembering bribing Kaylie—or maybe even Amy herself—to eat a few more spoonfuls of green beans, a few more spoonfuls of squash, a few more spoonfuls of beets.

When she closed the door to Gran's room, Kaylie, still in her babydoll dress and flats, stood talking to Solange. Amy said sourly, "I'm surprised you didn't put your hair in pigtails."

"Would have if I'd thought of it. How's Gran?"

"Asleep."

"Good. I'm going to take a shower."

"Not run off to see Cai?" Amy didn't know why she was being so nasty to Kaylie, except that the thought of Cai still made her chest ache and her head feel hopeless.

"Can't—he's working." Kaylie slipped off her dress. "And so are you. I just came from Myra Townsend. She says for you to report to her suite for the next scenario. Oh, and to wear something decent, which probably means not those yoga pants with that hole."

"Ha-ha."

"Have fun, sis."

*Ha-ha.*

# Twenty-two

## SUNDAY

A SEVEN-PASSENGER van carried the Lab Rats a long way from the city. Neither Myra nor Alex came along. Amy sat in the back row with Violet, who chattered about clothes, dance class, TV shows. At first Amy felt relieved. This was normal Violet—funny, sarcastic, effervescent—and Waverly had been wrong. But after a while Amy wasn't so sure. There were almost too many jokes, too many stories, too much effervescence, like cider whose pleasant bite was on the verge of turning sour.

"Violet," Amy said hesitantly as they got out of the van, "are you all right?"

"Cramped from sitting too long. Why?" Violet's gaze bored

down on Amy from her greater height, made even greater by four-inch Jimmy Choo ankle straps.

"Nothing. I just thought you seemed . . . oh, I don't know, a little on edge."

"Now, why would that be? Nothing to do with being cooped up in a hotel, cooped up in a van, cooped up in Myra Townsend's sadistic fantasies, hmmmm?"

That sounded more like Violet. Amy grinned.

The huge, dilapidated building in front of them sat in some sort of industrial complex, equally huge and dilapidated. Rusting pieces of machinery, none of which Amy could identify, led to empty overhead pipes. A vast parking lot, its asphalt cracked in crazy-quilt patterns, held only one truck with three missing tires and a broken axle. Windows on the building's lower floors were boarded over, those on the upper floors caked with grime. Over metal double doors a less faded rectangle of brick marked the place where a sign had once hung.

"Charming," Cai said.

Rafe said, "I know this place. It used to be a film factory, before everything went digital. Now the company can't even give it away because there's ground contamination from all the processing chemicals."

Waverly said, "Contamination?"

"Nothing that will hurt you if you're only around it for a few hours," Rafe said. "Not even in that get-up."

Waverly wore a miniskirt, high-heeled boots of buttery Italian leather, and a silvery top that looked as fragile as spiderwebs. Amy had on her mosaic-print miniskirt, white tee, and Fendi jacket; Violet wore silk pants, a ruffled blouse, and the Jimmy Choos. The boys, although dressed in expensive pants and jackets, at least wore sturdy shoes. Amy was glad of her Miu Miu sandals, flexible and low-heeled. Why had Myra sent them to an abandoned factory dressed like this? Then she realized.

"It films better if we're all tarted up," she said with resignation.

One of the double doors creaked open with a sound like fingernails scraping across a blackboard. A middle-aged man in greasy overalls came out and stared at them, unimpressed. "You the kids from that show?"

Amy grimaced. Who else would they be, in this forsaken place?

"Come on in, then."

The inside was so gloomy that at first Amy couldn't make out what lay on the metal table inside the door. Then she did: guns.

"You're going to be hunters," the man said with an unreadable expression.

Terrible images ran through Amy's mind: bullet guns, Tasers . . . That story she'd read for her lit class about men hunting each other for sport . . . But then her eyes adjusted more and she saw that the oversized guns included huge transparent chambers of colored liquids.

Tommy whooped, "Paintball!"

"Oh, really lame," Violet said.

Amy said, "Let's wait and see." If Myra planned this, it wouldn't be ordinary paintball.

Waverly said, "This top is Isabel Marant!"

The man spat on the very dirty floor. "Your boss rented the whole place. You kids are supposed to shoot anything you see moving. After the first ten minutes you can shoot each other, too. You lose ten points for every hit on them fancy clothes, gain ten points for every hit you get on somebody else, fifty points for every creature you nail. Each gun holds fifteen splats. Loser gets a booby prize. So pick a gun and go."

Only Tommy seemed enthusiastic. Amy hefted a gun with green paint, copying the expert way Tommy held his. She had never played paintball.

"Fan out," Cai said.

Before they did, Violet caught Rafe's and Amy's arms and whispered, "No shooting each other, OK? I'd like to preserve this outfit. Allies?" They both nodded.

The factory was filled with silent equipment, some of it

dripping liquids through cracks, some of it sagging in disrepair. Huge wooden boxes and rusting forklifts littered the aisles. Everything smelled dank, musty. The farther Amy went into the factory, the deeper the gloom. But she saw nothing that moved.

From the outside she'd counted five floors, which meant there had to be stairs somewhere. Her plan was to climb to the top, where there might be more light from the unboarded windows, and where she might be less likely to encounter the others. Maybe she could, in Violet's words, "preserve her outfit." If she lost the game in points, so what. Hunting should be as much about self-preservation as about prey. And what was the prey anyway? Undoubtedly some tech of Mark Meyer's. Or maybe more actors.

The stairwell, when she found it, had no light whatsoever and smelled of some animal that had died in there. Hastily Amy closed the door, her nose wrinkling.

Beside the staircase sat a freight elevator, a big cage with a metal grill over it. Amy pulled back the grill and stepped inside. Maybe it worked, maybe it didn't. Worth a try. She pressed the button.

The grill slid shut, rasping and wheezing, and the elevator rose. Amy heard Tommy call from somewhere below: "Nothing's moving to shoot!"

The top floor was lighter, although not by much because

the windows were both small and filthy. Amy tried to imagine what this place must have been like when it was a vital factory, full of workers earning good money doing necessary jobs. Where were they all now, since the Collapse? Gran's words came back to her: *A flash point. We're nearly there now.*

As she stepped out of the elevator, something moved in the shadows.

Amy raised her gun. The thing lurched forward, and when she saw it, she nearly laughed aloud. A zombie! Mark Meyer had created hologram zombies for the Lab Rats to shoot. Realistic—if you could use that word in connection with a zombie—but still cheesy beyond belief. Amy fired.

A glob of green paint hit the zombie and it immediately vanished. At the same time a jolt of electricity ran through Amy. She screamed and dropped her gun. Her hands tingled with pain.

So that was it! *Damn you, Myra!* Either play the game and get shocked, or don't play it and put yourself in line for the "booby prize," whatever horrible thing that was. Amy's eyes filled with tears of rage. When she examined her hands, the skin didn't seem harmed, and now the pain was fading. So—not enough electricity to cause injury, just pain.

She picked up her gun. Myra was not going to make a wimp out of her. She was going to use up every last gob of paint in this stupid weapon. Even though she would probably be experiencing the most pain; all the guns were identical, and she had the smallest body mass to absorb the shock. Possibly Tommy didn't feel much of it at all.

She moved forward cautiously, but even so she barely saw the next zombie before it reached her. She shot it and it vanished. This time, prepared for the electric shock, she didn't drop her gun. But it still hurt.

For the next several minutes she saw no more "prey." Neither could she see the machinery overhead in the rafters that must be generating them. Amy had just begun to relax when something scuttled along the floor to her left.

A rat.

She stifled a cry. Was it real or just another hologram? It was gone before she could decide, but the possibility of real rats—and why wouldn't there be rats nesting in an abandoned building?—set her nerves vibrating. Cautiously she moved toward one of the grimy windows, where she could see them better.

The freight elevator rasped behind her. Someone else on the fifth floor! Amy ducked behind a metal tank leaking viscous fluid from the many-armed pipes extending outward. Under the pipes she saw small brown droppings. The rats were real.

Whoever had come out of the elevator was silent, moving

stealthily. Maybe he or she didn't even know that Amy was on this floor. But the ten minutes were up; she was fair game.

As she stood behind the tank, trying to think what to do, the president of the United States came around the other side.

Amy was so startled that a bubble of sound escaped her lips. For a ridiculous moment she actually thought it was the president—wouldn't Mr. Taunton know a lot of important people? But of course it was a hologram. Amy raised her gun. The president smiled his famous smile and held up one hand. The illusion was so good that again Amy hesitated while all Gran's stories of assassination ran through her head. Gran remembered them all: President Kennedy murdered in Dallas, Ronald Reagan shot in front of a hotel in DC, this current president nearly killed by that lunatic in San Diego . . . Amy couldn't do it. Stupid though it was, she could not take aim and fire on the president of the United States . . . *A flash point. We're nearly there now*—

Something slammed into her right side and pain tore through her body. Amy screamed. It was the suddenness of the electric jolt, not the severity, since it wasn't any more than when Amy fired her own gun. But she hadn't expected the same shock when she was *hit*. Tommy whooped and ran from behind a piece of machinery. "Hey, Amy, I got you and—" He stopped dead.

The president was still waving and smiling. Tommy evidently knew who he was; his eyes widened and his gun wobbled. Then he dropped the gun and put his hand over his heart.

"Stop that, it's not the Pledge of Allegiance!" Amy snapped. The pain slowly drained from her body and she twisted to look at the back of her skirt. The Dolce & Gabbana mini was ruined, orange paint splattered all over the back. Paint had even reached her tee.

She pointed her gun at Tommy and shot him, and then she shot the president, who instantly disappeared. The double jolt of electricity hurt, but Amy was too angry to care. She'd never again own clothes this nice.

Tommy said, "You shot the president!"

"No, I didn't. Tommy, this is my floor. Go back down one floor in the elevator!"

"OK," Tommy said meekly. Amy hoped that all this was on film and that it undercut the competitive drama Myra was hoping for.

In the next five minutes she shot one more zombie, Mahatma Gandhi, and a rock star whose latest album had gone platinum. She saw no more rats. The elevator creaked again.

This time it was Cai. When she had him in view, she called, "If you shoot me you'll regret it!"

"I won't," Cai said. They approached each other warily, and sourness spread through Amy. Here were the makings of a genuine romantic fantasy of the type she used to spin for hours in her head: she and a gorgeous man, trapped in a situation of forced antagonism, wanting each other desperately but unable to touch, not only kept apart but also forced to be enemies by a cruel world that didn't understand the love of soul mates . . .

Except that Cai didn't love her, she was more concerned with rats than with soul mates, and what she wanted most was to get out of this building and see if the paint would come off the back of her skirt.

Cai shouldered his gun, a manly pose that would have looked great on him except for the red paint on his shirt and half his face. Amy said, "Who hit you?"

"Violet. She's firing like everything is real. This is a really lame scenario, you know?"

"Yeah. Even with the shocks."

"They're pretty mild," Cai said.

"Maybe for you. It goes by body mass."

"You sound like Rafe." Cai shifted his gun. "Amy, can I ask you something?"

"Sure." Her heart beat faster. "But remember that we're probably being filmed."

He leaned even closer, which—weirdly—did not increase her heart rate. Into her ear he said, "Does Kaylie *always* get her own way?"

Amy laughed. In those few words she glimpsed the entire Cai-Kaylie relationship. Oh, the poor guy.

"Nearly always," she said.

He looked unhappy. But before he could say more, a child crawled from an empty crate and said, "Help me! Please!"

Amy stared. No holograms had talked. The president had not said, "My fellow Americans . . ." Mahatma Gandhi had not urged nonviolent resistance. The zombies had not groaned. Was this an actor? The little girl was thin, filthy, ragged. . . . It wasn't hard to imagine her abandoned and taking refuge in this old building. In the worst neighborhoods of the city there were hordes of such children.

Cai started forward. A phantom leaped into Amy's mind: *lightning hitting a tree and igniting it*—

"Don't touch her, Cai!"

He stopped. "Do you think she's an illusion? She looks so real."

"I don't know." Amy grabbed Cai's arm and pulled him backward.

"Help me, please!"

He said, "If she *is* real—" just as the little girl's face morphed into a zombie's and she vanished in a burst of light and sound that blinded and deafened Amy so much she staggered backward.

"Shit!" Cai shouted. "A flash-bang!"

Leaning against a wall, panting, Amy waited for her senses to recover. She couldn't see, couldn't hear, her head rang as if hammered from the inside . . . but if she hadn't pulled Cai back and they'd both been standing closer to the hologram child, the effect would have been even worse. She gasped. "What's a flash-bang?"

"Law enforcement device. To make covering light and sound when a SWAT team goes in. You all right?"

Finally Amy straightened, inspecting the filth from the wall on her clothes. She had been dirtied, paint-shot, electric-shocked, frightened, and flash-banged. *Thanks, Myra.*

A gong sounded, echoing in the cavernous building, and a voice said, "Game over. Come to the front doors, players." A rat, startled by the voice, scuttled across the floor. Cai froze. Amy, made bold only because he was not, swallowed her fear and shot the rat with paint. Pain lanced through her, but the rat did not vanish.

In the elevator Cai said, "That was draining, in a stupid sort of way. What do you think Myra will use for list choices? 'Shot the president—and repented!'"

Amy laughed. But she was worried; she'd used only eight paint hits of her fifteen. Cai's gun looked nearly empty. What was the "booby prize," and would Amy get it?

They straggled from the factory floor to the double doors, one of which stood open. The clean sunshine beyond was the sweetest thing Amy had ever seen, even filtered through rusty machinery and sprawling weeds. Orange and blue paint stained Violet's clothes, and one heel of her Jimmy Choos had broken off. "I could have twisted my *ankle*," she snapped at no one in particular. Amy knew that for a dancer, a leg injury was worse than what Gran had always warned about: "Fall in those shoes and you could crack open your head!" Tommy, Cai, and Rafe likewise had multicolored splotches of paint, with Tommy so covered he looked like a broken kaleidoscope. But Waverly stood immaculate in her calf-length skirt, high boots, and Isabel Marant top. She wasn't even dirty.

"You went outside," Amy accused. "You just skipped the whole thing!"

"These are my own clothes," Waverly said, "not the show's. I'll take the booby prize instead. It will undoubtedly cost less."

"Don't be so sure," the man in overalls said. He gave them a nasty smile. For the first time Amy considered that he might belong not to the factory but to the show, as much in costume as all the rest of them. "Your booby prize is a firing squad."

Amy's mouth opened.

"I mean it—don't gape like that, youngsters. Raise your

guns. Fire on my count of ten. Sorry now, miss, that you didn't play fair?"

Waverly paled. Amy saw now that the evil man had subtly maneuvered Waverly so that she stood with her back to the closed half of the double doors. The sunlight fell on her from the left, creating dramatic shadows, and undoubtedly in line with the best camera angles. Everybody firing at once—the electric jolts would really hurt. What if they stopped Waverly's heart or something? No, Myra would have calculated that: enough electricity for maximum pain with minimum damage. And Amy could remember how even the double dose had hurt when she'd fired her gun at the same time as Tommy had fired at her.

"No," she said. "No one will shoot her. No one!"

Tommy, the only one who had raised his gun, looked puzzled. He didn't understand. He looked questioningly at Cai.

Cai said, "Lower your gun, Tommy."

The man bellowed, "It's in your contract!"

Amy said, "And in yours, I bet. But we won't do it. We *won't*."

Rafe muttered something Amy didn't understand; it might have been "Spartacus." But he was smiling.

The man said, "You could lose your jobs over this."

"Probably not," Violet said. She hobbled toward the door on her broken shoe. "Come on, gang."

The six filed out, Waverly still pale. The van was parked just around the corner. After they were inside, Waverly said quietly, "Thank you all."

Violet said, "We didn't do it for you." Which was correct but, Amy thought, unnecessary. The entire experience seemed to have put Violet into a mood of sour thoughtfulness. On the long ride back to the hotel, Amy couldn't get her to say anything at all.

# Twenty-three

## WEDNESDAY AND ON

THE SECOND HALF of the holographic-rats scenario ran on Wednesday night. Amy watched Kaylie grab Gran's purse to fight off the rats while Amy did nothing ("AMY: Freezes and cries!"). She hadn't actually cried, but neither had she acted bravely. Rafe announced loudly, "Yum! Rats!" and reached for one, licking his lips, before the rodents vanished ("RAFE: Picks up a rat to eat it!"). Waverly was swept into her chauffeur's arms and deposited inside her car ("WAVERLY: Is saved by someone else!"). Tommy and Violet: "Tries to run— and escapes the rats!" Cai and Lynn, like Kaylie, grabbed something to use as a weapon and "Fights off the rats!" Amy was sick of exclamation points.

The show proclaimed the winners, seven of them this time, each winning nearly a million and a half dollars. Then the first half of the *Romeo and Juliet* scenario ran. Evidently Myra had decided to pick up the show's pace. Amy watched herself, plus all the others, forced onstage in the middle of a performance, all but Waverly making fools of themselves in one way or another.

"Well," Gran said, and said no more. Amy felt grateful. Gran was resisting increasing the dosage in her pain pills, and for the next few weeks Amy was excused from work so she could stay with her. Often they talked, but not about what was happening to either of them. Gran, who'd always described herself as a citizen of the world, wanted to talk about the world: the Collapse, the new advances in biotech, the future of the Internet, the possibility of artificial intelligence. Amy listened, holding Gran's thin hand, watching the feverishly bright eyes, absorbing her grandmother's indomitable courage.

Gran insisted that Amy get some exercise, so every evening she took dance class with Violet, conveyed to a downtown studio and back in a closed car. It was all professional dancers, beside whom Amy was a disaster, but she didn't care. She just needed the distraction, which working out in the gym did not give her. The instructor, made aware of the situation, was tolerant. It was Violet who, in her new edgy mood, kept correcting Amy's pliés and kicks, occasionally even snapping at her. "Drop your shoulder, Amy—no, not like that! Watch!" Violet always apologized later, but something was not right.

Over the next few weeks, *Who—You* became even more intolerable to Amy. She was constantly on edge, waiting and watching—was this event the start of a scenario? Was that? Her neck ached with tension. Also, the filmed scenarios aired, two each week, starting with the one in which Mark Meyer had created "ghosts" of each participant's dead family member. Amy watched herself encounter her mother in the apartment stairwell with the connivance of Paul O'Malley, whom she'd thought was her friend. Fortunately, Gran had been asleep for that show. Next came the lobby attack, followed by paintball guns in the factory.

"Ratings are down," Alex told the Lab Rats, which of course they already knew from following the show's fate online. Viewers hadn't liked recent scenarios. The fake rats and fake zombies were called "cheats" and the dead relatives "a downer."

"So," Alex continued, "Myra and I have created a blog for the show, and each of you will now spend two hours a day on it, answering the e-mail we forward to you. Still no independent blogging, though, or posts about the show on Facebook, Twitter, or anywhere else. Make your answers as full and interesting as you can, preferably with snappy, quotable lines. Do any of you want a professional writer to help you with this?"

"Yes," Violet said promptly. "I want a professional writer to do it for me."

"I would think, Violet," Alex said dryly, "that you of all people would have no trouble with snappy quotable lines. Tommy, you'll have someone to help you. Amy, you can do this while your grandmother sleeps. Cai, your answers should reflect your personality, not Kaylie's. Rafe, not too erudite— nobody wants to read that ten-page history of medieval trial ordeals that you sent me last week. Everybody clear on this? OK, your first letters are already in your in-boxes. Forward all answers to me for vetting and I'll post them."

After Alex left, Amy asked, "Why hasn't he aired the pro- test outside the TLN building? That one wasn't a 'cheat.'" She shuddered, remembering being carried above the crowd, help- less and terrified of slipping underneath panicking feet.

Waverly said, "Problems with Legal," picked up her Fendi bag, and left the TLN suite.

"How does she know that?"

"Connections," Violet said wearily. "The rich are different from you and me. No, wait—somebody already said that."

Amy's forwarded e-mails were discouraging:

Dear Amy,

Why are you such a wimp? In the alley test you got caught by the bad guy. In the rats thing you froze. In the lame ghost bit you also froze. In the lobby with the cheesy fake robbers you did nothing. You don't belong on the show! Quit!

A Fan

Amy is a loser. She never fights or does anything interesting. Fire her now.

This show would be a lot better without Amy and Waverly. Waverly is a bitch and Amy just freezes every week. Get more like Cai! He's worth watching (drool drool drool).

i like Amy because she never does nothing i at least believe her but not the others its all fake

What was she supposed to write in response to those? Alex wanted answers "as full and interesting as you can, preferably with snappy, quotable lines." Sure, right.

Amy began, "Thanks for the e-mail. You have all seen only half of the ten scenarios we have filmed. I promise you that I am more active in the ones to come! Order of airing, which is not in my control, makes a big difference and—"

She hit Delete. She sounded whiny and apologetic, and "order of airing" was a stupid phrase. She'd even been betrayed into using an exclamation point. How was she supposed to answer this stuff? Alex had forwarded everyone's e-mail in a zip file; Amy's was the worst.

An e-mail popped up from Rafe: "Illegitimi non carborundum." What did *that* mean? She Googled it: it was a World War II mock-Latin saying originated by British intelligence, translated as "Don't let the bastards grind you down." Despite her mood, Amy laughed aloud.

As Violet's moods continued to be uncertain, Rafe was becoming the one bright spot in Amy's days. In the afternoons he came to her suite, listening to Gran when she was awake and playing chess with Amy while Gran took her fitful, unrefreshing naps. Kaylie and Cai made duty visits but it was clear that Kaylie wanted to be elsewhere. Cai was giving a lot of press interviews. "Are you doing that, too?" Amy asked Rafe.

"Not so much," he said, opening with the King's Gambit.

She declined the gambit and said, "But you're doing some interviews."

"A few, but not like Cai. I don't look like him." It was said without self-pity: just a fact.

"Are the others doing interviews? Waverly and Violet?"

"Yes."

"But not me."

"Myra knows you're occupied with your grandmother."

"It's not that, and you know it. The scenarios aired so far all have me looking ineffective! Rafe . . . what if they drop me from the show?"

"They won't."

"How do you know that? They explained Lynn's absence as 'illness.' They could do that to me, too. Have you heard anything? Please be honest with me!"

He looked up at her from the chessboard, and something moved in his brown eyes. "I'm always honest with you, Amy. The order of the shows was badly chosen. I think even Myra knows that now—don't you, Myra?" He cast his eyes to the ceiling; Rafe persisted in his belief that the suite of Amy's living room was constantly monitored. "They aired several scenarios in a row that fans found disappointing. Myra probably wanted to build week to week, with each scenario more dramatic than the one before, but that strategy isn't working. My guess is that next will come Lynn's meltdown in Myra's office, and you'll be the heroine. But right now, I think you need to get out of this suite for a little bit. Come down to the cafeteria with me."

"I can't leave Gran."

"Where's that nurse you had? Solange?"

"She only comes nights now. I want to be with Gran during the day."

"Fine, but she can stay alone for half an hour. I want a latte."

"We can send down to room service for lattes."

"Amy, take a walk with me!"

She hadn't heard that tone from Rafe before: half pleading, half commanding. He had something to tell her. Amy went.

Rafe had explored every inch of the vast hotel. He led her to a penthouse VIP lounge, which Amy hadn't known existed, and gained entry with a special key card, which Amy didn't have. The room had four glass walls and spectacular views of the city. French doors led to terraces planted with ornamental trees and bright flowers. A few people sat in leather chairs, reading newspapers or talking, sipping drinks provided by a bartender. The VIPs glanced up as Rafe and Amy entered, but they registered no reaction. Rafe and Amy went outside. She stood by a balustrade, her hands resting on the railing, gazing at the rooftops below her and the bay opening out to blue ocean far beyond.

Rafe said, "Gorgeous, isn't it? The privileges of the rich."

She smiled. "You sound like a throwback Marxist."

"Just a realist. Amy—why do you think there hasn't been a new scenario in so long?"

Amy had considered this already. "I think maybe Myra was waiting for data from viewers so she could decide what would play best."

"Well, she got data. But I think there might be another reason. I think she might be planning something really spectacular that took time to set up. Which means really dangerous."

Amy shook her head. "No, I don't think so. The only dangerous thing we've had so far is the mob of protestors outside the TLN building, and even you can't believe that Myra engineered *that*."

"No. But she might have augmented it, summoning actors to add to the protest after we all arrived for work. Just to see what happened."

"Rafe, you're paranoid."

"And you're beautiful. When the breeze blows your hair like that, it glints with about a hundred different colors."

Amy stared at him.

"Bronze, honey, cinnamon," he murmured. "Nutmeg, gold . . ." He leaned forward to kiss her.

Before she even knew she was going to react, Amy pulled away.

"Oh, Rafe, I'm sorry . . . I didn't mean . . ."

"I know what you meant." He turned his face, stony now, away from her.

"I like you as a friend but I don't . . . I don't have those kind of feelings for you."

"Do you still have them for Cai? Never mind, I know you do. I've seen how you look at him and Kaylie."

"I don't!"

"So now you can see your own face? How talented you are, Miss Kent. Just forget it, OK? Let's go play more chess."

"No, we should talk about this. I—"

"We should not talk about this. Why do girls always want to talk everything to death instead of just getting on with it? Forget the whole thing, all right?"

But she didn't, and she knew that he didn't either. The chess game was played in uncomfortable silence. Rafe won, threw her a look that said *You'd better not have lost that game on purpose*, and left.

"Amy?" Gran called from the bedroom, "Are you there?"

"Here!"

Gran's face looked drawn with pain. She said, "Dear heart . . . I think it's time for the stronger pills."

"Do you want the doctor? I can get him here fast!"

"No, just the pills."

Silently Amy brought them. Gran swallowed the pills, then sank back on the pillow and closed her eyes. Softly Amy touched her grandmother's cheek, and Gran smiled at her with sadness and the weight of things unspoken.

Myra said, "Yes, I've seen the ratings."

"What are you going to do about it?"

Myra told James Taunton her plans for the next scenario, finishing with, "And Mark is all ready to go."

"No."

Her stomach clenched.

"That's no different from the stuff that you've been doing. Novelty carried the first two weeks, but now you're giving me pap. We need more, especially since the merger. Step it up or the sponsors will bail."

"Yes, sir." He had given her an opening, and Myra took her courage in both hands. There had been no merger information from Taunton's office since the initial memo. "May I ask why 'especially since the merger'? Is Pylon unhappy with the show?"

"Let's just say that they're cautious." And then, "Myra— you and Alex *can* step it up, can't you?"

"Of course!" She forced a bright smile.

"I'm glad to hear it." He swiveled his chair away from her.

Myra strode confidently from his office, closed the door, and leaned against the wall. Her eyes squeezed shut and a tremor ran the entire length of her body. When she opened her eyes, Taunton's receptionist, a young girl of astonishing beauty, was gazing at her, openmouthed.

"Get back to work," Myra snapped.

"Yes, ma'am." But there were no secrets in a television station. Myra saw the girl's tiny, smug smile.

# Twenty-four

**A WEDNESDAY**

AMY WOKE WHEN a sprinkler came on over her bed, drenching her.

Smoke filled her nose, mouth, throat, lungs. Now she heard the alarms that, in her exhaustion, she had simply slept through before. The room was hazy with gray smoke pouring from a vent.

"Amy! Amy!" Gran called feebly from her room. Choking, Amy rushed to her room. There was less smoke there.

"It's a fire! Get out!"

"I—"

"Didn't you hear the alarm?"

Amy shook her head harder than necessary, trying to

clear it. She'd been conscious of nothing except her troubled dreams. She tried to think.

"Get out!" Gran said. She lay collapsed sideways on the bed and on top of the duvet, as if she'd tried to get up and could not.

"I'm not leaving you!" In her wet pajamas Amy rushed to the window, slamming the door to her own room on the way. Seventeen stories below, fire trucks screamed down the avenue, joining those already there. Police cars, more of them than Amy had even known existed, surrounded the building. Beyond them, people huddled in groups as vans arrived to take them away. But something was wrong—other people, some in body armor and some not, were jumping on the vans, throwing rocks at the police, being clubbed and dragged away. Seen from so far up, the scene had the monstrous feel of a battle waged in miniature, as if by human ants.

"It's not just a fire," she said to Gran, and was surprised at her own tone. Some switch had turned on in her brain. She felt not panicked or terrified, but coldly rational, as if facing a strong chess opponent. "Those are protesters, and SWAT teams! I think the anti-Pylon people have seized the building."

"And set it on fire?"

"I don't know. Most people seem to be out. How long ago did the alarm start?"

"About ten minutes. And someone pounded on the door. I tried . . . I tried to . . ." Gran's face crumpled.

"I know you did," Amy said, still in that hyperrational tone she hardly recognized as her own. And yet she did. It was hers, and she was the one going to get them both to safety. Wherever that was.

She ran into the main room of the suite and put her hand at the bottom of the door. Not hot—good. Cautiously she opened the door. No fire in the hallway. No people, either. "Hey!" Amy screamed. "Anybody here!"

Waverly ran into the hall, dressed in a satin bronze robe and combat boots, her hair tumbled on her shoulders. "I just woke up, I took two sleeping pills, I don't usually but yesterday—there's a fire!"

Amy wasn't interested in Waverly's drug routines. "I think the building's been taken by protestors. We have to get out." Already Amy was running back inside her suite. Waverly followed.

"Protestors? Then come on!"

"I can't leave my grandmother here!"

Amy darted into the bedroom. Gran looked at her with the sternest expression Amy had ever seen on that face. She said, "I told you to leave. Don't worry about me. Don't you think I know how close I am already to the end? Amy, do as I say!"

Amy ignored both words and expression. She hooked her arm under Gran's armpit and tried to ease her to her feet. Gran screamed in pain and Amy put her back on the bed. "I'm sorry, Gran, I'm sorry! But I have to carry you——"

"You can't. The elevators won't work in a fire, either. I told you to go and I mean it!"

"No!"

A sound behind her made Amy turn. Waverly was pushing a room-service cart into the bedroom. On it were dishes of half-eaten food: steak, salad, juice. With a single swipe of her arm Waverly sent it all crashing to the floor. "I didn't feel like seeing anybody for dinner last night. Come on, let's get her onto this."

Amy stared. Waverly repeated, "Come on!"

With two of them, they were able to lift Gran from both sides and lay the shrunken, light body on her side on top of the service cart. Amy had recovered her wits after the shock that Waverly—*Waverly!*—was thinking of someone besides herself. Amy said swiftly, "I'm going to make phone calls. Go in the bathroom and soak the towels in cold water, all of them, and put them on the bottom of the cart just . . . just in case."

"Got it," Waverly said.

Amy found her cell and punched in 911. A voice said, "Nine-one-one. State your emergency, please."

"I'm in the Fairwood Hotel and three of us are trapped on the seventeenth floor."

A tiny gasp on the other end of the line—were operators supposed to do that? The operator said something to someone at her end, and a different voice, male and authoritative, came on the cell. "You're on the seventeenth floor of the Fairwood?"

"Yes! We're going to go down the stairs to—"

"You can't. Protestors are occupying the first four floors, at least according to our latest information, and they're holding some hotel personnel hostage. They're threatening them with death if their demands aren't met. Listen to me carefully: There is a room on the sixth floor, where three armed men have barricaded some hotel guests and are prepared to defend them if necessary. Room 654. The fire is only on the top floors, and all guests were evacuated from there—why the hell weren't you?"

"We were asleep."

The man swore, and Amy didn't think that 911 operators were allowed to do *that*, either. He said, "The elevators won't work in a fire. Go down the stairwell and get to Room 654 as fast as you can. The—"

Amy hung up, put the cell on the cart beside Gran, turned to Waverly, and told her what 911 had said. "Ready?"

Waverly, pale under her sunlamp tan, nodded. Gran had

stopped arguing, from exhaustion or futility. Amy pushed the service cart into the deserted hall, Waverly steadying Gran's body on top of it. Even out here the fire alarm didn't sound very loud to Amy.

Waverly made a face. "They need a new alarm system. It can't—"

Amy said, "What was that?" A noise even more muffled than the alarm but distinct: *pop pop pop.*

Waverly said, "Gunfire. We shoot—my family shoots— and it's gunfire."

*We shoot.* Amy pictured a genteel party of skeet shooters aiming at clay birds, but the next minute came a harsher rattle she recognized from too many movies: automatic weapon fire. The silly, genteel picture vanished. Why was her mind throwing up this stuff now?

The girls reached the stairs. Waverly yanked the door open and Amy pushed the service cart through. The stairwell seemed to be free of smoke. "I'm going to take the bottom half, and you take the top. We have to hold it as level as we can, OK?"

"Wouldn't it be simpler if we just carried her between us?"

"It hurts her. And we're not going down all eleven floors," Amy said, panting. "There's an old unused freight elevator, with a locked door at the bottom, that Rafe showed me, but it only goes up as far as the fifteenth floor because they added on to the building and modernized the elevators. We can—"

Amy's cell rang. They had reached a turn in the stairwell where the cart was once more level, and Amy peered at Gran. Her eyes were closed, her body still. Frantically Amy felt for a pulse. Still there, and it seemed strong. Maybe Gran had just passed out from pain. The cell rang again and Amy grabbed it. Maybe 911 had something more to suggest—

It was Violet. "Amy, where *are* you?" Amy could hear shouting somewhere around Violet but muffled, as if through a door.

"Waverly and I are bringing Gran down to Room 654. Nine-one-one said it was safer because some cops were guarding hotel guests in there and—"

"The protestors took Room 654. A man just told me. Everybody there is dead."

Amy drew a sharp breath. Panic surged toward her, but then the coldly rational part of her brain was back in control. "OK," she told Violet. "Yes. Where are you?"

"Outside. We—"

"OK. Yes. Gotta go."

Waverly said, "Amy!"

"All right, Waverly, we have to keep moving. Change of plan to—"

"Amy! Down there! It's Rafe!"

Amy squeezed around the cart to see the bottom of the

flight of stairs. Rafe lay on his side, arms outstretched to claw at the steps above him. Blood streamed from his head.

She darted down the stairs. He was breathing. "Rafe! Rafe!" She slapped his face, because it was what she'd seen done in the movies and because she couldn't think what else to do. He didn't respond.

A phantom leaped into Amy's mind, only it wasn't a phantom but a memory: Rafe and she laughing at a café on Fenton Street. She seemed to see the picture from a great height, the way she'd seen the protestors attacking the building. She felt in his pockets and another picture sprang into her mind: Lynn in the alley scenario, stealing the wallet of the supposedly homeless man.

This was no scenario. This was Gran's flash point.

Waverly called, "Is he alive?"

"Yes. Unconscious."

"He was coming *up*. Trying to get to you, I'll bet. What are we—"

*Trying to get to you.* "We're going to take them both with us."

"With us *where*?" There was a hint of Waverly's haughty, I-know-the-world-and-you-don't superiority in the question, but only a hint.

Amy hooked her hands under Rafe's armpits and dragged him down the steps to the sixteenth-floor landing. He was surprisingly light; she would have had trouble moving Cai or Tommy. Amy raced back to the landing. "I'm taking this end of the cart. Ready?"

She and Waverly got Gran's cart to the landing. The bottom of the stairwell door, which Amy did not open, felt hot. Was the fire on this floor? If it was on the fifteenth . . .

*Don't think about that until you have to.*

On the way down the next landing—*carry the cart, try not to jostle Gran, go back for Rafe, try to not jostle him*—Waverly started to cry. "Amy, I don't want to die!"

The sight of tears on that usually cold face was so startling that Amy momentarily stopped dragging Rafe. She said fiercely, "We're not going to die!"

"There's smoke coming under that stairway door! Not much, but smoke!"

"Then we'll go down to the fourteenth floor. We can do this!"

Waverly didn't answer. But her tears disappeared and she lifted Gran's cart with as much straining care as if her own grandmother lay on it. A question flashed into Amy's mind: Would Kaylie have done as much?

Her cell rang. She ignored it.

The stairwell door to the fifteenth floor was indeed hot. The fourteenth was not, but when Amy cautiously opened it, wisps of smoke drifted through. She was going to close the door when more automatic gunfire sounded below them, terrifyingly close.

Waverly said, "I think they're on the next floor down!"

"Quick, get Gran and Rafe through!"

They got both the cart and Rafe's limp body onto the carpeted hallway of the fourteenth floor. "This way!" Amy said. She dragged Rafe.

Waverly followed with the cart. When they started choking with smoke, they draped wet towels over their faces, Gran's, and Rafe's. Sweat poured off Amy; the corridor was hot. Waverly's satin robe clung to her body in wet patches. Both their hair straggled limply into their eyes.

Waverly stopped. "Tell me where we're going or this is it for me!"

"Next door," Amy panted. "Linen room. The elevator is in the back and—"

The linen room door was locked.

Finally panicked, Amy rattled the door. The smoke was becoming thicker now, and the gunfire below them resumed. An old childhood game came back to Amy, one she and Kaylie had played: *Would you rather eat a worm or a spider? Would you rather kiss a boy's thing or a dog's ass? Would you rather fall off a cliff or a building?*

Would you rather be shot to death or roasted to death?

She rattled the door again. Waverly said, "Stand back."

"It—"

"I said stand back!" Waverly shoved Amy out of the way. Then she poised herself by the door, drew back one foot in the combat boot, and kicked the door handle. The door flew open.

Amy gaped. "You can—"

"Karate. I'm a brown belt."

"Then in the alley scenario—"

"I was wearing *heels*, Amy. And a Vera Wang! Come on, let's go."

There was less smoke in the small linen room. Shelves along three walls held sheets, towels, blankets, duvets, and an immense rolling vat of dirty bedclothes. The fourth wall consisted mostly of the iron grate of an ancient service elevator.

Amy said rapidly, "Get Gran into it. Rafe explained that this elevator isn't even on the electrical system—it's so old it uses counterweights. If it's not locked—".

It wasn't. Amy tugged at the grate and it creaked open like something from a horror movie. When they had crowded in, Amy pushed the Down button and squeezed her eyes shut. What if the mechanism was so old that the cables were rusted through or something—but no, in that case the thing would have been locked. The hotel didn't want lawsuits from its cleaning staff. The maids must still use this elevator.

The elevator rasped slowly, slowly, slowly down.

"The gunfire is louder," Waverly said. "Do you think Rafe will be all right?"

"How would I know?"

"Well, don't snap at me!"

"Sorry."

Amy's nerves felt ready to shatter. The elevator took forever, and as they passed each floor, she grew more shaken. By the time they reached the basement, her knees trembled. She locked them in place, seized Rafe again, and dragged him through a vast laundry area where the dirty linen from all nineteen floors ended up. At the far door, she pressed her ear to the door and listened.

"What?" Waverly said.

"I don't hear anyone. . . . But we won't know for sure until I open the door."

The girls stared at each other. Waverly's face was white as paper except for a long sooty smudge. She said, "Open it."

Amy eased the door open, peering out. Nobody. The door led to the basement storage room where Rafe had taken her. His key unlocked the door at the far end, it rasped open, and there was the tunnel, long and damp and low. Amy's relief was so great that for a moment her eyes filled. But there was no time for that.

"It's OK, come on!"

They hurried along the dim tunnel, which seemed to go on forever, silent except for pipes gurgling overhead. Just before they reached the end, Rafe moaned.

"It's OK, we're here," Amy said inanely.

"My . . . head . . ." Rafe said.

"I know. But we're safe now."

"We are?" Waverly said. "What's up those steps?"

"Fenton Street."

"*Fenton Street*? Like, Prada and Angelique's?"

"If you say so. Come on!"

Rafe mumbled, "Can . . . walk . . ."

He couldn't, but Amy got him upright and then it was easier to half-carry him. The nearness of safety somehow made this last stretch of their escape the worst piece. Amy trembled so much she could barely walk. Waverly, still pushing the cart, gave a single massive sob. But by the time they reached the rickety, cobwebby stairs up to the alley, Amy had herself under control.

"You go up," Amy said. "Get help. I'll stay with Gran and Rafe. Be careful!" What if protestors, and not cops, held Fenton Street?

No. This was Fenton Street. The police would let the Fairwood Hotel burn to the ground before they allowed damage to this enclave of riches.

Waverly scuttled up the stairs, the hem of her satin robe

catching on splinters and turning black with dirt. Amy's eyes had adjusted to the gloom of the tunnel. She saw that Gran's were open. "Gran? Are you OK?"

Gran whispered something. For a heart-sickening moment Amy thought it was good-bye. But then she repeated it, her quaver no more than a cobweb in Amy's ear. "Bravo, dear heart."

"They're down there!" Waverly cried. Then people pounded down the steps, someone said, "I'm a doctor," and Amy allowed herself to sink to her knees beside Rafe and let relief take her like a tsunami.

# Twenty-five

PEOPLE JAMMED the hospital ER: crying, shouting, moaning, swearing, looking for friends and relatives or demanding attention for the ones they'd already found. Amy heard the cops cursed, the protestors cursed—sometimes by the same people—the medical staff cursed, the economy cursed, the world cursed. The only quiet people were some of those who lay on the gurneys jamming the waiting room, the examining room, the corridors.

No gurneys were left for Rafe or Gran. Gran lay on the stretcher on which she'd been carried in from the ambulance. Rafe slumped in an orange plastic chair, holding his head. Waverly had been carried off by a cop to make a report. Amy, in her filthy pajamas, crouched on the floor beside Gran, and when a man in a bloody white coat went by, she grabbed the hem of his coat and said, "My grandmother! Please! She was in the fire and so was my friend——"

The doctor knelt beside Gran. "Burns?"

"No," Gran whispered. "I'm fine."

His hands went expertly over her, and somehow she found the strength to push him away. "Fine!"

"She inhaled smoke," Amy said, "and she has cancer!"

He looked at her for the first time, and recognition moved in his eyes. "You're a kid from that——"

"Yes. And so is Rafael Torres! I think he has a concussion!"

The doctor turned his attention to Rafe, peeled back his eyelids and shone a light, asked him some questions. Then he stood. "Neither of them is critical. Keep Rafael awake, preferably walking, for at least twelve hours. You'd actually do better to take them both home, there are so many badly off here that no one will see either of them for hours."

"I can't go——" Amy began, but the doctor was already gone. She and Gran were in nightclothes, but Rafe was dressed in jeans and a flannel shirt. "Rafe?"

"Perfectly coherent," he said, the words only slightly slurred. "You're holding up sixteen fingers."

"Does your head hurt?"

"President is Lady Gaga."

"Do you have your cell phone?"

"Two plus two is infinity. Yes, I do."

He produced the phone, a complicated piece of tech that Amy wasn't familiar with. She did discover that it was set to Vibrate and that he had eight missed calls from Myra. Kaylie wasn't on his speed dial and Amy couldn't remember her number, but Cai was there. Someone was wheeled past on a gurney. Someone else moaned. Someone screamed, "Those fuckers!"

"Indeed," Rafe said. "God, my head hurts."

Cai picked up on the first ring. "Rafe?"

"It's Amy. Is Kaylie——"

"Amy! Where are you? Are you safe?"

Before Amy could answer, Kaylie seized the phone. "Amy! Are you OK?"

"Yes, I'm in the hospital with Gran and Rafe and——"

"With Gran! How did you get out of the hotel? Violet said——"

"It's too long a story for now. Are you all OK?"

"Yes. We're at a new hotel. Myra got us there. Look, we'll come get you. Is Gran all right?"

Amy looked at Gran. She looked very fragile, very weak, and her breathing seemed hoarser. All at once her face spasmed and her eyes rolled back in her head. Amy leapt up from the floor and screamed, "Doctor! Nurse! Heart attack here! Oh, somebody come!"

A nurse rushed over, took one look at Gran, and yelled, "Code Blue. Code Blue. Get a crash cart over here!"

"Amy!" Kaylie screamed into the phone. "What's happening?"

Amy dropped the phone and seized Gran's hand. "Don't go, don't go, not yet!"

The next few minutes were a blur. The crash cart did not arrive. But a doctor gave Gran a shot of something, she was heaved onto a gurney, and an IV was attached to her. When the blur of fear eased, Gran lay breathing regularly, eyes closed, and Rafe stood beside Amy, holding her free hand. His head was still bloody. Chaos still raged around them in the ER.

"Admit her," a doctor shot at a harried nurse, and then raced off to the next patient.

Amy heard Rafe say into his phone, "She's all right." Oh—Kaylie was still on Rafe's cell. It didn't seem important, not even when Rafe said gently to Amy, "They're on their way."

"I'm not leaving."

"No," Rafe said, "I didn't expect you would."

Gran rallied. "She's a fighter," a nurse told Amy several hours later. "She's sleeping really peacefully now, probably until tomorrow morning. After that she'll most likely be moved out of the ICU. Some of these old people just have remarkable staying power. You should go home, clean up, get some rest."

Except that Amy didn't have a home. The old apartment's lease had been terminated and the few bits of furniture worth saving put into storage. The Fairwood Hotel was burned, or was a crime scene, or was still held by protestors: Amy had no idea which. There were no TVs in the Intensive Care Unit.

Cai and Kaylie arrived at the hospital, saw Gran, and brought Amy some clothes from somewhere. Now Kaylie sat outside in the waiting room since only one person at a time was permitted in the ICU. But when Amy dragged herself out there, only Rafe occupied the stiff, poison-green sofa. A bandage wound around his head and dipped near one eye.

"Jaunty," Amy said. She was almost too tired to stand.

"I'm aiming for that wounded-but-brave-soldier look. How is she doing?"

"Amazingly well, according to everybody. One doctor called her 'a tough old bird.' How are *you*?"

"Nothing to worry about. The staff has no time to worry about me, anyway. A slight concussion is small potatoes today."

She dropped onto the other end of the sofa. "Tell me."

Rafe didn't sugarcoat. "Six dead, at least fifty injured. A SWAT team retook the hotel. Criminal charges are being filed against the anti-Pylon group, and the other group, the looser Times Be Tough Man organization, have publicly dissociated themselves from the anti-Pylons. The president gave a press conference, with both stick and carrot. The stick is to send in the National Guard if the riots spread more——"

"Are they spreading?"

"Atlanta, L.A., and Detroit are on fire. Well, parts of them, anyway. The carrot is promised legislation of incredible scope. Something like the New Deal, to aid everybody at the bottom of the economic ladder, which is pretty much everyone. The rich are howling."

"So nothing will get passed."

"I think it will, Amy, this time. Even billionaires recognize that real revolution is a possibility, and revolution would bring down everything. The legislation will have to include some tariff protectionism and——"

"Stop, Rafe." She put a hand on his arm. "I don't have your grasp of politics, and anyway I'm too tired right now. Tell me later. For now—where are Kaylie and Cai?"

"They left. Myra summoned them."

Exhausted anger washed feebly through Amy. Kaylie preferred to go where Myra summoned—Kaylie, who wasn't even on the show!—rather than wait to see Gran again.

Rafe said, "A doctor told Kaylie to go home."

"Where's 'home'? Where are we supposed to go now?"

"Another hotel. The Carillon, on Portman Island."

That got Amy's attention. Portman Island, in the bay, was a beautiful, expensive resort. She'd seen pictures. "Well, I suppose there won't be any protestors there."

"Not unless the cleaning staff and kitchen help riot. But they won't. The security is massive. Since the Collapse, Portman practically has its own army."

"And you know this how?"

He held up his cell and grinned. "I've been waiting here to take you home. You can do a lot of research in all those hours."

Waiting to take her home. And Waverly had said that Rafe had been climbing the Fairwood Hotel stairwell to reach Amy. But she was too weary to deal with this now, or with the look in Rafe's eyes. She said, "Where's Waverly?"

"At the hotel. How come *she* came through for you?"

"It's complicated. But she did. Are Violet and Tommy OK?"

"Sure. They were outside with Cai and Kaylie, remember? One more thing: Myra gave a press conference. She said that TLN is looking into the possibility that the protestors attacked that particular hotel because of us. That we were targeted."

"That's ridiculous!" Amy said. "Those riots were bigger than some stupid TV show!"

"Of course. Myra misstepped badly. Now it looks like she's

325

piggybacking on everybody else's anger and desperation just to get free publicity. Come on, I'm getting you somewhere you can sleep."

"How? Portman isn't close . . . and how are we going to get to the studio every day?"

"I don't know about that. But I do know how to get you to the Carillon."

He stood and held out his hand. Amy took it reluctantly and dropped it as soon as she could. The look was still in his eyes, and she was too grateful to him, and liked him too much, to tell him she couldn't respond to that look. He was a good friend, but no more.

They took an elevator to the roof. Rafe, grinning mysteriously, made a call on his cell. A few minutes later a helicopter landed on the huge yellow cross that marked the helipad. The side of the helicopter blazed in red and orange TLN NEWS.

Rafe said, "That's probably the only time in my life I'll ever be able to summon an aircraft. I hope you're suitably impressed."

"I am!"

"Good." They climbed in and Rafe said, "Home, James." The pilot twisted to give him a sour look. Rafe grinned again, and they lifted into the sky. For a nauseating moment the view of everything far below—tiny cars, tiny people—reminded

Amy of looking down at the riots from the burning hotel. *Ants.* She shuddered and closed her eyes until they were away from the city, over the blue waters of the bay, sparkling in the morning light.

"No," Alex said. "We can't."

Midnight of the night before, and the conference room at TLN was lit like an operating room. *Surgical removal,* Myra thought—but not of her. She would do anything to keep that from happening.

She said calmly, "Let me make my case before you interrupt, Alex. Just grant me that courtesy."

"This is not a case anyone should make!"

Myra twisted her body so that her left shoulder was turned to Alex, her face toward James Taunton. He sat at the head of the mahogany table, his face inscrutable. Myra wasn't fooled by the lack of expression. She had erred badly with that press conference, and he was deeply unhappy with her. She was fighting for her life—for the one chance to regain the life she'd once had and had lost. And it was her only chance; Myra was under no illusions about that. Television had always been a sharks-in-the-water field and if she was fired now, in this economy, she would be so much bleeding meat.

"Mr. Taunton, we didn't cause the riots or the fire. No one

could possibly say that—and no one *is*. This is not a scenario. But it *is* an opportunity. At least three other stations are preparing quickie 'special news reports' on the hotel protest. That's because it's big news. Those reports will replay footage of the attack, the occupation of the premises, the counterattack, and then analysts will attempt to explain the behavior of everyone involved. Well, behavior is what our show is about! We can turn these news reports to the personal with the behavior of six individuals, three of which are pretty spectacular. We don't even have to include the voting, and we can explain why we're not including it—so as not to capitalize on tragedy. That ought to cover any objections from the bleeding-heart liberal crowd. What we can offer is a close-up, inside view of what happened, to complement and round out the outside view everyone else will have. Our show will almost be a historical document, focusing on teenage heroism."

Alex said, "You can't possibly believe that crap, Myra!"

"Alex—"

"Six people died, and we run it as entertainment?"

Myra opened her mouth, then closed it again. Taunton had shifted on his chair: a subtle shift, but she'd caught it and Alex had not. The best thing she could do now was shut up and let him come by himself to her idea. Under the table she laced her hands together so tightly that the rings on her right hand cut into the flesh of her left.

Taunton said, "We don't have footage of those three kids in the tunnel. Or the elevator, which we didn't even know existed."

"And neither did the protestors, which will be dramatic," Myra said. "We can re-create that part, with actors shot in soft focus and with towels over their heads against any heat, which is what Waverly told me they actually did. And—"

"Falsify footage?" Alex said.

"No, of course not—we say frankly that this part is a re-creation—a *faithful* re-creation. And we have footage of the girls loading the grandmother onto the service cart in Amy's suite. Visual and audio. Only visual in the hallway and stairwell, but it's dramatic. And we have spectacular shots of Rafe fighting free of the protestor who tried to eject him from the building, of the blow to his head, of him staggering up fourteen flights and then collapsing. He was trying to get to Amy! Now you tell me, what plays better than young love, unless it's young love in wartime?"

"Oh, Christ," Alex said, "give me a break."

Taunton said, "But the other three kids—"

"Not as dramatic, I admit. Cai, Tommy, and Violet were on the first floor and they were hustled out by the first wave of protestors, those nonviolent Times Be Tough people. But we still have close-ups, and Tommy especially looks terrified. An intimate reaction."

Taunton mused, "Too bad none of them was involved with that holdout group in Room 654. *That* was dramatic."

Myra kept her face blank. "But not as dramatic as the tunnel escape. And if—I'm just saying 'if'—we do decide to include voting, no one will predict heroics from Waverly. I was stunned myself."

"That's because you see the kids as one-dimensional dolls," Alex said. "And disposable dolls, at that."

Myra turned on him. "You produced a porn show, Alex! The people on *that* weren't dolls?"

"They were professional actors. These are kids who were in danger of their lives. Mr. Taunton, we can't do this."

Myra hid her sudden glee. James Taunton did not like to be told what he could or could not do. He said, "Do we have footage of the three emerging from the tunnel near Fenton Street?"

"Yes! Everyone up there had cell phones, and we've purchased some of the shots. Then I rushed in one of ours with a hand-held, in time to see the medics bring up the grandmother."

"She didn't die, did she? We can't use it if she died."

"She's in stable condition at Memorial Hospital. Out of the ICU already." This wasn't strictly true, but Mrs. Whitcomb might be moved to a ward in the morning.

Taunton said nothing. Myra held her breath. Into the prolonged silence Alex said quietly, "Mr. Taunton, if you do this episode, I will quit."

Taunton appeared to not even hear him. More silence. Finally Taunton said, "Put together a rough cut and let me see it tomorrow afternoon. We'll have to run it right away, to keep it timely, and shorten the rest of the show so both segments fit into the hour. The PR people will need time for advance spots, and Programming will have to dump something else. You'll need to bring in your staff right away, Myra."

"I can do that!"

Alex said, "Mr. Taunton—"

"I know, you're quitting. Best of luck to you, Alex. Not everybody has the guts necessary to work in television." He rose and walked out.

Alex said to Myra, "You exploitative bitch."

*You don't know the half of it.* But all she said to him was, "I'll miss working with you." And, to her own surprise, she found she meant it, although she couldn't have said why.

# Twenty-six

**THURSDAY**

THE CARILLON HOTEL on Portman Island
was set beside an expensive office park whose low buildings
were nearly hidden by trees. The whole area, bright with flowers and surrounded by open fields on one side and big estates
on the other, looked like something from a children's picture
book. No protestors here, no risk of attack, no city messiness.
Not, Amy noticed, so much as a discarded gum wrapper.

Nonetheless, the hotel had formidable security. Amy had
never seen lobby guards who were actually armed. More armed
men, some with exotic headgear, moved watchfully alongside
various hotel guests. "Bodyguards," Jillian explained. "The hotel hosts many foreign businessman involved in deals at the
corporate offices in the Park."

Amy smiled faintly. Jillian was their new liaison/chaperone/jailer from Taunton Life Network. Myra, Jillian explained, was very busy with the editing side of the show. Jillian looked about twenty-five, fresh-faced without being beautiful, well-dressed without Myra's style. She wore her hair in a bouncy ponytail. "Forty if she's a day," Violet breathed in Amy's ear, "and already had face work done."

Amy didn't see that, but since this was the first thing Violet had said to her since they arrived, she laughed obligingly. Violet stood with arms crossed over her chest, stony-faced. The six Lab Rats and Kaylie were getting a tour of the hotel.

"And your rooms are on the top floor," Jillian said as she pressed the elevator button for 3. "No suite this time, Amy, since your grandmother will probably be going to a nursing facility anyway. The——"

"I don't think she'll do that," Amy said.

"Beg pardon?"

"My grandmother. She'll want to stay with me."

"But Myra said——"

"I'm telling you what my grandmother will want." Amy heard herself sounding too shrill, and toned it down. "She's not a person who lets herself be shuttled around to where she doesn't want to be. And I want to be with her."

Kaylie did not say *Me too*.

Jillian frowned. "I'll check with Myra. Meanwhile, here we are."

The top floor of the hotel was a sprawl of thickly carpeted hallways, open sitting rooms, and at the far end, a glassed solarium in which three veiled Arab women sat at a table playing some sort of board game. In the corridor the Lab Rats passed a man in a turban accompanied by two bodyguards and a woman in Armani carrying a briefcase. Both looked curiously at the group.

Jillian unlocked the first of six doors in a cul-de-sac at the end of a hall, facing one of the pretty sitting areas. "This is your room, Amy and Kaylie. Kaylie, Serena had to guess at your size. Violet, you're in three seventeen, Waverly—"

Kaylie let out a whoop. Both of the double beds were piled with packages marked with their names. The room itself was nice but ordinary for a hotel room, at least from what Amy had seen in magazines and movies. She opened her packages. The contents were exact duplicates of the clothes Serena had chosen for her before, plus a small box from the hotel with toothbrush, comb, and other toiletries.

"Huh," Kaylie said sourly, and Amy turned.

Kaylie's clothes were nowhere near as expensive. Levi's, not jeans from 7 For All Mankind. Tops and a skirt that might have come from Macy's, not Prada. The colors, deep jewel tones, were good for Kaylie's dusky beauty, but Kaylie didn't care.

"'Cause I'm not on the show and you are," Kaylie said. She threw a red sweater onto the floor and stomped into the bathroom, slamming the door.

"Kaylie, you can wear mine!" Amy called.

"Like we're the same size," Kaylie yelled. The shower started.

It was true. Kaylie was taller and bustier. Amy picked up the sweater, folded it, and laid it on the bed.

She didn't want to be here. But unless she stayed at the hospital and watched Gran sleep for the next fourteen hours, there was nowhere else to be. Well, she could sleep, too. Once Kaylie was out of the bathroom Amy would take a shower, crawl into bed, and slide into welcome oblivion.

A knock on the door. Waverly stood there, even her hair clean and shining. Amy smiled. "You look great. All recovered from the tunnel? I want to thank you again for everything you did for—"

"I came to ask about the alliance," Waverly said, unsmiling. Her voice was cool. "I helped you, as you just pointed out. So the next time we're in a scenario, teamed or not, can I count on your help? Instead of you giving it to Violet or Rafe?"

Amy stared at her. "Was it just tit for tat, then? You only

helped save my grandmother's life because you expected something in return?"

"I asked you a question," Waverly said. "I'd like an answer."

It was incredible. Waverly acted as if Amy had never seen her cry, never seen her panic, never heard her choked longing for her own grandmother ("My grandmother was the only person in my entire family who was ever kind to me"). As if this was strictly a business deal.

Amy said, "I promised Violet and Rafe——"

"Who were no help to you in a crisis. Yes or no on your first loyalty, Amy?"

"I can't!"

Waverly's face didn't change. Quietly she closed the bedroom door.

Amy stood listening, but the thick hallway carpet muffled Waverly's footsteps. Misery swamped Amy. She couldn't break her promise to Violet—but didn't she owe Waverly, too? Why did Waverly have to make it seem so cold, such an impersonal deal? And then came a thought that Amy really didn't like. If Waverly had been as warm and all-girlfriend as Violet was—as Violet used to be—would Amy have answered her differently?

Bleakly Amy wondered if she'd ever understood anybody. Including herself.

* * *

The next morning, after a long and refreshing sleep, Amy took a cab to the hospital. When she left, Kaylie had not been in her bed and none of the Lab Rats was around, but the restaurant, lobby, and bellman's stand were thronged with focused-looking people in business attire, absorbed in intense discussions. No one paid her the least attention.

She expected to find Gran in the ICU, but the nursing desk told her that Mrs. Whitcomb had been moved to a geriatric ward; the ICU was now filled with victims of a commuter-plane crash just after midnight. Gran, to Amy's further surprise, was not lying in bed but sitting up in a deep plastic chair of hideous orange, watching TV.

"Gran!"

A newscaster said "—brought under control due to quick and efficient response by municipal police, although in Atlanta and Detroit—"

"How do you feel? Are you OK?"

"—a pointed harbinger of civil unrest due to—"

"Good morning, Amy. Let me just hear the rest of this."

"—major legislative initiative. Tonight the president will address the nation on—"

Amy waited impatiently. When the newscast switched to the plane crash, Gran muted it and turned a bright face to Amy. "It's going to be all right. Remember when I told you this was a flash point? It's galvanized those idiots in Washington and they're going to pass the Emergency Economic Restructure Act. This is radical, Amy, and in time it will—"

"I don't care," Amy said, more harshly than she'd ever spoken to Gran before. "How are *you*?"

"You should care about this legislation." Although her face looked drawn and weary, Gran's blue eyes sparkled. "This is going to save the country. With any luck, anyway. Do you realize how close we were to going up in flames? Yes, of course you do—you almost *did*. Amy, you were wonderful yesterday. You and Rafe and Waverly. Thank you."

"The important thing is that you're all right!"

"Well, I'm a tough old bird, as I heard someone say yesterday. Come here."

Amy crouched beside the orange chair. Gran put a rope-veined hand on her shoulder. "Listen to me, Amy. I've rallied this time, but there will be more like yesterday. Not brought on by a desperate escape from fire, I hope, but just because it's nearly my time. But I had a long talk with a doctor before you got here. My end will almost certainly come like yesterday, a simple stopping of my heart. It won't hurt and I might not even know when it happens. I'm lucky in that such a death is easy, love. I won't say that I'm not nervous about it, but . . . well, I don't want you to get all emotional before it even happens. I want that today you go to your job and carry on with your life."

"No."

"Yes."

"No!"

"Well, I can't force you, Amy, but I plan on spending the entire day watching news, witnessing what I think is going to be a genuine turnaround for this country. Do you know what the pundits are calling the legislation? The 'Raise-Up-Everybody Act'—isn't that wonderful? This is a historical moment. I want to learn everything about it, so don't talk to me while the analysts are on."

The analysts were on endlessly. Gran watched news: devoured it, Amy thought, which was more than she did to the lunch a nurse brought on a tray. Of course, Amy was glad that things were going to get better, if they were (TIMES BE TOUGH, MAN), but why did Gran need to hear it analyzed and debated and dissected and discussed and disagreed with and predicted and disbelieved and ardently believed and doubted and prayed for and illustrated with charts, graphs, numbers?

While Gran watched, Amy checked her cell. Strange that no one had called her. She found that the phone was dead. The charger had burned with the Fairwood Hotel, along with the computer TLN had provided her. She sighed and tried to concentrate on the news analysts.

Only once was Amy's attention fully engaged. A talking head said something about the president's speech being followed by political analyses tonight and by quickly prepared shows about the local protests tomorrow. "Including, strangely enough, one by Taunton Life Network as part of its schlocky teen show *Who Knows People, Baby—You?*"

The second talking head shuddered. "*That's* one I can skip."

"I agree. But at the same hour on CBS—"

Gran looked at Amy. "You know about this?"

"No!"

"Well, maybe you should find out more. Go on, honey, call TLN. Better yet, go to work and stop fidgeting here. You're distracting me."

Amy kissed the top of Gran's head—*tough old bird* didn't even begin to describe her—and escaped the ten-millionth analysis of a speech the president hadn't even made yet.

Back at the hotel, Jillian accosted her. "I wish you'd told me you wanted to go to the hospital!" Jillian's ponytail bobbed aggressively.

"I'm sorry," Amy lied. "But my phone is dead and the charger went in the fire."

"Oh. We'll get you a new phone. Right now everybody else

is at a day spa. TLN's treat. You could have gone, too. Anyway, a van will pick you all up at seven thirty a.m. tomorrow, so be ready. Wear jeans."

"Okay. Jillian, what about this special report on the show about the hotel fire?"

Jillian's voice turned guarded. "What about it?"

"Well, what will it be? How will it fit with any of the scenarios we shot? I don't get it."

"I don't know any more than you do. I guess we'll just have to wait and see."

A phantom sprang into Amy's mind: *a beach ball rolling down a steep slope.* Now, what the hell did that mean?

She had no idea.

The president's speech was exactly what the entire day of newscasts had said it would be. The Lab Rats all piled into Cai's room to watch it, but only Rafe gave the speech his whole attention. The rest watched intermittently. No one had any information on the "special edition" of the show promised for the next night, although everyone had speculations. Amy, sitting on the floor in front of the TV, tried not to look at the pair of Kaylie's panties under Cai's bed.

When the speech was over, Rafe said, "Perfect. It'll work. Despite all the yelling from special interests."

Violet said, "Thank you, Mr. Analyst. Now if you watch all the follow-up talk, you watch it alone. The rest of you, come with me. I found something terrific. Rafe isn't the only one who explores his environment."

Rafe glanced from the screen. "Violet, I told you this room—all our rooms—is probably bugged."

"Which is why we're not staying in this room. Come on!"

To Amy, Violet's voice sounded unpleasantly shrill, but if anyone else noticed, they didn't say anything. All six of them followed her to wherever she was taking them.

# Twenty-seven

IN THE ELEVATOR Violet took a plastic key-card from her bra and stuck it into a slot above the elevator buttons.

"For VIPs only. Which I just promoted us to being."

Cai said, "How did you get that?"

"I have my ways. . . ."

"I'll just bet," Waverly muttered. Violet ignored her.

Because the elevator ascended, Amy expected another roof terrace like the one Rafe had taken her to on top of the Fairwood Hotel. She was both right and wrong. This was a roof terrace, but not like the other. There was a whole other hotel up here. The long, flat roof of the three-story building held an outdoor restaurant at one end, an indoor club and spa at the other, and in between a garden with fantastic landscaping: topiaries shaped like rabbits or sprays of water, flowers so perfect they looked unreal, a small stream with tiny arched bridges and a waterfall splashing over varicolored rocks. The dusk smelled of blooms, of spices, of living water. Faint music drifted from the glass doors of the club. The whole was enclosed by an eight-foot-high concrete wall so that none of it was visible from below, but all was open to the sky.

Violet said, "Your ordinary business guests use the restaurant and bar on the ground floor. This is for security-vetted superguests only, so that everybody important doesn't have to fear being assassinated."

Cai said, "Let's go back down. I don't have any money."

Waverly said, "I got the tab." She gazed around with a distinct pout. Amy thought, *She's upset that she wasn't automatically given a card to this.*

Rafe said, "I'm no gardener but I don't think those flowers are in bloom yet naturally. They've been forced indoors and transplanted here. This one garden must take a huge amount of labor."

"Who cares," Kaylie said. "Let's see what that club is all about."

Violet said, "Except that this isn't where we're going."

They gaped at her. Rafe got it first. "Bugged. Security here will be higher than anyplace else in the hotel."

"Besides, we're underage," Violet said. "Just follow me."

She led them through the twilight toward the waterfall. The night had turned chilly, and no one else walked the garden. The pretty stream spouted from the top of an artificial hill covered with moss and ivy. It cascaded over rocks placed to produce maximum splashing, and then wound between flowerbeds. Violet ducked around the side of the hill and pulled aside a heavy swath of hanging ivy. Amy took a leaf between her fingers. It was plastic, but such a close match to the real ivy on the front of the hill that you had to touch it to tell.

Behind the ivy was a narrow door. Violet slipped in her keycard, pulled the door open, and flipped a switch. Light spilled out. "Hurry!"

The space under the hill was about ten feet square, sloping as the hill sloped, and littered with burlap bags that smelled earthy. Rakes, mops, buckets, trowels, and hoses hung on the walls, plus all sorts of things Amy couldn't identify. Above them, the stream babbled and ran. Low light plus the odors of loam, fertilizer, and water made it seem like a primitive cave beneath a river.

"A maintenance room," Rafe said. "You got that keycard from somebody on the maintenance staff."

"Natch," Violet said. "But that's not the best part. Ta-da!" She reached behind a pile of sacks and produced a bottle. "The very best third-rate Scotch."

"Ugh," Waverly said. "Not for me, thanks." She moved toward the door, fastidiously twitching her skirt away from the burlap sacks.

Amy had been going to say the same thing, although more politely, but something in Waverly's prissy, superior manner suddenly rankled. Just because Waverly came from money, why did that entitle her to think she was so much better than the rest of them? It wasn't like she'd earned the money by being brilliant or successful or anything. She'd just inherited it, or at least she would someday. All the humanity that Waverly had shown in the tunnel was gone again.

"I'll have some," Amy said defiantly to Violet. "Have you got glasses?"

"Of course." Violet produced a stack of plastic cups. To Waverly she said, "At least promise you won't sound the general alarm on us."

"Of course not," she said loftily, made a moue of disgust at the bags of soil, and slipped out the door.

Cai looked uncomfortable. "Tommy shouldn't drink, his doctor said so. I'll take him to his room."

"Are you coming back?" Kaylie demanded.

"I don't think so. I'll just . . . just wait for you downstairs."

Kaylie scowled. Cai and Tommy followed Waverly.

"Anybody else chickening out?" Violet said. "Rafe, you intimidated by being the only guy with this harem?"

"I'm fascinated," Rafe said. "Bring it on."

"Good boy."

Amy, Violet, Kaylie, and Rafe settled themselves onto bags of soil, which were surprisingly comfortable once Amy had wiggled her butt into an indentation. She could feel tension in every muscle of her body, over everything: Gran, the fire, the riots, the president's speech, Cai, money, her entire life. Anything that could ease her knotted neck, shoulders, *brain* seemed all at once infinitely desirable. When she'd worked in the restaurant kitchen, there had been a lot of drinking and drugs. Amy had steered clear of the drugs but once in a while had shared cheap wine with coworkers. It had relaxed her.

But not like this. The Scotch, which Violet poured halfway up the plastic cups, didn't really taste good. However, after just a few long sips she felt her body begin to loosen and her head to feel pleasantly light. She sipped more.

Rafe and Violet were arguing about the coming legislation to improve the economy. "You can't uncollapse the Collapse," Violet said. "We're permanently screwed."

Rafe said, "The legislation won't uncollapse anything. It will take the economy in an entirely new direction that—"

"I don't care," Kaylie said loudly. "Fuck the economy!"

"I think we already did that," Rafe said.

Kaylie turned on him. "You're always so smart! Pretending you know everything and are so much better than the rest of us. You're just like Waverly!"

"Ouch," Rafe said.

Amy said, "Waverly has unexpected depths." She was surprised that her words came out slightly wrong, although they were the words she'd intended. "She helped me with Gran. And with *you*, Rafe."

"For which I will be eternally grateful. But I think that was you. If Waverly had been alone when she saw me unconscious, she'd have left me in that stairwell."

Amy tried to decide if this might be true. Her brain seemed slow. She drank more Scotch, which didn't taste so bad now.

Kaylie said suddenly, "Cai is such a wimp!"

Violet purred, "But so gorgeous."

"He's always afraid of getting in trouble, breaking the rules, doing anything fun!"

Violet said, "And you like the bad boys."

"I'm only with him because—" Kaylie stopped and peered fuzzily at Amy.

Amy said, "You're only with him because you want to be close to the show, in case Myra somehow puts you in it."

"She might! I'd be interesting to watch!"

"I know," Amy said. "But you're fifteen, not legally an adult. And . . . and give me that glass. Gran wouldn't want you to be here, I shouldn't have let—"

"You don't 'let' me do anything—I make my own decisions! Saint Amy. You and Cai belong together. And . . . you know what? You can have him. I'm breaking up with that wimp."

Amy's heart behaved oddly: First it rose up in her chest, then it did a slow somersault, then it landed with a thud. "Bad dismount," she said.

"What?" Violet said.

"Nothing." What had she said? Nothing made sense, especially not Kaylie dumping Cai. If she really was going to.

Amy said, "You'll change your mind."

"Watch me. And you know what—this little party is stupid and lame. I'm leaving." She rose, staggered to the door, and fell. Rafe caught her and set her steadily on her feet. Kaylie twisted in his arms and kissed him deeply and long.

"Uh-oh," Violet said.

Amy felt something else happen in her chest, but she didn't know what. Kaylie was kissing Rafe. He wasn't protesting. Kaylie shouldn't kiss Rafe. Kaylie—

Rafe pushed her gently away. "You're so pretty, Kaylie. And that felt terrific. But you're not the one I want."

Kaylie let out a cry of frustration, yanked open the door, and slammed it behind her.

Violet said, "And then there were three. Amy, your sister has real issues, she does."

"I have to go after her," Amy said. "She won't—" Won't what? Won't break up with Cai, like she promised? No, it wasn't that. . . . Amy's head felt even more floaty than before.

"Kaylie'll be fine," Violet said.

Amy said, "I can't let her worry Gran. But Gran is in the hospital."

"Right," Violet said.

"I'm responsible for Kaylie. And Gran. And everybody."

"And why is that, I wonder?" Violet said.

Amy wasn't sure what she'd said. Her mind fumbled after a thought. She found it. "It goes by body mass."

"What does?" Rafe said.

"The electric jolt from the paint gun," Amy said. But that wasn't it, she couldn't think what she had meant. . . .

Violet reached out and took Amy's glass. "I think you've had enough, One Two Three."

Amy said, "You're not really eighteen, are you? And your name isn't Violet Sanderson."

Violet was still for a long moment, her plastic cup in one hand, Amy's in the other. Finally she said, "Who told you? Myra?"

"Waverly. So it's true?"

"It is."

Rafe looked surprised. Amy felt pleased that she'd actually known something he didn't. She said to Violet, "You're twenty-six."

"Yes."

"And you have a criminal record."

"Very minor. Well, relatively minor. One count of possession and two of shoplifting. I was very broke and very hungry."

"And Myra knows?"

"Of course Myra knows," Violet said impatiently. "There isn't anything that Myra doesn't know about every single one of us, right down to what color panties you wear and what you got in math in the third grade."

"Is this why you've been so weird lately? And why did Myra let you on the show if you're twenty-six?"

"I don't know yet. But I'm sure it will come out eventually. Myra plans way ahead. Meanwhile, I'm getting exposure, and the dance offers are coming in for when this hellish experience ends. Two more scenarios in our contracts. Which I'll bet, Saint Amy, you never read."

Amy ignored this. Violet looked angry. Amy didn't want Violet angry at her. She said, "But you're a real dancer. I know because I fook . . . *took* class with you. You're so good!"

"Oh, Amy," Violet said in a different tone, "you can't stand to be on the outs with anybody, can you? Not even the horrible Waverly. You think that if you just try to get along with people

and do the right thing and work hard, that's all it takes to succeed. The world isn't like that. Grow up!"

"Violet, don't leave, sit back down again——"

"Not a chance. Have fun, kids. But treat her gently, Rafe——
I'd bet next week's salary that she's a virgin. Unlike little sister
Kaylie." Violet went out, slamming the door behind her.

"Everybody slams the door," Amy said wonderingly. "The
hill shook."

Rafe laughed. In the gloom she could see that his eyes
were very bright and very shiny. Small brown eyes . . . A sudden
picture sparked in her mind, so strong that at first she thought
it was a phantom. It was not. Merely Cai's eyes, blue as pieces of
sky, deep as oceans . . .

Was Kaylie really breaking up with Cai?

Rafe said, "I think I'm a little drunk. But not as drunk as
you."

"I want to ask you something."

Rafe tensed. But Amy's thoughts had wandered away
from both him and Cai, even from Violet. "It's something that
I've wondered about for a long time. Why do they watch?"

"Why does who watch what?"

"The people. The show. Us." Her mind fumbled, then found
what she wanted to say. "Most of us on most episodes end up humiliated and embarrassed. When I was like that, all my 'fan' mail

told me what a wimp I was. Then when I wasn't like that, my mail told me I was just faking doing well. Why do they want to see us fail and resent it when we don't? Except for Cai."

"Cai," Rafe said in a different tone. Amy, too absorbed in what she was saying, didn't notice.

"OK, with Cai it's the girls. But for all the rest of us— why do they watch? If I weren't on this sick show, *I* wouldn't watch it."

"You're not in that audience," Rafe said. "You don't want to sneer at people. They do."

"But *why*?"

"Because they're so ground down that it's a little bit of re- lief to laugh at someone worse off than they are."

Amy frowned. "I don't get it."

"I know you don't. You're not the kind of person who would get it. That's why I—shit, I'm sick of explanations!" Rafe grabbed Amy and kissed her.

This wasn't like the previous time he'd attempted to kiss her. This was hard, his lips pressing into hers, and his arms surprisingly strong around her. He wasn't much taller than she was, but his body felt firm and taut against hers, and some- thing stirred in Amy's chest. In her breasts, in her body. Star- tled—for *Rafe?*—and more than a little drunk, Amy pushed him away.

Instantly he released her. In the dim half-light of the maintenance cave his face went bleak. "So," he said.

"Rafe—"

"It's Cai, isn't it?"

She wanted to tell him no, but she wasn't sure that was true. Kaylie was breaking up with Cai. Cai would be free for another relationship. . . . But Rafe's kiss had felt both exciting and sweet. . . . Amy couldn't find words. The eloquence of just a few moments ago seemed to have used up her total supply.

"I—"

"Don't lie to me, Amy. Anything but that. I saw your face when Kaylie said she's dumping Cai. You have a very transparent face." He scowled. "It's like falling in love with Saran Wrap."

*Falling in—*

"And now I see your face again. Don't look so appalled. I won't bother you with my stupid feelings again."

"Rafe—"

But his pride had apparently taken all the beating it was going to. He left the maintenance cave.

*At least he didn't slam the door.*

Amy stood up from her burlap sack. Her legs wobbled under her. With one hand braced against the wall, she groped her way to the door and outside. A light drizzle had started to fall. The gorgeous, meticulously maintained flowers dripped gently as she stumbled down the winding paths, over the miniature bridges, to the elevator that needed no VIP keycard to carry her down. You were only a Very Important Person if you were on your way up.

Myra's cell rang at two a.m. She and two exhausted techs had been working on the hotel-fire footage for sixteen hours straight. By six o'clock tomorrow—no, today—it had to be finished and on its digital way to the affiliate stations for the eight o'clock special show. Myra glanced at her cell, planning to ignore anyone but Taunton.

It was Mark Meyer. He had, fortunately, been on vacation for several days with his appallingly scruffy girlfriend. Away, he couldn't interfere. Myra didn't trust Mark. He was like rain: necessary but unpredictable, and out of her control. She didn't like things she couldn't control, and a part of her suspected that Meyer was capable of deluges, storms, floods. The only thing to do with such phenomena was to keep a close eye on them. She answered the cell.

"Yes, Mark."

"I'm back."

"Good. Did you have a nice vacation?"

He ignored this, as he ignored all personal questions. How had he even acquired a girlfriend?

"I want to know what time tomorrow."

"Tomorrow?" Her mind had gone blank.

"For the scenario," he said impatiently. "Our plane was late—it sat on the tarmac for six fucking hours. That's illegal here but not in Fiji. I just got in and I want to get at least a little sleep. Can we push back the scenario from eight o'clock to eleven? I can do it earlier if you want because everything is set, but I'd rather not."

Tomorrow's scenario. In the rush to get the special-edition show edited, Myra had forgotten all about it. Her first impulse was to cancel the whole thing; next to the ratings gold she had in her editing machine, the planned scenario looked too tame. On the other hand, after tomorrow night the show was sure to finish out the season, and she would need the episode. And it would keep the pesky talent occupied and controlled for the day.

She was a little surprised that Mark hadn't mentioned the TV ads for the upcoming special edition. But if he'd been slogging through airports and waiting on tarmacs, perhaps he hadn't seen the promos. He had called after the riots themselves, to make sure everybody was safe, but Myra had said nothing to him then about the precious footage of the tunnel escape.

"Yes, eleven o'clock is fine. I won't be there but you can handle it."

"Sure." He hung up.

Myra went back to editing. She found a close-up of Waverly's face twisted with fear. "Cut that into the tunnel sequence with the actors."

"But we said the tunnel sequence was only a simulation of—"

"Just do it!"

At least four more hours of work. Myra poured herself another cup of strong coffee.

Mark didn't go straight to bed. He never went to bed without a final check of certain tech, not even when he was so tired he swayed on his feet. Elena lay crumpled across their bed, asleep fifteen seconds after her head struck the pillow. Mark meticulously checked his tech. His sagging eyelids flew open.

"Shit!" he said.

# Twenty-eight

**SATURDAY**

WHEN HER ALARM went off at six thirty, Amy woke with what she supposed—never having had one before—was a hangover. She wanted to be at the hospital when Gran woke. Her head hurt, and her stomach felt queasy. Cautiously she eased herself off the bed, lurched across the dark room, and tripped over one of Kaylie's shoes.

Kaylie lay heavily asleep in the other bed. Here, not with Cai. That would need thinking about, but at the moment thinking wasn't possible. Memory of the events in the maintenance cave made her just as queasy as the hangover. First Kaylie had attacked her, then Violet, then Rafe—why was everyone so mad at her? She hadn't *done* anything.

*No self-pity. Get to Gran. No, wait, Jillian had said a van was coming at seven thirty . . .*

In the bathroom Kaylie had scrawled lipstick across the mirror: YOUR RIDE NOT TILL 10:00. Thoughtful of Kaylie, even though it meant that Amy had to peer at herself through smears of L'Oréal Cherry Red.

A shower, three aspirin, and a cup of coffee helped her physical state, although not as much as she'd hoped. She was just leaving the hotel lobby for the taxi stand when Mark Meyer came in.

"Amy. Where you going?"

"To the hospital to see my grandmother."

"No, you're not. We have a scenario in less than an hour."

"But there was a message from Myra's office that we didn't need to go to the conference room until—"

"I *said* in less than an hour."

He looked terrible. The skin under his eyes, dark and bruised-looking, sagged as if he were twenty years older than his age. His clothes were rumpled and stained, as if he'd been wearing them for days, and he smelled. Amy said, "Are you all right?"

"You can't go to the hospital now."

She said, with great and deliberate emphasis on each word, "I. Am. Going. To. See. My. Grandmother."

Something moved behind his eyes. He glanced at his watch. "OK. I'll drive you. One quick look and back here."

"Mark—"

"Come on!" He strode out the door, elbowing past a group of Asian businessmen who eyed him with distaste.

In his Porsche he said nothing, driving expertly and too fast over the long causeway off the island. At the hospital he went with her to Gran's floor, sank into a plastic chair near the nurse's station, and pulled a tablet from his pocket. "I'll wait here."

"Mark," Amy said firmly, and over the throbbing in her head, "I'm not going back with you. I'm staying here today with my grandmother."

"No, you're not," Mark said, not looking up from his tablet. "You have a contract, and the scenario is brief. But go see how she is."

Gran was asleep. A young nurse was adding something to her IV. She looked questioningly at Amy.

"I'm Amy Kent, Mrs. Whitcomb's granddaughter and her next-of-kin. Is she—"

"You're the girl from the TV show! *Who—You!*"

Amy scowled. The nurse didn't notice. "I really love that show, and you're great on it!" All at once she turned professional. "Mrs. Whitcomb is doing really well. She had a very restful night. The doctor will be here in a few minutes and you can talk to him. But can you just give me a hint what this special edition of the show is about tonight?"

Amy was saved from answering by the appearance of the doctor, a small harassed Indian who didn't recognize Amy. He said that Gran was "progressing with great magnificence," and Amy immediately fell in love with him. Or at least with his musical accent and charming way of reassuring her. "She will sleep a few more hours, we will have a meeting with the cardiologist and some case worker, and all will be decided. Perhaps your grandmother will go to nursing, perhaps to hospice, perhaps stay here a time longer. All will be decided."

"What time is the meeting?"

"Three o'clock."

"I want to be here."

"Yes, certainly." He vanished out the door, white coat flapping behind him.

Amy kissed Gran, who didn't stir. Certainly Gran looked better: good color, steady heartbeat on the pinging monitor. Amy could do Mark's "brief" scenario and be back in plenty of time.

She lingered a few moments longer, studying the numbers on various monitor screens, wishing she knew what they all meant. Rafe would probably know. Rafe would be at the scenario, and Violet, and Cai. Oh, joy. But there was no help for it, not really. "Nursing" or "hospice" or "stay here a time longer." They all depended on the medical benefits attached to Amy's job. She went back to Mark Meyer.

On the drive back he was even ruder than usual, ignoring her attempts at conversation, until she just gave up. At every traffic light his frown deepened. But when they waited in line for valet parking, Mark turned to her.

"Listen, Amy, I'm going to tell you something."

"OK," she said warily.

"I'm telling you this because you're the only girl who hasn't hit on me in an attempt to get advance knowledge about my tech. As if." Mark drummed his fingers on the steering wheel. "All I'm going to say is this: 'Think twice what is real.'"

Amy stared at him. But he had turned away, getting out of the car and handing the keys to the valet.

The Lab Rats were driven to yet another unmarked brick building. There was little talking in the van. After last night, Amy felt embarrassed to look at Rafe, at Violet, even at Cai. Waverly sat wrapped in a disdain so thick that you could practically see it. Amy wedged herself in the first seat beside Tommy, who drummed his fingers nervously on his knee for the entire ride. Jillian made a few sprightly attempts at general conversation, which met with such stony silence that she gave up.

Another sparsely furnished waiting room. Jillian said, "This is another one-by-one scenario. Amy, you're first again, so that the van can take you back to the hospital."

"Thanks," Amy said, with what she knew was not enough gratitude. Her head hurt, and she'd had no breakfast because the thought of food was still nauseating.

Jillian led her down a corridor to a plain metal door, unlocked it, and smiled. "Good luck."

"Thanks," Amy repeated, again without enthusiasm.

The room beyond the door was a blank cube: white walls, ceiling, floor of rough stucco. Its small size reminded her unpleasantly of the maintenance cave the night before. The only object was a white birch tree growing incongruously from a hole in the floor, and in the top branches of the tree, a whimpering puppy.

Amy blinked. Hadn't she already done this one—fake dog in a tree? Before she'd even known she was in a scenario. What the—

A tiny door opened on the wall across from the tree, an opening no more than six inches high. Three spiders crawled out.

Amy gasped. She wasn't more than ordinarily afraid of spiders—it was rats that terrified her—but these spiders were really repulsive, and *huge*. Each hairy dark-brown body looked the size of her palm and just as tall, with eight legs extending out another three or four inches. Each leg bristled with hair. The spiders began to crawl.

She could hear the faint click-click-click of small claws on the white floor, a horrifying sound.

Amy backed away from the crawling spiders. They looked like tarantulas—but what did she know about spiders? They were moving steadily across the floor, but not toward her. Something seemed to draw them steadily toward the tree.

In the high branches the puppy whimpered.

For just a moment vertigo swept through Amy, sagging her against the wall. But then sense returned. These spiders weren't real. Mark Meyer had just told her as much: "*Think twice what is real.*" And not even Myra would subject her lab rats to venomous spiders on national television. If Amy kicked one of these spiders, her foot would go right through it.

She moved to the closest one—then hesitated. The Miu Miu sandal exposed her bare toes. If she was wrong—

She wasn't wrong. These were more of Mark's clever holograms. She raised her foot to stomp on the spider.

It reared back, raised its front legs into the air, and *hissed*.

Amy jumped back. Then she felt ridiculous—Mark was a tech genius, but so what—followed by feeling furious. He was a tech genius and he used that formidable talent to terrorize people more gullible than she. Tommy, for instance—

Fury took her, aided by exhaustion and her hangover. Amy swooped down to grab at Mark's collection of pixels and laser light. Her hand closed on a hard furry body.

She screamed and threw the spider away from her. It hit the opposite wall and slid lightly down, leaving black hairs on her skin that almost immediately began to itch. Meanwhile, the other two spiders had reached the tree and begun to climb it.

*Real.* Oh, the bastards! But Mark had said—

*Think twice.*

Cautiously, staying as far away as possible from the spider on the floor, Amy took her cell phone from her pocket. She approached the tree. So did the third spider; evidently the tree had something in it or on it that attracted spiders. Amy got within a few feet of the branches, took careful aim, and tossed her cell phone at the puppy. If she knocked it free, she could dart in and grab it before the spiders change course. But she didn't think she'd have to.

The cell phone went right through the puppy.

Amy retrieved her phone from where it had hit the floor and went back to the door. She could just imagine the stupid voting choices for this scenario: Who rescued the puppy? Who just stood and screamed? Who stomped on the spiders? That would be one or more of the boys, whoever was wearing boots and didn't have arachnophobia. Not Violet or Waverly in their high heels.

All at once the whole thing bored Amy. These stupid scenarios, these endless fake choices . . . She was sick of *Who—You*. One more scenario after this and her season's contract was done. With any luck, the show would then be canceled. The ratings had been sagging steadily.

She waited for the door to open, watching the real spiders climb the real tree toward the fake dog.

Gran was awake and alert. Not, however, her usual self.

Amy had turned on the noon news, which was full of excited men and women debating the passage of the Emergency Economic Restructure Act. But Gran merely waved her hand—such a thin hand, blue-lined and brown-dotted as a road map—at the television. "Turn it off."

"Off?"

"Yes. Come here, Carolyn."

*Carolyn. Her mother's name.*

Startled and disturbed, Amy took the chair next to the hospital bed. Gran's eyes seemed too bright, too big, in their sunken sockets. But she smiled broadly, and her voice sounded strong. "Remember when you were three, Carolyn? We took you to the zoo, along with the neighbor girl, Elizabeth. And somehow Elizabeth just slipped away from your father. Just skipped off when he took his eyes off her. We both rushed around frantically, me carrying you, and you kept saying with such satisfaction, 'Maybe the *lions* ate her. Maybe the *tigers* ate her.' It turns out you didn't like Elizabeth."

Amy's hand tightened on her grandmother's. It had been Kaylie that had said that at the zoo, when Amy got lost.

"And remember when you painted your sister's Barbie doll green and said it was an alien? You even gave it some unpronounceable name, like the ones in those dreadful alien-invasion movies."

Amy had never had a Barbie doll. Maybe her mother had, or maybe Gran was wandering even farther back in time to her own childhood. For the next hour Gran told stories that jumbled Carolyn, Kaylie, Amy, and some other names—Eddie, Christy—that Amy vaguely remembered as being cousins of either her mother or grandmother. Maybe. The stories grew more animated and more chaotic, and Gran's hand tightened on Amy's, until abruptly she fell asleep.

"Nurse!" Amy rain into the hall. "Something's wrong!"

The nurse came in, examined Gran, listened to Amy's rushed account. Then she said gently, "You have to expect this, my dear, with this sort of illness. But she's not in any pain, and you say she didn't seem distressed."

"No, she seemed happy to talk like that!"

"She probably is. But I'm going to ask the doctor for something to make sure she sleeps right after dinner and on through the night, to conserve her strength a bit. She might wake again this afternoon, though, if you want to stay."

Amy stayed. At the 3:00 meeting the cardiologist, case worker, and Indian doctor decided that Gran should stay for now in the hospital. Gran did wake, to tell a few more stories with the same animated relish, the same confusion of time and people. She seemed perfectly content. After she had her sleeping pill, Amy took a cab to the hotel.

She was glad that Gran seemed to feel such pleasure. She was also glad there was no chance that Gran would see the "special edition" tonight of *Who—You*. Whatever stupid thing it was that Myra had put together about the riots and the hotel fire, at least Gran wouldn't have to go through it again.

# Twenty-nine

THEY GATHERED IN Cai's room to watch the show: Cai, Kaylie, Tommy, Rafe, Violet, Amy, even Waverly. The good thing was that even though the old camaraderie was gone, so was the extreme awkwardness of the morning in the van. The reason was the spider scenario, in which all of them had realized that the spiders were real and the puppy was not. Nearly everyone had thrown something at the hologram.

"Let Myra make 'voting choices' out of *that*!" Rafe said. He wouldn't look directly at Amy, but otherwise he seemed himself. "I threw my watch at the fake dog."

"My cell," Waverly said.

"Me too," Amy said.

"My shoe." Violet.

"My boot," Cai said. "I was hoping to knock it into my arms. Tommy, what did you throw?"

"Nothing," Tommy said. "Did you see those spiders? Beauties!"

They all stared at him. Tommy rushed on, his words tumbling over themselves. "*Theraphosidae.* I don't remember the other word right now. They make silk for their burrows, and they can climb trees, and the girls make two thousand eggs in a baby sac! And they've been around at least sixteen million years. That's a very long time!"

Cai managed to speak first. "It really is. Tommy, how do you happen to know so much about spiders?"

"Sam let me have a book. With pictures. And there were spiders in the Insitution, although not *Theraphosidae.* I always want one for a pet, but they cost a very lot."

"Tommy," Violet said, "weren't you afraid of the spiders?"

"Oh, no. They were defanged. I looked real close. Anyway, a *Theraphosida* bite won't really hurt you, no more than a wasp."

Violet laughed and shook her head. Amy held out her hand. "Why have I got this red itch? It didn't bite me, you're right about that."

"That kind of spider throws little tiny hairs at you if you threaten it. See, I've got itching too. It will go away by tomorrow."

Tommy burbled on, bouncing up and down on the edge of Cai's bed, while Amy tried to sort out her thoughts. Mentally challenged, but he had learned all this about something he genuinely cared about. *"The Institution."* Was that why Tommy was on a show he obviously hated—because his uncle had told him that was the only way out of some badly run and spider-infested institution? Tommy had refused to tell Amy about his uncle when she'd asked him before, but in his present excitement he'd let it slip. Did Myra know? What could be done about it?

"Sshhhh," Kaylie finally said, "the show's starting." She flicked the remote to turn up the sound, then snuggled close to Cai. Evidently she had reconsidered dumping him. For now, anyway.

The atonal, vaguely menacing music came up under the show's title but the usual emcees were absent, replaced by an older man with moussed hair, expensive suit, and the solemn look of someone being sworn in to office. None of the Lab Rats had ever seen him before. He intoned, "Any tragedy produces heroes, cowards, bystanders, and innocent victims. The recent riots in our city are no exception. Some people behaved with that outstanding and glorious concern for others that we call heroism, even at the risk of their own lives. This show has always been dedicated to the examination of human behavior—"

Violet snorted.

"—including what the great statesman Benjamin Disraeli called the legacy of heroes: 'The memory of a great name and the inheritance of a great example.'"

"Oh, sure," Rafe said. "Us and Ben Disraeli, best buddies."

"Our producers deliberated long and hard about what you are about to see," the announcer continued. "We decided—"

"Like he's part of the production team," Cai said.

"—after much soul-searching, to air this episode of *Who Knows People, Baby—You?* We do so *not* to trivialize what happened at the Fairwood Hotel, but to illuminate it. And perhaps along the way, we can all learn something from what happened, and from the heroes it produced. TLN is fortunate to have had cameras positioned to capture the stirring acts of courage, determination, and love that you are about to witness. To begin, tonight you must make your voting choices within the next five minutes, before the—"

Amy gasped, "They're going to vote on people's *deaths*?"

Rafe said, "As long as it isn't one of ours. Although that might have made an even better show."

Waverly leaned forward, staring at the television. Abruptly Violet rose and stalked out of the room. Amy said, "Violet—" but Violet kept going, her long black hair swinging behind her.

Tommy said, "What's wrong with Violet?"

Cai said, "We'll ask later, Tommy. We need to see this."

None of others so much as twitched in their seats, although Amy felt her stomach tighten until it hurt. This show was so ghoulish, so outrageous, so insensitive. . . . And she would be a part of it.

Two lists flashed on the screen, one with the faces and names of the six Lab Rats, one with voting choices topped with a large red WHO:

1. Tried to save someone else—and succeeded!
2. Tried to save someone else—and was rescued instead!
3. Escaped the building easily!
4. Escaped the building with difficulty!
5. Was never in any danger!

Amy said, "I cannot believe they're doing this. Turning violence and death into off-track betting."

Rafe said, "There'll be a huge backlash."

Cai said, "But by that time they'll have the ratings."

Rafe held up his tablet. "I think they already do, according to the blogosphere, anyway."

"Sshhh," Waverly said.

Five minutes of the voting grid, intercut with exterior

shots of the hotel at various hours of the day and night. The normal street traffic, the arriving guests, the unloading of luggage somehow ratcheted up the tension: None of these people knew what would happen to them this night.

The man's deep voice said, "Voting is now over," and the screen exploded into sound and motion. Protestors thronged the streets, shouting and waving placards. Cars were overturned and set on fire. Cops clubbed protestors and released canisters of tear gas, which sent a bunch of people fleeing inside the hotel. Amy had seen this footage before on various news channels, but she couldn't look away. A woman was clubbed by a policeman, fell, and was hauled away in cuffs. Someone near her pulled out a gun and shot the cop.

Rafe said quietly, "That was what really did it. That changed the protest into a blood battle. The start of what could have been a real revolution."

*I was still asleep upstairs*, Amy thought. *If Gran hadn't called out over and over—*

The picture changed to low-resolution, black-and-white images inside the hotel. Rafe said, "Security-camera film—I wonder what those copies cost Myra?" No one answered. The film showed people pouring out of their rooms, jamming the elevators and stairwells. The security tapes had no sound, but TLN had supplied a soundtrack of screams, shouts, alarms.

Fires broke out, although it was impossible to say who had set them.

The picture, still black-and-white, changed to what Amy recognized as the first-floor bar, although she had never gone inside it. Gunfire and shouts sounded in the lobby and everyone looked startled—evidently this film had been shot before the previous segment. A sudden enlargement zoomed in on one table of three.

Kaylie said, "There I am!"

"In the bar?" Amy blurted. Like that mattered now!

Kaylie gave her sister a tolerant look. "Everybody has fake ID, sis."

"I don't," Tommy said, but probably he didn't need it. He and Cai looked older than they were. Or maybe Kaylie had bribed the bartender, or Myra had for better footage over time, or—who knew? Nothing was as it seemed.

Tommy said, "I didn't like that restaurant."

"Well," Kaylie retorted, "you didn't have to come with us."

Cai said, shockingly, "Shut up, Kaylie." Kaylie looked startled.

The camera pulled back for a long shot as protestors poured into the bar. People started screaming. But these protestors, evidently the milder Times Be Tough Man group, just waved everybody out. That led to a stampede across the lobby, which reminded Amy sickeningly of the anti-Pylon protests. But she didn't see anyone trampled.

Again the image zoomed in on Cai, Kaylie, and Tommy. Cai held Kaylie's arm, and he and Tommy formed a bulwark around her. The three of them made for a side corridor off the lobby, leading to the gift shop and rest rooms. A fire door marked DO NOT OPEN: ALARM WILL SOUND gave them access to an alley, and if an alarm sounded, it became part of the manufactured soundtrack.

Amy thought: *Escaped the building easily.* Immediately she hated herself.

The picture switched to Rafe. He, too, was outside the building, but he was fighting his way toward it. Small and quick, he ducked through the screaming crowd, until he joined a group of rioters armed with bats and guns and was swept into the lobby.

Kaylie said, "You're going *inside!*"

So Rafe had not told anyone else what had happened that night. Apparently, neither had Waverly. This would all be new to Kaylie, to Cai, to Tommy. Amy hoped that her sister would shut up now. Amy had no hope that Cai, despite his one reprimand to Kaylie, could actually make her stay quiet. Cai didn't have that much strength of personality.

Rafe fought his way across the lobby. The elevators had stopped working and stood open. The soundtrack softened long enough to hear the elevators' computerized voice say, "The elevators are inoperative during a fire. Use the stairs—"

Rafe did. He darted into a stairwell and began climbing. Several floors up, a group of protestors flung themselves into the stairwell from above. One of them pointed a gun at Rafe.

The picture changed to Waverly's bedroom. She leapt out of bed, dressed in a silk nightgown that showed off her beautiful breasts and tiny waist.

She said bitterly, "They told us there would be no filming inside our bedrooms."

"Surprise," Cai said, and Amy realized it might be the first sarcastic thing she had ever heard him say.

Waverly yanked a satin robe over her nightgown and dashed to the door. In the hallway she pounded on all six Lab Rats' doors, yelling, "Get up! Fire! Get up get up get up!"

*She might dislike us all*, Amy thought, *but she didn't think only of herself*. But, then, Amy had already learned that Waverly was more complex than she had first believed.

None of the doors opened—where was Violet?

On-screen, smoke drifted down the hallway—just wisps, but a sprinkler came on in dramatic close-up. Waverly went back into her room. The camera switched to Amy, getting drenched in bed by another sprinkler. Gray smoke poured from vents. Gran called, "Amy! Amy!"

So the wiring in the bedroom had had sound, too. Amy

thought of all that Myra must have heard, all that Amy had believed was private.

The on-screen Amy rushed into Gran's room, which was much less smoky. Gran cried, "It's a fire! Get out!"

"I—"

"Didn't you hear the alarm? Get out!" Gran lay collapsed sideways on the bed and on top of the duvet as if she'd tried to get up and could not.

It was terrible to relive all this, knowing what was coming, unable to change any of it. Rafe glanced over at her, but Amy kept her gaze on the television.

On-screen, Amy cried, "I'm not leaving you!" and rushed to the window. "It's not just a fire. Those are protestors, and SWAT teams. I think the anti-Pylon people have seized the building."

"And set it on fire?"

"I don't know. Most people seem to be out. How long ago did the alarm start?"

"About ten minutes. Maybe fifteen. I tried . . . I tried to . . ." Gran's face crumpled.

"I know you did," Amy said. She ran into the main room of the suite and put her hand at the bottom of the door, then slowly opened it. "Hey! Anybody here!"

Waverly's door opened. Now she wore combat boots with

her satin robe. "I just woke up, I took two sleeping pills, I don't usually but yesterday—There's a fire!"

"And I think the building's been taken by protestors. We have to get out." Both of them left the hallway, and the camera image switched.

Waverly said, "Protestors? Then come on!"

"I can't leave my grandmother here!"

Amy darted into the bedroom. Gran said, "I told you to leave. Don't worry about me. Don't you think I know how close I am already to the end? Amy, do as I say!"

Amy tried to lift Gran, who screamed in pain. "I'm sorry, Gran, I'm sorry! But I have to carry you—"

"You can't. The elevators won't work in a fire, either. I told you to go and I meant it."

"No!"

Amy turned. Waverly pushed a room-service cart into the bedroom, laden with dishes of half-eaten food: steak, salad, juice. Waverly sent it all crashing to the floor. "I didn't feel like seeing anybody for dinner last night. Come on, let's get her onto this. . . . Come on!"

The two girls lifted Gran on top of the service cart, and the camera image shifted to Violet.

It was again a black-and-white security-camera image. Violet, dressed in a hotel terry-cloth robe with a towel wrapped around her head, emerged into a corridor. A close-up of the door behind her showed its sign: LADIES' SAUNA. Sweat filmed Violet's face. She looked wildly around her, then pulled her cell from her robe pocket.

Amy had an inane thought: Did steam and high temperatures hurt cell phones? Why would Violet have hers in the sauna?

As she listened to her phone, Violet's mouth made a round wet O. She ran down the corridor.

Rafe frowned. He said to no one in particular, "She's going the wrong way. Into the fighting."

Violet pushed through a set of double doors and into a group of rioters. One had a blowtorch.

Another camera switch: back to Rafe in the stairwell, facing the rioter's gun. He threw his hands over his head and began talking very fast, although the film was without words. The rioter made a disgusted face, lowered his gun, and pushed past Rafe.

Kaylie said, "What did you say to him?"

Rafe didn't answer her. On-screen, the rest of the rioters pushed past Rafe on the stairwell. The last one swung his baseball bat and caught Rafe on the side of the head. He fell forward, blood streaming from his head, and lay still.

The real-life Rafe chewed on his bottom lip hard enough to pierce it.

No one spoke for most of the rest of the broadcast. Amy watched herself make the phone call to 911 that told her there was a safe room on the sixth floor, and receive the call from Violet that said there wasn't. She watched herself and Waverly discover Rafe and heard Waverly say, "He was coming *up*. Trying to get to you." She heard herself say, "We're going to take them both with us."

Back to Violet, who had to fight and claw her way to safety, but eventually made it. *Escaped the building with difficulty.*

For the rest of the broadcast the camera stayed on Amy, Waverly, and Rafe. Amy was careful not to look at the other girl when the on-screen Waverly started to cry and said, "Amy, I don't want to die!" But when the camera caught Waverly kicking the linen-door lock open with her combat boots, Amy drew a breath of relief. There would be no cameras in the linen cellar, the freight elevator, or the tunnel. It was over.

Except that it wasn't.

The image got much blurrier, but it was still in color. Everyone was seen from the back, without close-ups, as the girls carried Gran and Rafe to safety. Waverly said, "That's not us!"

Rafe said, "I think it's actors. This is a simulation of what happened."

Amy said, "*The bastards.*"

It got worse. The simulation put rats in the tunnel, where there had been no rats. Pipes overhead dripped thick

disgusting liquid onto them, where there had been no dripping. Worst of all, at one point Amy stopped dragging Rafe,
forcing Waverly to stop pushing the cart. The blurry Amy said,
"If I don't make it and you do, tell Rafe I was in love with him."

"What!" Amy exploded. Tears of pure fury sprang to her
eyes. "I never said that!"

Kaylie said uncertainly, "It was your voice . . ."

Rafe said, "Voice sequencer. The software takes individual
words you said in another context and joins them together to
make sentences you never said." He didn't look at Amy.

Amy said, "Can I sue? I will sue!"

A moment later she realized that this might hurt Rafe's
feelings. Suing TLN over the statement that she loved him—
didn't that imply he was too horrible to love? That wasn't what
she meant at all. But the whole thing was so cheesy, so melo-
dramatically stupid, even for television.

"Sshhh," Kaylie said. Even though now there was no
sound except the fake dripping of the fake pipe liquid.

The sequence ended with the rickety, cobwebby stairs
up to the alley off Fenton Street. Now the image was not
only blurry but bobbing up and down: shot with somebody's
cell phone, maybe. Waverly, at the top of the stairs, cried,
"They're down there!" People lifted Gran and Rafe from the
tunnel and Amy, in her filthy pajamas, followed. The screen
went black.

Long portentous moment, and then the soundtrack burst into cheering. What cheering? It didn't matter. The announcer in the dark suit reappeared, saying, "Acts of courage, acts of heroism, acts of love. In that terrible night, three brave survivors. Amy's grandmother and Rafe have both recovered completely. And all six of our participants will be back next week to test what *you* know about people, baby!"

The cheering rose in volume. A voice-over, barely audible over the din and speaking as quickly as the disclaimers in medication commercials, said that some parts of the preceding broadcast were re-creations. Amy had to strain to hear it. The list appeared on the screen, this time completed so voters could see how they'd done:

AMY: Tried to save someone else—and succeeded!

CAI: Escaped the building easily!

WAVERLY: Tried to save someone else—and succeeded!

RAFE: Tried to save someone else—and was rescued instead!

TOMMY: Escaped the building easily!

VIOLET: Escaped the building with difficulty!

Tommy seized the remote and turned off the TV. "I don't like that show."

Cai said, "No. None of us do. Rafe, have you got anything on the Internet?"

Rafe had been working his cell nonstop. Without looking up, he said, "Somebody at TLN 'leaked' response numbers. Higher than any other show this month, including the legitimate news specials on the riots. A lot of outraged posts about the whole thing, but outrage doesn't condense easily into numbers. Oh, and——" He stopped.

"And what?" Kaylie said.

"One more burn victim from the riot just died in the hospital."

No one said anything. Amy got up and stumbled from the room, back to her own. Sickened, she only wanted to never again see anyone connected in any way with Taunton Life Network.

# Thirty

BY THE NEXT morning, the death threats had appeared.

Amy would not have known this if Cai hadn't called her. She stared at the ID. It was six thirty in the morning—why would Cai be calling her unless something had happened to Kaylie?

"Cai! What's wrong?"

"Have you seen your e-mail? On the show site?"

"No, of course not, I just got up to get ready to go to the hospital and—why?"

"Take a look. Jillian just called me. Myra doesn't want anyone to leave our floor of the hotel, not even to go to the restaurant. We're supposed to order meals from room service."

"I'm going to the hospital."

"Just look at the e-mail first, OK?"

As soon as she clicked off, her cell rang again. Jillian. "Amy, I'm calling everyone. There are some threats being made against all of you connected with the show, so please don't leave your floor until you hear from us."

"I'm going to the hospital to see Gran!"

"That's not a good idea," Jillian said. "Really. The FBI will be here very soon."

The FBI?

Amy brought up MAIL on the cell. She had more than five thousand, automatically forwarded from the show's website. Quickly she read a handful:

Who do you think you are, turning other people's deaths into so-called entertainment? You're a fucking bitch!

I used to like you on WKPB-Y, but not now. You should not do that. People died or got burnt in those riots. You have no heart.

You all deserve to die, you exploitative fuckers, and I intend to see that you do.

Amy groaned. If the FBI was involved, somebody was taking this very seriously. But she was still going to the hospital.

Quickly she brushed her teeth, threw cold water on her face, and tossed on clothes. Outside her door stood a man the size of a small building. Amy stifled a scream.

"Sorry to scare you, Miss Kent. I'm Ethan, your bodyguard."

"My what?"

"Bodyguard," he said patiently. Bald and heavy-jowled, he had a face like a bulldog. "From TLN. I stay with you from now on."

Amy drew herself up straight, trying to look taller than five-foot-two. "I'm going to the hospital to see my grandmother."

"Yes, ma'am. And I'm going with you."

"But Jillian said—"

"I don't know who Jillian is. Ms. Townsend sent me."

Amy glanced down the row of closed bedroom doors. No one else had a bodyguard. Evidently Myra decided that everyone else would stay in the hotel. If Amy left now, she might avoid the whole FBI thing—another plus.

"OK, let's go, Mr.—"

"Ethan."

He kept close to her in the deserted lobby, sat beside her in the cab, trailed her watchfully in the hospital. She could not get him to stop calling her "ma'am." At Gran's room he waited respectfully outside the door, and Amy decided she liked him.

Gran was awake, and fully herself. She didn't confuse Amy with her mother, and she wanted to watch the news. "That's good," she said of the progress of the "Raise-Up-Everybody Act," which the president was ramming through Congress. "It'll cost him reelection, but it'll save the economy. The opposition knows that and they'll castigate him until it all succeeds, and then they'll take credit for it themselves."

"Does it always work like that, Gran?" Amy asked. She was thinking of the show, not the country.

"Always. Some try to do the right thing, some try to do the best thing for themselves, and most of us just muddle through, not sure what we've done until we see the consequences. Sshhh—I want to hear this part."

Amy didn't particularly want to hear that part. Of course she was glad that the economy would improve (if Gran was right), but the details seemed confusing. Well, wasn't that what Gran had just said? "Most of us just muddle through."

Midmorning, Kaylie turned up. "Hey, Amy. Is Gran asleep?"

"Yes. How did you get out of the hotel?"

Kaylie scowled. "Why wouldn't I be able to get out? I'm not on the show, remember? Nobody's sending *me* death threats."

"Is everybody else getting them?"

"Yes. And the show's ratings went through the roof, and Myra is giving you all a huge bonus so you won't quit, and it's all just great."

"Uh-huh. Did you break up with Cai?"

"No. And I want your advice."

Amy blinked. Kaylie never wanted her advice. She said cautiously, "About what?"

"Mark Meyer. He's not so old, you know? And he's sort of cute. If I hit on him, would it improve my chances of getting on the show?"

Amy put her head in her hands. "No. That's been tried. Kaylie, don't you ever want to earn anything for yourself, without using some guy to get it for you?"

"It's been tried? Really? Did you try it?"

"*No.* But Mark told me Waverly tried to seduce him for information, and I saw Violet come on to him, and it just made him dislike them."

"Oh. Thanks for the info. I—hey, Gran!"

"Kayla. Hello, honey."

For the next hour Kaylie devoted herself to Gran. She made herself Kaylie-at-her-most-magnetic, telling funny stories and asking questions and listening to Gran's answers, even when they wandered a bit. When Gran said she was cold, Kaylie ran to get another blanket, and in the way that Kaylie pulled it up to Gran's chin, Amy saw genuine tenderness. Kaylie was not performing. In her own way, she did care about Gran, even if this turned out to be her only visit. Which Amy suspected it might be.

But Kaylie was not Gran's only visitor. In the afternoon, to Amy's surprise, Rafe walked into the room.

"Hello, Mrs. Whitcomb. Amy."

Gran's eyes brightened. Amy didn't meet Rafe's gaze. He sat down beside Gran and immediately they plunged into a discussion of the economic package. Rafe had all the interest in details that Amy lacked. The discussion went on until Gran tired too much.

"Rafe——" Amy said, her first word in half an hour.

"Yeah, I've got to be going. Wonderful to see you, Mrs. Whitcomb."

"Come anytime."

"Amy, can I see you in the hall for a minute?"

In the corridor, between a rolling cart filled with cleaning equipment and an empty wheelchair, Rafe handed her a cell. "Here, you need this. You can't just be out of touch with the world in here."

"But——is this yours?"

"My old one. Jillian gave me a new one this morning. She

doesn't know that this one actually came through the fire."

"Rafe—did you come all the way down here just to give me a cell?"

He didn't answer, avoiding her gaze and saying instead. "Don't reply to your e-mail. In fact, don't even look at it."

"I already did. Jillian gave me a phone last night. Kaylie said everybody's getting death threats."

"Yeah. We're under more security than the Oval Office."

"Then how did you get out and come here?"

Finally Rafe looked at her. He grinned. "Security's focused on keeping intruders out, not us. I just slipped out through the kitchen and hitched here."

All at once Amy wanted to kiss him. Astonished at herself, she wondered why: Was it just gratitude for his thoughtfulness, admiration for his brains, what? Rafe didn't seem to notice anything. He said, "Well, bye," and loped down the hall.

*Most of us just muddle through.*

Amy went back into Gran's room. Gran was asleep again. Only she didn't wake up; she had slipped into a coma.

This, the doctors said, was probably the final coma, and it would all be over in a few more days. Gran looked peacefully asleep. Kaylie came each day to bring Amy fresh clothes, and at night the nurses wheeled in a cot for her. Time felt suspended.

Amy watched TV, but not *Who—You*. The first time she turned it on, she saw that it was the scenario with the real spiders and fake puppy, and suddenly she didn't care who had done what. She clicked off the TV before she saw anyone's responses.

Violet never answered her cell, which both surprised and hurt Amy. Mostly Amy watched TV. Now that Gran was no longer able to care about the Raise-Up-Everybody package of laws, Amy concentrated on them until she finally understood what the laws were supposed to do and how they would radically restructure the American economy. On her cell she played anonymous online chess, a lot of chess, with strangers who had no idea who she was. Daily she checked the TLN website. The death threats fell off as the loonies turned their attention elsewhere, but the outrage over the hotel-fire show didn't subside. Nonetheless, TLN withdrew Ethan from the hospital door. And after each airing of the show, the ratings sagged more. Viewers could send in comments, and Amy was always surprised at how many did: Didn't these people have anything better to do?

Boring.

Really lame. Who cares if a pretend dog gets rescued?

**The Frustration Box thing was just stupid. I'm done
watching.**

**Give us something REAL, like the riot where that girl
takes her clothes off or, even better, the hotel fire.
More like that!**

Amy stared a long time at that last comment.

There were other, gentler ones, some even positive, but
these were in the minority. Eventually she gave up reading
any of them. Violet did not call her. And the ratings continued to sag.

Then, on the last afternoon of Gran's life, Waverly came
to see Amy, and Amy realized that nothing was close to being
over.

# Thirty-one

**THURSDAY AND ON**

WAVERLY WORE D&G capris, a black silk top slashed into strategic ribbons, sandals studded with more rivets than a Boeing 747, and a sulky expression. Amy looked at the clothes and realized it must be summery outside. She looked at the expression and said, "What's wrong?"

"I'm quitting the show." Waverly tossed her purse, a cute clutch, on a plastic chair. "I wanted to tell you because, well, we went through a lot together."

"Oh." Waverly didn't exactly look vulnerable—Amy had seen her that way only once, under extreme circumstances—but she did look more open than usual.

Waverly said, "I'll probably never see you again, Amy. I

mean, let's not kid ourselves—we don't exactly move in the same circles. But you're not a bitch like Violet or a total opportunist like Kaylie, so I want to tell you why I'm leaving and give you some friendly advice."

This speech struck Amy as condescending in so many different ways that she didn't know where to begin to answer it. However, Waverly evidently didn't expect an answer.

"The show is finished. Unless Myra comes up with something really spectacular, it will be canceled after this season. I—"

"How do you know that?"

"I know. I told you, my father has connections. I made a huge mistake thinking that *Who—You* would be an attention-getting way to launch my TV career. It's the wrong kind of attention. I'm marked now with the general sleaze of the show, and it will take me a long time of different exposure to overcome that. Fortunately, Daddy is willing to help, which I should have let him do in the first place. I had this stupid idea that I wanted to do it all on my own."

"Maybe it wasn't such a stupid—"

"Yes, it was. I'm here to tell you that you should get out, too. Get a lawyer to break your contract, which is what I'm doing. You'll have to forfeit that last big bonus, of course. But you'll avoid all the bad publicity coming over the whole FBI thing."

"What bad publicity? What FBI thing? You mean the death threats?"

Waverly retrieved her purse and poked around in it for a lipstick. "Oh, Amy, you have been out of touch, haven't you? The FBI doesn't care about those death threats. 'Too vague and generic to warrant investigation.' I care, which is another reason I'm getting out. But the FBI is more concerned with fraud. They've asked a lot of questions about rigged voting."

"Rigged voting? But the show has given away millions of dollars!"

"I know." Waverly applied her lipstick, which was a peculiar shade of blue-black. On her, with that outfit, it looked weirdly alluring. "I don't understand it, and I don't really care. Something about violating interstate commerce laws. You'd think they'd have something better to do with their time, wouldn't you? Anyway, if there are subpoenas and testifying and all that shit, I don't want any part of it. My advice to you is get out now."

Amy didn't know what to say. One thing she did know: Waverly might blithely "get a lawyer" and forfeit the TLN bonus, but Waverly had her father's money behind her. Amy did not. On the other hand, she wanted nothing more than to leave the TV show.

"One more thing," Waverly said. "They'll need to replace me for the final scenario, whatever it is."

"So? Who will they . . ."

Waverly gazed steadily at her.

Amy said, "Oh my God. Kaylie."

"I don't know that for sure. But I guess yes. She's there, she knows the drill, she's photogenic, and she's a wild card. Just what Myra likes."

"She's only fifteen!"

"Not according to Kaylie. She says she had a birthday."

Amy juggled dates in her head. Kaylie's birthday had been two days ago, and Amy had completely forgotten it. Life in a hospital did that: erased time, erased any events except those connected with Gran.

"Bye, Amy," Waverly said. "Have a good life." She left, her walk sexy in the riveted sandals.

For several minutes Amy stared at the empty doorway, her mind a jumble. Kaylie's birthday, Waverly's quitting, the FBI . . .

Then all at once a phantom slashed into her mind, by far the strongest she'd ever had. Clear and bright, the phantom almost seemed outside her mind, a living thing in its own right. It was her mother's face from Gran's photograph, except that now her mother was smiling, a smile so warm and loving that Amy felt her heart rise in her chest.

The next moment, there was movement behind her. Amy whirled around. Gran sat up in her hospital bed, spine straight and eyes shining, and said joyously, "Carolyn!"

Amy rushed forward. She caught Gran as she toppled sideways, and she knew even before she called for the nurse that her grandmother was dead.

Amy never remembered the next hour. A nurse must have come, and a doctor, and someone must have led her away, someone must have taken Gran away. But all Amy could see was that phantom of her mother, appearing just before Gran called her mother's name in that strong voice ringing with joy. Had it really been a phantom? A premonition? Something manufactured by her mind because deep down she knew what must come? Or had the phantom been something else, its own thing, unclassifiable but very real? A message?

*"Carolyn!"*

Whatever it was, it sustained Amy through the next days. It sustained her through Kaylie's burbling phone call—"They put me in the show!" It sustained her through the brief funeral service. Gran had died happy, of that Amy was absolutely certain. If she knew nothing else, she knew that.

And the phantom of her mother's face would sustain Amy through quitting *Who—You*. If Waverly could do it, so could she. Let Myra sue her for breach of contract. You couldn't get money from someone who had none. Amy no longer needed medical coverage for Gran. Amy was getting out.

✳ ✳ ✳

"You can't!" Kaylie cried.

"Kaylie—"

"It's not fair! No! I won't let you do it!"

Amy stiffened. "You won't 'let' me?"

"No!"

They stood facing each other across Kaylie's bed at the Carillon Hotel. The bed was strewn with clothes, most of them Amy's; evidently Kaylie had been trying them on. Her face contorted so much with anger that she actually looked ugly. Her green eyes narrowed to slits.

"You've outshined me my entire stupid life, Amy, and now I finally have my one chance and you are not going to ruin it for me! Do you hear me—you're *not*! I've worked hard to get on this show and—"

"Worked hard how? By pretending to love a boy you don't?"

"I never told Cai I love him! You can afford to be so fussy and holier-than-thou because you were born with all those brains and talents, school and chess and gymnastics and everything—well, I wasn't! All I have is my looks and my personality and you can sneer all you want at how I use them but I'm not you! I'm not Saint Amy, and I sure the fuck don't want to be! Just don't screw this up for me!"

"I'm not, I—"

"Yes, you are! If you quit, the show would be down two people that viewers know and maybe Myra will cancel the whole thing! Don't you see—this is my *chance*. Everybody says Myra has to do something spectacular to get the ratings up and I need to be part of it. I need to get something of my own!"

"You can get something else, something that isn't a sleazy TV show that just exploits death and tragedy to—"

"No, I can't get anything else! God, don't be so selfish! If you won't do this for me, do it for Gran!"

Amy frowned. "What do you mean, 'for Gran'?"

"She wanted you to go to college, you know she did! It was her dream! She didn't have any dreams for me, did she, but let's pass over that for a minute. Gran wanted you to go to college and for that you need one of those 'bridge' schools that teach you all the stuff you lost by doing short-form high school instead of the real thing, and for that you need money. The amount of Myra's bonus, in fact!"

"How do you know all that?" Amy said, but of course Kaylie would know from online research and from Cai. Kaylie didn't bother to answer, instead plunging ahead.

"You have to go to college for Gran and you have to go on the show for me and not just throw it all away like you always do! You get good things hand-delivered to you and then you just rip them up—like this!"

Kaylie seized Amy's layered silk top from the bed and tugged at it. The fabric tore with a horrible rending sound like fingernails on a blackboard. Kaylie threw it to the floor and grabbed Amy's Fendi jacket. She put her teeth to the soft buttery leather.

"No!" Amy leaped onto the bed, then onto Kaylie. They crashed together to the floor, where Kaylie struggled briefly and then began to cry.

"Please, Amy, I need this, I do, please . . ."

"All right!" Amy was furious with Kaylie for begging, furious with herself for giving in, furious with Gran for dying, furious with Myra for everything else. It didn't feel good. She got up off the floor, clutching her jacket. After a minute she hurled it away from her. She wasn't doing this for a hunk of designer leather.

"Thank you," Kaylie said.

Amy said, "You're not all that welcome. And you know what? Later on you'll actually think less of me for giving in to you!"

To Amy's surprise, Kaylie actually considered this, head cocked to one side and face thoughtful. "I'll try not to."

"Good," Amy said sourly. She knew it was the best she was going to get. Now all she had to do wait for Myra's last scenario, hoping the wait would not be long. Amy didn't want Myra to wait "out of respect"; she just wanted the final scenario over.

It came the next day.

# Thirty-two

**TUESDAY**

AMY'S CELL RANG. She had been dreaming about Gran, a vague but peaceful dream in which Gran smiled at her and fixed her oatmeal with raisins, Amy's favorite childhood breakfast. The dream had none of the joyful, preternatural force of that last phantom image of her mother (*"Carolyn!"*), but it was pleasant and Amy resented being woken from it by her cell. In the other bed Kaylie groaned and turned over. She'd stopped sleeping in Cai's room, leaving him looking dazed and bruised and unhappy. Amy didn't want to think that Kaylie had dumped Cai because she was now on the show and had no further need of him—but it sure looked that way.

"Hello?" Amy said. She hadn't seen who was calling.

"This is Myra. Be dressed in outdoor clothing and in the lobby in half an hour. Same for Kaylie." She clicked off, just as a text came in.

"Kaylie, get up. We're on." She fumbled with the phone, trying to access the text. The time said 4:30 a.m.

Kaylie bolted upright. "Really? *Really?* Showtime!" She bounded out of bed—Kaylie, who never woke before ten, and who needed another hour to remember her name. "I get the shower first!"

"We only have half an hour!"

Amy switched on the bedside light, blinked, and squinted at the text. It was from Mark Meyer, and consisted of just two words, set in all capitals: LAST TIME.

Well, she knew this was the last time for a scenario—why would he bother to text that? And at four thirty in the morning? Amy stumbled out of bed and gathered up her clothes, waiting for her turn in the shower.

Which she didn't get. Kaylie took so long that all Amy had time to do was brush her teeth, wash her face, and put on minimal makeup. Kaylie, on the other hand, looked fabulous. She'd made up her eyes to look huge, with a pale mouth and gleaming dark curls. She wore her own jeans and boots but a new top—Myra must have sent it last night—in a shade of green that made her eyes glow emerald and showed the tops of her spectacular breasts. Amy, in jeans and white tee, felt like a wren beside a parrot. A very tired wren.

She said, "Come on, Kaylie. You don't want to be late for your television debut."

"No!" Kaylie said, utterly missing the sarcasm. The last time Amy had seen her sister this innocently excited had been before the All-City Talent Show, which seemed a million years ago.

And look how that had turned out.

In the elevator on the way down, both of them clutching their jackets, Kaylie said, "If Myra wants 'outdoor clothing,' should you be wearing those sandals?"

"They're all I was given this time around. Too bad Waverly took away her combat boots."

"Yeah." Kaylie looked down at her boots, heavy and high. "Want to switch?"

"Your feet are about two sizes larger than mine."

"Oh, yeah, right."

Had Kaylie made the offer from concern over Amy's sandals or from a desire for the designer footwear? Amy didn't know. Maybe both.

Violet and Rafe waited in the lobby with Jillian, and a moment later Cai and Tommy joined them. Kaylie was the only one who looked fully awake; not even Jillian was perky at five in the morning. She got them all into a van, where coffee and muffins waited. The van took them to the airport.

"Hey," Kaylie said, "where are we going?"

Rafe said, "I don't know. But we're going there in a helicopter."

"Cool!"

By the time the helicopter lifted off, pink stained the sky. They left the city and flew out over the bay, then the ocean. As they approached a small island that looked all green from the air, the copter abruptly dropped so that they came in low and all Amy could see was a landing area on the edge of a steep cliff. The sun had not yet risen above the horizon, and the sky was a glorious tapestry of gold, red, orange. Below the cliff, mild waves broke white on the rocks. Amy, jumping down from the helicopter, saw a low wooden building set in a stand of trees.

"This is pretty," Tommy said. "I like this place." He gazed at the trees in half-bud, the wild roses ringing the wooden building, the fresh May morning.

Cai said, "But where are we?"

Rafe was working the GPS on his cell. He said, "Holtz Island. Privately owned. Undeveloped."

Jillian said, "Inside, everybody."

The low wooden building, which seemed very new, was furnished with only a few tables and chairs, rough wooden shelves along one wall, and a man in a Park Ranger uniform even though Rafe had said this wasn't a public park. The shelves held cardboard boxes, a dorm-style refrigerator, a microwave, and a small television. On the opposite wall were two doors, both closed.

Jillian said, "Welcome to Maze Base. This is Ranger Compton. He has something to tell you after I explain the scenario. First, however, I need to collect all your cells, tablets, and other technology. It will all be here when the scenario is over."

Everyone emptied their pockets onto the table. Jillian swept all the electronics into a large tote labeled TLN. For the first time that morning, Amy felt the old tightening in her stomach and tensing along her neck. Whatever she had to face lay just beyond one of those wooden doors.

"Wait!" Violet suddenly said, sounding almost desperate.

They all looked at her. Violet lowered her head and shook it, like a bull going into the ring. Amy couldn't see Violet's eyes through the swinging curtain of long black hair. Violet seemed to want to say something, but then she straightened, smiled, and said nothing. She took an elastic band from her pocket and pulled her hair into a bun.

Jillian said, "Violet, are you OK?"

"Never better!"

"Then I'll begin. Behind that door"—she pointed dramatically—"is a maze. It's enormous, covering nearly a third of the island. It took days to construct. You'll be divided into teams. Each team's task is to get through the maze, which will bring you back out that second door there." She pointed.

Amy waited, but there didn't seem to be more. Kaylie said, "That's it? Just go through the maze?"

Rafe said, "I think the point is what's in the maze."

Jillian smiled. "You're right. There's a treasure in the maze. You'll know it when you see it. There are other things in there, too: food, water, prizes. But you'll have to find them. Like I said, it's a *big* maze. Everybody put on one of these lanyards—that little button at the end is a microphone, to call us in case of emergency."

Amy almost laughed aloud at this transparent ploy. The mics were to record the Lab Rats, of course. But no one said anything as Jillian draped the lanyards over each of their necks.

"The teams are Kaylie and Cai, Rafe and Amy, Tommy and Violet. You are required to stay with your team member at all times."

Of course they were—otherwise there would be no conversation to record. But there must be more going on than just a maze; Myra needed a big last scenario. What else lay behind that door?

Jillian's face turned serious. "Ranger Compton has something to tell you, too."

Compton stepped forward. Tall, straight-spined, sunburned, he looked like a recruiting poster for somebody's army. His face was as serious as Jillian's. "Since the maze finished construction, a coyote was found dead on the island. Because of certain unusual aspects of the corpse, an autopsy was performed. The coyote died of Keegan's syndrome."

Rafe let out a long, low whistle. Everybody else looked blank. Amy vaguely remembered hearing something about Keegan's on the endless news shows she'd watched with Gran—but what?

"Keegan's syndrome," Compton continued, "is one of the new diseases that have appeared since the Collapse. Like flu, it mutates easily. Like rabies, it attacks the brain. It is *not* rabies. But it's dangerous, and we know that it can jump species far more easily than most viruses. Most mammals can be affected by it, including humans. Two days ago a second coyote was seen near the helipad with the symptoms of Keegan's syndrome, which include staggering on weak legs, foaming at the mouth, and atypical behavior, including unprovoked attacks. The animal was shot. It carried Keegan's. Taunton Life Network contacted us and we did a complete inspection of the maze. It is perfectly safe. No infected coyote, if indeed there are any left on the island with Keegan's, can get through the walls of the maze. Coyotes cannot climb, and infected ones are too disoriented and weak to dig beneath the walls.

"The virus is fast-acting, more so than anything the CDC has seen before. But there is a completely effective antidote. It must, however, be administered within two hours of the bite, or else the victim undergoes quite a bit of pain and possible residual brain damage. In the unlikely event that one of you is bitten—although I don't see how that would happen if you remain in the maze—you can call for help with your microphones and you'll be taken out of the scenario. We have syringes of antidote stockpiled right here." He pointed to the wooden shelves on the side wall. "Any questions?"

Before anyone could ask one, Jillian said earnestly, "We at TLN wanted to be perfectly straight with you. Now that you know the facts, are you still willing to run the maze?"

Amy stared at her. Jillian was completely sincere; Amy was sure of it. She was one of those people who believed what her employers told her, carried out tasks with all the ability she had, and cared about the outcome. She was, in fact, what Amy had been before she went to work for TLN.

Violet said, "We can opt out? Without violating our contracts?"

"Yes and no," Jillian said. "You can opt out and TLN will of course take no legal action, but you forfeit the last bonus you received and the one for this scenario, too—which I'm happy to say is the same huge amount as the last one! The bonuses depend on completion of all specified services, as per your original contracts. It's a lot of money, people."

It was indeed. With two bonuses that size, Amy could not only do a bridge course to prepare herself for college, she could pay for the first year at university. And Kaylie could maybe go to some sort of school, too—modeling? acting?—or launch some kind of career, doing something . . .

That was what Gran had so desperately wanted for her granddaughters.

"I'm in," she said to Jillian.

One by one, the others agreed. Only Rafe hesitated. He thrust his hands deep in his pockets, hunched forward as if protecting his own body, and said, "Keegan's attacks the amygdalae directly. Those are the parts of the brain that control and inflame primitive emotion."

"That's right," Compton said.

"In West Virginia two cases have been found with squirrels as carriers."

"Yes. But this isn't West Virginia, son. Here only coyotes have been found as carriers. And this is an island. Squirrels can't cross that much water."

Rafe chewed on his bottom lip. Then he glanced over at Amy, shrugged, and nodded.

"Great!" Jillian said. "If you'll all just sign these brief statements saying that you were told about the coyotes . . . terrific! Let's get you started!"

She walked to the left door and flung it open, looking as if offering them the entrance to Eden.

Amy scanned the paper, signed it, and passed the pen to Kaylie, who didn't bother to read it at all. Joining Jillian, Amy peered through the door. A small square space enclosed with rough wooden walls set with three more doors. Except for the fact that the walls were ten feet high, it could have been a dog run behind a particularly shabby trailer. The three doors presumably led to the maze beyond.

Jillian said, "Amy, you signed first, so you get to choose which starter passage you and your teammate Rafe will begin with!" She had ramped up the perkiness so high that Amy looked for the hidden camera. She didn't spot it. But then, she rarely did.

She said, "We'll take the middle door."

"Great!"

Another few minutes and the door had closed behind her and Rafe, and Amy heard a key turn in the lock. They were in.

More ten-foot-high walls, these about four feet apart, like a long hallway of unsanded, unpainted walls. The lumber was so new that it still smelled of fresh sawdust. Openings led to other branches of the maze. The ground underneath was dirt, interspersed with weeds and the occasional rock.

Rafe said, "I love what they've done with the place."

"Do you want to go left or—"

"Just a minute, I want to check something first." He slipped the lanyard over his head and held it up to his eye. From his pocket he pulled a small folding knife, carefully pried the back off the microphone, and examined the innards. "OK," he said finally, "I think it *is* just a mic. Not also a camera. They can hear us but not see us, at least not through these. Although I imagine microcams will film us at strategic points along the maze. Hi, Myra!" He waved.

Amy said, "I have an idea. We should mark each turn we take so we don't end up just going in circles. You can use your knife to cut notches in the wood."

"Good. We'll do it."

They marked the first turn they took, branching to the left. Rafe said, "We should also keep the sun in mind as a marker, as well as remember that it's moving through the sky. I have a feeling we're going to be here all day. We're facing the sun now. If we keep trying to turn our back to it, we'll be at least heading back in the direction of Maze Base, which is where the second door is too."

But the available maze passages didn't let them turn their

backs to the sun. They plodded on for an hour, marking turns, until Amy felt completely confused. The sun grew hot and she took off her jacket and slung it over her shoulder. They never heard the other two teams; the maze must be enormous. Weeds poked through the sides and tops of Amy's sandals, scratching her feet. The unending vista of rough wooden boards grew monotonous, and then faintly claustrophobic. The blue sky overhead helped, but it carried no clouds to shield them from the sun.

Another turn, and they came upon a metal ice chest. "OK," Amy said. "This will be a magic carpet to fly us out of here."

"Too low-tech," Rafe said. "It'll be jet packs, prototypes from Pylon's super-secret research plant in the Arctic, and fueled by teeny-tiny nuclear reactors."

"No, it'll be the opening to a tunnel that goes down to the center of the Earth. All we have to do is squeeze through that little opening."

"Not the center of the Earth—it leads to a fabulous underground palace, complete with fountains of chocolate and dancing girls."

"You can have the dancing girls, I'll take the chocolate. Open it already."

The ice chest held bottled water, sandwiches, apples, and

cookies. Amy took off her lanyard and dropped it into the ice chest. "Come on, let's have lunch without listeners."

"You didn't read the paper you just signed, Amy. We're supposed to keep it on."

"Oh. OK. Then we won't talk." She reached out and took off Rafe's lanyard, put it soundlessly in the ice chest, removed all the food, and closed the lid.

Rafe laughed. They sat with their backs to a wall, drank deeply from the water, and ate the food. Amy was surprised at how comfortable she felt with Rafe, given everything that had been said between them. He was acting like a friend, not a rejected lover. At the same time, that very fact piqued her a little. Had he changed his mind about her already? She remembered her impulse at the hospital to kiss him. What if she tried to do that now? Would he push her away?

Did she want him to?

Instead she said, "Tell me more about Keegan's syndrome."

He wiped his mouth on his sleeve; the ice chest had omitted napkins. "I said most of it back there. The virus releases a neurotoxin in the brain that really messes it up. The CDC is worried. What they know for sure is that it's one of the fastest-mutating viruses they've seen, more so than influenza, and that's fast. So far it's been confined to mountainous areas. I'm surprised it's here."

"Do you think it really is? Or that TLN is messing with our heads again and there isn't any Keegan's on the island?"

"I thought of that. Could be."

"Did you always want to be a doctor?"

He smiled. "Well, when I was four I wanted to be a hooker. I heard the word and I thought it meant a fisherman, putting bait on hooks."

"Did you do a lot of fishing where you grew up?"

"Fishing, hunting, trapping. If we hadn't, we wouldn't have eaten."

This was new information. At the café on Fenton Street, Rafe had evaded saying anything about his background. Now he crumpled up his sandwich wrappings, glanced once at Amy, then gazed at the opposite wall of bare boards as he talked. Its shadow slanted across his face, striping it in dark and light.

"You can't imagine how I grew up, Amy. It was in the West Virginia mountains, where Latinos aren't exactly common. Or welcome. My father died when I was six. He was distilling meth in a lab that blew up—they do that, you know. Tricky stuff. My mother raised me and my brother alone. She fed us squirrel stew, fish from mountain streams, stuff from the neighbors. When she couldn't make that work anymore, we left the mountains for DC and she worked as a maid in a hotel. Six months later she dropped dead while cleaning somebody else's toilet, and I went into foster care."

There was no self-pity in his voice, and Amy didn't touch him. She only said, "That must have been hard."

"Yes and no. At least it got me sent regularly to a decent school. In the mountains and then in the hovel my mother could afford in Anacostia—which is *not* a good neighborhood in DC—the schools mostly tried to keep kids from killing each other. They didn't always succeed. I was small and smart and couldn't fight well, so I got beat up a lot. But even though my foster parents were pricks, keeping kids for the money, they lived on the edge of a good school system filled with kids whose parents wanted them to succeed. I never fit in—too poor, too geeky, too unathletic—but my teachers loved me. You, too, I bet."

"Yeah. For all the good it did me."

"It will. We're both going to earn these bonuses and then get ourselves to college. I'm going to be a doctor and you're go-ing to be a neurologist."

"Fine with me. What happened to your brother?"

Rafe's face shut down. "Dead of an overdose. You don't want to know the details. Come on, we better get back to work."

They put on their lanyards and resumed walking. Amy wanted to take Rafe's hand, but now his face looked so closed up that she didn't dare. Probably he regretted saying so much. Why had he told her at all? Maybe she should reach for his hand . . .

Then he said something that shattered that possibility. "I'm glad your sister's here. I'll bet Myra is, too. Waverly is photogenic, but Kaylie is the most beautiful girl I ever saw. And when I saw her last night talking to Tommy——you weren't there——I realized that I've misjudged her. She's really sweet underneath. She——what is it, Amy?"

"Nothing," Amy snapped. "Keep walking. We need to get out of this stupid maze."

# Thirty-three

**TUESDAY**

TWO HOURS. THREE. The maze went around and around, or maybe it didn't. Maybe it just led straight on forever. More than once they rounded a bend to find carved into the wood their symbol that said they'd been there before. The sun rose high in the sky and beat down steadily. Amy felt sweat soak her hair, run between her breasts, break through her underarm deodorant. Her Fendi jacket, slung over her arm, felt like a hot compress. She and Rafe came across another ice chest of food and drink, a pair of lawn chairs, a plastic wading pool filled with fluffy stuffed penguins, and a cardboard box of tennis balls. Amy had no idea what they were supposed to do with any of it.

"Nothing," Rafe said, "except remark that the stuff is here, so that the cameras that are also probably here can pick us up. Well, we're doing that. Have a tennis ball." He threw one playfully at Amy, who made no effort to catch it.

He said, "What's eating you?"

"Nothing. I'm just tired."

"Let's rest a few minutes."

They sank to the ground, Rafe so near her that Amy could feel the heat from his thin body. It stirred her, and she castigated herself. *Sure,* now *you decide you like him just because he's switched his interest to Kaylie. You're an idiot, Amy, and perverse as well. You always want what you can't have and ignore what you can. Stupid!*

"Amy," Rafe said, and at the choked sound in his voice she turned to him. His eyes were pleading. "I know I said this once before and shouldn't say it again, but—"

"EMERGENCY!" blared Amy's and Rafe's lanyards, so loudly that Amy jumped. "This is an emergency! We must evacuate the island. Repeat, this is an emergency and NOT part of your scenario! Find the blue dot on the side of your lanyard and press it three times. That activates the homing device. Just go in whatever direction keeps it beeping to return to your start. Please, people, come in now!"

Amy had not known Jillian could sound so desperate.

Rafe said, "Do you think this is part of the scenario?"

"I don't know. She said not. I don't know." She found the blue dot and pressed it three times. A strong *blatt* sounded. When Amy turned one direction, it softened and then ceased. In the first direction, it stayed loud. "We better follow it."

Amy and Rafe walked quickly, following the blatts. Amy kept expecting some of Mark Meyer's weird holograms to jump out at them, but nothing did.

In half an hour they were back at the start of the maze. Cai and Kaylie had already arrived. They both stared at the television blaring from the shelves.

"Amy!" Kaylie cried. "The president's been assassinated!"

"—has set off a fresh round of riots in a nation already tense from economic collapse," said the voice of a newscaster over images of rioters. "Burning and looting in several cities has not yet been brought under control. The former vice president, sworn in scant hours ago, has ordered out the National Guard. She—"

One of the cities burning was theirs. Amy watched as an explosion took out the State House with its distinctive green dome—the *State House*.

"—equipped far better than previous rioters, including some with what seems to be military hardware. Shoulder-mounted grenade launchers have—"

Cai said to Rafe and Amy, "It's all so well organized!"

Rafe said, "Who was the assassin? What was his agenda?"

"They don't know yet. He blew himself up. Jillian says we're aborting the scenario and going back to the mainland. She's outside with the copter pilot. We're just waiting for Violet and Tommy."

Kaylie said wonderingly, "The news guy said it's a *revolution*."

The monstrous images began to repeat as the newscaster scrambled for new information he didn't yet have. Amy clasped her hands together tight. *Oh, Gran—you were so sure we'd dodged the flash point!*

Jillian ran back inside just as Tommy burst through the door from the maze, his lanyard still blatting. The ugly noise stopped at the same moment that Jillian said, "Where's Violet!"

"She's gone!" Tommy screamed, almost hysterical. Tears ran down his broad face and his entire huge body trembled. "She got bit by a naked dog and then she acted all weird and then she got out of the maze and she's *gone*!"

Amy's mind raced. A naked dog—that could be Tommy's description of a coyote. The coyote could be one of Mark's tech inventions, a hologram . . . except that Tommy had seen it actually bite Violet—hadn't he?

She seized his sleeve. "Tommy, tell us what happened. Everything. Don't leave anything out!" When she saw that her agitation was only adding to his, she forced her voice to be soothing and calm. "It's all right, you're safe, we just need to know what happened to Violet. Tell me everything."

Tommy looked over Amy's shoulder at the TV. "Somebody killed the president!"

"I know, and we can talk about that later. Just tell me what happened to Violet, everything you can remember."

Her soothing was working, at least a little. Jillian snapped off the TV. Tommy clutched Amy's hand. Cai moved to Tommy's other side and put an arm around his shoulders. "Steady, big guy. You can do it."

Tommy's face scrunched with effort. "Violet and me walked through the maze. She put marks on the wall with lipstick so we knew where we went. She had three lipsticks in her pocket, different colors."

Of course she did. Ah, Violet!

"Then we went around a bend and this naked dog—"

Cai said, "Naked dog?"

Rafe said, "Coyotes undergo heavy shedding when warm weather comes."

"It jumped out at us and it bit Violet!"

Rafe said, "How did the dog behave?"

"All weird!" Tommy cried. "When it ran it fell down and it had spit all around its mouth! And it bit Violet!"

Amy said, "You actually saw it bite Violet? Not just jump near her and maybe her body was between you and the dog so you didn't see the actual bite?"

"I saw it! I saw her blood! And she told me to help her tie a piece of her shirt on it and I did but it kept bleeding through the cloth."

A shudder ran through Amy. Impossible to not believe Tommy, or blood. Violet had been bitten by a coyote carrying the Keegan's virus.

Jillian, very pale, said, "Where is Violet now?"

"I don't know! We tried to walk real fast but she fell down and I tried to call you on this"—he held up the lanyard—"but I couldn't figure out how it works and Violet had her eyes closed and wouldn't help me! So I tried to follow the lipstick marks back here but I got lost and then this thing started to make noise and said to follow the noise. Cai, you have to find Violet!"

"We will," Cai said, but at the uncertainty in his tone Rafe looked at him sharply.

The helicopter pilot strode into the room. "Jillian, you have two minutes to get everybody aboard."

"One of our participants is still in the maze."

"Then get him out!"

"There's been a . . . an unforeseen incident that—"

"Listen," the pilot said, "my family is in that area of the

city where there's fighting. My wife is eight months pregnant and our baby is two years old. I'm flying this bird back to the mainland and getting myself home no matter who is or is not with me. Do I make myself clear? This job is not worth my family's life. Now, anybody who's going, get yourselves aboard *now*."

Jillian said, "Just let me call Myra to——"

"Call whoever you want. I'm lifting the copter in two minutes flat. I'll send someone back for you later if I can't come myself." He strode from the room.

Jillian cried, "Get on the copter, everyone!"

Amy said, "You can't leave Violet here! If she's bitten, she needs the antidote you have here!" She seized Jillian by the shoulders. "Or were you lying about the antidote?"

"No! It's there! But I'm not staying—if the city really is burning down, who knows when anybody will get back here!" Jillian wrenched herself free of Amy's grasp, threw her a look somewhere between fear and dislike, and ran out the door.

Amy said, "Kaylie, get on the copter. You, too, Tommy." He would be no help here. "Rafe and Cai and I will look for Violet."

Kaylie said instantly, "I'm staying!"

Cai said, "I'm going."

Amy looked at him. She saw what she'd always known was there: the weakness under the spectacular looks and sweet nature. Cai was kind, but he was passive. Otherwise he would not have let Kaylie dominate him so completely. And to think she had once preferred him to Rafe! Amy hadn't even considered whether Rafe would stay; she knew he would.

But Kaylie was a surprise. Did she want to stay for the humanity of saving Violet, or for the drama? Either way, Amy wanted her little sister somewhere safe. She opened her mouth to say this but Kaylie cut her off.

"Don't *start*," she said savagely. "I'm staying. This is my decision!"

Cai, stiff-backed, walked from the room. A few moments later Amy heard the copter lift.

"OK," Rafe said, not entirely steadily. "Let's go find her."

They ransacked the cardboard boxes on the rough shelves, tearing open cartons and spilling the contents onto the floor. "Here are the syringes with antidote," Rafe said. "Three of them, preloaded. Let's hope they don't need to stay cold, or that we find Violet soon." Carefully he wrapped them in his denim jacket. "We can— Oh, shit!"

"What?" Kaylie cried, spinning around and squinting at the door.

"The tote bag with all our tablets and cells is gone. Jillian must have loaded it onto the chopper for the trip back before all this came down. Efficient Jillian."

"Well, don't say 'oh shit' like that," Kaylie said crossly. "I thought you saw an infected coyote!"

Amy said, "Here's some rope. We should take it with us."

"Why?" Kaylie demanded. "Oh—in case we have to tie up Violet. Here are spoons, forks, and oh! Some steak knives. Everybody take one."

Amy said, "A blanket, bottles of water—how are we going to carry all this stuff?"

Rafe said, "Make backpacks out of these garbage bags."

"Stylish," Amy said. "You'll see them on the runway in Paris." The joke fell flat. Amy's fingers trembled as she checked the batteries in three heavy-duty flashlights. Surely they wouldn't need those, surely they'd find Violet before nightfall. . . .

"Ready?" Rafe said, looking determined. "Let's go."

With garbage-bag packs on their shoulders, the three of them entered the maze.

It was easy to find the first lipstick marks in the maze passage that Tommy and Violet had taken. They followed the marks, running in single file. A drum beat started in Amy's head: *two hours two hours two hours*. That was how long they had to get to Violet with the medicine before there "might be brain damage." How much damage? How certain was "might be"?

After several turnings of the maze, Amy said. "Wait—I

have an idea. Rafe, boost me to the top of the wall. If it's wide enough, I can walk up there and see farther. Maybe I'll spot her."

Rafe cupped his hands. Amy shed her share of their gear, put her foot into Rafe's hands, and vaulted upward. The top of the wall was an inch wide; not enough to balance on, not even if she took off her sandals. She wasn't that good of a gymnast.. "This won't work. I'm coming down."

Rafe caught her, and for a moment her body slid down against his. Amy flushed. She avoided looking at either him or Kaylie.

Rafe said, "I guess it's the lipstick trail, after all." His voice was husky.

Amy said, "I wish I'd thought of that at Maze Base. I could have stood on the top of the camp building and maybe seen more."

"Do you want to go back?"

"No. Let's go on."

Another twenty minutes and Amy said, "Wait—she's going in circles. Here are two sets of lipstick marks but in different colors."

Kaylie, a little way ahead of them, said, "Cai and I went in circles, too. It's so confusing. We— Fuck!"

She had turned another corner. Amy and Rafe raced to

join her. A section of the fence had been smashed in with one of the ice chests. A corner of the chest was dented as if it had been used as a battering ram. Two boards had given way, leaving a hole about a foot above the ground, just above the horizontal railing to which the upright boards were nailed. On one edge of the hole, blood stained the raw wood.

Amy stooped and looked through the hole, hoping to see another part of the maze, another weed-strewn walled path. Instead she saw bushes and, in the near distance, trees. Kaylie said flatly, "She escaped."

Amy straightened. Anger swept over her: at Violet, at Myra, at TLN, at Keegan's syndrome, at the world. Why should she go through that hole after Violet? Why should Amy have to feel so responsible? For Violet, for Kaylie, for Gran, for Tommy in the Frustration Box, for the entire world? Why always *her*?

Responsible. Response-able. She was able to respond. Well, great, fine, wonderful—"able to" wasn't the same as "compelled to." So why did she always feel compelled to help, to arrange, to comfort? All at once she was sick of it. Let somebody else take responsibility for a change!

Only there wasn't anybody else. Not right here, right now. If she said she was not going out into the island, with its infected coyotes, then Rafe wouldn't go either. He was here to protect her, not Violet. Probably not even Kaylie would go alone, away from any cameras. There was only Amy to make the decision, only she right now at this place in this particular awful moment among the awful moments her life had somehow become.

She flung her leg over the smashed wood and prepared to squeeze through the hole.

"Wait," Rafe said. "Don't come in contact with her blood." He wrapped the bloody edge of the wood with cloth torn from the blanket in his garbage bag, and Amy climbed through. Rafe and Kaylie followed.

The ground sloped down for a few feet. They could clearly see where Violet had slid in the loose gravel. Next came a strip of weeds and torn-up ground rutted with deep tire marks, probably from construction equipment. At first it wasn't hard to follow Violet's trail. She had dropped a used-up lipstick, shed her jacket, torn a bit of silk on a thorny bush. Once into the trees, however, it became more difficult.

"Listen," Rafe said. "Hear that? I think it's the sea. If Violet is thinking at all, maybe she'd head that way to search for a boat, or to circle around back toward the start of the maze. The helipad is on that small cliff right beside the ocean."

Amy said, "It's not much to go on. We don't know how rational Violet still is."

Kaylie said, "She was rational enough to break out of

the maze. Besides, I don't have any better idea—do you?"

Amy shook her head.

Kaylie said, "You know, it's funny—the show was supposed to be about predicting people's behavior, and here we are predicting Violet's. Don't you think that's funny?"

"Hilarious," Amy said sourly. "Come on."

Rafe said, "Stay together. I'm going first and looking ahead. Kaylie, you keep a watch on either side, and Amy, you watch behind us. If you see, smell, hear, or anything else the first sign of a coyote, yell. They're primarily nocturnal but I've seen them out in daytime, and anyway their behavior will be changed if they're infected."

"I have no idea what a coyote even looks like," Kaylie said. "Wait! I have an idea! We should carry torches, like when people are attacked by wolves in the movies!"

"I thought of that," Rafe said, "but it would take too long to find pine pitch and coat branches with it, and otherwise the branches will just burn too soon."

"Too bad," Kaylie said, and Amy turned to stare at her sister. Kaylie was *enjoying* this.

They moved cautiously through the trees. Rafe was proved right in his choice of direction; almost immediately they found one of Violet's shoes in a little clearing. Rafe said, "If the disease causes fever, she's going to take off as many clothes as possible."

Now Amy could hear surf through the trees. Not loud, it wasn't a windy day, but steady. Waves breaking against rocks. They found Violet's other shoe.

Something moved through the trees. Amy gasped and said "There!" The shape picked up speed. Amy's heart thudded as the three of them backed into each other. Rafe and Kaylie took out knives. Rafe said "Careful—"

A deer broke cover and bounded away.

Kaylie laughed shakily. "Bambi. And we react like it's Shere Khan."

Shere Khan—the tiger from *The Jungle Book*. Gran read it to them when they were small. Amy was surprised that Kaylie remembered. Somehow, despite all reason, that made her feel better.

Several minutes later, as the surf sounded more strongly, Rafe picked up a bloody scrap of silk from on top of a stand of weeds. Violet's blouse. He dropped it again, careful to not touch the blood.

The trees thinned. As soon as they cleared the forest entirely, they saw Violet. She sat beneath a stunted pine, one of a little grove on the edge of the cliff, the trees bent from years of salty wind. Violet, in jeans and bra, had her knees drawn up to her chin and her bare arms wrapped around them. She rocked back and forth, singing.

"OK," Rafe said. He took a length of rope off his belt. "I'm going to tackle her and—"

"Ha!" Kaylie said brutally. "She's way taller than you and twenty pounds heavier, even slim like she is. *I'll* tackle her and you two tie her."

"No!" Amy cried, without thinking.

"Still the big sister?" Kaylie said. "Knock it off, Amy." Kaylie started forward.

Amy stuck out her foot and tripped her. Kaylie sprawled on the ground, her face sliding across dirt. In a second she was up, lip and cheek bloody, fists clenched. "Why did you do that? Amy, you don't own me!"

"It's too dangerous!"

"But I'm the biggest one here!"

Too true. Kaylie was nearly as tall as Violet, and without Violet's dancer's slimness. Kaylie had breasts, hips. But Violet had muscular legs and arms from her constant dance classes, and Amy didn't want Kaylie anywhere near Violet. Amy pretended to turn away and hang her head, and Kaylie twisted to again look at Violet. Instantly Amy was on her, the sheer weight of her attack carrying both of them to the ground. "Rafe!" Amy called. "Tie her!"

But Rafe was gone.

Both girls realized this at the same second and sprang to

their feet. Rafe had dropped his pack and was halfway to Violet, who also stood up and looked poised to run. But even as Amy ran forward, she saw Violet stagger and fall. Closer, and Amy could see Violet's eyes: wild, rolling from side to side, crazy.

Violet shouted something incoherent. She flailed on the ground, clearly unable to rise. Rafe, intent on getting to her before either Kaylie or Amy, held a length of rope in his hands. But his words, coming to Amy over the surge of waves, were calm and soothing. "It's OK, Violet, I'm not going to hurt you, it's OK—"

He reached her, the length of rope stretched between his hands, the shadow of the spindly pine only partly darkening both their figures. Then something fell or leapt from the tree branches above and fastened itself on Rafe's neck.

He screamed. The thing did not let go. Amy, stopped cold in horror, saw that it was a squirrel. Rafe tore it off him and it ran a few steps, staggered, and fell. She saw the foam around its mouth. Then the squirrel ran again, floundering, and plunged over the side of the cliff.

Rafe had fallen to his knees. Blood soaked his collar. Amy heard the ranger's condescending voice in her head: *This isn't West Virginia, son. Here only coyotes have been found as carriers. And this is an island. Squirrels don't cross that much water.*

But one had.

"Shit!" Kaylie cried.

And Violet jumped to her feet, not shaking or flailing, her eyes dark with emotion. She said, "I didn't know about this part. Please believe me, Rafe—Myra didn't tell me anything about this!"

# Thirty-four

AMY STOOD TRANSFIXED. Gooseflesh rose on her sweaty arms. She started forward and Violet said, "Don't touch him! It can be transmitted by blood!"

Kaylie said, "You whore. You were faking!" She leapt at Violet. Both girls went down. Kaylie outweighed Violet but Violet was stronger. A few rolls on the ground and Violet had Kaylie pinned. Strands of Violet's black hair straggled loose and fell into Kaylie's mouth.

"I'm letting you up, Kaylie, but don't try that again! It's Rafe you should be thinking of, not your own stupid revenge for what you don't even understand!"

Amy barely heard her. She ran back for Rafe's makeshift

pack and fumbled in the plastic garbage bag for the syringes, carefully wrapped in his jacket. She got one out, then hesitated. "I don't know how to . . . or how much. . . ."

"Give it to me," Rafe said. "I can still do it." He looked normal, except for the torn flesh and blood on his neck. Amy, remembering the squirrel fastened to him like a leech, shuddered. Rafe took the needle and injected himself in the bend of his left elbow, emptying the syringe. His voice trembled.

"That should do it. But I don't know if the symptoms come on anyway and then the medicine catches up, or what. The virus can cross the blood-brain barrier but I don't know if the antidote can, or if it works indirectly. I might show some symptoms. Give me something to cover my neck, and *don't touch my blood or saliva*. OK, Amy?"

She nodded. He was trusting her.

Rafe rose, shakily. "Let's go while I can still walk."

Kaylie said, "Not till this whore gives us some answers!"

Amy said, "It can wait. And I want to get away from the cameras!" She had figured out that much, anyway.

Kaylie had not. "Cameras?" She looked up into the tree branches.

"Somewhere. Come on!"

Across the open stretch, into the trees. Clouds had rolled in, blocking the oppressive sunshine, but also making it dimmer beneath the trees. They couldn't find the path. After what seemed a long while but probably wasn't, Amy said, "This way?"

"I don't know," Rafe said. "It's so hot here—"

He fell down.

Immediately Amy dropped to the ground beside him. "Rafe—can you get up?"

He didn't answer. Violet and Kaylie watched, Violet wrapping her arms around her skimpy bra, Kaylie uncharacteristically quiet, with her hands on her hips. When Rafe staggered to his feet, Amy slipped her arm under one of his shoulders. Violet darted to his other side but Kaylie shoved her away.

"You've done enough, bitch!"

Through the trees, trying to remember which way they'd come—"This way," "No, that way"—but finally they got through the little forest, although not at the same place they'd entered. Clouds had rolled in, obscuring the sun, and a wind sprang up. Across a stretch of scrub and weeds rose the maze, seemingly miles of rough upright boards. It looked like a stockade, Amy thought, a pioneer barrier keeping out predators. If there were more infected animals on the island, wouldn't the humans be safer inside the maze?

"Amy," Kaylie said softly, "look at Rafe's mouth."

Saliva pooled at the corners of his mouth, foaming spittle. His brown eyes looked unfocused. They rolled back in his head.

"Put him down!" Amy said.

On her knees beside him, she said, "Rafe? Can you hear me?"

He started to speak, stop, and grinned crazily. Spittle flew from his mouth. Then he began to *sing*, a tuneless and almost wordless mumble.

"He's going weird," Violet said.

Kaylie suddenly laughed, a sound so shocking that both Amy and Violet stared at her. Kaylie said, "I know that song! Our stupid choir teacher at school liked all those lame old musicals . . . listen!"

Rafe's voice grew stronger. His eyes grew wilder. Finally Amy distinguished the words croaked out in Rafe's tenor: *"Once in love with Aaaamy, al-ways in love with Aaaamy—"*

Kaylie said, "Don't quit your day job, Rafie. God, you geeks are all alike."

Rafe turned his head at the sound of Kaylie's voice and lunged for her.

She was too quick. She leaped backward and his jaws closed on air. Kaylie said, "He tried to *bite* me!"

Violet said, very low, "We can't wait any longer to tie him."

But Rafe had the rope. It still hung from his belt. Rafe swayed on his feet, grinning crazily. He was obviously very ill—didn't that mean he would be easy to seize and tie? They were three against one. Amy glanced at Violet and they began to circle Rafe carefully. Kaylie, taken over by her own anger, stood fused to the ground and glared at Rafe.

"You fucker—you tried to bite me!"

"Kaylie——" Amy began, but too late she caught Kaylie's expression: rage, the kind of primal fury that stops all thought, that hijacks all action. "No, Kaylie!" Amy shouted, but that was too late, too.

Kaylie raised her fists and hurled herself at Rafe. Amy screamed. *He would try again to bite her and this time he would succeed, his teeth would sink into her and*—

It didn't happen. Rafe was not yet as physically weak as he looked. He leaped backward, away from Kaylie's attack, and then he was gone, running into the trees behind them, as fast as ever.

Violet said shakily, "Adrenaline surge." She wrapped her arms around her bare upper torso.

Kaylie didn't pursue Rafe—not that she could have caught him. She stood with her head down, panting hard, fists closing and unclosing.

Amy said, "Did you . . . did you see his face?"

"No," Violet said. "What about his face?"

"He *knew*."

Violet put a hand on Amy's arm. "Knew what?"

"Knew he was dangerous to us. Knew he'd tried to harm Kaylie. He ran away to keep *us* safe from *him*."

Violet said nothing. Kaylie snapped, "Romantic bullshit! He tried to kill me!" Her fury turned on Violet. "This is all your fault!"

"Some of it, anyway," Violet said. "Not all of it."

Amy said, "We can argue about this later. For now we have to . . ." Have to what? She tried to think. "We have to get inside Maze Base, away from any infected animals. We can get there by following the maze wall." She pointed to the upright boards, dull now under the increasingly sullen sky. "That copter pilot said he would come back or would send somebody back for us. As soon as he finds out his family is safe from the riots. Then we can get help for Rafe."

Violet said, "There are no riots."

Kaylie whirled to face her. "We saw them on TV! It's a revolution!"

"There is no revolution. You saw a CGI simulation that Mark Meyer put together."

Unreality swept over Amy. None of this could be happening. It had nothing to do with normal life: with getting up in the morning, getting dressed, caring for Gran, going to work. That was what real people did. Real people didn't end up on an island with infected animals, a foaming-at-the-mouth friend, another friend who was nothing like what she appeared, and a manufactured version of history in bright Technicolor. Real people also didn't cause any of that to happen, as Myra Townsend and Mark Meyer apparently had.

She said to Violet, "Tell me. Now," and at the tone in Amy's voice, even Kaylie shut up.

Violet said, "There are no riots. The president wasn't assassinated. I wasn't bitten by a coyote. It was a trained animal, a shaved dog, and I had that fake blood that actors use, hidden under my blouse. Tommy was easy to fool."

"So the whole thing was part of the scenario." All at once Amy remembered Mark Meyer's text message to her that morning: *Last time.* She'd thought he meant this was the last scenario. He'd really meant that Amy should remember the last time, when the spiders had been real animals but harmless.

Violet said, "I was part of the scenario, and so was the fake coyote attack, and me leaving the maze. But *not* the real infected squirrel that bit Rafe. I don't think even Myra knew that was here."

"I think she did. I think she had it brought here to bite one of us."

Violet stared. "I thought I was the cynical one here. She would be breaking about sixteen laws if she did that. Including maybe attempted murder."

"Only if anybody can prove it. Violet, why did you do it?"

"I can't tell you that. But I hope you'll believe I had a good reason."

"Not good enough! What's happening to Rafe—this virus thing is new and so is the antidote and nobody really knows how bad he could be! Wait—was that ranger fake, too? Compton?"

"Yes."

"But not the squirrel?"

"No! I swear to you I didn't know that would happen! There were supposed to be cameras in those trees, but not infected squirrels!"

"If Rafe has any brain damage, I swear I'll hunt you down. No matter what it costs me."

"He injected himself with the antidote!"

"Yes, and how do we know that the antidote is even real?"

Both Violet and Kaylie stared at her. Finally Kaylie said, "Not even Myra would—"

"Really?" Amy said bitterly. "Are you sure about that? The only thing I'm sure of is that as soon as we get to Maze Base, we'll be back on camera for TLN. Maybe we even are right now. Smile, Violet. You're on TV."

# Thirty-five

SILENTLY THE THREE girls headed across the scrub-dotted open space toward the maze. Violet shivered in her lacy bra as the wind picked up even more. In the distance, surf pounded. Amy squinted at the sky, trying to guess where the sun was. There—it broke through the clouds for just a moment. So that was west. From what Rafe had said this morning, they should turn left at the maze wall in order to head back to the helipad.

Rafe. Where on the island was he? Was the antidote real? It had to be; not even Myra would arrange for real infected squirrels and a fake antidote—would she? Tension stiffened Amy's neck and shoulders so much that she almost groaned.

"How far is it to base?" Kaylie said. "Does anybody know?"

"No," Amy said. "It's too confusing to judge. But if we follow the fence, we'll get there."

"Stop for a minute," Kaylie said. "I have to show you something."

Amy and Violet stopped. Kaylie pressed her lips together and her gaze swung uncertainly back and forth between Amy and Violet. She wasn't even glaring at Violet anymore, which scared Amy more than anything else.

"Kaylie, what is it? Are you— Oh God, did something bite *you*?"

"No, no," Kaylie said, "nothing like that. It's just that . . . I have to show you something."

Kaylie bent over. Amy and Violet watched, Amy's apprehension mounting. Kaylie reached into her boot and pulled out something small and gray. She closed her hand over it, as if hanging on to its identity until the last possible moment.

But Violet knew. "Kaylie . . . Christ, I guess I'm lucky you didn't shoot me with it."

Amy said, "You have a *gun*?"

Kaylie opened her fist. The gun was no more than five inches long. Small, innocent-looking, it seemed like a toy. Violet said, "A mousegun!"

Amy exploded. "Where the hell did you get that?"

"From James. In the band."

Violet said, "Band?"

"I was in this band, Orange Decision. I was sleeping with James, the lead guitar, and he got me—Amy, don't look like that, it's just a gun!"

*Just a gun!* "Do you have a permit for that thing?"

Violet snorted, then said gently to Amy, "Of course she doesn't have a permit. She's too young. But, One Two Three, there are a lot of museguns floating around the city, especially since the Collapse. My roommate Deirdre had one. People have to defend themselves."

"Yeah," Kaylie said, "don't be such a dork."

Amy demanded, "Is it loaded?"

"Yes. It shoots five bullets. Other kinds shoot more but they're not as powerful. Ryan told me."

"Kaylie, you're an idiot! What did you think you were going to shoot here?"

"I should shoot Violet!"

"No, thanks," Violet said. "Kaylie, you know you can't hit anything with that more than about five yards away? And that's only if you're a good shot."

"I'm not very good," Kaylie admitted. "But I can shoot a coyote if we see one, or maybe a squirrel if it's not going too fast."

"Just don't shoot Rafe. When he was going to bite you—"

"It happened too fast," Kaylie said, scowling at Violet. "I didn't have time to get the gun out! But next time . . . I won't let him bite Amy!"

Amy looked at her sister. Kaylie—defending her? The sense of unreality came back, sweeping over her in a dark cloud. She said to Kaylie, "Give me that thing."

"No."

"Kaylie—"

As they glared at each other, Violet's hand darted out, quicksilver, and plucked the gun off Kaylie's palm.

"Give that back!"

Violet held the gun behind her back. "Kaylie, listen to me. You act impulsively—you know you do. You shouldn't have a gun, especially one that doesn't have a manual safety catch, unless Ryan bought it legally in California or Massachusetts, which somehow I rather doubt. I know you don't think I deserve to have this gun either, and you're probably right. So I'm going to give it to Amy, and then we're going to all find the building by the helipad and get inside before twilight falls and we can't even see any attacking animals, and then we're going to use the cells and tablets we left there to call for help for us and Rafe. And we're going to do all this calmly and quietly, so that Myra doesn't get anything else to film. OK?"

Amy held her breath. Kaylie balled her hands into fists. Amy saw her sister gauging the distance to Violet, weighing her chances in a fight. And if there was a fight and that stupid gun went off . . . no *safety catch* . . .

The moment seemed to go on forever. The wind blew harder. A bird made a raucous sound: *caug caug caug.*

Kaylie said sulkily, "Give it to Amy, then."

Violet handed the gun to Amy. It felt shockingly light: no more than a pound. She held it gingerly, pointed at the ground. She'd never held a gun before. Violet should have it, not Amy—but in her present mood, Kaylie would never agree to that. And Amy wasn't sure she trusted Violet either. Violet had been a plant to bring off Myra's scenario, just like Lynn Demaris and Paul O'Malley. Rafe was out there somewhere, crazed with sickness, and maybe the antidote wasn't real either. And who knew what other infected animals were still loose on the island.

"Come on," she said roughly to Violet and Kaylie. "We need to get to Maze Base." Even if they couldn't call the mainland from there, the building would still be safer than being out in the open.

They trudged in silence, following the maze wall, while the sky darkened into dusk. Every time a bush or stand of weeds rustled in the wind, Amy's stomach roiled—was that a coyote?

A squirrel? Was it infected? Squirrels were just rats with fluffy tails. She could almost taste the tension in Violet and Kaylie, their bodies taut and jumpy. On the other side of cleared land between the wall and the forest, the trees rustled and whispered, telling her something she couldn't understand, but it felt bad.

*Get a grip, Amy.*

"OK, almost there," Kaylie said as they rounded a jagged outcropping of maze and the helipad came into view. A few more steps and Amy could see the rough wooden building.

Violet said, "Was the door left open like that when they all went for the helicopter?"

"I don't remember," Amy said. Everyone had been in such a hurry: Cai and Jillian and Tommy and the pilot. And then Rafe and Kaylie and she had ransacked the shelves before heading into the maze to find Violet—*had* the outer door been ajar?

Twilight was deepening into night. The door seemed to open into a black hole.

Kaylie said, "Who has the flashlights?"

They slung the garbage bags off their backs. Kaylie pulled two flashlights from hers. Amy said, "Oh my God!"

"What?" Violet said, spinning around. "Do you see something. *What?*"

"No, no, it's not that. . . . Nobody brought Rafe's garbage

bag, after he dropped it. We didn't think. The rest of the antidote syringes are in there!"

The three girls stared at each other in the gloom. Finally
Kaylie said, "Well, then, nobody else better get bit. We can't go
back for it. If the antidote is even real in the first place." She
turned on a flashlight, handing the other one to Amy. Violet
grimaced but didn't argue. Kaylie would be a long time forgiv-
ing Violet, if ever.

The beam of flaring light was reassuring. Warily, Kaylie
led them through the door. The room was empty, with the
cardboard boxes they had pulled from the shelves still scattered around the floor. No animals, no Rafe. Amy felt a little of
the tension leave her neck and shoulders.

Then Violet screamed.

Amy whirled around, swinging her flashlight. Violet
pointed toward the door. They hadn't closed it behind them.
An animal crouched there, square in the doorway, bigger than
a cat but surely smaller than a coyote—a woodchuck? Badger?
Amy didn't know, but she knew the foam around its mouth,
the stagger in its walk as it crept forward.

"Shoot it!" Kaylie cried, just as Amy opened her fist,
aimed the miniature gun, and fired. The muzzle of the tiny
gun flipped upward, and she missed, but the sound seemed to
enrage the creature. It leaped forward, fell, lurched again. It

was coming at her. Amy fired a second time. No effect on the animal. She needed to be closer, she had to let it get closer, she couldn't let it get closer or it would be close enough to—

Amy was lifted bodily off her feet and thrown backward. Violet, who had done the throwing, crashed into her. Kaylie was just ahead. She slammed the door on the slavering animal.

They were behind one of the three doors at the far end of the room. They were in the maze.

"You all right?" Violet said. Her voice shook.

"Yeah, I . . . yeah."

Kaylie said, "At least you didn't drop your flashlight. But you didn't hit that thing, either. What *was* it?"

"Do I look like a naturalist?" Amy snapped. All at once she realized that her hand burned. She dropped the gun; red welts crossed her palm. But slowly her stomach was sinking back to its normal place. She wasn't going to throw up after all. Good. OK. They were in the maze. The thing was on the other side of the door.

Violet picked up the gun. "Maybe that thing wasn't even infected, just startled. Or maybe the virus jumped another species. Rafe would know."

Kaylie snapped, "Well, we haven't got Rafe."

"Like I haven't noticed?"

Amy said slowly, "I think Rafe might have left that door open. Unless Jillian did when they ran for the copter. Does anyone remember?"

Kaylie and Violet shook their heads. In the upward slant-ing beam from the flashlights, their faces looked eerie, full of strange shadows. The miniature gun dangled from Violet's hand. Amy struggled to pull herself together.

"OK, here's the deal. There's a limit to how long Myra can leave us here. There are no riots in the city, no presiden-tial assassination. Even if she pretends that somehow nobody is watching the film, it's nearly night. They have to come back for us very soon or face who-knows-what lawsuits. So we stay someplace near cameras, which is probably right here—this is one of the maze starts, after all." Amy turned her face upward and shouted, "You hear me, Myra? We're here, Rafe is infected, and it's getting dark. Come get us!"

Kaylie said, "Don't ask that bitch for anything!"

"I'm not asking, I'm demanding. We stay right here, with light and walls, and where we can hear the helicopter. Violet, there's a blanket in my garbage bag; put it around your shoul-ders. I don't think we'll be here long."

Violet said, "And what if a sick squirrel comes over the walls? They can climb, you know. I've seen them go right up the side of a tree."

"I'm hoping the sick ones don't climb. If there even are more sick ones on the island."

"We know there's a sick something. Was that thing you tried to shoot a woodchuck?"

Amy didn't answer. Violet passed her the miniature gun when Kaylie wasn't looking. All at once Amy wondered if Waverly would have been able to hit the maybe-a-woodchuck. *"My people shoot."*

The girls settled onto the ground, backs against the walls, the flashlights aimed down the maze in case anything approached. Violet had wrapped herself in the blanket. Kaylie's stomach growled loudly. She said, "Some of those ice chests in the maze had sandwiches and cookies. I could just go and—"

"No!" Amy said. Kaylie didn't argue.

If it was Rafe who'd left the outside door open, then he was in the maze with them.

With the sun gone, the evening grew cold. Amy shivered. Her feet were covered with tiny red nicks where weeds and sticks had poked between the straps of her sandals. Her palm burned red from the gun, which she must have been holding wrong. She was starving. She said nothing about any of that because she didn't want to give Myra anything else to film.

Myra. Could a human being really have brought infected animals to the island and left teenage kids alone there, just to have something exciting to film? Myra wasn't some human being from way back in history—the Romans sending gladiators into the arena to fight to the death, Ivan the Terrible butchering peasants for sport—but a human being right now, in twenty-first-century America, an executive at a TV station. Someone who looked normal, polished, successful. Did that mean that "normal" wasn't what Amy had always assumed? Was in fact—

"Listen!" Kaylie cried. "I hear the chopper!"

Amy got to her feet and strained to listen. Yes, there was something . . . yes, the helicopter! Violet, holding one of the flashlights, rose and brushed dirt from the seat of her jeans. Kaylie, still sitting cross-legged on the ground with her back against the maze wall, closed her eyes in gratitude.

Rafe dropped onto Kaylie from the roof of the maze base.

Kaylie screamed. Violet swung the flashlight wildly, the beam flashing on sawed boards, the ground, Rafe and Kaylie. She was fighting him off, but her legs were crossed under her, a bad position to attack from. He snarled, like a dog, and lunged his mouth at her shoulders and neck. Amy, two feet away, got one clear glimpse of his lips drawn back over his teeth, gleaming white in the flashlight's beam.

*Rafe*, so smart and sweet—

Kaylie, her sister—

Amy raised the tiny gun and fired. At this distance, not even the mousegun could miss.

Rafe let out a shrill, inhuman scream. Then he collapsed on top of Kaylie. She shoved him off while Violet shouted, "Are you bit? Are you bit?" The whole world went red for Amy, saturated in a fine scarlet mist, and then black. The ground rose to slam into her. For the first and only time in her life, she fainted.

But only for a moment. She was staggering back onto her feet when a second, louder gun fired beyond the door and something heavy hit the floor. Then the door burst open and there were men in uniform shoving through the door, and a woman with EMT on her shoulder patch was turning over Rafe's still body to see if he breathed, if he lived, if Amy had done the terrible thing she'd always feared most: irresponsible harm to someone she loved.

# Thirty-six

AMY AND KAYLIE sat on hard plastic chairs in the corridor outside Rafe's hospital room. It was midnight but the corridor was as busy as if it were noon. Doctors went in and out, men in suits made notes, nurses carried out vials of blood. "Rafe won't have any blood left," Kaylie said.

"It's for the CDC," Amy said.

"What's that, again?"

"The Centers for Disease Control. They need to see what's going on in Rafe's body because of the virus and the antidote."

"I thought the brain scans did that."

"Those too," Amy said.

A nurse approached. "I'm sorry, but visiting hours are long over. You'll have to leave."

"No," Amy said simply.

The nurse frowned and turned to call security. Kaylie said pleasantly, "You just came on shift, right? We've been through this with all the other nurses. We're not going and if you make us go, we'll make the biggest stink you ever saw because we were with Rafe on that island where he got infected. I mean, you can't even imagine how much fuss I'm capable of making. So the other nurses said we can stay, and if you check their notes or tablet or whatever the hell you guys do, I'm sure you'll see that we're allowed here."

The nurse blinked, looked uncertain, frowned again. She hurried to the nurses' station at the other end of the hall.

Kaylie called after her, "Have a good night!"

Amy pulled at the skin on her face. She was tired beyond belief. She and Kaylie still wore their clothes from the island, ripped and dirty. She had told her story at least six times, to six different people. But it was a version of the story that left out Violet's pretending to be bit, and she made Kaylie also leave that part out. They said only that they were all actors on the TV show *Who Knows People, Baby—You?*, filming a scene on the island. A squirrel had bitten Rafe and he had started to act strangely. Amy, Kaylie, and Violet had helped him back to the film crew helicopter. The medical people all accepted this; they weren't interested in a TV show, only in the virus, its rodent carrier, and the use of the antidote.

During a bathroom trip Kaylie had demanded fiercely, "Why are you protecting Myra?"

"I'm not," Amy had said. "Oh, I'm not, believe me. I'm not even protecting Violet. I—"

"Yes, you are!"

Amy had had time to think over Violet's story. "Kaylie, Violet didn't know about the infected animals. I believe that part. Violet didn't know anybody would be hurt, only scared. That infected squirrel, at least, was Myra's doing. Has to be. It's just too coincidental otherwise."

"So what are you going to do about Myra?"

"I don't know yet! Stop itching at me! Right now I just want Rafe to be all right!"

Kaylie's face changed. She stopped rubbing her hands under the automatic blow-dryer and put still-damp fingers on Amy's arm. "I know. You're in love with him."

"I didn't say that!"

"But you are. Even though he looks like a skinny toad."

"He does not!"

Kaylie had smiled. "See how you defend him?"

Now Amy waited on a puke-yellow plastic chair—why were hospital chairs always such awful colors?—and thought about Rafe, about Violet, about Myra. About Gran, who had died looking joyous and with her beloved daughter's name on her lips. Gran had really liked Rafe, and—

A doctor came out of Rafe's room, older than the rest of the medical staff, with kind eyes. "Ms. Kent? You can go in now for a few minutes."

Amy's weariness vanished. She dashed into the room. Rafe, propped on pillows, smiled at her. Emotion almost swamped Amy, so much emotion that she couldn't speak.

"Hey, Amy, Kaylie," Rafe said.

Kaylie said, "You're you again."

"Yeah. Being Julius Caesar was getting wearing."

"But they let you keep the toga."

Rafe laughed. His eyes were clear, although the skin beneath them sagged with exhaustion. Amy still couldn't speak. He said, "Amy?"

Her eyes filled with tears.

Kaylie said elaborately, "Excuse me, but I need to use the ladies' room." She left on exaggerated tiptoe.

Amy finally choked out, "You're completely OK?"

"Yep. Brain working and everything."

"Rafe—" Then she was by his bedside, stooping to kiss him.

He yanked his head to the side to avoid her kiss.

Hurt, Amy straightened. Of course he didn't want her to kiss him, not after the things she'd said, not after he knew she'd preferred Cai—Cai! How stupid had that been, she hadn't known what Rafe was like, what Cai was like, what she herself was like, stupid to think Rafe would still—

"Amy, my saliva," Rafe said. "I can't kiss you yet, but oh God I wish I could, Amy——"

She knelt by his bed and put her arms around him and hoped Kaylie would not come back for a long time. Into Amy's mind leapt a phantom: *a gold coin, solid gold, like pirates used to bury, covered with seaweed and dirt but still shining on the palm of a bruised and sunburned hand.*

When the night shift did eventually throw Amy and Kaylie out of the hospital, Kaylie decided to go peacefully. Rafe was all right. Besides, TLN had sent a limo for them, and Kaylie loved limos. It was Amy who made a fuss, refusing to go back to the Carillon Hotel. So some poor TLN flunky was awakened in the middle of the night to book them into a different hotel a block from the hospital.

The next morning she slept until nine. Leaving Kaylie asleep, Amy went to the row of shops that were part of the hotel and bought a sexy sundress, sweater, underwear, and makeup. Then——*the hell with it, let TLN pay*——she added a lot more clothes and a rolling suitcase, charging everything to her room. She showered, dressed, and walked to the hospital, pulling along her new wardrobe in her new suitcase. The day turned warm, sweet with the scent of fresh-cut grass, and she took off the sweater.

"Wow," Rafe said, sitting up in his hospital bed with a lunch tray in front of him. "You look terrific."

"Can I kiss you yet?"

"No. But you can—Mark!"

Amy turned. Mark Meyer stood in the doorway, dressed in his iconic leather jacket, despite the heat. He came close to the hospital bed and studied Rafe. "You OK?"

"I'm fine. Just your normal bout of mutating, brain-attacking, personality-altering virus."

Mark said somberly, "I didn't know about the infected mammals."

Amy heard his faint emphasis on his first word. "Mark—are you saying that somebody did know?"

"Stop." Mark took a device from his jacket pocket, pressed a button, and began to move it around the room. Amy, fascinated, watched in silence. Finally Mark said, "No bugs. Talk."

Amy said, "Did Myra deliberately bring an infected squirrel to the island, to the tree with the cameras where Violet was told to go, so that the show would get footage of someone—"

"I can't prove anything."

"But do you think—"

"Look, if you can't prove anything, it's like it never happened. In law, anyway. Do you understand, Amy? You fling accusations around Myra without any proof and it's you that will go down. She has an entire legal team behind her. She also has a TV station. But the squirrel isn't why I came here. I have something else for you."

Mark pulled on a pair of latex gloves. Then he fished something from another pocket—maybe all those pockets were the reason for the leather jacket. This item at least Amy recognized: a tiny tape player. Mark set it on Rafe's bed, turned it on, and adjusted the sound so that both Rafe and Amy had to lean close to hear.

*"Violet!"* Myra's voice said. *"Call Amy now. Ask where she is. She'll say in a stairwell. If she asks about Room 654 being safe, tell her that it's not anymore. Tell her the militants took the room and there was a firefight that killed someone and nobody is there now."*

Violet's voice: *"Did protesters take the room?"*

*"Just do it!"*

*"No. Not if you're just sending Amy into more danger for your fucking show!"*

*"I'm not, I promise you. She has a clear, safe passage out. Just do as you're told or else it's you who will be in danger and you know what I mean!"* Click.

Amy couldn't speak.

Finally Rafe said, "Play it again."

Mark did. In Amy's mind rose clear images, like a movie, of the night of the hotel fire. She and Waverly in the stairwell, carrying Gran on the room-service cart. Amy's call to 911, who told her about the "safer" room on the sixth floor. Then Violet's call, full of concern for her, telling her to not go to Room 654. Where in actuality it *was* safe. Where she and Waverly and Rafe could have holed up with off-duty cops until the SWAT team took the building back. That was what Violet had prevented. Violet, her friend.

Rafe watched her closely. He said nothing.

Amy said to Mark, "How did you get this?"

He waved his hand, as if even asking the question was dumb. "It's an illegal recording, of course. I monitor Myra's cell. I don't trust her."

Rafe said, "What are you going to do with it?"

"I'm going to give it to you." He pulled off his latex gloves. "But if you tell anyone where you got it, I'll deny it. My fingerprints are not on it. It's not traceable to me."

Rafe said levelly, "And you're willing to work for this person?"

For the first time, emotion appeared on Mark's face, gone in a moment. "I like my job. Most of the time, anyway. I want Myra gone, but I'm not deluding myself that you kids can accomplish that. This recording is illegal, you'd never get it admitted in any court. You could take it to James Taunton, but he backs Myra as long as he can stay in official ignorance of how she gets her ratings. No, that's not fair—he *is* in ignorance, but only because he chooses not to ask questions. I work on other shows for TLN, better shows, and I want to go on doing that. The work suits me. I'm giving you this tape so *you* will quit."

Amy said hotly, "But she'll just put others in the same danger!"

Mark shrugged. "I can't control the world. But I like you two. You're both honest and smart, although not smart enough to take on Myra Townsend. You don't have the resources or the experience or the ruthlessness. I just wanted to show you why you should get out of TLN while you can."

Mark strode out of the room, leaving the miniature tape recorder on Rafe's bed tray beside the orange juice. Amy looked at it as if it were a bomb.

"Amy——" Rafe said.

"I need to see Violet. Now. Do you have a cell?"

"No. They took everything electronic off the island, remember?"

"OK, wait here. I'll be right back." Amy stood, looked down at Rafe, hesitated, and then bent and swiftly kissed the top of his head. Before he could react, she was out of the room and on her way to the nurses' station. "May I make a phone call, please?"

"Pay phone in the lobby," said a cold-eyed nurse behind the desk. Probably she had heard about Kaylie's threats of the night before. No help here.

In the lobby she stopped three people before an elderly woman would consent to listen to her. The woman wore a fur cape despite the heat. She was accompanied by a man in uniform, who held one arm as she made her way slowly toward the front door. Her spine curved painfully forward.

Amy said, "Please, ma'am, could I have fifty cents to make a phone call? I lost my purse and I'm just desperate!" She tried to sound young and near tears.

The uniformed man said, "No soliciting in the hospital, miss. Move along!"

"Wait," the old woman said. She fumbled for her purse.

It took a long time for her to find her change purse inside her purse, to bring out a few quarters, to hand them to Amy. Amy gushed her thanks, ignored the man's hard scowl, and sprinted for the pay phone, praying it would work. No one used pay phones anymore.

It did work. There was even a phone book.

"Good morning, Carillon Hotel. How may I direct your call?"

"I'd like to be connected to the room of a guest, please. Violet Sanderson. No, wait—"

Myra had had them all register under fake names, to discourage the hate-mail crowd. What had Violet used? What? Amy couldn't remember. She couldn't remember any of their aliases except her own and, bizarrely, Tommy's. "I mean, please connect me to Insect Man's room."

"Just a moment, please."

The phone rang. *Please let Tommy be there*—

"Hello?"

"Tommy, it's Amy."

"Hi, Amy." And then, "Are you mad at me?"

"No, Tommy, I'm not mad at you. But can I talk to Violet? It's really important. Please go to her room and knock on the door and tell her to come to your room to talk to me on the phone. OK?"

"OK. I'm glad you're not mad at me. Cai said you are because him and me left the island without you. He said that Kaylie—"

"I'm not mad at you! Just get Violet, OK?"

"OK."

A long wait. Amy stared at the people crossing the lobby without really seeing any of them. What if Violet refused to come to the phone?

She didn't refuse. "Amy?"

"The hospital cafeteria. In half an hour. Be there." Amy hung up, unwilling to say more. Violet's phone could be tapped.

Was she being paranoid? No, she hadn't been paranoid enough. But it had become so hard to tell what was real and what was not. That's what the show had done to her, to all of them.

Time to even the score.

# Thirty-seven

**WEDNESDAY**

IN THE NOISY cafeteria, Amy sat at a table in the corner and waited. She was hungry but had no money to buy food. She should have snagged something off Rafe's tray.

Violet appeared in twenty-two minutes. She looked terrible: haggard, with uncombed hair. She must have jumped straight into a cab on Portman Island. "Is Rafe—"

"Like Rafe was ever your first concern." But then Amy relented. "He's fine. They'll probably release him today. Violet, why did you do it?"

"I told you on the island, I had no idea about the infected squirrel, I thought there would just be a bit of melodramatic acting and—"

"Not on the island. The phone call during the hotel fire,

466

telling me that everybody in Room 654 was dead and there was no safe place to go. When there was."

Violet went very still. A busboy clattered past with a cartful of dirty, rattling dishes. "How do you know about that?"

"It doesn't matter how I know. Why did you do it? Waverly and I could have been killed. People were shot during that hotel riot, and there was fire on the upper floors."

"I didn't know how bad it was for you! I didn't know until after it was all over, and Myra told me in that phone call that you had an easy, safe passage out!"

That much was true. Amy studied Violet, trying to see beneath the surface. How could you ever be sure what anybody's motives really were?

She said quietly, "What hold does Myra have over you?"

Violet didn't even hesitate. She spoke like someone glad to unburden herself. "She has evidence that I was betting on the show. Through a friend of a friend. I already knew who behaved how, of course, from talking to all of you. That's what the FBI was sniffing around after. It violates interstate commerce laws."

Amy blinked. Whatever she'd expected, it wasn't that. "Did you win?"

"One point three million dollars. I was going to start my own dance studio."

"'Was'?"

"Myra traced us. I thought I was being really careful but I guess not careful enough. She has recordings, film. She took back all the money and said if I do what she asks on the show, she won't give any evidence to the FBI."

"Why does the FBI care about a stupid TV show?"

"I told you, it violates some sort of interstate law."

Amy considered. "I don't believe it."

"You don't believe me?"

"I don't believe Myra. I think she found out about your cheating and made up the FBI stuff to get you to cooperate. God, Violet, the whole country is falling apart! Do you think the FBI has time to worry about TV betting?"

"But Waverly said some agents with ID came to ask her—"

"She told me that too. But I'll bet that Myra hired a few actors to pose as agents, to make her whole scam on you look more legitimate."

Violet leaned back in her cafeteria chair. A group of doctors in scrubs went past, carrying coffee and talking in low tones. Finally Violet said, "You've changed, One Two Three."

"And you never were what I thought you were. Come upstairs. You're going to tell Rafe all this."

Violet looked unhappy, but she agreed. Kaylie had arrived and was sitting with Rafe. Amy surveyed her sister's outfit: upscale and pulled together. *Good.* Amy said, "Kaylie, I need you to say absolutely nothing while Violet talks. I mean it, it's really important, and I have something important for you to do afterward. Nothing at all, OK?"

Kaylie glared at Violet but nodded sullenly, perhaps lured by the "something important to do." Violet told Rafe her story. Kaylie, miraculously, didn't interrupt. When Violet finished, Rafe took a sip of water and said to Amy as if Violet weren't there, "What are you going to do?"

"*We're* going to do it. Myra will be here soon, I think."

Kaylie said, startled, "Myra?"

"If Tommy's hotel phone is bugged, which I suspect it is. Kaylie, I need you to do something really fast. Fenton Street is four blocks west of here. Beside the Tuileries Café is Nang's Electronics, a high-end electronics store. Go down there and steal a microcam, anything with both visual and audio. Steal it quick. And don't get caught."

Kaylie, Rafe, and Violet all stared at Amy. Then Kaylie said, "What have you done with my real sister?"

Violet choked out, "I have some money and a credit card—"

"No. This has to be untraced. Kaylie, go! We don't have much time!"

Kaylie sprinted from the room just as a nurse entered it to give Rafe a sponge bath. He argued, but lost. Violet and Amy were banished to a waiting room, where a boisterous family joked and laughed about finally taking home a patient named Horatio. Or maybe Horatio was their dog; it wasn't clear. Beneath the din, Violet said quietly, "Are you going to throw me under the bus, Amy?"

"No. I'm not."

"I don't see how you can confront Myra without implicating me. I wasn't supposed to tell you anything, ever. Not that I don't deserve being made a scapegoat."

"Too bad you don't play chess, Violet."

"*Chess?* What the fuck does chess have to do with anything?"

"By the third move the board can have 71,852 different configurations. There is *always* a huge choice of moves to make next."

Kaylie returned, carrying nothing. Disappointment lanced through Amy. But then Kaylie pulled something from her bra: an impossibly small something, round and metallic, connected by a thin wire to something only slightly larger.

Violet, despite everything, smiled. "Now, I could never do that. Not wearing a thirty-four A."

"It's video *and* sound," Kaylie whispered, although she could have shouted and her words would still have been lost in the din about Horatio. "You just—"

"Myra!" Amy said.

"Hello," Myra Townsend said. "It's lovely to see so much support for Rafe. How is he?"

She stood behind Kaylie, who kept her back to her. Over her shoulder Kaylie said, "I don't want to talk to you!" and flounced into the ladies' room. Amy saw why it had taken Myra this much time to arrive; she was impeccably dressed and groomed. Slim silk trousers, cream summer-weight jacket, makeup fresh and dewy under her blonde bob. The queen gliding regally across the chess board.

Amy said cordially, "Rafe is fine. A nurse is with him, but we can go back into his room in just a minute." What did Myra think that Amy knew?

Everyone stood in awkward silence until the nurse came out of Rafe's room. Violet rose and led the way back in. Amy and Myra followed, and then Kaylie from the ladies'. Myra began to gush over Rafe, who said nothing.

"You're looking so well! Rafe, it's remarkable the way you—all of you—can take a situation gone horribly wrong and turn it into acts of bravery and heroism. It's so inspirational for our viewers! I've authorized a bonus for all of you four, of course, twice as large as your previous one. And you, too, Kaylie, our newest heroine."

Kaylie lounged against the far wall. On the front of her

shirt was a curious pin: a knot of silver chains, ends dangling at different lengths, like something Waverly might wear. In the middle of the chains, practically unnoticeable, was a small glass circle. Kaylie gave a tiny nod to Amy.

They were live.

Amy interrupted Myra. "We have something to say to you. We know you deliberately brought an infected squirrel, and maybe other animals as well, to the island to make the show scenario more dangerous and exciting."

Myra looked shocked. "Amy! That's ridiculous! We would never put you participants at risk! Why that's just—Amy!"

Amy had hoped that Myra would say "Prove it," which might have been at least a half-assed admission of guilt. But Myra was too wily for that. She'd declined the gambit. Amy brought out her next attack.

"I can't prove anything about the squirrel, no. But here is something I *can* prove. The night of the hotel fire, I called 911 and they told me to try to get to Room 654, which was the safest place in the hotel. But you called Violet and told her to call me and lie that the cops in Room 654 were already gone."

Violet tensed. Myra looked even more shocked and began to protest her innocence. Rafe took Mark's miniature tape recorder from the drawer of his bedside table and played the tape.

*"Violet!"* Myra's voice said. *"Call Amy now. Ask where she is. She'll*

*say in a stairwell. If she asks about Room 654 being safe, tell her that it's not anymore. Tell her the militants took the room and there was a firefight that killed someone and nobody is there now."*

Violet's voice: *"Did protestors take the room?"*

*"Just do it!"*

*"No. Not if you're just sending Amy into more danger for your fucking show!"*

*"I'm not, I promise you. She has a clear, safe passage out. Just do as you're told—"*

Amy clicked off the machine before the part where Myra revealed that she had some kind of hold over Violet. Amy said, "But Violet didn't listen to you. She tried to call my cell, and then Rafe's, to tell us we should go to Room 654. Only mine had slid off the cart that Waverly and I were maneuvering down the stairwell, and I never got the message. Neither did Rafe, because he was hurt and unconscious. But we found Violet's message later, after everything was over, on his cell. She tried to get us to safety despite what you told her."

Myra looked directly into Amy's eyes. Amy had never seen a gaze that steady, that hard, that unrelentingly cold. "No," Myra said, "that can't be right. If you never got this horrible message that you said I told Violet to convey—and that's not true, Amy dear, I just don't know why you're saying this!—if you never got that message from Violet, you would have gone to Room 654. But you didn't. You didn't even try to get to the sixth floor. I'm afraid you're contradicting yourself, my dear. You're confused."

"No. I'm not confused. We didn't try to go to the sixth floor because *you* called me then and said that everyone in Room 654 was dead."

"I did not! You're lying!"

"There are cell phone records of the call."

Watching Myra's face, Amy saw the moment that the older woman realized. Myra had called Amy's cell during the hotel fire, just as she'd called everyone's cell, with her fake checks on whether they had gotten out all right. But although the cell-phone records at Verizon would show that Myra's call to Amy had taken place, it would not show the content. If Amy said that Myra was doing her best to send Amy and Waverly into deeper danger, Myra had no way to disprove that. And her earlier call to Violet lent it plausibility.

That Amy was lying did not bother her at all. This woman was evil.

For just a second Myra's eyes flared with hatred. Then she had control of herself again. She was good, Amy had to give her that. Amy had hoped to provoke her into an admission of guilt, but instead Myra said gently, "I'm afraid you *are* confused, Amy dear. Of course I called your cell, I called all of you.

Alex and Mr. Taunton and I were so worried! Until we knew that you six, and Kaylie too, of course, were safe outside the hotel, we were just beside ourselves with anxiety. Of course I called your cell. And Cai's and Waverly's and Tommy's and Violet's and Rafe's."

Rafe spoke for the first time. "But we still have that recording of your call to Violet. That looks pretty incriminating, Myra."

"Does it? I don't think so. I think you faked that recording, pieced it together from other speeches you somehow recorded of mine that—"

"You mean, the way you did for 'dialogue' of Amy and Waverly during the hotel fire re-creation in the tunnel? You can't get around that call to Violet. You made it. You sent two young girls and a sick old lady away from safety and into danger just to make your show more exciting, and you put infected animals on Holtz Island for the same reason."

"Oh, Rafe, I think the infection is still addling your brain. Perhaps it's a good thing that all your contracts with TLN are over." Myra swept from the hospital room, looking sad, concerned, and not at all guilty.

Amy dropped into a plastic chair and sagged with disappointment. "She didn't admit anything. I thought that if we pushed her enough—Kaylie, you can stop filming. We don't have anything that could take on TLN's lawyers, anything that would really hold up in court."

Kaylie said, "So now you're a lawyer, too, on top of everything else? You don't know that!"

Rafe chewed his lower lip, which all but disappeared between his teeth. Finally he said, "Amy's right. I'm not a lawyer either, but that one recording of Mark's—it isn't enough. They could twist it every which way. They could say, for instance, that Myra genuinely did believe Room 654 had been taken by militants. I'll bet Myra could even bribe witnesses to say that they were with her when somebody else told her that. Then Myra would look like she was trying to save Amy and Waverly, not kill them."

Amy said, "So we're screwed. It's over. There's nothing we can do."

Rafe leaned forward in his bed. His brown eyes gleamed brightly. "Not necessarily."

Kaylie demanded, "What do you mean?"

Rafe said, "Myra holds all the artillery of her generation: lawyers, courts, television. But we have our own generation's artillery."

Violet said, "Speak English!"

Rafe said, "I am. *Who—You* was all about electronic voting. And the show shaped public opinion—including opinion of us—on the Internet. That's where things happen now."

Amy got up from her chair. With great deliberation, she walked toward Rafe. Saliva or no saliva, she intended to kiss him.

A piercing scream in the corridor stopped her. Then another, even more horrible. Shouts, and a phantom leaped into Amy's brain: *a huge golden lion, wounded and bleeding, trying to bite a rearing snake.*

All four of them tore into the hall.

Tommy stood over Myra, who crouched on the floor with her hands over her head. Tommy held an IV pole grabbed from a patient in a wheelchair. The patient cowered in his chair. Tommy raised the IV pole and brought it down on Myra, shouting, "You did it! You made the squirrel bite Rafe! And I'm not going back to Sam like you said, I'm not getting locked in that insitution again, I'm not I'm not I'm not! You told Sam he would get money for letting you use me but I hate the show and hate it and hate it! And Cai said you made the squirrel bite Rafe! You're a bad person a bad person a bad person—"

Myra screamed at the blow from the metal IV. It landed on her shoulder, not her head, but with enough force to send her sprawling across the floor. An orderly rushed toward Tommy, who continued to yell. The orderly tried to grab Tommy, but he was nowhere near Tommy's size and Tommy threw him off.

"I won't go back to Sam and the insitution I won't—" He raised the IV pole again.

Myra pulled a gun from her purse and fired.

Tommy screamed and went down.

Then the orderly grabbed Myra, joined by two more men who rushed from nearby rooms. Amy darted toward Tommy but was immediately blocked from getting to him. The men jumped on him, pinning him to the floor. A nurse was shouting into a phone. Patients yelled in nearby rooms, and people caught in the corridor either stayed flattened to the wall or tried to flee.

The orderly had Myra's gun. Blood gushed from Tommy's arm but it seemed to Amy that he wasn't dangerously hurt. He wasn't fighting the men pinning him, and he wasn't shouting anymore. In fact, his broad face had smoothed out, looking almost peaceful. The men looked at each other, then cautiously eased off. Tommy sat up, cradling his arm, and looked down the corridor. "Hey, Amy," he said. "Rafe, I see your ass!"

Hastily Rafe clutched his hospital gown, open down the back, around himself.

Violet laughed. Kaylie touched first Amy's arm, and then her camera lens in its nest of chains. "Got it. All of it."

"Where'd you get those chains, anyway?" Violet asked.

"Tore them off the tampon dispenser in the ladies' room. They were holding it to the wall."

Violet made a noise that could have meant anything. Cops burst into the corridor. Myra struggled to stand, but the orderly wouldn't let her. A doctor bent over Tommy's arm. Amy, light-headed, suddenly had to sit down. She turned to go into Rafe's room, saw Rafe standing there clutching his ridiculous hospital gown, and walked straight into his arms. His lips felt full and soft.

Behind her she heard Violet say softly, "Thank you, One Two Three." But it didn't matter. At this moment, at least, only Rafe mattered. At this glorious moment.

# Thirty-eight

THEY RAN THE VIDEOS on a laptop Violet bought with her credit card; she was the only one who had one. Amy refused to let Kaylie steal anything else. They also bought a cell, putting it in Rafe's name. "We'll never get back the ones taken by the copter," Rafe said regretfully. "They'll all just conveniently be misplaced."

Rafe had been released from the hospital that afternoon, after police officers had taken all their statements as witnesses. Amy warned everyone to tell the cops only that Myra had come to check on Rafe's progress. Otherwise they might have been stuck giving depositions forever. Tommy stayed in the hospital while his arm was being treated; he didn't seem to mind. "I got her," he told Amy. "But I didn't kill her."

"No," Amy agreed, fervently glad that he had not. She wasn't sure whether Tommy was under arrest for assault. A bored-looking cop guarded his door. Well, the Lab Rats would deal with that when they had to.

Rafe, Violet, Amy, and Kaylie did minimum editing on the two videos, the one of Myra in the hospital room and the one of Tommy going berserk in the corridor. All they did was cut out Amy's disappointed statement about Myra ("She didn't admit anything"), plus Amy's questioning Myra about the infected squirrel ("I don't know for sure," Rafe said, "but that might open Amy up to charges of libel"). He added, "I don't know if they can tell whether we tampered with the video, but just in case, let's not. I'm going to make six DVD copies and we need to put them in six different safe places. OK, Amy, you're on."

Amy stood self-consciously in front of a blank white wall in the hotel room they'd rented, again on Violet's credit card. Kaylie recorded on her stolen microcamera. "My name is Amy Kent. You may have seen me on the TV show *Who Knows People, Baby—You?* If you didn't, the show has six kids—wait, there were seven in the beginning, right? We had Lynn and—"

"Cut," Violet said. "Amy, you're no actor. Just say the speech the way we wrote it. Start over again."

Amy grimaced and began over. "My name is Amy Kent. You may have seen me on the TV show *Who Knows People, Baby—You?* If you didn't, the show has six kids thrust into various scenarios, and then viewers vote on how they think each will react. The show is produced by Taunton Life Network. But TLN didn't just create harmless scenarios for us six. They used terrifying, real-life events like the Fairwood Hotel fire during the city riots. That might be objectionable, but it's legal. What is *not* legal is to deliberately send some of us into real danger—and that's what Myra Townsend, the executive producer, did. I and another participant, Waverly, were told by Myra to take my dying grandmother"—Amy faltered, but caught herself and went on—"directly into the path of a fire and of people shooting automatic weapons. What you are about to see is some of us confronting Myra about that, and our evidence. Then you'll see Tommy, a mentally challenged show participant, make his own accusations against Myra—and her violent response. You might have seen something about the hospital shooting in the news, but here is the *real* story."

"Good," Kaylie said. "You look pathetic."

"I don't want to look pathetic."

"Well, you do."

They put Amy's introduction at the head of the video, titled the whole thing "The Truth About Hospital Violence: Why Tommy Shot TLN Producer," and added Rafe's new cell number. "OK," Rafe said, "here goes." They uploaded to You-Tube.

They each produced tweets on their newly opened Twitter accounts.

They took turns on the laptop e-mailing everyone they could think of to look at the YouTube video. "The problem," Rafe said an hour later, when their hit rate was still low, "is that there are millions of things on YouTube, most of them junk. We have to get people to look at ours. If we could just reach somebody really influential!"

Kaylie's stomach rumbled. She said, "How about we go out for—" when the communal cell rang. Rafe answered. "Yes?"

A deep voice said, "Amy Kent, please," and Rafe passed the cell to Amy, who put it on speakerphone.

"This is Amy."

"This is Harrison Tollers."

Amy, Rafe, Violet, and Kaylie looked at one another and shrugged; nobody knew the name.

"I'm Waverly Balter-Wells's father. My daughter just showed me your YouTube video. I would ordinarily discount this sort of hole-in-the-wall slander—James Taunton is a business acquaintance of mine—but Waverly assures me that you are not the sort to make things up or play stupid hoaxes. Is it true that this Townsend woman actually put my daughter in great danger in the hotel fire? Greater than occurred by chance?"

Amy drew a deep breath. "Yes, sir. She did."

"And that tape you played of the phone call to . . . Waverly, what was the name of . . . oh, yes, to Violet—that tape is legitimate?"

"Yes, sir. It is. We have it."

"Where did you get it?"

"I can't tell you that."

"Then why should I believe it's legitimate?"

"It is. Waverly told you that I don't lie." A ridiculous statement—how many lies had Amy told in the last twenty-four hours? But she plunged ahead. "Besides, sir, would I take a risk like this if the tape weren't legitimate? I think I might be opening myself up to libel charges."

"You most certainly are. But if what you say happened really happened and my daughter's life was deliberately endangered, you will have all the legal help you need, as well as a countersuit. I'm sending a car for you immediately. Where are you?"

Amy gave the name of the hotel. She added, "But the others involved in making the tape are coming, too. My sister Kayla Kent, Rafael Torres, and Violet Sanderson. Waverly knows them all."

"Very well. Be out front in half an hour, Ms. Kent." He hung up.

*"Waverly,"* Violet said. "Who would have thought."

Kaylie said, "Does *he* have a TV station, too? Are there roles available on his shows, do you think?"

"He doesn't have a TV station," Rafe said. "He has a bank. And a brokerage house."

"Oh."

Amy turned to the others. "Listen, we stick together on this. Kaylie, you say nothing against Violet, do you hear me? I mean it."

"Saint Amy," Kaylie said sourly. She was disappointed that Waverly's father had no TV station. "Do I have to be nice to Waverly, too?"

"Yes!"

Violet had ducked her head. When she raised it, her eyes were watery. She tried to smile at Amy.

"Come on," Amy said. "Let's pack up."

Rafe said, "I'm just going to check YouTube one more time before I shut down the—oh my God!"

"What?" Kaylie bounded forward.

"Half a million hits. And it's going up."

Amy closed her eyes. The room had suddenly quivered a bit. No phantom came to her mind, but a thought did, clear and shining even if it made no sense:

*Thank you, Gran. Thank you.*

# Forty

TLN EXECUTIVE ARRESTED ON CHARGES OF
INTENT TO ENDANGER SHOW PARTICIPANTS

**ASSAULT CHARGES DISMISSED AGAINST
TOMMY WIMMER, "HOSPITAL BERSERKER"**
Extenuating Circumstances Cited

## MYRA TOWNSEND FIRED FROM TLN

## TOWNSEND TRIAL TO BEGIN TODAY

## TOWNSEND COUNTERSUIT AGAINST TV "LAB RATS" QUIETLY DROPPED

Says plaintiff lawyer caught off the record: "You can't win against that much public opinion, no matter what the law says. That's not the way the system works."

## CANCELED TV SHOW BECOMES CULT FAVORITE ON INTERNET

Notorious "Who Knows People, Baby—You?" Spawned Scandal, Court Cases, Largest Viral YouTube Video Ever

## MYRA TOWNSEND CONVICTED OF RECKLESS ENDANGERMENT IN FIRST DEGREE

Could Get Five Years in Jail

# Epilogue

## ANOTHER SPRING

"HEY, AREN'T YOU Amy Kent?" the gardener asked, straightening up from the flowerbed on the university quad. He'd been weeding azaleas in full purple bloom.

"No," Amy said, hurrying past.

This had been easier in the winter. Hoods, scarves, people rushing to class with their heads lowered against the fierce New England wind. She had scarcely ever been recognized, except in class or in the dorm. Either her classmates, after a few curious stares and some tentative questions not too difficult to evade, had dropped the subject of the TV show, or else she had dropped them. The circle of friends that she and Rafe had built up regarded them as who they were on campus, not before.

Anyway, most people were more interested in their own lives than in others'. Gran had always said that.

But not everybody, and here it was spring with its light, revealing clothing, and the kind of people interested in defunct TV shows and public scandal and court cases were going to recognize her again. Ah, well. In the most pragmatic terms possible: The money was worth it. Amy's final two bonuses from TLN had gotten her through the bridge course and to college, and the settlement won from them by Waverly's father's lawyer would keep her here until she earned her degree.

But the degree wasn't on her mind today. Kaylie was. Kaylie, and the reunion.

Rafe rounded the corner of the science building and waved at her. He had bulked up a little in the past year, but not much. Often he forgot to eat, especially when he stayed at the lab all night. Rafe had tested out of most freshman classes and was officially a second-year student, but he was taking mostly junior classes. In another year and a half he would apply to med school. Amy's heart quickened at the sight of him. His kiss was deep and sweet.

"Where is this meeting, again?" he said when the kiss was over.

"You know, Rafe, you used to keep track of everything and now I'm the only one who ever knows what we're doing."

"I know what *you're* doing," Rafe said, "every little thing."

It was true. He was interested in her classes, her activities, her mind and heart, just as Amy had always longed for. *You feel too much, Amy*, Gran had always said. But with Rafe it was safe to feel that much, because he returned it.

She said, "The reunion is at Di Capa's."

"Kaylie?"

"She said she would be there." Amy's voice was grim.

"So, all of us except Cai."

"No, Cai's coming."

"He is! How did that happen?" He took her hand and they began walking.

"Tommy persuaded him. But I think the real reason is that Cai is finally over Kaylie. He's bringing a girlfriend."

"I see!"

"Tommy's bringing a girlfriend, too. I think it's more interesting that Waverly will be there."

"Slumming, I'm sure."

Amy laughed. "Either that or she's lining up a future doctor for her future old age."

"No, I'll bet she just wants to remind us how much we owe her father. Subtly, of course."

Amy sobered. "Well, we do."

"He owes you, too. Waverly might not have gotten out of that hotel fire alive if it hadn't been for you."

"Oh, rot. Waverly always gets out alive. Who's paying for this meal?"

"You are. I got it last time. Besides, I had to requisition more guinea pigs."

Both of them had enough money to cover the costs of college, but not much more. Rafe could use the university lab equipment for his extra experiments only if he paid for the supplies himself. Research into the effects of various toxins on the amygdalae in the brain was expensive.

Amy's own classes were going well. She might never find out what her phantoms really were, but she enjoyed her biology classes, she was on the dean's list, and more scholarships were open to her. She could afford the next three years if she was careful—and if Kaylie didn't need any more lawyers.

They reached Di Capa's, an Italian restaurant off-campus, not so far away that the city became dangerous but not so close that many students would be there. Especially not at three in the afternoon. Cai, Tommy, and two girls were already seated at a table in the back. "Hey, Amy!" Tommy called. "Hey, Rafe!"

Cai smiled. Amy smiled back, feeling nothing. Cai was more gorgeous than ever, his dark hair falling across his forehead, his muscular body perfect in a white tee that made his skin even more golden, his blue eyes like a sunny ocean. Next to him, Rafe looked like a scrawny, monochromatic chicken.

Amy didn't care. She was more interested in the girl beside Cai, who was—

Oh my God. It was Aliya Brandon.

Amy managed a smile. Rafe frankly stared, and kept at it so long that Amy wanted to pinch him. Aliya Brandon's beauty made even Cai look plain. Well, no, nothing could do that, but Aliya was not only spectacular, she was famous. Her skin, the color of milk chocolate, seemed to have no pores and to glow with an inner light. Her hair, deep auburn, framed a delicate face with black eyes and full red lips. Amy had seen that face blown up to ten feet across on a movie screen. And even ten feet across, she'd still had no pores.

Tommy had evidently been learning to do formal introductions. His brow scrunched with the effort to get it right. "Amy Kent, this is my girlfriend, Natalie Smith. And this is my friend Aliya Brandon. Natalie, Aliya, Amy Kent. Rafe Torres, this is my girlfriend, Natalie Smith. And this is my friend Aliya Brandon. Natalie, Aliya, Rafe Torres."

"Hi," Amy managed. Natalie, a quiet-looking girl with masses of ringlets, smiled shyly.

"Hello." Aliya's smile and her Caribbean accent, musical and husky, seemed to finish off Rafe. Amy had to poke him.

"Hi!"

"Hello," she said again.

Tommy was practically bouncing in his chair. "I haven't seen you since a long time!"

"I know. How are you doing, Tommy?" Amy and Rafe sat down.

"Good! I'm doing good!"

"And you still like your group home?"

"Oh, yeah, it's awesome. And Sam is in jail. Did you know that Sam was in jail?" Natalie nodded vigorously at everything Tommy said.

"Yes, I did."

"He can't get at me. But I'm sorry that Kaylie is in jail, too."

Amy glanced at Aliya. "She's out. Aliya, how did you and Cai meet?"

"Surfing. I sneaked away from the studio to Malibu, and he was there. I had to sneak because they don't like me to surf."

Of course not. Break one of those exquisite bones, chip one of those perfect teeth, and an entire movie could be delayed.

Aliya said in her seductive accent, "I fell in the water and the board hit my head—a beginner's mistake, really. Cai rescued me."

Amy nodded. Cai was a rescuer—look how he continued to see Tommy—as long as it didn't put Cai in personal danger. Like with Violet on the island. Now Cai blushed faintly, and his long fingers fiddled with his water glass. Was he still embarrassed about how they had all parted? Maybe. Yet he'd come today for Tommy.

Or maybe to show off Aliya.

But it could easily be both. Amy knew now how mixed anyone's motives could be. Look at—

"Violet!" Tommy shouted. He half stood, shaking the table, before his face twisted in concentration. "Violet Sanderson, this is my girlfriend, Natalie Smith. And this is my friend Aliya Brandon. Natalie, Aliya, Violet Sanderson."

"Hello," Violet said. She kissed the tops of Amy's and Rafe's heads. "You all look great."

It was Violet who looked great. Her long black hair was twisted in a high chignon. Her body looked toned and fit, kept that way by dancing in a show in New York. She'd taken the train up for this reunion. Things had gone well for Violet since the trials ended. She had resumed her own name, Jane Patterson, but Amy could never think of her as anything but Violet. Now she looked critically at Aliya, who gazed coolly back. Amy waited for the moment of recognition, but it didn't come. Then Amy realized that of course Violet had already known about Aliya and Cai, and was refusing to act impressed.

Amy realized something else, too—Waverly knew. Aliya was the reason Waverly had deigned to join this party—not gratitude to Amy nor interest in Rafe's medical career. Waverly hoped that Aliya could help her. Waverly had had a few bit parts in TV shows over the past year, but as the notoriety over the case had faded, so had her acting career. Amy had actually seen one of the shows, practically the only television she'd watched since her classes started. Amy didn't think Waverly had been very good in her role. Somehow she'd seemed . . . flat. Lifeless. She—

"Waverly!" Tommy stood, again jostling the table. This time Rafe's water glass tipped over, but he caught it deftly. "Waverly Balter-Wells, this is my girlfriend, Natalie Smith. And this is my friend Aliya Brandon. Natalie, Aliya, Waverly Balter-Wells."

"Hello," Aliya said.

"Hello." Big smile. Waverly, in a Carolina Herrera dress that toned down her punk-socialite style and that probably cost as much as Amy's rent for the year, sat down gracefully. She said to Aliya, "I'm a big fan of your work. Particularly in *Morning Light*."

"Actually," Cai said easily, his arm across the back of Aliya's chair, "we were hoping to have a lunch free of industry gossip."

Waverly's smile became slightly strained. Amy looked at Cai: "*We* were hoping"? Like industry gossip was something he had to be burdened with too. And the proprietary way he spoke up for Aliya . . . What had Amy ever seen in Cai? Kaylie had had his number much earlier.

And yet he was so good to Tommy. Mixed motives.

Where was Kaylie? Amy's gut tightened. *Oh, please, not another "incident"! Kaylie was out on bail. If she was arrested again . . .*

Rafe was telling Cai about his experiment with guinea-pig brains. Cai didn't look very interested, but Aliya did. Tommy was telling Waverly about Sam's being in jail. Amy knew she should join one of the conversations—Waverly needed rescuing—but she was too nervous to speak. The waitress took their order, so absorbed in looking at Aliya that she barely glanced at anyone else. Now Kaylie was ten minutes late, and Amy reached for her cell. Although Kaylie didn't always answer.

For the last year, Kaylie had been drifting. The island episode of *Who—You* had never aired, blocked by some sort of injunction by one of the lawyers. Kaylie was not recognized on the street (an "honor" Amy would gladly have done without). She'd had no offers of TV parts. She'd left school and worked part-time, low-wage jobs, when she could get them. Between jobs, Amy had given her money and Kaylie had hated Amy for it, and then hated herself for her own ingratitude. Two weeks ago she'd gotten arrested for shoplifting. Amy had scraped together bail, knowing that if Kaylie didn't show up for her court date, Amy would have to leave college to make up the bail for-feiture.

And come to think of it, how did Tommy even know that Kaylie had been in jail?

"—and cut out the diseased brains to centrifuge them," Rafe was saying to Cai. Amy poked him and whispered, "Stop it!" She knew what Rafe was doing: getting even with Cai for leaving them on the island. Cai hated grisly descriptions.

"Kaylie!" Tommy cried. "You came!"

Amy let out a long breath and turned in her chair.

Kaylie looked terrible. She'd lost weight, and her tee sagged on her. It had a small food stain on the front. Her hair could have used shampooing, although it still curled becom-ingly around her face. Nothing could dim the emerald of her eyes, but the skin under them was shadowed and stretched. Amy's worst fear was that Kaylie would become hooked on some of the terrible designer drugs on the street, although so far as Amy knew, she wasn't yet.

"Kaylie," Tommy said, "this is my girlfriend, Natalie Smith and my friend Aliya Brandon. Aliya, Kaylie Kent."

"Amy's sister," Aliya said. "Hello."

"Hi." Kaylie dropped into a chair, obviously determined to not be impressed by Aliya's presence. "Hi, sis. Rafe. Everybody."

"Hi," Cai said neutrally. Rafe, seated beside Kaylie, hugged her. The waitress brought their salads.

"Would you like to order, miss?"

"Just black coffee."

Amy burst out, "Kaylie, eat something!" and immediately regretted it. Kaylie hated to be ordered around.

This time, though, Kaylie surprised her. "OK. A small salad, please. When they have their entrees."

Aliya said, "A salad is all I'm having too." She studied Kaylie closely, and Amy grew angry. OK, Kaylie looked a wreck compared to everybody else, but it was rude of Aliya to stare at Kaylie's poor grooming and tired face. And why was Kaylie so tired, anyway? What had she been doing?

Then Aliya said, "Actually, Kaylie, it's you I came here to meet."

"Me?" Kaylie looked startled, then suspicious. "Why?"

"Do you by any chance have an agent?"

"A what?"

"No? Then I can talk directly to you." The longer Aliya spoke, the prettier her accent became, but also thicker so that everybody at the table leaned slightly forward in an effort to decipher every word. Amy began to realize why Aliya's movie roles featured such short speeches.

"A friend of mine saw you in that TV show *Who Knows People*, the pirated uncut footage when you took off your clothes to get the attention of that flash mob to prevent a stampede. He says you have a magnetic quality on-screen. He is putting together an independent film, very small, no studio backing although he does have distribution. When he knew Cai and I were coming East to see Cai's family and that I would see you, he asked if I would see if you're interested in auditioning for a role in the film. Two scenes only, he says, but good scenes."

Kaylie's eyes widened. Waverly shifted in her chair, and Amy didn't dare look at her. Amy didn't dare look anywhere, in case she somehow screwed this up for Kaylie. But then another thought hit her, and despite herself she blurted, "You said your friend saw Kaylie take off her clothes. Is this film porn?"

Aliya laughed. "Oh, no, no. It is a respectable film. The part is a girl who is trying to find her father, who has gone missing. She gets murdered in her second scene, which propels the plot. My friend wrote the screenplay, and he is very good."

Kaylie said, "Then why aren't you in it?"

Aliya said gently, "I don't do small indie films."

Of course not. She was an international star. Even if her dialogue was partially incomprehensible.

Aliya continued, "If you agree, you can fly back with us and stay with me for the audition. My friend will cover your expenses. We leave Saturday."

"Yes!" Kaylie said. "Oh my God, yes! Except—"

The court date. Amy figured rapidly. She said, "If you're back by next Thursday, that would work."

Aliya said, "We can have you back by next Thursday. Why?"

"I'm in a wedding. Well, the wedding is Friday, but there's a rehearsal."

*Good catch, Kaylie,* Amy thought.

"A wedding," Aliya said. "How nice." She looked pointedly at Rafe and Amy. Amy shook her head, dazed. Marriage? Although maybe Aliya didn't know how old she and Rafe were. She loved Rafe, but Gran would have killed her if Amy made a decision like that at seventeen.

Gran. Amy wished that Gran could see Kaylie get this chance. If it turned out to be a chance. It might not, but maybe . . .

Waverly stood. "I'm sorry, but I have to leave. I have another appointment. Aliya, nice to have met you."

Amy stood too. "Don't go, Waverly."

"I really have to."

The two girls looked at each other, and Amy knew that Waverly saw Amy's pity for her disappointment, and also that Waverly resented that pity. Somehow Amy never could do the right thing with Waverly. Except that once, in a hotel on fire and under siege. Not exactly the basis for an ongoing friendship.

"Well," she said awkwardly, "stay in touch. Good luck."

"Thanks."

Aliya watched Waverly walk away, and Amy had the impression that Aliya knew exactly what Waverly had wanted and why she was leaving. Aliya was shrewder than she looked. And yet she didn't know about Waverly's grief for her own grandmother, or how she had stayed to help Amy with Gran when both their lives had been in danger. Aliya saw Kaylie's talents but not her jealousy. Cai saw Kaylie's ruthlessness but not her courage. And what things didn't Amy know about any or all of them?

She sat back down at the table. The conversation turned general. They joked and laughed. No phantom invaded Amy's mind, but she pondered that *nobody* knew other people, baby. Not all the way through. Nobody.

Just muddling through.

# BLOG POSTING:
## ODDITIES OF OUR FAIR CITY

by Don Owens, "Our Own Town Crier"

Maybe leopards do change their spots. In a strange little nonevent yesterday, a state-of-the-art miniature camcorder was returned to the store from which it had been stolen nearly a year ago. "This has never happened before," said Nang Min Ho, owner of Nang's Electronics on Fenton Street. "I have no idea how the thief got the camcorder out of the display case a year ago, or back into it today. But I'm glad he did, because it's quite expensive."

If this becomes a trend now that the economy is showing such definite improvement, maybe someone will return the good old days when everyone had a job. Although thanks to the bold and decisive nonpartisan legislation passed by Congress in response to the so-called Flash-Point Riots a year ago, we're at least halfway there. And I'm always glad to report on a repentant thief who returns merchandise. Even if we'll never know why.

# ACKNOWLEDGMENTS

I would like to thank both my editor, Sharyn November, and my husband, Jack Skillingstead, for their many patient readings of this manuscript, and their many valuable suggestions for improving it.